Close to the bustl[illegible]le of London Bridge, t[illegible]ross Way, lies Crossbones g[illegible]neath the brick and rail surrounds lie the remains of around [illegible]00 mostly forgotten women. They were known as the Winchester Geese.

Licensed by the Church, abused by the powerful, abandoned by the world.

I wrote *The Winchester Geese* to honour women who lived in the shadows, who were sold and silenced and made monstrous by the very institutions meant to save them.

To imagine a world where these women did not vanish but fought back.

I hope this novel brings the Geese into the light, and, in some small way, gives them the justice history denied. I also hope you enjoy the time spent sharing it.

Thank you for walking this path with me.

Jeffrey Day

In memory of Elaine, and in dedication to her daughter, my wife, Kerry.

Two formidable women.

Prologue

Agnes bit down on the leather strap, her teeth sinking deep as another wave of pain tore through her body. Sweat ran in rivulets between her breasts, soaking the rough shift that clung to her like a second skin. The cathedral cellar stank of blood, piss, and fear, the air thick with the midwife's muttered prayers and Agnes's muffled screams. Torchlight cast long, dancing shadows across the stone walls, turning the faces of the two clergymen into leering masks as they watched from the corner, vultures waiting for the weakest moment.

"Push, girl. Push now or lose the babe," the midwife hissed, her gnarled hands pressing against Agnes's swollen belly.

Agnes arched her back, a howl rising from the depths of her being as fire spread between her legs. The leather strap fell from her mouth.

"Holy Mother of God!" The blasphemy tore from her throat, echoing off the damp stone walls. One of the clergymen stepped forward, his face twisted in disapproval, but the midwife waved him back.

"Let her curse if she wants. Pushing out a child earns you the right," the old woman said, her voice as rough as gravel. She wiped Agnes's forehead with a damp cloth. "Another one coming. Ready yourself."

Agnes clutched at the rough edges of the makeshift bed, little more than straw piled on planks, hidden away in this forgotten corner of the cathedral where the sounds of her labour wouldn't reach the ears of the devout above. Her body, once her strength, had become a torture chamber, contracting and expanding without her consent, working toward an inevitability she could neither control nor escape.

The taller clergyman shifted, the wooden cross around his neck catching the light. "How much longer?" His voice carried the sharp edge of impatience.

"Babies come when they come," the midwife answered without looking up. "Even bastards born in secret."

Agnes felt her insides twist again, a pain so acute she saw white spots dance before her eyes. Her fingernails dug into her palms, drawing blood as she fought against the scream building in her chest. The sheets beneath her were soaked through with sweat, blood, and fluid, the stink of it rising like an accusation.

"Mother of Christ," she gasped, her voice a ragged thing. "Take it from me."

The midwife chuckled, a sound devoid of humour. "Too late for that, my lady. Your legs spread easy enough nine months ago. Now you pay the toll."

The truth of it stung worse than the pain. Agnes had known men before, rough hands and hurried couplings in alleys and backrooms of the stews, but none had left her with child. Until him. Until the man whose name she never spoke aloud, whose ring glinted in the shadows as he knelt between her thighs, whose whispered promises turned to threats when her belly began to swell.

Another contraction ripped through her, and this time Agnes couldn't hold back the scream. It tore from her throat like a living thing, raw and primal.

"I see the head," the midwife announced. "Crown of dark hair, this one."

The shorter clergyman stepped closer, peering between Agnes's spread legs with detached curiosity. "Remember our agreement," he said, his voice soft but threaded with steel. "The child belongs to the Church."

Agnes felt something shift inside her, a bone-deep change that had nothing to do with the baby fighting its way into the world. A cold clarity washed over her, cutting through the haze of pain. They would take her child. They would disappear this evidence of sin, this product of a holy man's weakness. The truth of it settled in her chest like a stone.

"Push now," the midwife ordered. "Push like your life depends on it."

And Agnes did. She gathered every scrap of strength left in her broken body and pushed, a sound halfway between a growl and a prayer escaping her lips. The burning sensation between her legs intensified until she was certain she was being torn in two, split open from the inside out. Then, suddenly, release. A slippery, wet feeling of emptiness followed by a thin, angry wail.

"A girl," the midwife announced, her voice softening for the first time. "Strong lungs on this one."

Agnes fell back against the sweat-soaked straw, her chest heaving. The pain didn't stop, it merely changed form, settling into a dull, throbbing ache that radiated from her core. She watched through half-lidded eyes as the midwife wiped the blood and mucus from the squalling infant with a scrap of linen.

"Let me see her," Agnes whispered, her voice cracked and dry.

The midwife hesitated, glancing toward the clergymen, but something in Agnes's face must have moved her. She wrapped the infant loosely and laid her on Agnes's chest. The tiny body was warm and impossibly light, the skin mottled and red, the face scrunched in outrage at the cold, harsh world it had entered.

Agnes traced a finger along the curve of her daughter's cheek. The baby's cries softened at her touch, dark eyes blinking open to stare up with unfocused intensity. In that moment, Agnes felt something crack open inside her chest, a fierce, burning love she had never known existed.

"She's perfect," she murmured, counting tiny fingers, marvelling at the miniature nails.

The taller clergyman stepped forward, his shadow falling across the bed. "You have little time," he said. "Acquaint yourself briefly with her before she goes; it is the father's wish that she be taken."

Agnes looked up at him, this man who spoke of her child as if she were a package to be delivered. His eyes were flat, empty of compassion. Behind him, the shorter priest nodded, already reaching for the bundle in her arms.

"Please," Agnes said, infusing her voice with a weakness she no longer felt. "A moment alone with her. To say goodbye properly."

The clergymen exchanged glances. The midwife was busy between Agnes's legs, tugging gently on the cord to deliver the afterbirth.

"Very well," the taller one said finally. "We shall wait outside. Do not tarry."

They moved toward the door, their robes whispering against the stone floor. The midwife finished her work, cutting the cord with a sharp blade that she set aside on a small table near the bed.

"I'll clean this up," she said, gathering the soiled linens. Her eyes met Agnes's briefly, and something passed between them, a flash of understanding, even solidarity. Then she too was gone, leaving Agnes alone with her daughter and the guttering torches.

Agnes waited only long enough to hear the door latch before she moved. Pain seared through her as she pushed herself upright, the child clutched to her chest. Blood and excrement coated her thighs, ran down her legs in sticky streams. She swayed, momentarily dizzy, but forced herself to stay conscious.

The blade the midwife had used to cut the cord gleamed in the torchlight. Agnes snatched it up, tucking it into the fold of the cloth wrapped around her child. Then, with every muscle screaming in protest, she eased herself off the bed.

Her legs trembled beneath her, threatening to fold. She pressed one hand against the wall, leaving a bloody smear as she shuffled toward the small door at the back of the cellar, a servant's entrance she had noted when they first brought her down here three days ago, when her waters broke.

The door creaked as she pushed it open, revealing a narrow corridor lit only by a single torch in a distant bracket. Agnes paused, listening. From the other side of the cellar, she could hear the murmur of the clergymen's voices. Not yet returning, but they would soon grow impatient.

The baby stirred against her chest, making a soft mewling sound. Agnes pressed her lips to the tiny forehead. "Hush now," she whispered. "We're leaving this place."

She moved into the corridor, forcing her battered body forward one painful step at a time. The rough stone scraped against her shoulder as she used the wall for support. Every movement sent fresh blood down her legs, but Agnes ignored it, focused only on escape.

The corridor ended in a set of narrow stairs that wound upward. Agnes paused at the bottom, gathering what remained of her strength. The baby sensed her mother's desperation and remained quiet, tiny fists curled against Agnes's skin.

Climbing was agony. Each step sent shards of pain through Agnes's torn flesh, but she gritted her teeth and continued, one hand supporting her child, the other gripping the wall. Behind her, she heard a distant shout, they had discovered her absence.

At the top of the stairs, a small wooden door stood between Agnes and freedom. She pushed it open and stumbled out into the chill night air, the shock of it momentarily stealing her breath. She found herself in a small courtyard, the cathedral's massive shadow looming above her. The streets of Southwark waited beyond a low wall, dark and tangled like the web of a monstrous spider.

"There! By the servants' entrance!"

The shout came from her right. Agnes turned to see the shorter clergyman pointing at her, his face contorted with rage. Behind him, the taller one was already moving forward, surprisingly fast for a man of his size.

Agnes ran.

She had no plan beyond escape, no destination except away. Her bare feet slapped against the cold cobblestones as she fled the cathedral grounds, plunging into the warren of alleys that made up Southwark's underbelly. The smell hit her immediately, an assault of piss and rot and human misery that even the night air couldn't disperse.

"Stop her!" The voice echoed behind her, closer than she'd expected.

Agnes ducked into a narrow passage between two crumbling buildings, the walls so close her shoulders scraped both sides. The baby whimpered against her chest, disturbed by the jostling motion. The pain between Agnes's legs had become a constant burn, each step leaving a trail of blood behind her.

She emerged onto a slightly wider street, where a few scattered lanterns cast pools of dim light. A drunk stumbled past, too lost in his cups to register her bloody, half-dressed state. Agnes veered left, then right, trying to lose herself in the labyrinthine alleys she had known these past few years. But her pursuers knew these streets too. She heard them behind her, their footsteps splashing through puddles of filth, their voices calling to each other as they split up to hem her in.

"The woman cannot have gone far," one shouted. "She's injured and weak."

Agnes pressed herself into a shadowed doorway, trying to quiet her ragged breathing. The baby squirmed against her, making small, distressed sounds. Agnes looked down at her daughter's face, so new to the world, already experiencing its cruelty.

"I won't let them take you," she whispered fiercely. "I swear it."

Footsteps approached, slow and deliberate. Agnes peered around the edge of the doorway to see the shorter clergyman moving down the alley, a lantern held high. His face in the wavering light was a mask of righteous anger, his free hand curled into a fist.

She waited until he had passed, then slipped out of her hiding place and darted in the opposite direction. Her body was beginning to fail her, each step more difficult than the last. Blood trickled steadily down her legs, marking her path like a hunter's trail. The streets grew narrower, the buildings leaning in as if to crush her between them. Agnes recognized this part of Southwark, she was nearing the river, where the poorest of the poor made their homes in lean-tos and abandoned boats. And closer, just three streets away, lived Margaret.

Margaret, who had taken in Agnes when she first escaped her husband. Margaret, who asked no questions and expected no payment beyond an occasional shared meal. Margaret, who had no children of her own, except for the one lost a few weeks back, and room in her heart for so many more. Agnes changed direction, her steps more purposeful now. She had a destination, a plan forming through the haze of pain and fear. She would not be able to keep her daughter, not now, not in her condition, not with the Church hunting her. But Margaret might.

The sound of running footsteps jerked her from her thoughts. Agnes glanced back to see a dark figure sprinting toward her, not one of the clergymen, but a younger man in priest's robes. They must have summoned reinforcements.

"Stop in the name of the Church!" he shouted.

Agnes stumbled forward, her bare feet slipping in the muck of the street. The baby began to cry in earnest now, her wails cutting through the night air like a beacon. Agnes pressed her closer, trying to muffle the sound against her body as she fled.

The priest was gaining on her. Agnes could hear his breathing, harsh and determined. She rounded a corner, hoping to lose him, but her weakened legs betrayed her. Her foot caught on an uneven cobblestone, sending her staggering into a wall.

The impact jarred her entire body. She managed to twist at the last moment, protecting the baby with her shoulder, but the collision still drove the air from her lungs. She slumped against the rough bricks, gasping.

The priest appeared at the corner, his face triumphant as he spotted her. "There you are," he said, advancing slowly now.

"The child belongs to the Church. Hand her over, and you may yet receive mercy."

Agnes straightened, bracing herself against the wall. One hand slipped into the baby's swaddling, fingers closing around the blade hidden there.

"Come no closer," she warned, her voice surprisingly steady.

The priest smiled, a cold twisting of lips. "You can barely stand, woman. Do not make this more difficult than it needs to be."

He lunged forward, hands outstretched to grab the baby. Agnes moved with the last reserves of her strength, pivoting away from his grasp. As he stumbled past her, she drove the blade into his side, feeling it slip between his ribs with sickening ease. The priest made a choked cry; more surprise than pain. He staggered back, looking down at the spreading stain on his robes with disbelief. Then his knees buckled, and he collapsed into the mud of the street.

Agnes didn't wait to see if he would rise again. She pushed herself away from the wall and continued, each step a battle against her failing body. The streets blurred around her, familiar and strange all at once. She was moving on instinct now, drawn by the memory of safety.

Finally, she turned onto a narrow lane lined with timber houses leaning drunkenly against each other. The third door on the left, which was Margaret's. Agnes staggered toward it, her vision darkening at the edges. She raised a fist and pounded on the weathered wood. "Margaret!" she called, her voice cracking. "It's Agnes."

The door yanked open, revealing a stout woman with a face lined by hardship but softened by kindness. Margaret took in Agnes's bloody state with a single glance, then reached for the bundle in her arms.

"Sweet Jesus, what have they done to you?" she whispered.

Agnes surrendered her daughter, watching as Margaret gathered the child to her breast. "Godspeed and look after her. Her name is Marion. They'll come looking," Agnes warned. "Keep her hidden. Keep her safe."

Margaret nodded, already pulling the baby close, her body angling protectively. "And you?"

Agnes shook her head, stepping back. In the distance, she could hear shouts, the sound of the search intensifying. "I can't stay. They'll find her if I'm with her."

As if to emphasize her words, two guards appeared at the end of the lane, their torches blazing as they scanned the darkened street.

"Go," Margaret urged, already backing into her home. "I'll protect her as my own."

Agnes's eyes locked with her daughter's one last time. The tiny face was calmer now, the dark eyes blinking solemnly as if trying to memorize her mother's features.

"Live," Agnes whispered. Then she turned and slipped into the shadows between buildings, her blood-smeared figure melting into the darkness like a ghost returning to the grave.

Margaret closed the door, clutching baby Marion to her chest. Outside, the guards moved down the lane, their torches illuminating empty doorways and abandoned carts, finding no trace of the woman who had passed like a shadow through their midst, leaving behind only her most precious possession and the mystery of her fate.

Chapter One

The Bishop's Seal

The Thames wafted its rotten breath across Mare's face as she picked her way through the sludge. The Spring dawn was announced by a dirty smear of light behind the London skyline. She tugged her hood lower, the weight of sleeplessness hanging from her eyelids. No one with honest intentions trudged through riverside filth at this ungodly hour, herself included.

Only villains, wretches, and those owed money by worse yet braved the banks at first light. She stopped, cocking her head. The wind carried the scrape of oars from upriver, a wherry, some poor sod rowing hard against the morning tide. Farther down, the shouts of dockhands tangled with the wet slap of nets. She smirked. Saints claimed God's mercy renewed each morning, but the Thames' mercy came in the form of fog thick enough to hide a murder or a midnight rendezvous, if you knew where to stand.

Mare did. She'd mapped every rotten timber and piss-stained jetty by memory before her breasts had come in, tracing the hem of London like a seamstress fitting a shroud. She'd been born into mud and got her first lessons in the virtues of filth. How a slippery embankment made for swift escapes, how a layer of river muck dulled the shine on stolen goods, how nobody looked twice at a child plastered head to toe with the city's run-off. No one with honest intentions ever haunted this liminal place at such an hour; it was a parade route for the desperate, the avid, the doomed. She fitted right in.

Her boots squelched with each step, the mud sucking at her heels like a hungry mouth. The stench was familiar, fish guts, human waste, and the repulsive odour of river water that had seen too many bodies. Mare's nostrils had long since given up on rebellion. Southwark's stink was her stink now, had been since she was small enough to slip between market stalls and lift purses with fingers nimble as water spiders.

Across the water, the city was stirring. The distant clatter of shutters being thrown open, the occasional shout of a boatman, the persistent jangle of bells. Behind her, Southwark's taverns and brothels still leaked light and noise; places like The Cardinal's Cap never truly closed, just cycled through different varieties of sin as the hours passed. Mare knew their rhythms as intimately as she knew the calluses on her palms.

Something caught her eye, a shape that didn't belong among the driftwood and rubbish. A splash of white in the brown-grey landscape, partially submerged in the muck where the river had deposited it during the night's high tide. Mare stopped, her body tensing like a bowstring. She'd seen enough dead things to recognize another.

"Shit," she muttered, scanning the riverbank. Empty, save for a few gulls picking at something nearby. She approached cautiously, hand sliding beneath her cloak to grip the hilt of her dagger.

The corpse lay face-up, half-swallowed by the Thames mud. A man, or what remained of one. The crows had been at him already, his eyes and the soft flesh of his cheeks torn away, leaving him with a startled, hollow expression. Blood had soaked through his fine linen robes, once white, now a canvas of slurry and mud. A clergyman, by the look of his attire, quality cloth and gold thread that still glinted dimly at his collar.

Mare crouched beside him, her dagger now drawn, though the man was clearly beyond presenting any threat. His throat had been opened with a practiced hand, one clean slash that would have emptied him in heartbeats. This wasn't river rubbish or some drunken fool who'd stumbled into the Thames. This was deliberate work.

"Who were you, then?" she whispered, tilting her head as she studied his ruined face. The man's hands were soft and uncallused, save for an ink stain on his right middle finger. That's when she saw it, clutched in his rigid palm like an accusation. A brass seal, its surface catching the strengthening dawn light. Mare's stomach clenched. She knew that seal, had seen it pressed into wax on documents that could raise a man to prosperity or condemn him to the gallows.

The Bishop of Winchester's personal mark.

"Fuck me sideways," she breathed, glancing over her shoulder again before leaning closer.

Mare slid her dagger between the corpse's stiff fingers, working the blade carefully. The seal was stuck fast, pressed so hard into the flesh that it had left a perfect inverse impression. Not placed there gently after death, forced into the palm as the man died, a message or a signature. The Bishop's mark, branded into dead flesh.

The seal came loose with a wet sound that turned Mare's stomach despite herself. She wiped it against her cloak before examining it. Heavy and cold, the brass was slick with river water and something darker. Mare had overseen enough of the Bishop's correspondence to recognize the intricate pattern, the wolf of Winchester surrounded by Latin inscription, power captured in metal.

She pocketed it, the weight of it immediately seeming heavier than its physical mass should allow. Her mind raced like a cornered rat. The Bishop of Winchester did not lose his personal seal. It did not find its way into a dead man's hand by accident or coincidence.

"You weren't what you seemed, were you?" she murmured, her breath forming ghosts in the chill air.

With practiced hands, she searched the body more thoroughly. The dead man's throat had been opened with a single, practiced slash, not the jagged wound of a desperate cutpurse, but the clean cut of someone who knew exactly how to separate a man from his life without fuss.

Mare turned her attention to his hands. The right one still clutched at nothing, frozen in its final gesture of futile defence. She pried the fingers open gently, studying the palm. Calluses, yes, but not from a labourer's tool, these were the marks left by a quill pressed too hard against flesh for too many hours.

Mare's fingers skimmed the sodden robes, near the small of the back, her touch registered an irregularity in the lining, a hidden pouch, sewn with small, precise stitches between the layers of cloth. The kind of hiding place only its maker would know to look for.

"Clever," she muttered, using her knife to slice the stitches. "But not clever enough to keep you breathing."

Inside the pouch, protected from the river's corruption by layers of oiled cloth, was a small parchment. Even with this protection, blood had seeped through one corner, blossoming across the yellowed surface like spilled wine. Mare held it closer to the lantern, squinting at the tight, cramped script.

Latin. Of course it would be fucking Latin.

Mare's lips moved silently as she translated the words. The Bishop hadn't wasted coin on her education for nothing, though he might not appreciate how she was using it now.

"Sub scaena prelo," she murmured aloud. "The press beneath the stage."

A barge horn blared in the distance, making Mare twitch. The tide was beginning to turn. Soon enough, this stretch of bank would see traffic; fishermen, mudlarks, the city watch if some fool had reported a body. She needed to be gone before then. Standing, Mare cast her eyes across the horizon once more, methodically searching for watchers. The windows of the buildings along the bank stared back, dark, and empty. The cathedral rose behind them, its spire piercing the dawn sky like a warning. Even from here, Mare could make out the Bishop's residence attached to its side, a handsome stone building where Richard Wickham conducted the business of both God and man with equal ruthlessness.

The seal sat in her pocket like a burning coal. Report the discovery and earn the Bishop's fleeting gratitude, he rewarded useful information, particularly when it concerned his interests. But a man with the Bishop's seal pressed into his dead hand? That wasn't information; that was a noose waiting to tighten around whatever neck was foolish enough to present itself.

Keep it to herself, then. Learn what it meant before deciding how to play it. The Bishop had taught her that lesson himself. Knowledge hoarded was leverage gained. Still, if Wickham discovered she'd found his seal and kept it secret... Mare's hand drifted unconsciously to the thin scar along her left palm, a souvenir from her first lesson in the Bishop's displeasure.

The rising sun cast long shadows across the water, and for a moment, the cathedral's silhouette stretched all the way to the riverbank where Mare stood, as if reaching for her with fingers of darkness. The dead man stared up with his hollow eyes, his secrets cut from his throat and spilled into the Thames mud.

Mare felt the Bishop's seal against her thigh, heavy as guilt, cold as opportunity. A splash in the water startled her from her thoughts. Mare's hand flew to the dagger at her belt, but it was only a water rat, its eyes gleaming red in the lantern light before it dove back into the river's murk. Then she heard them, the deliberate sound of footsteps on the muddy bank, approaching with cautious intent. Not the uneven stumbling of a drunk or the hasty tread of a cutpurse. These were the steps of men who knew where they were going.

Mare extinguished her lantern with a quick, practiced movement. Darkness enveloped her like an old friend as she slid backward into the shadow of a rotting wharf piling, her body pressed against the slimy wood. The seal and parchment disappeared into her bodice, tucked safely against her skin.

Two figures materialized from the gloom, cloaked and hooded against the shade. They moved with the confidence of men who didn't fear the dark, or what lurked within it. Mare held her breath, her fingers curled around her dagger's hilt.

A sound, the unmistakable squelch of a boot in mud jerked her from her thoughts. She slid backward into the deeper shadows beneath the riverbank's overhang, her body pressed against the damp earth, the parchment and seal tucked securely away. They stopped before the corpse, looking down at it with the dispassionate interest. "This is the one?" The first voice was cultured, with the crisp pronunciation of someone who'd had Latin beaten into him by expensive tutors.

"Yes, that’s him alright." The second man was older, his voice a gravelled rumble.

The first man nudged the corpse with a booted foot. "The tide will soon take him downstream and wherever he washes up he won’t be unduly noticed."

"No, not unduly," said the older man, "He made a grave miscalculation. He thought himself a player in this game when he was merely a pawn."

The older man knelt beside the corpse, his cloak dragging in the mud as he examined the dead man's face. The bishop's spy is dead, but the fake seal is missing. That means the Order must have it and can use it for forging papers, we should report this to Francis."

They began to drag the corpse toward the water's edge. Mare remained perfectly still, hardly daring to breathe. The seal in her pocket and the parchment clutched in her hand suddenly felt like burning brands, marking her for discovery. They spoke for a few minutes more, their voices dropping to murmurs too quiet for Mare to catch. Then they dragged the body fully into the river, watching as the current pulled it slowly toward the heart of the Thames.

Only when the sound of their footsteps had faded completely did Mare allow herself to breathe normally again. Her heart hammered against her ribs, as if trying to break free from the cage of her chest. The seal and parchment felt heavier now, weighted with implications she didn't fully understand.

"The press beneath the stage," she whispered again, the words taking on new weight. Whatever this meant, it had cost a man his life, and who were "the Order" that somehow implicated the Bishop of Winchester, the man who'd pulled her from the gutter and fashioned her into his useful tool.

Mare retreated from the riverbank, her steps silent but her mind thundering with questions. The Bishop's seal and the dead man's message weighed heavier than their physical presence should allow. She moved like a shadow through Southwark's narrow streets, suspicion and possibility churning in her gut like bad ale.

The words meant little on their own, but Mare knew Southwark's geography of secrets better than most. The Bishop's double spy murdered. The Order's next move. The press beneath the stage. Mare slipped away from the riverbank, keeping to the shadows as naturally as breathing. Her mind churned with questions and suspicions, none of them pleasant. She'd stolen from dead men before, it was normal behaviour in Southwark, but never had she felt so distinctly like she'd picked up something far more dangerous than a brass stamp.

Whatever game was being played in the shadows of London, she had just unwittingly made herself a player in it. And in her experience, unwitting players could soon become corpses.

The Cardinal's Cap squatted on the corner of Pike Lane like a toad waiting for flies, its windows glowing yellow through the river fog. They say the house was built on bone and bad debts before it became a brothel masquerading as a tavern. All the whorehouses traded as drinking establishments following the law change that had banned them from the mid part of the century. It had previously been a crumbling wine merchant's hall, red-bricked and ivy-choked, sitting just off Clink Street like a secret no one wanted to remember. Its rafters creaked like gallows and the walls sweated damp year-round. But it had three things no other place did; thick shutters, cellar space deep enough to bury a horse, and a tunnel that ran beneath it straight to the Thames. And that made it Mare's favourite hub from which she conducted the Bishop's covert work.

Mare pushed through the door that late afternoon, the familiar wall of stench hitting her like a fist, sweat, spilled ale, piss, and too many unwashed bodies sharing the same air. The tavern's patrons barely glanced up as she entered. In a place where everyone had something to hide, curiosity was a luxury few could afford.

Mare nodded to the barkeep, a mountain of a man with a face like a badly butchered side of beef. He grunted in recognition and reached for a mug without being asked. The Cardinal's Cap wasn't the sort of establishment that prided itself on variety, you drank what they poured and were grateful if it didn't blind you. He slid her a tankard without a word, knowing her preference for the least watered-down ale he kept under the counter. It was an arrangement they'd maintained for years; she occasionally provided information that kept his establishment from being raided by the bishop's men, and he occasionally pretended his ale contained real barley.

She took her drink to the corner table where she always sat, back to the wall, clear view of both the door and the narrow staircase that led to the rooms above. Old habits. The Bishop had tried to train them out of her, to make her move and sit like a lady, but some lessons went deeper than his teachings. Survival trumped manners every time.

The smoke hung thick as a London fog, the air barely disturbed by the occasional half-hearted swing of the door. Candles guttered in pools of their own wax, casting more shadow than light. Perfect for Mare's purposes. She placed her mug on the scarred table and carefully withdrew the Bishop's seal and the bloodstained parchment from her cloak.

The brass caught what tiny light there was, its surface still bearing traces of river mud despite her attempts to clean it. The wolf of Winchester stared up at her, its tiny brass eyes somehow managing to convey the same cold calculation as its owner. Mare ran her thumb over the Latin inscription that circled the beast. Sigillum Episcopi Wintoniensis. The seal of the Bishop of Winchester. A small, heavy circle of metal that could condemn a man or elevate him, depending on whose hands it graced.

The parchment was beginning to curl at the edges as it dried. The bloodstains had turned a rusty brown, obscuring some of the writing, but the phrase remained clear enough. Prela sub scaena. The press beneath the stage. Mare turned the words over in her mind, assessing them against what she knew of Southwark. The district had no shortage of stages, bear-baiting pits, and makeshift platforms where street performers plied their trade but only one playhouse this side of the river. But a press? That suggested printing, which meant books or pamphlets, which meant ideas. Dangerous things in dangerous times.

Around her, the tavern hummed with life, or some approximation of it. A pair of prostitutes in the corner, their painted faces cracking with exhaustion, counting coins and comparing notes on the night's clients. Three sailors huddled over a game of dice, their whispered accusations of cheating growing less whispered with each round of drinks. A man in a merchant's coat, far too fine for this establishment, slumped over his cup, either passed out or dead, it made slight difference to the barkeep who kept charging for each refill.

These were Mare's people, though the Bishop would hate to hear her say it. For all his efforts to polish her into something useful, she remained, at heart, a creature of Southwark's shadows. She understood their language, their codes, their desperate slight schemes to survive another day. The Bishop used her for precisely this reason; she could move between worlds in a way his other agents could not.

Around her, the tavern's patrons continued their nightly rituals of drinking, whoring, fighting, and plotting. A pair of doxies in the corner compared the wounds left by customers, while a one-eyed sailor tried to convince a group of wide-eyed boys that he'd seen a mermaid off the coast of Spain. At the bar, a man with hands like shovels arm-wrestled for drinks while a crowd placed bets on the outcome.

None of them mattered. None of them knew that Mare sat among them with objects that men had killed for, objects that represented secrets important enough to draw mysterious figures to a corpse in the night. She turned her attention to the parchment, carefully unfolding it beneath the table. The bloodstain had dried to a rusty brown, obscuring part of the Latin text, but the phrase she'd deciphered earlier remained clear: "The press beneath the stage." There were other words, partially legible; something about "printers" and "forbidden texts," but the blood made it impossible to read with certainty.

"You look like you've seen a ghost."

The voice startled Mare from her thoughts. She'd been so focused on the seal and parchment that she'd missed the approach of Bess Quickly, a newcomer mistake that would have earned her a slap from her first mentor in the thieving trade.

"Sit down, Bess," Mare said, quickly concealing the items in her lap. "You're blocking my view of all the handsome men."

Bess snorted and dropped onto the bench across from Mare, setting down two fresh tankards. Her hair was a mess of faded red curls piled atop her head, her face bearing the map of a hard life lived without apology. She wore a dress that had once been fine before time and numerous stains had their way with it. Mostly a barmaid now, though Mare knew she'd been other things before, things that required different skills but the same absence of squeamishness.

"Handsome men, my arse. This lot would scare a hungry dog away from a butcher's bin." She pushed one of the tankards toward Mare. "You look like you need this more than I do, and that's saying something considering the day I've had."

Mare accepted another ale with a nod of thanks. She and Bess had an understanding born of shared circumstances; both had crawled their way up from Southwark's gutters through whatever means necessary. Neither asked too many questions about the other's business.

"Bad day?" Mare asked, not really caring but appreciating the distraction from her own troubles.

"Three sailors with the pox trying to hide it, one merchant who couldn't get his cock to stand to attention even with me and Polly both working on it, and a bloody priest who wanted to 'save my soul' but not before sampling the goods." Bess took a long drink. "The usual. But you" Her sharp eyes narrowed. "You've got that look. The one that says you're in it up to your neck already and still digging. You all right?"

"Just tired," Mare replied, casually sliding the parchment into her sleeve. The seal, however, remained on the table, too late to hide it without drawing more attention.

Bess snorted, not buying the excuse for a moment. "Tired looks different on you. This is something else." Her shrewd eyes flickered to Mare's hands, then back to her face. "His Grace got you running strange errands these days?"

The question was casual, but nothing was ever casual with Bess. They'd known each other too long for that—back to the days when Mare was still learning to survive Southwark's cruel lessons and Bess had occasionally slipped her scraps from the tavern kitchen as well as share her bedroom.

Mare hesitated, then made her decision. She nudged the seal forward slightly, letting Bess get a better look. "Found this. Thought you might have heard something."

Bess's eyes widened, her hand darting out to cover Mare's, stopping her from exposing the seal further. "That's trouble you don't want to be holding, love," she warned, her voice dropping to barely more than a breath.

"I gathered that much," Mare said dryly. "But why? It's just a seal."

"That's not just any seal, and you bloody well know it." Bess glanced around nervously before leaning closer. "Where did you find it?"

"In the hand of a dead man by the river, this morning."

Bess's face paled beneath her rouge. "Fuck my old boots, Jesus, Mary, and Joseph. You need to take that back to him right now. Right now, Mare. Don't stop for anything."

"Back to who?"

"Don't play stupid with me. It doesn't suit you." Bess's fingers tightened around Mare's wrist. "The Bishop. Take it back to him and tell him exactly how you found it. And then forget you ever saw it, if you value that pretty neck of yours."

Mare studied her old friend's face. Bess wasn't easily frightened, she'd survived three husbands, countless lovers, and the sweating sickness that had emptied half of Southwark two winters past. Yet now her eyes darted to the door every few seconds, her throat working as if she were struggling to swallow.

"What do you know, Bess?" Mare pressed, turning her hand to grip Bess's in return. "What's got you scared?"

"I don't know anything," Bess replied too quickly. "And neither should you. There's been whispers, that's all. Men in fine clothes asking questions they shouldn't. People disappearing. The Bishop's name coming up in conversations where it doesn't belong." She pulled her hand free and stood abruptly. "I've said too much already."

"Bess"

"No." Bess cut her off with a sharp gesture. "We've been friends a long time, Mare. That's why I'm telling you to drop this. Whatever game the Bishop is playing, it's bigger than you. It'll swallow you whole and won't even notice the lump you make going down."

Bess knew people, heard things. She might recognize the seal or know something about the cryptic message.

"Ever heard anything about a press beneath the Rose Theatre?"

Bess's expression didn't change, but her fingers tightened imperceptibly around her tankard. "Can't say that I have," she replied too casually. "Why?"

Mare studied her friend's face, noting the slight tension around her eyes. Bess was lying, and not very well. Interesting.

"Just something I overheard," Mare said with equal casualness. She took a risk and slid the seal partially out from under the table, just enough for Bess to glimpse the silver gleaming in the dim light.

Bess's eyes widened, and a flash of genuine fear crossed her face before she schooled her features back into practiced indifference. She leaned forward, her voice dropping to a whisper that wouldn't carry beyond their table.

"That's trouble you don't want to be holding, love. The kind that gets a person's throat cut and their body dumped where even the rats won't find it."

"You recognize it, then."

Bess glanced nervously at the door, then back to Mare. "Put it away. Now."

Mare complied, tucking the seal back into her bodice. "Tell me what you know, Bess."

"I know nothing, and if you're smart, neither do you." Bess's usually brash demeanour had vanished, replaced by something Mare rarely saw in her friend, genuine concern. "There are things in this city that it's better not to see, Mare. Things that see back."

"That's not an answer."

"It's the only one you're getting from me." Bess's gaze darted around the room again. "There are ears everywhere, and not all of them belong to beggars looking for coin, you better than anybody should know that."

Mare leaned forward. "The Bishop…"

"Don't," Bess hissed, gripping Mare's wrist with surprising strength. "Not here. Not anywhere." She released Mare's arm and stood abruptly. "I've got customers waiting. Forget whatever you found, Mare. Throw it in the Thames and walk away."

With that, Bess melted back into the crowd, leaving Mare alone with her ale and her thoughts. The tavern continued its drunken revelry around her, but now Mare studied the faces with new wariness. Were there watchers here? Ears that reported back to the mysterious "Order" the men had mentioned?

She drained her ale and stood, careful to move naturally despite the urge to flee. The seal and parchment felt heavier than before, weighted with implications that grew darker by the hour. Whatever she'd stumbled into, it was big enough to frighten Bess Quickly, a woman who'd once stabbed a constable in broad daylight for grabbing her arse.

Mare left coins on the table and made her way to the door, keeping her pace unhurried despite the prickling sensation between her shoulder blades. The early night air hit her face, carrying the eternal stench of the Thames and Southwark's open gutters. It smelled like home, like danger, like life and death commingled, as so it did to the man stood in the shadows who watched her leave.

The seal pressed against her skin, and the parchment crinkled with each step. The weight of Southwark's secrets pressed down on her shoulders as she melted into the fog-shrouded streets, her mind churning with questions that had no answers, only consequences.

Chapter Two

Whispers in the Clink

Dawn crept over Southwark with a dim light barely penetrating the river fog as Mare was marched through the streets. The Bishop's men had found her not an hour past, hadn't bothered with explanations, just rough hands closing around her arms and a curt "His Grace requires you." The seal and parchment burned against her skin, hidden beneath layers of clothing and lies, as they steered her toward the looming shadow of the cathedral.

Mare Fleet was escorted by the Bishop's personal men, not the common watchmen who patrolled Southwark's streets with bored indifference. These wore matching leather jerkins with the wolf of Winchester stamped on their shoulders, their faces hard as coins and about as expressive. The taller one had fingers as fat as sausages, digging into the meat of Mare's upper arm with unnecessary force. The shorter compensated with enthusiasm, his grip tight enough to leave bruises.

"I can walk without assistance," Mare said, her voice flat as a blade. "Or does His Grace think I'll bolt like a spooked horse?"

"Shut it," the taller guard grunted. "You'll speak when spoken to."

They pushed her past the morning beggars and early market folk, who averted their eyes with practiced caution. Association with the Bishop's displeasure was contagious, a disease no one wanted to catch. The fog swallowed their passage, turning the familiar streets into a grey purgatory of half-seen buildings and muffled sounds.

The Clink precinct rose from the mist like a stone fist, the Bishop of Winchester's domain in Southwark, where his authority outweighed even the King's men. Its walls separated God's representative from the sins he controlled but secretly taxed and managed. Mare had passed through these gates many times before, but never with hands forcing her forward.

The first checkpoint came at the outer gate, a bored guard barely glancing at her escorts before waving them through with a knowing smirk. The second was more formal, with ledgers to mark her entrance and dead-eyed men taking note of her name. By the third checkpoint, the world had changed entirely.

The streets of Southwark fell away, replaced by the Bishop's inner sanctum. Cold marble floors stretched beneath her feet, the stone worn smooth by centuries of powerful men walking the same paths to conduct their business of souls and silver. Oil lamps cast long fingers of light that never quite reached the shadows gathering in corners. The air changed too, the reek of the Thames replaced by stone dust, beeswax, and the cloying sweetness of incense.

Distant chanting floated through the corridors, monks at their morning prayers, their voices rising and falling like tired waves against a shore. The sound should have been comforting. It wasn't. Mare had learned early that the holiest men often harboured the darkest secrets.

The guards brought her to an ornate door carved with biblical scenes, angels with swords, sinners in torment. Subtle, the Bishop was not. They knocked once, then pushed her inside without entering themselves. Smart men. They knew better than to witness whatever happened in the Bishop's private chambers.

Bishop Richard Wickham sat behind a desk that could have fed a Southwark family for a year. The wood gleamed with polish, its surface inlaid with mother-of-pearl that formed the shape of the

Winchester arms. Behind him, tapestries depicted saints in glory and sinners in agony, the eternal choices the Church offered its flock.

The Bishop himself was a statue carved from ageing flesh, a tall man grown solid with power rather than fat. His face bore the deep lines of sixty years, yet his eyes remained sharp as a blade newly honed. Those eyes fixed on Mare now, cold as river stones in January. His fingers drummed impatiently on the desk, the sound sharp in the silence.

"I've been waiting," he said finally, his voice carrying the refined accent of education and authority. "I dislike waiting."

"Blame your men Your Grace, they marched me here, and it was at their pace" Mare replied, keeping her tone carefully neutral. "I only knew of your requirement of my presence."

"Do not play games with me today, Marion." He used her full name deliberately, a reminder that he knew exactly who and what she was. "I am not in the humour for it."

Mare inclined her head slightly, a performance of deference she'd mastered years ago. Her mind raced behind the mask of subservience. How much did he know? Had he somehow discovered she'd found the seal? Was this summons about the dead scribe dressed as a clergyman, or something else entirely?

The Bishop studied her face for a moment, then seemed to reach a decision. "There is a matter requiring your particular talents for... discretion."

"I live to serve, Your Grace," Mare replied, the words practiced and hollow.

"A body has been discovered downstream by the Thames. A clergyman." His eyes never left her face. "This could present complications I cannot afford at present."

Mare's expression remained carefully blank, though her heart stumbled in its rhythm knowing what she had uncovered the previous day. "Bodies by the river are hardly uncommon, Your Grace."

"This one wears the robes of a man in my service." His fingers stopped their drumming, coming to rest flat against the polished surface. "I require this matter overseen with absolute thoroughness. Any evidence that might have been left behind and spirited about Southwark is to be recovered and brought directly to me. Any whispers or words on the street about this reported back."

The brass seal pressed against Mare's ribs like a burning coal. Her thumb twitched near the concealed dagger at her waist, a reflexive gesture she immediately stilled.

"Is there something specific I should be looking for, Your Grace?" she asked, injecting just enough sarcasm to maintain her usual demeanour without revealing her knowledge.

He stood slowly, his height allowing him to look down at her with practiced disdain whilst ignoring the thrust of the question. "I've replaced more valuable assets than you, Mare."

The threat hung in the air between them, as tangible as the incense smoke that curled from censers in the corner. Mare's hand moved unconsciously to the thin scar that ran along her left palm, a souvenir from her first lesson in the Bishop's displeasure, delivered when she was sixteen and thought herself cleverer than she was.

"I understand perfectly, Your Grace," she said, the words like ashes in her mouth.

"See that you do." Wickham sat back down, dismissing her with the gesture. "Failure in this matter will not result in a scar, Mare. It will result in your end. The body will vanish, any witnesses must be silenced, and any items recovered must come directly to me."

Mare bowed, the motion allowing her to hide the momentary flash of calculation in her eyes. She straightened, face once again an unreadable mask. She knew the body would vanish, the Bishop had already taken care of that, but the forgery seal, which was what he wanted and that was what she already had hold of, not beyond a yard of where he stood over her.

"Consider it done, Your Grace."

She turned and walked to the door, feeling his eyes on her back like the point of a knife. The seal and parchment seemed to grow heavier with each step, her possession of them now a death sentence should the Bishop discover her deception. The game had indeed changed, and the stakes were no longer merely survival, but the manner of her death should she lose. Mare closed the door behind her with a soft click that sounded final as a coffin lid.

Mare's footsteps echoed on the marble as she left the Bishop's chambers, her mind churning like the Thames at high tide. The corridor stretched before her, empty save for the shadows cast by guttering oil lamps and the weight of centuries pressing down from the vaulted ceiling. She needed time to think, to plan, the Bishop's demands hanging around her neck like a noose waiting to tighten. The brass seal felt impossibly heavy against her ribs, a secret that could see her floating face-down in the river by sundown. Why did she not offer it up there and then?

"The Bishop's favourite shadow looks troubled this morning."

The voice slid from the darkness like a knife from a sheath. Mare didn't startle, she'd spent too many years in Southwark's alleyways to betray surprise, but her hand instinctively shifted toward her concealed dagger before she recognized the speaker.

Thomas Walsingham, relative to the Queen's spymaster and principal secretary, Francis Walsingham, emerged from an alcove with the precise timing of a man who'd been waiting specifically for her. The Bishop's page wore a doublet of deep blue velvet that had clearly been made for someone else, the shoulders too broad, the sleeves ending a finger's width short of his wrists. New clothes but not newly made. Hand-me-downs from some noble's castoffs, meant to elevate him above his station.

His smile sat unnaturally on his face, like a mask that didn't quite fit. "Been swimming in troubled waters, have we, Mare?"

"Nothing I can't navigate," she replied evenly, noting how he positioned himself to block her path, not completely, but enough to assert his imagined authority. "Did you need something, Walsingham, or do you simply enjoy loitering in corridors?"

He wore his hair in the same severe style as the Bishop, though on his younger face it looked like a boy's attempt to imitate his father. His fingers, stained with ink at the tips, tapped against his leg in the same rhythm Wickham's had drummed on his desk moments before.

"His Grace has entrusted me with delivering this to you." Walsingham produced a sealed parchment from his sleeve with a flourish that aimed for elegance and landed squarely on pretension. "Additional instructions."

Mare took the offered message, noting how his fingers lingered on the parchment a moment too long, the way his eyes flickered to the broken seal that had clearly been reattached with careful precision. So, Walsingham had read it, then. Interesting that he wouldn't bother hiding that fact from her.

"The Bishop's patience wears thin these days," he added, eyes darting past her shoulder to check if they were being observed. "I wouldn't delay in addressing his concerns."

"His Grace just dismissed me with his concerns quite thoroughly articulated," Mare said, tucking the message into her bodice without reading it. Let him wonder at her apparent lack of curiosity. "Or perhaps you weren't listening at the door as carefully as usual."

Colour flashed across Walsingham's cheeks before he mastered it. "I serve His Grace directly. I don't need to resort to common eavesdropping."

"Of course not," Mare agreed with a smile that didn't touch her eyes. "You're far too valuable for such tasks."

The sarcasm wasn't lost on him. Walsingham stepped closer, invading her space with deliberate intimidation. He smelled of expensive cologne applied too liberally, as if trying to mask the lingering scent of his humble origins.

"We all serve in our ways, don't we? His Grace values loyalty above all else." His voice dropped lower. "Even from those he plucked from the gutter."

Mare's expression remained neutral, though internally she reassessed the man before her. Walsingham was playing a deeper game than she'd credited him with. The reference to her background wasn't casual, it was calculated to remind her of her precarious position.

"How fortunate that his definition of loyalty is so... flexible," she replied. "Stealing His Grace's correspondence to satisfy your curiosity seems an interesting interpretation of the virtue."

Walsingham's lips twitched, not a smile, nor a snarl. "Careful, Mare. The Bishop may value your special talents, but you aren't irreplaceable. None of us are."

The echo of Wickham's earlier threat wasn't coincidental. Either Walsingham had indeed been listening at the door, or the Bishop had shared his intentions regarding Mare's potential disposability.

"Except you, of course," Mare said, her tone light as feather. "I'm sure your position is entirely secure."

She watched him absorb the implication, saw the flicker of uncertainty behind his eyes. Walsingham cocked his head slightly to the right, another unconscious mimicry of the Bishop's mannerism when considering a problem.

"His Grace has expressed concerns about divided loyalties within his household," Walsingham said, studying her face carefully. "Particularly regarding those who maintain connections to their former lives."

Mare recognized the trap for what it was. Walsingham was fishing, hoping she'd reveal something in defence of herself. Instead, she simply shrugged.

"The Bishop knows exactly who and what I am," she said truthfully. "That's why he values me."

"Values you enough to send you chasing after a dead clergyman and whatever he might have been carrying?" Walsingham's eyebrows rose slightly. "Curious errand for his favoured shadow."

And there it, confirmation that Walsingham knew more than he should about the Bishop's personal business. Mare filed that information away, another piece in the increasingly complicated puzzle she was assembling.

"I go where I'm sent," she replied, sidestepping the implication. "As do we all."

She moved to pass him, deliberately brushing against his shoulder as she did so, a small assertion of her own lack of intimidation. The sealed message sat unread against her skin, alongside the stolen seal and bloodstained parchment. Three secrets, three potential deaths.

"One last thing," Walsingham called after her. "There are rumours of Puritan sympathizers within the Bishop's household. His Grace has asked me to compile a list of those whose loyalties might be... compromised."

Mare paused but didn't turn. "How fortunate that you're so ideally positioned for such a task," she said, voice carrying in the stone corridor. "Being above suspicion yourself."

She continued walking, spine straight, pace unhurried despite the urge to flee. Behind her, she felt Walsingham's eyes burning into her back, a boy playing at power games while dabbling in matters that could see them both swinging from Tyburn Tree.

The message from the Bishop could wait. First, she needed to understand what game Walsingham was playing, and whether he was a pawn or aspiring player in the larger scheme that had left a clergyman dead in the Thames mud with the Bishop's seal clutched in his hand.

Mare moved through the cathedral's side passages with practiced nonchalance; her ears pricked for any useful fragment of conversation. The Bishop's summons and Walsingham's veiled threats had set the board for a game she hadn't agreed to play, yet here she was, a piece in motion without knowing all the rules. Information was currency in Southwark, often more valuable than silver and Mare needed to be rich before her next move.

The cathedral entrance loomed ahead, its cavernous archway swallowing light rather than welcoming it. Morning prayers had just concluded, and black-robed clergymen spilled from the inner sanctum like ants from a disturbed hill. Mare needed a vantage point, somewhere to observe without being observed, to listen without being heard.

She found it in a small alcove near the entrance, a forgotten saint's niche that had long since lost its statue to time or theft. Only a stone pedestal remained, gathering dust where holy feet had once stood. The alcove was deep enough to conceal her if she pressed her back against its cold stone yet positioned perfectly to catch conversations as people passed.

Mare slipped into the space and crouched down, making a show of adjusting her boot laces for any casual observer. Her hood fell forward, shadowing her face while her fingers worked at knots that needed no tightening. Her position offered a clear view of the entrance while keeping her features obscured, a hunter's blind in the heart of the cathedral.

The measured cadence of footsteps approaching made her fingers slow their work, her body tensing like a cat sensing prey. Two clergymen walked toward the entrance; their heads bent together in the universal posture of shared secrets. The taller wore the robes of a senior deacon, his face thin and sallow with ambition. The shorter man's attire marked him as a secretary or scribe, but his bearing suggested greater importance than his position would indicate.

"...cannot allow these Puritan dogs to dictate terms," the taller man was saying, his voice barely above a whisper yet carrying in the stone chamber. "The Bishop may counsel patience, but the time for action approaches."

"Patience has its merits," the shorter man replied. "Though I agree that certain measures must be taken before the situation worsens."

They paused near the entrance, just feet from Mare's alcove. She remained perfectly still, her breathing shallow, her eyes fixed on her boot laces as if they presented a puzzle requiring her full attention.

"The brothels are the key," the tall man continued. "We burn them out, blame the Puritans for the fires. The people will turn against them when their pleasures are threatened."

The shorter man chuckled, the sound dry as autumn leaves. "An elegant solution. The Winchester Geese scattered, the Puritan faction blamed, and the Bishop's coffers unaffected since he'll collect rebuilding fees."

"Indeed. Though this assumes Wickham's fall doesn't come first."

Mare's fingers froze on her laces, her mind suddenly sharp as a blade. The Bishop's fall? This was no idle gossip between churchmen, this was conspiracy, spoken openly within the Bishop's own domain.

"His Grace's position is not as secure as it once was," the shorter man murmured. "The Queen's ear has been poisoned against him, and his protection of the theatre companies grows increasingly problematic. The time approaches when new leadership will be required."

"And you believe…"

The taller man's words died as his gaze swept across the entrance hall and landed on Mare's crouched form. His eyes narrowed, suspicious as a miser counting coins.

"You there," he called, his voice shifting to the authoritative tone used for servants and beggars. "What business have you here?"

Mare stood slowly, her face a mask of deference that she'd perfected over years of playing the invisible observer. "Forgive me, your reverence. Just tightening my boot before I depart. The cobbles outside are treacherous when wet."

The clergymen exchanged glances, a silent communication that Mare couldn't fully interpret but recognized as dangerous.

"The cathedral is no place for loitering," the shorter man said, his earlier conspiratorial tone replaced with public piety. "We were just discussing the upcoming feast day preparations. Such a holy time for reflection on our mortal sins."

The abrupt change of subject was as subtle as a tavern brawl. Mare lowered her eyes, the picture of chastened humility.

"Of course, your reverence. I'll be on my way directly."

She moved past them with measured steps, neither too hurried nor too casual. Her face remained impassive, but behind the mask, her mind raced like a hunted fox. The Bishop's fall. Burning brothels. Puritan factions. The theatre companies. Each piece connected to the next in ways she didn't yet understand but knew instinctively were tied to the dead clergyman and the seal hidden against her skin.

The guards at the Clink precinct's outer gate barely glanced at her as she passed. Mare was a known quantity, the Bishop's shadow, his street ear, his deniable asset. She nodded to them with the perfect balance of familiarity and distance that her position required. They returned the gesture with equal disinterest, already turning their attention to a wagon attempting to enter.

Outside, the Thames fog rolled in thick as wool, shrouding Southwark's streets in grey obscurity. Perfect weather for secrets and lies. Mare pulled her cloak tighter around her shoulders, feeling the weight of the brass seal and bloodstained parchment in her hidden pockets. The morning crowd parted around her, market women with baskets, apprentices rushing on errands, sailors stumbling from a night's debauchery.

None of them knew the game unfolding in their midst. None of them saw the gathering storm that threatened to consume the district; Puritans against the Bishop, clergymen plotting to burn the very brothels that put coin in their master's purse, whispers of Wickham's fall from grace. And at the centre, a dead man in the Thames mud, his throat cut, his hand clutching a seal that now rested against Mare's ribs like a burning coal.

The Winchester Geese, the prostitutes who worked under the Bishop's protection and paid his taxes, had no idea their livelihoods and their lives hung in the balance of power shifting within the cathedral walls. They were hocks, as Mare had once been. As part of her still was.

She disappeared into the fog like a ghost, her mind calculating loyalties and betrayals, power, and survival. The Bishop demanded she discover any evidence of the dead clergyman. Yet that same evidence might be her only leverage if Wickham's position truly was precarious. The question that pressed against her mind with each step was simple yet impossible to answer with certainty: Which side of the coming war offered the best chance of survival?

Mare's fingers closed around the seal and parchment in her pocket as she vanished into the grey morning, leaving no trace of her passing save footprints in the mud that the next rain would wash away.

Hunger gnawed at Mare's belly like a rat at a corpse. She blinked awake in the grey half-light, the silence pressing against her ears like water. No coughing. No muttered prayers. No scrape of the cooking pot. Just nothing. Her eyes found the still form on the pallet across the single room—her mother, lying motionless beneath a thin blanket, face turned to the wall.

"Ma?" The word died empty and lost in the airless hovel.

Mare pushed herself up from her nest of rags in the corner. Her legs wobbled, weak from days without proper food. The floor felt cold against her bare feet as she crept toward her mother's bed.

"Ma, I'm hungry."

She knew before she touched the shoulder. Knew from the stillness, from the absence of breath sounds, from the smell that was different now, no longer sweat and sickness but something else, something final. Mare's small hand connected with cloth covering bone. She pulled gently, rolling her mother toward her.

The face that greeted her wasn't her mother's anymore. The plague had hollowed her cheeks and blackened the flesh beneath her eyes. Her lips were pulled back in a grimace that showed teeth too large for the shrunken face. The marks on her neck had turned the colour of spoiled meat.

Mare didn't cry. Tears were for when Ma could stroke her hair and whisper comfort. There was no comfort in this room anymore, just a body that used to hold her mother and now held nothing at all.

She backed away from the bed. Her stomach growled again, reminding her that death didn't end hunger. Death didn't end anything but the dead. The living still needed to eat.

Mare pulled her only dress over her shift. It was too small, the hem barely reaching her knees, the sleeves stopping halfway down her skinny arms. She found her worn leather shoes beneath the bed and slipped them on without stockings. No time for stockings when hunger clawed at your insides.

At the door, she paused, looking back at the figure on the bed.

"I'll come back, Ma," she lied, knowing she wouldn't. Knowing the body-collectors would come eventually. Knowing there would be nothing to come back to.

The London streets swallowed her whole. Mare had never felt so small, a twig caught in a rushing river of flesh and noise. Bodies pressed past her, men with shoulders wide as doorways, women with skirts that swept her aside like refuse. Everyone moved with purpose, with destination. Everyone except Mare.

The market square heaved with activity. Fishwives shouted their wares, their faces red with effort and ale. Apprentice boys scurried between stalls, carrying messages and goods. A pair of city watchmen leaned against a wall, picking their teeth with disinterest. The smell of roasting meat from a vendor's cart made Mare's stomach twist painfully.

She slipped between bodies, light as a ghost, eyes scanning for opportunity. A dropped coin, an unattended loaf, a moment's distraction from a fruit-seller, any of these could mean the difference between eating and starving. But the market folk knew her kind, kept their goods close and their eyes sharp.

"Hungry, little mouse?"

The voice came from behind, startling her. Mare turned to see a man squatting to her level. His face was a ruin—pockmarked skin stretched across sharp bones, gaps where teeth should be, a smile that twisted rather than reassured. His clothes stank of fish guts and piss.

"Got bread back at me place," he said, revealing blackened stumps when he spoke. "Cheese too. Fresh milk, even. All for a pretty little thing what's polite."

Mare's belly answered before her brain could warn her. It growled loud enough for the man to hear, his grin widening in response.

"That's right. Proper hungry, ain' t ye? Come on, then. Not far."

His hand closed around hers, calloused palm, fingers sticky with God-knew-what. Warning bells rang in Mare's head, distant memories of her mother's cautions about strangers, but hunger was louder, more insistent.

He led her away from the market, down a narrow alley where the buildings leaned together as if whispering secrets. The sounds of the street faded with each step. Sunlight struggled to reach them here, trapped between the overhanging upper stories of the buildings.

"Just down here," the man said, pulling her deeper into the shadows. "Nice and private, like."

The alley ended in a small courtyard walled by the backs of buildings. No windows overlooked it, just blank stone, and weathered wood. A dead end. The only way out was the way they'd come in.

"Where's the bread?" Mare asked, her voice small but steady.

The man's grip tightened painfully around her wrist. "After." His other hand went to the front of his breeches. "Turn around first, little mouse. Bend over and close your eyes."

Understanding dawned, cold, and sickening. Mare tried to pull away, but his fingers dug deeper, bruising. He spun her, pushing her toward the damp wall.

"Don't fight, now. Be good and ye'll get your food after. Fight, and ye'll get worse than empty belly."

His breath hit the back of her neck, hot and reeking of rot. Mare squeezed her eyes shut, her body rigid with terror. The blow came with a sound like a melon splitting. The man's grip vanished. A thud followed, the heavy sound of a body hitting cobblestones.

Mare spun around. The man lay crumpled on the ground, a dark stain spreading beneath his head. Above him stood a girl, not a woman yet, fifteen or sixteen. She held a length of wood in her hand, the end of it wet and dark.

"Fucking bastard," the girl spat at the prone figure. "I told ya last time I'd split your skull if I caught ya with another child."

She turned to Mare, her face softening slightly. Her hair was a tangled mess of blonde curls, her dress worn but clean. Sharp eyes assessed Mare quickly.

"You all right, then? He didn't touch ya proper, did he?"

Mare shook her head, still too shocked to speak.

"Good. I'm Bess. What's your name?"

"Marion," she whispered.

Bess nodded, dropping the bloody club beside the man's body. "Well, Marion, you best come with me. This rat will wake up angry if he wakes at all." She extended a hand, cleaner than the man's had been. "Where do ya live?"

Mare hesitated, then pointed vaguely in the direction they'd come from. "Ma's dead. Plague took her."

Something shifted in Bess's expression, recognition, understanding. "Show me."

They walked through streets that seemed different now with Bess beside her. The bigger bodies still pushed past, but Bess pushed back, carving a path for them both. When they reached the hovel, Mare hung back, unwilling to enter again.

"In there," she said, pointing at the door.

Bess disappeared inside, returning moments later. Her face was grim. "Plague, sure enough. They'll take her to the pit by sundown." She looked down at Mare. "You've nowhere else?"

Mare shook her head.

"Then you'll come with me. My ma's being taken today too. Same plague. Come on."

Bess led her through winding streets to the riverside, where a small group of people had gathered. A cart stood waiting, already laden with shrouded bundles. Men in vinegar-soaked masks lifted another, Bess's mother, wrapped in a sheet. The smell of lavender hung thick in the air, fighting unsuccessfully against the stench of death.

A priest mumbled words over the cart, his face turned away from the bodies, his nose pinched between thumb and forefinger. No one wept. No one spoke. The cart creaked as it pulled away, taking the dead to a pit outside the city walls.

"That's that, then," Bess said, her voice flat. "Come on."

They walked to a narrow building squashed between a cooper's shop and a chandler's. A wooden sign hung above the door—a red hat with a tassel. The Cardinal's Cap.

"I live upstairs," Bess explained, leading Mare through a taproom that stank of spilled ale and sweat. Men glanced up from their cups, eyes lingering too long on Bess, barely noticing Mare's small form behind her.

The room at the top of the stairs was small but clean. A bed assumed one wall, a small table and stool occupied another. A cracked window let in a square of grey light.

"Sit," Bess ordered, pointing to the stool. She rummaged in a box and produced a hunk of bread and a piece of hard cheese. "Eat slow or you'll sick it back up."

Mare's hands trembled as she took the food. The bread tasted better than anything she could remember.

"You can stay here," Bess said, watching her eat. "But when I have... friends visiting, you'll need to wait on the stairs. Understand?"

Mare nodded, not understanding at all but willing to agree to anything for the safety of this room, this food, this girl who had saved her.

Bess smiled, the expression softening her sharp features. She reached into the box again and pulled out a cloth doll, its face smudged, its dress torn but carefully mended.

"Here. This was mine when I was small as you."

Mare took the doll with reverence, her fingers tracing the stitched face. She hugged it to her chest, happiness bubbling up through the fear, hunger, and grief. But the doll squirmed in her arms. Its stitched mouth opened in a silent scream. It wriggled free of her grasp and leapt to the floor, running toward the door on stuffed legs that shouldn't move.

"No!" Mare cried, reaching for it. "Come back!"

The doll turned, its thread mouth now a gaping hole, and laughed. The sound tore through the room like ripping fabric.

Mare jerked awake, a cry dying on her lips. The dream clung to her like river fog, images of her mother's plague-ravaged face dissolving into the reality of a rented room in Southwark. She sat up, heart hammering against her ribs, the taste of old fear bitter in her mouth. The room was different, larger, cleaner, with a proper bed and chest, but the squalor of her childhood was never far, always waiting in dreams to remind her of the girl she'd been. Of Bess who'd saved her. Of the life she'd escaped, only to trade it for different dangers.

Mare pressed the heels of her hands against her eyes, willing the dream away. The Bishop's seal pressed against her ribs, the dead man's secrets heavy as stones. No time for ghosts when the living posed such immediate threats.

Chapter Three

The Playwright's Quill

The Rose theatre, stood like a wooden ghost against the midnight sky, its timbers creaking in the gentle wind like an old man's joints. She had seen it built, its Octagonal pit and three stories of timber clad boxes merging into an amphitheatre that delighted London's massing populace. Mare approached from the shadows, her footsteps silent as death on the damp earth. The Bishop's seal pressed against her ribs beneath layers of wool and linen, a constant reminder of the dangerous game she'd stumbled into. She knew the theatre would be empty of its usual crowd, the players and patrons who filled it with life during daylight hours but not entirely deserted. He would be waiting, as he always did when he sent word.

She circled the structure twice, checking for watchers, a habit that had kept her breathing when others had stopped. Satisfied, she slipped through the side entrance, a narrow door used by stagehands and players that was never properly locked. The hinges protested with a soft whine that made her wince. Mare paused in the darkness, letting her eyes adjust to the deeper blackness inside, her senses extending like fingers into the gloom.

The theatre's emptiness had a presence all its own. Without the pressure of bodies and voices, the vast wooden structure held its breath, storing echoes of past performances in its beams. The smell hit her first, wet timber softening in places where rain had found its way through the thatched roof, tallow candles burned down to stubs, their greasy smoke still hanging in the air. Beneath that lay the metallic trace of stage paint and the musty odour of costumes stored too long without washing. Death, glory, and pretence, all mingling in the stale air.

Mare moved along the edge of the gallery, keeping to the shadows. The stage lay before her, a half-constructed forest scene abandoned mid-creation. Wooden trees stood like sentinels, painted green leaves drooping toward the boards. Scattered props, a crown, a wooden sword, a fool's bauble, lay waiting for the next day's performance. The trapdoor in the centre of the stage was slightly ajar, a darker square in the darkness.

She sensed rather than saw him at first, a shift in the shadows, a presence that disturbed the theatre's empty slumber.

"You took your time," Christopher Marlowe said, stepping out from behind a painted backdrop. He held a single candle, the flame casting his sharp features into harsh relief, cheekbones like knife edges, eyes deep-set and burning with an intensity that had drawn her to him from their first meeting over a year ago. "I was beginning to think the Bishop had finally discovered your divided loyalties."

"The Bishop knows exactly where my loyalties lie," Mare replied, remaining where she was, one hand casually near her hidden dagger. "With whoever keeps me breathing and fed."

Kit, as everybody called him, smiled, the expression not reaching his eyes. "How refreshingly mercenary of you, my dear."

He was dressed simply for a man of his reputation, dark breeches and a shirt of decent linen, ink stains on his fingers that no amount of washing ever seemed to remove. His hair fell in unruly waves around a handsome face that women found either captivating or unsettling, with little middle ground. Mare had always leaned toward the former, though she'd learned to distrust that impulse.

"You asked for me," she said, finally approaching. "Here I am."

"Here you are indeed." His eyes moved over her with familiar hunger, but there was something else there too, a calculation, an assessment. "Looking remarkably untroubled for someone carrying death in her pocket."

Mare's hand moved unconsciously to where the bloodstained parchment lay hidden, and she saw Kit track the movement. Damn him and his observant eyes.

"Speak plainly or not at all," she said. "I've had enough riddles today to last me till Judgment Day."

Kit glanced toward the partially open trapdoor, then back to her. He moved closer, close enough that she could smell the wine on his breath and beneath it, the ink and paper scent that clung to him always.

"Prela sub scaena," he whispered, his lips almost brushing her ear. "The press beneath the stage. That's what they're whispering about in the taverns, in the palace corridors, in the Bishop's own halls. A nest of sedition right under the noses of the authorities."

Mare kept her face impassive, though her heart quickened. The same Latin phrase that was on the dead clergyman's hidden parchment, now spoken aloud by Kit.

"And what would I care for a printing press?" she asked, moving past him to examine the stage more carefully. Her eyes noted every detail, the worn spots on the boards where trapdoors were most often used, the shadow beneath the partially open centre trap, the smell of ink that seemed stronger near certain areas.

"Because, my sweet Southwark rose, this press prints words that could topple giants." Kit's voice took on the passionate cadence he used when performing his own works, part sermon, part seduction. "While Queen Elizabeth's court fiddles with its jewels and courtly dances, common men are learning to read. And what they read shapes what they think."

Mare glanced back at him, at the fervour in his eyes that both attracted and alarmed her. "Pretty thoughts for a university man," she said.

"More than thoughts." Kit moved to stand beside her, looking down at the trapdoor. "These pamphlets circulate among the common folk, giving voice to ideas that would never be spoken aloud in polite company. Ideas about the natural rights of men, about the tyranny of the church, about the corruption that flows from Westminster to the farthest corners of the realm."

As he spoke, his hands moved in expansive gestures, painting visions in the candlelight. Mare watched those hands, elegant despite the ink stains, capable of writing words that moved audiences to tears and of opening a man's throat with equal skill. Kit was many things, few of them safe.

"Pretty words don't fill empty bellies, Kit," she said, cutting through his rhetoric with Southwark's brutal practicality. "People who spout such things tend to lose their heads, while the hungry stay hungry and the rich stay rich."

Kit's expression hardened for a moment before shifting to a smile that didn't touch his eyes. "Such cynicism from one so young. Has the Bishop taught you so well to distrust hope?"

"Hope is a luxury," Mare replied, her fingers brushing against the raised edge of the trapdoor. "Like clean water and untorn stockings. I prefer more tangible currencies."

"And yet here you are," Kit countered, "carrying something that brought death to its last owner. Is that tangible enough for you?"

She turned slowly to face him, her expression carefully blank. "What exactly do you know about what I'm carrying?"

"I know that a man who worked for the Bishop was found in the Thames with his throat cut," Kit said, his voice dropping lower. "I know that certain items went missing from his person before the body was discovered by the authorities. And I know that you have a habit of being in precisely the wrong place at the wrong time."

The hidden seal seemed to burn against Mare's skin. She maintained her composure with the skill of years spent hiding her thoughts from men who would kill her for them.

"Interesting theories," she said. "You should write them into your next play. The groundlings love a good murder."

Kit's laugh was soft and dangerous. "My dear, we're all already in the play. Some of us just don't know which part we've been cast to perform." He stepped closer, the candle flame illuminating the intensity in his eyes. "The question is whether you're playing the hero or the fool."

Mare felt the weight of the parchment in her pocket, the embossed brass of the seal against her skin, and the growing certainty that she was caught between forces far larger than she'd imagined. Kit stood before her, beautiful and treacherous as a poisoned cup, offering knowledge that might save her or condemn her.

Kit's words hung between them, heavy with implications and dangers neither could fully voice. Mare stepped closer, close enough to see the slight tremor in his hands as he held the candle, the way his throat moved when he swallowed. Political fervour had always stirred something in him that mirrored desire, the two passions tangled in his poet's soul until they became indistinguishable. She knew this, had used it before. Her hand reached up, fingers brushing against his cheek, a calculated touch that could be mistaken for tenderness if one didn't look too closely at her eyes.

"You play with fire, Kit," she whispered, her voice rough-edged in the theatre's emptiness. "And fire is not particular about what it burns."

His free hand caught her wrist, holding it against his face. His skin was hot, feverish, burning with the same intensity that filled his words that spoke of revolution and justice. "Some things are worth burning for."

"Pretty sentiment from a man who's never been cold," Mare replied, but she didn't pull away. Instead, she moved closer, her body pressing against his with deliberate purpose. Information had its price, and her body was currency she'd learned to spend carefully.

Kit's breath hitched, his eyes darkening with a hunger that had nothing to do with politics. The candle wavered in his grip, casting wild shadows across the painted backdrop behind them. "You mock my privilege," he said, "but you benefit from it all the same."

Mare's laugh was sharp as broken glass. "Is that what we're calling it now?"

She took the candle from his unresisting fingers and set it on a nearby prop table, where it cast just enough light to see by. Then her hands were on him, not gentle, not loving, but purposeful. Kit responded with equal urgency, backing her against the wall of the backstage area, his fingers tangling in her hair, pulling it free from its careful arrangement.

The wall was rough against her back, splinters catching at the wool of her cloak. Mare felt the familiar weight of desire pool low in her belly, but kept it leashed, controlled. This was business as much as pleasure, a transaction where her body purchased secrets her ears might never hear. Kit's mouth found her neck, his teeth grazing the sensitive skin there as his hands worked at the fastenings of her bodice.

"Tell me about the press," she gasped as his fingers found bare skin. "Where is it? Who runs it? Who writes the pamphlets?"

Kit laughed against her throat, the sound vibrating through her. "Even now, you're working," he murmured, pulling back to look at her with a mixture of admiration and hurt. "Do you ever stop being the Bishop's creature?"

Mare's hand snaked between them, finding the hardness straining against his breeches. She squeezed, hard enough to make his eyes flutter closed. "I'm no one's creature but my own."

Their coupling was swift and urgent, as it always was, clothing pushed aside rather than removed, bodies joining with the efficiency of long practice. Mare hitched one leg around his waist, her back pressed hard against the wooden wall. She kept her eyes open, scanning the shadows around them even as Kit lost himself in her body. Her scarred palm pressed flat against his chest, feeling the thundering heart beneath his ribs. That scar, the Bishop's first lesson in obedience, compelled against Kit's skin like a brand, a reminder of loyalties she couldn't entirely surrender.

Mare watched Kit's face as pleasure overtook him, the vulnerability there, the momentary surrender of his sharp intellect to something more primal. She allowed herself to follow, but even in release, a part of her remained vigilant, alert to the creaking theatre around them and the secrets it harboured beneath its wooden floors.

Afterward, they separated with practiced efficiency, rearranging clothing in the dim candlelight. Kit's hands trembled slightly as he retied the laces of his shirt, his eyes not meeting hers. The fire of his earlier passion had banked to embers, replaced by a wariness that Mare recognized all too well. They both knew this dance, bodies shared while secrets remained carefully guarded.

"Your hair," Kit said finally, gesturing to the tangled mass that now fell past her shoulders. He moved behind her, his fingers gentle as they gathered the dark strands, twisting them back into a semblance of order. Mare felt his hands working, but also the subtle shift of weight as his other hand moved to her cloak, hanging on a nail nearby.

She pretended not to notice the slight rustle of paper, the careful sliding of something into a hidden pocket. Information had its price, and she'd just paid it, whether she wished to or not.

"There," Kit said, settling the cloak around her shoulders with unusual care. "Presentable enough that the watchmen won't mistake you for one of the Winchester Geese."

Mare snorted. "The Geese dress better than I do. Wickham sees to that."

Kit's expression darkened at the mention of the Bishop's name. "How long will you serve him, Mare? A man who taxes the very flesh of women, who profits from the suffering of your neighbours while pretending to moral authority?"

"Until a better option presents itself," she replied pragmatically, adjusting her cloak so that it hung properly, feeling the new weight in its folds. "Unless you're offering me a position in your household? I could mend your stockings and listen to you compose sonnets all day."

The bitterness in her voice was real, and Kit flinched from it. "You deserve better than either fate."

"Deserving has nothing to do with surviving in Southwark," Mare said, moving toward the theatre's side entrance. "Words won't change that, no matter how pretty you make them."

Kit followed her, the candle casting their shadows long and distorted against the wooden walls. "You're wrong," he said, his voice taking on that fervent quality again. "Words can change everything. The right words, printed and distributed, read aloud in taverns and marketplaces, they become thoughts, and thoughts become actions."

Mare paused at the door, turning to face him one last time. "And actions become corpses floating in the Thames. I've seen where your words lead, Kit."

"Not my words," he insisted. "Not yet. But soon, perhaps." He reached for her hand, his thumb brushing across her scarred palm with deliberate gentleness. "Be careful, Mare. The game you're playing has more pieces than you know."

"I'm not playing a game," she replied, pulling her hand away. "I'm just trying to stay alive. Something you might consider as well."

As she turned to leave, her gaze caught on the stage's central trapdoor, slightly ajar as it had been when she arrived. Prela sub scaena. The press beneath the stage. The dead clergyman had died for whatever lay beneath some wooden boards, could it be those? Kit could not be that stupid could he, or could he? A press printing words that threatened the powerful. Words that Kit clearly knew about, even wrote.

The realisation settled in her stomach like a stone. The murdered man in the river, the Bishop's missing seal, the parchment with its Latin phrase; all connected to this place, to Kit, to whatever conspiracy bubbled beneath London's surface like a pot about to boil over.

Mare slipped out into the night, the frigid air a shock after the close warmth of the theatre. She moved through the shadows with practiced ease, putting distance between herself and the wooden playhouse that harboured more secrets than players. Only when she'd reached the relative safety of an alley three streets away did she reach into her cloak's hidden pocket.

The pamphlet was small, crudely printed on paper that felt rough against her fingers. Even in the dim light of the alley, she could make out the bold heading: "On the Natural Rights of Men to Worship According to Conscience." Below it, in smaller type: "With Observations on the Corruption of the Bishops."

Mare's expression hardened as she tucked the treasonous document away. Kit's dangerous idealism would get him killed, and now he'd tried to make her complicit in his crusade, using her body as the battlefield for his recruitment. The trust between them, already stretched thin, had finally snapped like a frayed rope.

She moved deeper into Southwark's familiar darkness, the weight of papers and seal and secrets dragging at her like stones tied to a drowning woman's ankles.

Chapter Four

The Order Revealed

The tunnels beneath Southwark were older than the city above, older than the river, older, Mare sometimes suspected, than God's patience for the people who squatted atop them. Most folk wouldn't have braved those warrens for a sack of coin and a promise from the Queen herself. Mare picked her way through them on nothing, but a sodden scrap of parchment, a gutful of nerves, and the Bishop's brass seal chafing her tit.

Southwark's underbelly didn't smell any better than bad guts, but at least down here the river stink was cut with the sharp tang of mildew, burnt tallow, and piss. The torches had long since guttered out, so she moved by the faintest hint of phosphor from the mould crawling the stones and the occasional echo of some other poor bastard scrabbling for safety or a place to die.

She paused at every junction, comparing the twisting script on the parchment delivered by Walsingham, to the crude marks scrawled on the tunnel walls, a broken crucifix here, a row of teeth there, a cock-and-balls rendered in excruciating detail and then, for good measure, labelled as the prior of St. Mary's. Mare smirked. Southwark's poor couldn't read, but they drew with savage precision.

Her boots squelched in mud, the sort that sucked at your foot and tried to keep it as a trophy. Every few paces the ceiling dipped low enough to force her into a crouch, and once she had to duck around a spot where the stone had caved in and left a puddle of black water too wide to step over. She kept her head down and her mind sharp, remembering the last time she'd let her focus drift in these tunnels, two months healing a cracked rib courtesy of the Winchester Geese, and a matching scar she never bothered explaining.

Left at the cracked statue of a weeping angel (the only angel in Southwark with both tits and a cock), straight past the catacomb that reeked of old meat, then a right at the archway shaped like a gaping mouth. If she hadn't spent her youth filching bread and running from pimps, she might have been lost within three turns. Instead, she moved with the half-mad confidence of someone who'd already decided she wasn't going to die today, so fuck the odds.

The Bishop's seal burned against her breast, a cold accusation she kept pressed under two layers of damp linen. It was supposed to buy her entry, or at least safety. Instead, it felt like a beacon screaming her secrets into every shadow.

She nearly missed the last turn. The "door" was a slab of wet oak wedged into the wall and disguised with a rotting tapestry, St. Ursula, but with the saint's eyes scraped off and red paint oozing from the sockets. Subtle as a dog's bollocks, Mare thought. She knocked, three short and two long, as directed.

The panel slid back, and two women stared her down from the gloom. Both wore men's clothes, the kind stitched to allow for quick movement and concealed weapons. The taller had a nose broken in at least three places, the other a shiv tucked into her sleeve. Neither smiled.

"About time" said the big one.

"I'm not a clock," Mare replied, holding up her hands.

They stepped forward in tandem, the shorter circling behind to check for a tail while the big one patted Mare down with the practiced enthusiasm of a constable shaking a drunk for loose change. Her hands went everywhere, ankles, calves, thighs, groin, and up under the arms, pausing only to linger at the spot where the seal was hidden. Mare tensed, but the big woman just grunted and moved on.

"Light," she barked.

The other woman struck a spark and lifted a lantern to Mare's face, as if expecting her to flinch from the truth. Mare stared back, unblinking. Her interrogator grinned, a flash of rotten teeth in the dark.

"Cute. Go ahead."

The door swung inward, and Mare ducked past them into a tunnel that opened into what looked like the crypt of a forgotten church. The air inside was warmer, thick with the sickly-sweet breath of too many bodies in too little space. Tallow candles crowded the walls in iron sconces, each flame spitting and guttering in the faint current.

Twenty women sat in a rough semicircle, perched on overturned barrels, and scavenged crates. Most wore their hair hidden beneath dark scarves, but a few let it fall in wild tangles. The clothes were a patchwork of brothel rags, cutpurse leather, and stained wool that had seen more rain than sunshine. Their faces were a catalogue of what happened when you survived Southwark for more than a decade, old bruises fading to yellow, new bruises blooming purple, and the kind of haunted, razor-edged attention that never let its guard down.

At the centre stood a woman Mare recognized even before the guards announced her. Sister Agnes. She was taller than Mare remembered, or that was just the authority she wore like a second skin. Her hair was the colour of dirty snow, scraped back so severe it made her cheekbones look like they could cut glass. Her face had once been beautiful but now it was a map of hard choices and harder winters. The only ornamentation she allowed herself was a scar at her left wrist, jagged and white, where a rope or blade had nearly done for her once and failed.

As Mare entered, every eye in the room followed. The semicircle adjusted, gaps closing, as if to make sure there'd be no easy exit for her. Sister Agnes waited until the candlelight had caught Mare's features before she spoke.

"Another lost lamb seeking shelter?" Her voice was pure cathedral, but with enough gutter on the vowels to let you know she'd worked for every inch of her authority.

Mare bowed her head. "Depends on who's offering."

A ripple of laughter moved through the room, low, not friendly, more the sound of predators enjoying a rare moment of entertainment.

Sister Agnes stepped forward, and Mare's guards melted into the shadows behind her. "We don't get many from the Bishop's flock down here. Usually, he prefers his girls with more skin and less wit."

"I don't work for the Bishop," Mare said, careful to keep her tone respectful but not weak. "I work for myself. Sometimes that means crossing his path, sometimes not."

"Everyone works for someone, girl," Agnes replied. "That's how the world stays broken."

Another laugh, this time with a bitter undertone.

Agnes gestured, and one of the other women, small, sharp-chinned, fingers stained with ink, produced a half-empty bottle of gin and two chipped mugs. She poured for Agnes first, then for Mare, and retreated to her perch.

"Sit," Agnes commanded, and Mare sat, ignoring the scrape of splinters on her thighs.

The circle watched her with blank faces, waiting for the next move.

Sister Agnes raised her mug. "A toast, then. To freedom, and the women who fight for it."

Mare clinked her mug and drank. The gin burned like truth on the way down.

The candles hissed, the shadows inched closer, and Mare realized, with a mixture of awe and dread, that these women weren't just survivors. They were building something. Not a brothel, not a gang, not a church, but, for the first time in Southwark, a sisterhood that would kill for each other instead of letting the world do it to them.

Sister Agnes set her mug down and fixed Mare with a look that saw straight through every mask and lie.

"So," she said. "Why are you here?"

And for once, Mare hesitated before answering.

Mare took the moment's pause as a chance to scan the crypt again, this time with both eyes open and a different calculus at work behind them. There were alcoves to the sides, three, she counted, each holding a pallet and a woman or girl not sitting with the group. One slept or pretended to; her arm was bound in splints and propped on a stack of rags. Another lay curled tight on her side, face blackened with healing burns, hands clutching a rosary with all the tenderness of a drowning child clinging to driftwood. The third girl stared straight at Mare, eyes huge and unblinking, the whites gone yellow with some slow fever.

Agnes waited. It was a good tactic, letting the silence chew at Mare's nerves. If Sister had ever been a nun, she'd kept the patience and lost the mercy.

"I'm here because the Bishop wants me dead," Mare said, keeping her voice steady. "And because the last time a man tried to collect the bounty on me, I left him with less balls than God gave him. So, I figured it was time to find better company."

A lie, but not a complete one. The best kind.

Sister Agnes smiled, the effect more frightening than friendly. "Which man was that?"

"Does it matter? They're all the same once you see them from below."

More laughter from the group. Agnes paced around Mare, hands behind her back like a magistrate waiting to pass sentence.

"You've worked the brothels," Agnes said. Not a question.

Mare nodded. "And the gaming dens, and a bit of honest picking before the Bishop's men got their claws in me."

"Honest picking," Agnes repeated. "You hear that, girls? Our guest here is a model citizen."

A woman with a mashed nose and cauliflower ears spat onto the stones. "More honest than a priest," she said. The others grunted agreement.

Agnes held up a hand and all fell silent. "You know what they call us, in the ledgers?" she said to Mare, voice rising so all could hear. "Winchester Geese. Like we're poultry, plucked and caged for the Bishop's table. The Bishop eats, the Queen eats, and if you're lucky you get the bones."

"I know," Mare said, meaning it. She glanced at the girl with the burns, then the one with the broken arm. "I'm not here for pity, though."

Sister Agnes drew closer, close enough for Mare to smell the cloves she chewed to cover the stink of cheap gin. "No, you're not," she said. "You're here because you want to live."

"Is that so rare?" Mare shot back.

"In Southwark? Wanting to live is the most dangerous trait you can have."

A new voice piped up, one Mare hadn't noticed, a kid no more than fifteen with the look of someone who'd seen every dark trick the district had to offer. "She's got the look, Sister. She's not one of the Bishop's birds."

Agnes looked at Mare, then back at the girl. "You trust her?"

The kid shrugged, shoulders bony as a chicken. "Trust her more than I trust the men up top. If she's lying, we'll know soon enough."

That got another round of dark chuckles.

Sister Agnes turned her full attention to Mare, eyes searching for the crack in her story. "We're not a charity," she said, "and we're not a brothel. If you want to stay, you must earn it."

Mare looked at the huddle of faces, the broken but not beaten, the scars on their bodies and the steel in their eyes. She thought of her own scars, old and new, and the Bishop's seal still burning against her.

"I can pull my weight," she said.

Agnes nodded. "We'll see."

She turned to the assembly. "Show her what we do."

One by one, the women told their stories. Mare listened, arms folded, face impassive.

The girl with the fever had worked the Rose Tavern before she was old enough to bleed. When a Puritan preacher tried to "save" her, she laughed in his face. He had her dragged behind the theatre and beaten till her spine cracked. Agnes found her in the mud and put her back together with splints and vinegar.

The burn victim had been set alight by a client who wanted to watch a witch burn. When the church investigated, they declared the matter closed; after all, she'd survived.

The girl with the broken arm was sold by her own mother to a debt collector. When she tried to run, the Bishop's men caught her. They broke her arm as a warning.

Every story had the same core: a system designed to consume women, then discard them when they stopped being profitable or pretty.

When the last testimony faded, Agnes addressed Mare again. "Do you see why we exist?"

Mare nodded, feeling a weight in her gut that had nothing to do with hunger.

"The church takes everything from us," said the burn victim, voice raw. "Even the right to curse their names."

"That's why we started the Order," said the kid with the sharp face. "Not for charity, but for vengeance."

The group muttered, some crossing themselves, others just spitting on the floor.

Agnes pulled up a crate and sat, finally at Mare's level. "You know the Bishop's methods," she said. "How he keeps the Geese in line. His private men, his ledgers, his taxes. Tell us how he does it. Tell us what you know."

Mare hesitated, which wasn't like her. She chose her words carefully. "It's not all organized. Some of it's just old habit. If you pay your taxes, the Bishop's men leave you alone, unless you're too pretty, or too loud, or someone higher up wants you for himself. Then the taxes become leverage."

"And if you don't pay?"

"You disappear," Mare said. "Or worse, sometimes they make an example."

Agnes grunted. "So nothing has changed in thirty years."

"They're clever about it," Mare added. "The Bishop gives some of the girls a taste of power, lets them run errands or collect debts. Makes them think they're in the inner circle, but really, he's just using them to track the others."

"That's true," said the woman with the mashed nose. "My sister worked for him. Thought she was untouchable. Then she crossed him, and they found her in the river."

A shiver passed through the group.

Sister Agnes leaned forward, her scarred wrist visible on the crate. "What do you want, Mare? Sanctuary? Or something more?"

Mare didn't answer immediately. She stared at her mug, the dregs swirling. "I want him gone," she said quietly. "But I know that's a wish for fools."

"Maybe," said Agnes, "but we make our own luck down here."

A commotion near the entrance broke the tension. One of the guards appeared, dragging a man by the collar. He was thin, ragged, face half-hidden by a blood-soaked kerchief. The women tensed, some rising, ready to fight.

"He tried to follow," said the guard, shoving the man forward. "Should we kill him now, or later?"

Agnes motioned for calm. "Let's see who he is first."

Mare recognized him, barely, a minor clerk from the Bishop's office, one who sometimes delivered messages and sometimes blackmailed girls for favours. He looked at Mare with bloodshot eyes and spit on the ground.

"Fucking whores," he croaked. "You'll all hang for this."

The group surged forward, but Agnes held them back. She walked to the man and slapped him, open-palmed, with enough force to snap his head around.

"Try again," she said.

He glared. "Wickham will find you."

"Tell Bishop Wickham we're ready for him," Agnes said, her voice cold and clear. "And if he wants to meet, he knows where to find me."

She nodded to the guards, who dragged the man away, their fists already working him over as they went.

Agnes turned back to Mare. "That's what we do," she said. "We send messages."

The group relaxed, some laughing, others just breathing easier. The girl with the fever caught Mare's eye and smiled, slow and tragic. Mare smiled back, barely. Sister Agnes poured two more drinks, handed one to Mare. "You ever killed a man, Mare?"

Mare didn't blink. "A few."

Agnes nodded. "Good. We may need you soon."

She raised her mug again. "To vengeance, then."

They drank. The candles flickered, the shadows leaned in, and for the first time since she'd taken the Bishop's coin, Mare felt like she was somewhere she belonged. But belonging, she knew, was just another way to get yourself killed.

Sister Agnes stood, adjusting her battered tunic. "One more thing," she said, her gaze pinning Mare to the spot. "What do you know of the Bishop's personal seal?"

Mare's fingers twitched, betraying her before she could stop them.

"Nothing," she lied. "Never seen it up close."

Agnes's smile was as thin as a razor. "You're a poor liar, Mare. And you're hiding something."

The circle of women leaned in, eyes glinting.

Mare braced herself, ready for the next question, or the blade that might follow if her answers didn't satisfy. Mare took a slow, steady breath and forced her fingers to unclench. She'd lied to better women than Agnes before, but few had the habit of sniffing out bullshit with such economy. She let her eyes wander the circle, taking in the faces. No one moved, not even to scratch an itch. She'd met less attentive audiences at royal executions.

"The Bishop's seal," she said, stalling, "isn't for show. It's for control. Every letter, every edict, every order to punish or protect, nothing leaves his hand without the mark. Most men don't even know what it looks like, but the ones who do know to shit themselves if it shows up at their door."

Agnes's head cocked a fraction, either curious or amused. "And what does it look like?"

"Brass," Mare said, "about the size of a thumbprint. The wolf of Winchester on the face, Latin round the edges. He keeps it on a chain round his neck, except when he wants to remind someone who's boss, then he presses it into their palm himself. Leaves a mark for days. Sometimes longer if he's feeling generous."

Agnes gave nothing away, but a few of the women in the circle shared wary glances. Mare felt the power shift, subtle as the tide on a windless day. She knew enough to be useful, even dangerous.

"You've seen it," Agnes said. Not a question.

"Once. When he wanted to make sure I remembered my place. I still do," Mare replied, flexing the fingers of her left hand in memory.

The moment hung between them. Then, surprisingly, Agnes nodded approval.

"Well," she said, "that makes you more honest than most who come through these doors. Most people think the Bishop's seal is just a bit of wax and theatre."

"It's the theatre that kills," Mare said, meaning every word.

"Indeed." Agnes rose from the crate, motioned for the circle to stand down. "Mare, come with me."

She led Mare deeper into the crypt, past a row of ancient columns and into a side chamber. Two women waited there, one leaning against the wall, arms crossed, and the other hunched over a table strewn with scraps of parchment and broken wax seals.

"This is Blackwood," said Agnes, nodding to the wall-leaner. "She oversees security. If you have a problem with her, you won't have it for long."

Blackwood didn't smile. She had a fighter's build, all muscle and scar, and fingers that drummed on her biceps with a boredom that could turn deadly in a heartbeat.

"And this is Thimble," said Agnes, gesturing to the table. "She forges the Bishop's hand better than the Bishop himself. She's also the best lockpick in the district, if you ever need a door opened that shouldn't be."

Thimble glanced up, eyes sharp behind a fringe of prematurely grey hair. "Ever picked a bone lock?" she asked, voice raspy from years of candle smoke and gin.

"Only the ones attached to men," Mare said, earning a snort from Thimble and a twitch of amusement from Blackwood.

Agnes shut the chamber door and sat at the edge of the table. "You're not here by accident," she said. "Wickham's got his hand in everything these days, and if you're on the run, it means he's either lost patience or you've outlived your usefulness."

"I'm not on the run," Mare said. "I'm looking for a way to hurt him."

Blackwood grunted. "So's half the city. Most end up in the river for their trouble."

"I plan to last longer than that," said Mare, keeping her voice even.

Agnes nodded. "We'll see."

She pulled a battered ledger from beneath the table and flipped it open. The pages were a litany of debts, names, crimes, and the kind of careful notes you made if you planned to outlive your enemies by knowing all their secrets. She pointed to a line on the page.

"Walsingham," Agnes said. "Bishop's new page. Likes to visit the Geese after hours, promises salvation, but takes his payment in flesh. He's due for a lesson. Do you know him?"

"Too well," Mare said. "He's clever, but cowardly. If you squeeze him, he'll bleed."

Agnes smiled. "Excellent. We're planning a little demonstration. Thimble here will forge a message from the Bishop, summoning Walsingham to a rendezvous. You'll deliver it, and Blackwood will make sure he doesn't walk home with all his parts intact."

Mare's lips twitched. "You trust me with this?"

"Not a bit," said Blackwood. "But you've got the face and the wit for it. If you're working for Wickham, he'll be watching you. So don't fuck up."

Mare nodded, adrenaline already sharpening her thoughts. "Where's the meeting?"

"Old tanner's yard by the bridge," Blackwood said. "Midnight. Don't be late, or we'll do the job without you and blame you for the mess."

Agnes closed the ledger and locked eyes with Mare. "Do this right, and we'll let you stay. Do it wrong, and you'll wish for the Bishop's mercy instead of mine."

Mare met her gaze, unflinching. "I won't fail."

Thimble slid a folded note across the table, the wax seal still cooling on its edge. "For you, darling. Make it look good."

Mare tucked the message into her sleeve and turned to leave. Blackwood stepped into her path.

"One more thing," said the security chief. "If you try to warn Walsingham, I'll know. And I'll find you."

Mare grinned, sharp as a razor. "If I wanted him alive, I'd just let him keep doing what he's doing."

Blackwood stepped aside, and Mare slipped out, heart hammering. The meeting in the crypt had left her with more questions than answers, but at least now she had a direction, one that might just bring the Bishop down, if she could stay ahead of the knives at her back.

As she ascended into the night, the chill hit her vigorously. The Bishop's seal burned against her chest, a reminder of what she was risking, and why. Her mind spun with schemes, with memories, with doubts.

For the first time in years, Mare allowed herself the smallest flicker of hope.

Then she buried it deep, where nothing and no one could reach.

The market writhed with bodies, a serpent's nest of silk and wool and linen all rubbing against each other. Mare's small form slipped between them, invisible as a ghost, her eyes sharp as a crow's as she studied the passing purses. Three years under Bess's wing had taught her the rhythm of the hunt, which pockets hung heavy, which men were too distracted by wares or women to notice small fingers at their belts, which constables were watching, and which were sleeping off last night's ale.

"The fat ones," Bess had told her that first winter, when hunger had sharpened Mare's desperation to a point fine enough to pierce her fear. "Fat men with clean hands and red cheeks. They've never missed a meal, so they won't miss a few coins neither."

Mare watched a merchant now, his belly straining the buttons of a wool doublet that had been expensive before sweat and food stains had dulled its sheen. He stood with a cloth trader, their heads bent together over a bolt of imported linen, fingers evaluating the weave as their mouths shaped numbers too large for Mare to comprehend. Perfect. Distracted by business, blind to the street around them.

She moved with practiced casualness, neither too fast nor too slow. Just another street child weaving through the crowd, unremarkable as dirt. The merchant's purse hung from his belt, a soft leather pouch that clinked with each shift of his considerable weight. Mare sidled closer, timing her approach to coincide with the haggling's climax.

"Twelve shillings per yard is highway robbery!" the merchant bellowed, his face flushing darker.

In that moment of outrage, with every eye drawn to his performance, Mare's fingers did their dance. The knife, small but sharp, another gift from Bess, sliced the purse's strings with a single practiced motion. The weight of coins dropped into her waiting palm, and she was moving again, drifting away before the leather had fully settled against the merchant's thigh.

Her heart drummed against her ribs, not with fear but with the thrill of success. This was power, this was control, the ability to take what wasn't given, to eat when others starved. Mare turned a corner, then another, putting distance between herself and the inevitable discovery. Only when she'd reached the relative safety of an alley did she examine her prize.

Silver winked up at her from her palm, six shillings and a handful of pennies. A good take. Enough for bread and cheese for a week, if they were careful. Mare tucked most of the coins into the hidden pocket Bess had sewn into her dress, keeping just two pennies visible in her hand as she emerged back into the flow of the street.

At a baker's stall, she handed over the pennies for a loaf still warm from the oven. The man barely glanced at her, but she kept her face blank, expressionless. Bess had taught her that too, never show satisfaction after a lift. Satisfaction drew notice, and notice was death in their trade.

With the bread tucked under her arm, Mare made her way back to the Cardinal's Cap. Bess would be entertaining a "friend" until midday, but Mare could leave the food in their room for when she finished.

"Brought you something," Mare said when she found Bess alone, brushing her hair at the small, cracked mirror they shared. The room smelled of sweat and the cheap rose water Bess used to mask the scents of her profession.

"I'll have it later, I ain't hungry," Bess replied, not looking away from her reflection.

"I'll save it for later, then," Mare said, breaking off a piece for herself.

Bess nodded, finally turning to look at her with that strange mixture of hardness and affection that had been Mare's only constant these past three years. "Good haul today?"

Mare grinned, patting her hidden pocket. "Fat merchant. Too busy shouting about prices to notice me."

"That's my girl," Bess said, a rare smile softening her features. "Just remember…"

"Don't keep all my eggs in one basket," Mare finished for her. "I know. I've got it well hidden, all over. "

After eating, Mare slipped out again while Bess prepared for her next client. The Thames beckoned, its stink familiar as family, its muddy banks a patchwork of secrets and opportunity. Mare made her way to the docks, weaving between sailors and cargo with practiced ease.

Her first cache was beneath a rotting wharf piling, where the mud and water created a natural hollow that hands larger than hers couldn't access. Mare glanced around, making sure no eyes followed her movements, then quickly deposited three of her shillings into the space, wrapping them first in an oiled cloth to protect against the damp.

Southwark was a maze of hiding places if you knew where to look, the loose brick in the wall behind the butcher's shop, the hollow in the oak tree in the small yard behind the tavern, the space beneath the third step of the chapel's side entrance where even God seemed to look the other way. Mare had been caught empty-handed once before, when a gang of older boys had cornered her after a lift. They'd taken everything, left her with nothing but bruises and the knowledge that wealth carried in one pocket was wealth easily lost.

Never again. Now she was a squirrel with winter always on her mind, stashing bits of security against the inevitable cold seasons of life. By late afternoon, Mare had visited three of her hiding places, each taking a small tribute from the day's success. The remaining coins she would give to Bess for their lodging, keeping just enough to justify her day's absence. But first, one more lift. Just one more, to round out a good day's work.

The market near London Bridge catered to a different clientele, merchants coming in from the south, travellers from the continent, men with heavier purses and sharper eyes. More risk, but better rewards. Mare slipped into the crowd, her gaze settling on a man in a dark cloak, his purse fat as a summer tick on a dog's ear.

She followed at a distance, waiting for her moment. The man paused at a stall selling imported spices, his attention caught by a display of pepper and cloves. Mare moved in, fingers ready, breath held in her lungs like a prayer.

The moment her hand dipped toward his pocket, a vice closed around her wrist. Mare looked up into a face hard as stone, eyes that held no mercy, no understanding.

"Come along, little madam," the man said, his grip tightening until her bones seemed to grind against each other. "I've someone who wants to see you."

Mare kicked and twisted, her free hand clawing at his grip. "Let me go! I didn't do nothing!"

But her cries drew no sympathetic glances, no intervention. This was Southwark, where every soul minded their own troubles. The man dragged her through streets that grew progressively cleaner, toward the looming shadow of the cathedral and the Clink precinct beside it.

Terror froze the blood in Mare's veins. The Clink was where people disappeared, where screams echoed at night and bodies were conducted before dawn. She had heard the stories, seen the broken men who sometimes emerged, shadows of their former selves.

"Please," she begged, her voice cracking. "I'm just a child. I was hungry is all."

"Save your breath," the man replied, not slowing his pace. "The Bishop doesn't concern himself with the excuses of thieves."

The Bishop. Mare had heard of him, the Wolf of Winchester, they called him in tavern whispers. The man who controlled Southwark's sins like a puppeteer controls his wooden actors. Her struggles redoubled, panic lending strength to her small limbs, but the man's grip was implacable.

They passed through gates, past guards who nodded with deference to her captor. Into courtyards of swept stone, through doors of carved wood, down corridors where her dirty feet left marks on polished floors. Finally, they stopped before a door that swallowed light rather than reflect it.

The man knocked once, then pushed her inside.

Behind a desk that stretched like the Thames sat a man whose eyes cut through Mare's defences as easily as her knife had cut the merchant's purse strings. Neither old nor young, his face bore the lines of one who smiled rarely but effectively. His hands, resting on the wooden surface before him, were perfectly still, the kind of stillness that spoke of complete control.

"So," Bishop Richard Wickham said, his voice carrying the refined accent of education and power, "this is the little shadow that's been causing such concern in my markets."

Mare jolted awake, her heart hammering against her ribs like a trapped animal. Sweat slicked her skin despite the night's chill, the memory of those cold eyes still sharp as a blade after all these years. Beside her, Bess snored softly, older now but still the same in all the ways that mattered. Mare's breathing slowly steadied as the familiar shadows of their room at the Cardinal's Cap replaced the ghostly image of the Bishop's study.

Fifteen years had passed since that first meeting, yet Wickham's hold on her remained as tight as her captor's grip had been that day. The brass seal against her ribs reminded her of the Bishop's hold on her and the risks of trying to escape.

Chapter Five

The Puritan's Pyre

Mare pulled the plain woollen shawl tighter around her shoulders as she slipped through the barn door, a grey ghost among shadows. The rough cloth scratched against her neck, a constant reminder of the role she played tonight, not the Bishop's agent, not Sister Agnes's conspirator, but a vengeful sister of the faithful, eager for righteous fire. Her pulse fluttered against her throat like a trapped bird, but her face remained a mask of pious solemnity as she surveyed the gathering of Puritans huddled in the flickering half-light of tallow candles.

The barn sat squat and forgotten on Southwark's edge, far enough from the watchful eyes of the Bishop's men that its occupants could speak treason without fear of immediate consequences. Mildew and rotting hay perfumed the air, mingling with the sharp tang of unwashed bodies packed too close in the humid night. Two dozen people sat on benches that seemed built by hands skilled in farming rather than carpentry. Their faces were maps of hardship, sunken cheeks, calloused hands, and eyes burning with the peculiar fervour of those who had replaced earthly comforts with heavenly promises.

Mare found a spot near the back, positioning herself beside a post that would conceal her if needed. She kept her head bowed, eyes downcast in the manner of a modest woman, but beneath lowered lashes, she catalogued faces and matched them to names she had heard whispered in Southwark's taverns. The cloth merchant with the missing finger. The widow whose husband had died in the Bishop's debtors' prison. The blacksmith's apprentice caught distributing seditious pamphlets and escaped with only a flogging due to his master's connections.

At the front, standing atop an upturned crate that creaked dangerously beneath his weight, John Stubbs held court. Mare had heard of him, everyone in Southwark had. Formerly a respected scholar, he lost his hand during a violent struggle arising from his support of Thomas Cartwright, the Puritan leader, and was subsequently incarcerated in the Fleet Prison, located north of the Thames and east of Fleet Street. The loss had transformed him from critic to zealot. His remaining hand clenched into a fist as he pounded the air for emphasis, the empty sleeve of his other arm pinned neatly at his side.

"The whores of Babylon flourish in our midst!" Stubbs roared, his voice like stones grinding against each other. "While the so-called men of God count their coin and turn blind eyes!"

Spittle flew from his lips, catching the candlelight like tiny stars before disappearing into the gloom. The gathered faithful murmured their agreement, a sound like insects stirring in dry grass.

"Their papal protector sits in his palace, growing fat on the sins of the flesh!" Stubbs continued, his gaunt face twisting with disgust. "Bishop Wickham, who claims to serve Christ while he taxes the very bodies of fallen women!"

Mare flinched internally at the mention of the Bishop's name but kept her expression appropriately outraged. Her fingers twitched beneath her shawl as she committed Stubbs's words to memory. The zealot's hatred for Wickham was not news, but the specific fury in his voice tonight suggested something had changed, something that had turned simmering resentment into active plotting.

A woman near the front punctuated Stubbs's accusations with a fervent "Amen!" Others joined, the word rippling through the barn like a wave. Mare echoed it softly; her voice lost in the chorus of righteous anger.

"God's patience grows thin," Stubbs declared, lowering his voice to a growl that somehow carried more menace than his shouts. "And so does ours. The time for words has passed. Now comes the time for cleansing fire."

The silence that followed was absolute, broken only by the soft hiss of candle flames. Mare felt the shift in the air, the moment when talk became conspiracy, when thoughts became plans.

Stubbs nodded to a bearded man in the front row, who produced a roll of parchment from inside his jerkin. As he unrolled it across an improvised table of planks and barrels, Mare recognized a crude but effective map of Southwark. Her heart quickened as red crosses appeared, marking locations she knew all too well—The Rose, The Crane, The Maiden's Head. Every brothel under the Bishop's protection received its designation, along with his residence and the collection houses where his men gathered the district's taxes.

"Three nights hence," Stubbs said, his finger jabbing at the map, "while the Bishop attends court, seeking further favours from those in power, we shall deliver God's judgment upon his earthly kingdom."

Mare's fingers curled into her palm, nails biting flesh as she fought to maintain her placid expression. Three nights. Dozens of women, Winchester Geese, yes, but women, nonetheless, sleeping in those marked buildings. Women like the girl with fever in Sister Agnes's crypt. Women like Bess. Women like Mare herself, once upon a time.

"We begin here," Stubbs continued, tapping The Rose Tavern. "And here." His finger moved to The Crane. "The night watch is thinnest between the hours of two and four. "The Bishop's men will be distracted near the bridge," he said, nodding to a grim man who gave a slight smile. "The fire will spread quickly through the wooden buildings."

The gathered faithful leaned forward, their faces transformed by the dancing shadows and their own vicious anticipation. Mare shifted slightly, angling for a better view of the map and the plotters clustered around it. Names and faces, dates, and times, she recorded each detail in her memory with the precision of a scribe. This information would be worth more than gold to Sister Agnes. Worth more than the Bishop's seal.

"God's judgment comes by fire," Stubbs declared, his voice rising again to fill the barn's rafters. "As it was with Sodom, as it was with Gomorrah, so shall it be with the dens of iniquity that pollute our Southwark!"

"Fire!" someone shouted from the crowd.

"Cleansing fire!" called another.

The cry spread quickly, turning into a low, threatening chant. Mare joined in, her voice carefully modulated to blend with the others while her mind raced through the implications of what she had learned. The Bishop, for all his cruelty and corruption, at least offered a certain protection to the women under his taxing hand. If the Puritans succeeded, that fragile shield would vanish in flames, along with any women too slow or too stubborn to flee.

Stubbs raised his hand, and the chanting subsided. His face changed, and his eyes reflected the candlelight. "The Lord's work requires careful hands," he said. "And righteous hearts. Are you prepared, brothers and sisters, to be God's instruments of justice?"

The crowd responded as one: "We are!"

Mare's lips formed the words along with them, though her throat produced no sound. In the shadows of the barn, with the smell of damp straw and tallow smoke thick in her nostrils, she felt herself balanced on a knife's edge. A single lapse could expose her true purpose. The Puritans would show no more mercy to a spy than they planned to show the Winchester Geese.

As Stubbs bent again over the map, outlining escape routes and gathering points, Mare committed every word to memory. Whatever came next, whether she followed through with Sister Agnes's plan for Walsingham or brought this new intelligence to bear, the women of Southwark would not burn without warning. Not while she still drew breath.

The crowd parted as a thin-faced woman stepped forward, her movements sharp and efficient as a butcher's knife. From a satchel at her hip, she produced small linen pouches tied with twine, each no bigger than a child's fist. The barn fell silent save for the soft shuffling of feet as she began distributing them, one to each man and woman who approached with outstretched palms. Mare watched through narrowed eyes, keeping her place among the shadows, as the woman placed a pouch into a young man's trembling hands and whispered something that made his face harden with resolve.

"God's cleansing agent," the woman announced, her voice carrying the distinctive clip of education despite her rough attire. "Handle it with care, brothers and sisters. Its power serves our purpose, but carelessness invites premature judgment."

Mare inched closer, careful to maintain her posture of reverent attention. The pouches contained some kind of powder; she had seen similar concoctions in the arsenals of soldiers and the workshops of alchemists. Saltpetre or a basic accelerant. Whatever its composition, its purpose was clear enough: to ensure that righteous flames spread quickly and burned hot.

"Three measures mixed with lamp oil," the woman continued, demonstrating with empty hands how to prepare the mixture. "Place it where wood meets wood, where wind might feed the flame. God's breath will do the rest."

A burly man with a blacksmith's shoulders raised his hand. "The watchmen patrol in pairs. How do we avoid detection?"

Stubbs nodded to a wiry fellow near the front, who stood and faced the gathering. Mare recognized him vaguely, a former soldier, judging by the way he carried himself and the distinctive scar that twisted his mouth into a permanent sneer.

"We've mapped their routes," he said, tapping the parchment spread on the makeshift table. "The Bishop's men are creatures of habit. Seven patrols, fourteen men total, following the same paths at the same intervals every night. Predictable as the tide."

He demonstrated a series of hand signals, fist raised for danger, palm flat for clear passage, two fingers for retreat. The group mirrored his gestures, practicing until Stubbs nodded his satisfaction. Mare copied them precisely, committing each to memory along with the patrol information. Knowledge that might mean life or death for the Winchester Geese in three nights' time.

"What of the whores themselves?" asked a pinch-faced woman near the back, her voice dripping with distaste. "Some may resist evacuation."

Mare's stomach clenched at the casual cruelty in the woman's tone. Not "women" or even "sinners," but "whores" stripped of humanity, reduced to their function. It was a familiar reduction. The Bishop did it with ledgers and taxes; the Puritans with righteous disgust. The result was the same: lives treated as disposable.

The ex-soldier's face darkened. "Any who resist God's cleansing will be dealt with appropriately," he said, his hand drifting to the knife at his belt. "Their souls require... forceful salvation."

A murmur of approval rippled through the barn. Mare's jaw clenched involuntarily, a momentary lapse in her careful composure. The thought of Bess or the fever-stricken girl from Agnes's crypt facing "forceful salvation" at this man's hands made something primal and violent stir in her chest.

"Brother Timothy and his men will ensure no one raises an alarm," Stubbs added, nodding toward a cluster of hard-faced men. "Silently and efficiently, as God's work demands."

Mare composed herself, though it was already too late. From the corner of her eye, she caught movement, a man watching her, his face pitted with old pox scars, his eyes narrowed with suspicion. He had noticed her reaction, that flicker of revulsion she'd failed to mask. She cursed herself silently. Carelessness killed in Southwark, whether in dark alleys or firelit barns.

"Haven't seen you before, sister," the pockmarked man said loudly, his voice cutting through the low rumble of conversation. Heads turned, eyes fixing on Mare with sudden interest. The thin-faced woman paused in her distribution of pouches, one hand still extended.

Mare felt the attention like a physical weight. The moment balanced on a knife's edge, one wrong word, one false note in her performance, and these righteous men and women would show her exactly how efficiently God's work could be done.

"Brother Ezekiel raises a fair point," Stubbs said from his position at the front, his single hand gripping the edge of the crate he stood upon. "We must be vigilant against the Bishop's spies. They are everywhere, even in the houses of the faithful."

Mare straightened her shoulders and met Ezekiel's gaze directly. Then, with deliberate contempt, she spat on the dirt floor of the barn.

"My own sister was taken by those devil-houses," she snarled, injecting every ounce of the genuine rage she had felt at the casual discussion of murder into her voice. "Three years gone now. Bishop's men said she owed a debt that couldn't be paid except on her back."

The raw bitterness in her tone silenced the room. Mare let her hands clench into fists at her sides, visible proof of her anger. It was not difficult to summon the emotion, she'd seen too many girls forced into the Bishop's service, too many broken bodies discarded when they were no longer profitable.

"I've been in Kent," she continued, the lie flowing smoothly. "Working as a laundress until I could save enough to return. I heard of your gathering from a woman at the market, said you were doing God's work against the flesh-peddlers." She fixed her eyes on Stubbs. "I want to see them burn. All of them. Every brothel, every tax house, every place that profits from women's flesh."

The silence stretched, taut as a hangman's rope. Ezekiel's suspicious gaze did not waver, but others in the crowd showed signs of softening, nods of understanding, murmurs of sympathy.

Finally, Stubbs nodded, a slow inclination of his head that carried the weight of judgment. "Another soul seeking righteous vengeance," he declared. "Welcome, sister...?"

"Ruth," Mare supplied without hesitation, offering a common name that would raise no eyebrows.

"Sister Ruth," Stubbs repeated, "whose pain gives her purpose in God's cleansing fire."

The tension dissipated like morning mist, the gathered faithful returning their attention to the preparations at hand. Even Ezekiel seemed mollified, though his eyes lingered on Mare a moment longer than comfort allowed.

The thin-faced woman approached, offering Mare one of the linen pouches. "For your sister," she said, pressing it into Mare's palm. "Justice comes to those who wait in faith."

Mare accepted the pouch, feeling its weight, heavier than it looked, with the grains of powder shifting inside like whispered threats. "Thank you, sister," she murmured, tucking it carefully into her pocket. Evidence, should she need it later.

The meeting progressed with renewed purpose. The ex-soldier continued detailing escape routes, while others discussed how to create fire traps that would spread quickly through the wooden brothel structures. Mare watched and listened, her face now a perfect mask of vengeful anticipation, while her mind raced ahead to the consequences of what she was learning.

Three nights. Dozens of buildings. Hundreds of lives in the balance. The women of the brothels, yes, but also the children who often slept in the attics, the elderly servants who cooked and cleaned, the bouncers and doormen who had nowhere else to go. All sacrifices on the altar of purification.

As the Puritans rehearsed their roles, who would light the first flames, who would block the exits, who would ensure the Bishop's men could not organize a response, Mare filed away every detail. Names matched faces; tasks matched locations. By the time Stubbs called for them to practice once more their hand signals, she had composed in her mind a complete map of the coming destruction.

The pouch in her pocket seemed to burn against her thigh, a physical reminder of the stakes. Whatever game she had been playing between the Bishop and Sister Agnes, between survival and revenge, had just become far deadlier. The Puritan plot would force her hand, one way or another.

Stubbs raised his single fist toward the rafters. "In a week, Southwark will be cleansed," he declared. "And the Bishop will return to find his kingdom of sin reduced to ashes."

"Amen," chorused the faithful.

"Amen," echoed Mare, and tasted ashes on her tongue.

"Let us pray," Stubbs intoned, his voice dropping to a reverent growl that carried to the rafters. The Puritans formed a ragged circle, hands linked, heads bowed like penitents before an invisible altar. Mare joined without hesitation, slipping between a gaunt woman with work-roughened hands and a young man whose face still bore the soft edges of youth. Their fingers closed around hers, one set calloused as bark, the other damp with nervous sweat—forming a chain of righteous intent that made Mare's skin crawl beneath her placid expression.

"Lord of cleansing flame," Stubbs began, his remaining hand raised toward the barn's darkened ceiling, "guide our hands in the coming purification. Let the fire of Your judgment sweep through the dens of iniquity that corrupt our Southwark. Let it consume the flesh-peddlers and tax-collectors who grow fat on the sins of the weak."

"Amen," murmured the circle. Mare's lips formed the word without sound.

"Three nights hence, when your servant Wickham cavorts with the powerful, seeking to expand his kingdom of sin, we shall strike in Your name. The brothels shall burn. The collection houses shall burn. The very ground where Satan's work is done shall be cleansed by righteous flame."

Mare's mind raced behind her lowered eyelids. The Bishop's monthly visit to court, she had forgotten. Wickham always spent the first weekend of the month currying favour with courtiers and officials, securing his position with gifts and promises. His guard dropped, and Southwark's defences weakened.

"Grant us Your protection as we do Your work," Stubbs continued, his voice rising with fervour. "Shield us from those who would defend corruption. Strengthen our resolve against the screams of the wicked. Let Your holy fire purify what men have defiled."

The hands gripping Mare's tightened unconsciously. Around the circle, faces gleamed with sweat and anticipation in the candlelight. She recognized the expression, it was the same fever-bright look she'd seen on men before battle, on gamblers before a ruinous bet, on zealots of every stripe when they believed righteousness justified any action.

"In three nights, Southwark shall be born anew from the ashes of sin. So it was in Sodom, so it shall be in London."

"So it shall be," echoed the faithful.

Stubbs lowered his hand, and the circle broke apart. The meeting was concluding, its purpose achieved. The gathered faithful began to disperse in twos and threes, never larger groups that might attract the night watch's attention. They murmured quiet farewells, exchanged knowing glances, tucked their pouches of "God's cleansing agent" into various hiding places on their persons.

Mare lingered, pretending to help an older woman fold the rough benches and stack them against the wall. Her every movement calculated to appear helpful while allowing her to gather final scraps of information from the conversations around her.

"...midnight at the old well..."

"...five men at the bridge to create the distraction..."

"...ensure the back exits are blocked first..."

Each fragment was a piece of the puzzle, another detail to help Sister Agnes and the Winchester Geese prepare for what was coming. Mare stored them away methodically, her face betraying nothing of the urgency building inside her chest.

"Brother Timothy will distribute the remaining materials tomorrow night," Stubbs announced to those still present. "Same time, beneath the chandler's shop on Fish Street. Those assigned to the northern brothels should attend."

Mare nodded along with the others, committing the location to memory. Another meeting, another opportunity to gather intelligence, if she survived this one.

She felt eyes on her back and turned to find the pockmarked man, Ezekiel, watching her again. His suspicion had not fully abated, despite her convincing performance earlier. He approached with the deliberate casualness of a predator trying not to startle prey.

"Sister Ruth," he said, the name sitting awkwardly on his tongue as if he were tasting it for falsehood. "These streets aren't safe for a woman alone, especially one newly returned to Southwark. Allow me to escort you to your lodgings."

His smile did not reach his eyes. Mare recognized the tactic, he wanted to know where she was staying, wanted to verify her story. A trap disguised as chivalry.

"Kind of you, brother," she replied, matching his false warmth with her own. "But I'm to meet my cousin's boy at the crossroads. He's waiting to walk me to his mother's house, where I'm staying." She gestured vaguely eastward. "Good Christian folk who took me in when I returned."

"I could at least see you to the crossroads," Ezekiel persisted, stepping closer. The smell of him, onions, and stale sweat, filled Mare's nostrils. "These are dangerous times. The Bishop's spies are everywhere."

"Indeed, they are," Mare agreed, allowing a hint of steel to enter her voice. "Which is why discretion serves us all. My cousin would ask questions if he saw me with a strange man, even a brother in faith. Questions lead to talk and talk leads to discovery."

Stubbs appeared beside them, his good hand coming to rest on Ezekiel's shoulder. "The sister speaks wisely," he said. "We disperse separately for good reason. God's work requires caution as well as courage."

Ezekiel hesitated, then nodded reluctantly. "Of course. Forgive my concern, sister."

"It's a credit to your vigilance," Mare replied, forcing gratitude into her tone. "I'll see you at the chandler's shop tomorrow night."

With a final nod to Stubbs, she slipped out of the barn and into the embrace of Southwark's foggy night. The air outside was cool against her face, damp with river mist and the peculiar thickness that came before dawn. She pulled her shawl tighter and set off at a brisk pace, ears straining for the sound of following footsteps.

Once she'd put sufficient distance between herself and the barn, Mare abruptly changed direction, ducking into a narrow alley between a cooper's shop and a decrepit tavern. The passage stank of piss and rotting vegetables, but it provided cover from watching eyes. She moved quickly, her feet finding the familiar path through Southwark's labyrinthine backways.

Left at the abandoned wellhouse, right at the slaughter yard, through the gap in the fence behind the tannery where the stench was so foul even the Bishop's men avoided patrol. Mare navigated the urban maze with the confidence of someone who had memorized its secrets in childhood, when knowing the hidden paths meant the difference between eating and starving.

Only when she was certain no one followed did she slow her pace, allowing her mind to fully process what she'd learned. Three nights until Southwark burned. Three nights to warn dozens of women scattered across the district's brothels. Three nights to prepare defences against fanatics armed with fire and self-righteousness.

And still, Sister Agnes's task for Walsingham awaited her. The forged message from the Bishop sat in her sleeve alongside the pouch of incendiary powder, two quite different missions with lives hanging in the balance of each.

Mare emerged onto a wider street, the fog swirling around her ankles like ghostly cats. The dim shapes of Southwark's buildings loomed through the grey murk, The Rose in the distance, The Crane closer at hand, the spire of the cathedral where the Bishop would return in three days to find his domain in ashes if the Puritans had their way.

Her heart pounded against her ribs, not from exertion but from the weight of responsibility settling across her shoulders. The Winchester Geese, women like her, women who had few choices and fewer protectors, would be sleeping in those marked buildings when the zealots came with fire. They would have no warning unless Mare gave it to them.

The Bishop's seal pressed against her breast, a cold reminder of where her loyalties were supposed to lie. But the seal's head was away at court, indulging in the very sins he taxed others for committing. He would not burn, but the women under his protection would, unless Mare chose to betray one master to save them.

She quickened her pace again, decision solidifying with each step. Sister Agnes needed to know what was coming. The Geese needed time to prepare. And if that meant the Bishop's interests suffered, well, it was time to pay the debt she owed to the women of Southwark rather than the man who had plucked her from their ranks for his own purposes.

The fog parted before her like a tattered curtain as Mare headed towards The Cardinal's Cap. Her mind calculated paths and possibilities, escape routes and defensive positions, all while the weight of dozens of lives pressed down upon her like stones.

Less than a week. It would have to be enough.

Chapter Six

Whispers and Daggers

The back room of The Cardinal's Cap stank of fear and cheap perfume, a familiar blend that Mare had long since learned to ignore. She shouldered through the low doorway, ducking beneath a beam that sagged with the weight of secrets and time. The single candle on the table guttered in a draft that found its way through cracks no carpenter had ever bothered to seal. The light caught the edges of faces she trusted as much as she trusted anything in Southwark, which was to say, just enough to risk their lives but not enough to turn her back.

Bess Quickly sat closest to the door; her wiry frame perched on a three-legged stool that wobbled with each of her nervous movements. Her fingers danced across an old coin, flipping it between knuckles gone white with tension. The coin, Spanish, by the look of it, disappeared and reappeared as if by magic, a habit Bess had carried from her pickpocketing days.

"Better late than never," Bess muttered, her eyes never settling on any one spot for more than a heartbeat. They darted from Mare to the door to the single grimy window, cataloguing threats with the precision of someone who had survived by seeing danger before it saw her.

"Some of us have been waiting since nightfall," added Katherine Howard. from the far side of the table, a woman fallen from her station. Despite the grime that clung to every surface in the room, Katherine's posture remained as rigid as if she were sitting for a portrait. Her gloves, once the fine calfskin of nobility, now patched in three places – rested on the table before her, fingers aligned with painful precision. Her composure cracked only when the floorboards above creaked under a heavy step, her shoulders jerking upward before she mastered herself again.

Mare closed the door behind her, testing the latch twice before she was satisfied. "The Bishop's men are out in force tonight," she said, crossing to the table in three economical strides. "And there's more than usual to avoid."

She reached into her cloak and withdrew the pouches she had collected, one from the Puritan meeting, another from her own supplies. They hit the table with a soft thud that nonetheless made Katherine flinch.

"What's this, then?" Bess asked, the coin vanishing into a hidden pocket as she leaned forward. "Doesn't look like the Bishop's usual tithe."

"Because it's not from the Bishop," Mare replied, untying the first pouch. She spread its contents on the scarred tabletop – a fine grey powder that caught the candlelight with a dull gleam. "It's from the Puritans. They are calling it 'God's cleansing agent.' Mixed with lamp oil, it burns hot enough to take down a building before the nightsoil men can piss on it."

Katherine's composure slipped again, her eyes widening. "They're planning to burn the brothels."

It was not a question. Mare nodded anyway.

"The Rose, The Crane, The Maiden's Head," Mare confirmed, her scarred palm tracing invisible maps across the tabletop. "Three nights from now, while the Bishop's at court currying favour with whatever noble cock he's sucking this month."

Bess swore, the words crude enough to make even Katherine's carefully neutral expression crack into something like appreciation.

"Stubbs is leading it," Mare continued, gathering the powder back into its pouch with careful fingers. "They've got watchmen's routes mapped, accelerant distributed, even a distraction planned for the bridge to keep any help from coming."

"How many dead are they planning on?" Katherine asked, her voice as calm as if she were inquiring about the price of bread.

"They didn't specify a number," Mare replied. "But they weren't planning on knocking first."

The candlelight threw Mare's shadow, growing against the wall as she straightened, a dark giant looming over the cramped room. She rubbed her scarred palm with her thumb, a habit she had developed years ago when plotting moves that might get her killed.

"That's not all," she said. "The Order is recruiting. Sister Agnes held a meeting in the crypt last week. More women than I've seen gathered in one place outside a church or brothel."

Bess's face darkened. "The nun with the scar?" She made a gesture across her own wrist.

Mare nodded. "The same. She is building something bigger than just shelter for broken women. They've got weapons, plans, a whole network running beneath Southwark like rat tunnels."

"And where do we stand in all this?" Katherine asked, reaching for her gloves and drawing them on with methodical care. "Between Puritan fire, the Bishop's tax, and the Order's... whatever it is."

Mare sat, the stool creaking beneath her weight. The question hung in the air between them, heavy as a gallows rope.

"We stand with the women who'll burn if we do nothing," Mare said finally. "Winchester Geese or not, they deserve warning."

"Warning them defies the Bishop," Katherine pointed out, her voice neutral but her eyes sharp.

"Letting them burn defies something worse," Mare replied.

Bess snorted. "Getting pious in your old age, Mare?"

"Getting practical," Mare corrected. "Dead women pay no taxes. The Bishop loses either way. But if we warn them, we gain something he can't buy, loyalty."

Katherine nodded, a single precise inclination of her head. "And the Order?"

"We watch them," Mare said. "Learn what Sister Agnes is building. See if it's something we can use."

"Or something that'll get us all killed," Bess muttered.

Mare did not contradict her. Everyone understood survival in Southwark was never assured, just temporary.

"Each of you takes a brothel. The Rose to Katherine, you still pass for quality enough to get past the door. The Maiden's Head to Bess, you know which girls to trust there. I'll manage The Crane and the smaller houses."

The women took the packets without question, tucking them away with the practiced ease of those accustomed to hiding contraband.

"What do we tell them?" Katherine asked, adjusting her gloves.

"Tell them fire's coming," Mare said. "Tell them to be ready to move, or fight, or both. Your choice how much more to share."

Bess's eyes narrowed. "And if they ask who sent the warning?"

Mare's lips curved in a smile that did not reach her eyes. "Tell them a friend. One who remembers what it's like to sleep above a tinderbox with no way out but the window."

The three women regarded each other across the table; the candle's flame reflected in their eyes. Bess's sharp and restless, Katherine's cool and assessing, Mare's dark and unreadable. No further words were needed. They had all survived Southwark long enough to know that in these streets, trust was a luxury afforded to the dead.

Mare stood, signalling the meeting's end. "End of the week," she reminded them. "After that, we see which way the wind blows the ashes."

The others rose, Bess already calculating routes through the back alleys, Katherine mentally rehearsing whatever story would get her past The Rose's discerning doorman. Neither questioned Mare's authority, not because they couldn't, but because they recognized the weight she carried in her shoulders, the responsibility she'd claimed when others had looked away.

As they prepared to slip back into Southwark's darkness, Mare felt the Bishop's seal press against her ribs, cold as a dead man's touch. She wondered, not for the first time, whose game she was really playing, and whether anyone would survive the final move.

The candle had burned lower, stretching their shadows across the grimy walls like tortured spirits. Bess produced a flask from somewhere within her bodice and splashed amber liquid into three chipped cups that hadn't been clean since the old queen's funeral. Katherine hesitated before drinking, her gloved fingertips hovering over the rim as if searching for the least offensive place to touch. Mare knocked hers back in one practiced motion, the gin burning a familiar path down her throat, loosening something in her chest that she usually kept locked tight as a miser's purse.

"Fuck me, but we need this," Bess muttered, refilling Mare's cup without asking. "Three days 'til they try to burn us out. Might as well enjoy what's left."

Katherine sipped delicately, her Pinky extended in a habit she'd never managed to break despite years in Southwark's filth. "You've always had a talent for finding the bright side of catastrophe, Bess."

"Talent's all I've ever had," Bess replied, her quick eyes darting to the door as footsteps passed outside. They continued down the hall without pausing, but Bess's shoulders remained hunched. "That and quick fingers."

Mare settled back against the wall, letting the gin warm her blood. "Tell them," she said quietly. "They should know who they're trusting their necks to."

Bess shot her a look that might have been annoyance, might have been something else. She tossed back her own drink and wiped her mouth with the back of her hand.

"Not much to tell that you can't guess," she said, spinning the empty cup between her palms. "Grew up in the shit end of Southwark. Mother died pushing out another baby that didn't live. Father drank what he earned and beat what he couldn't drink."

Her hands never stopped moving as she spoke, the cup dancing between her fingers like the coin had earlier. Mare recognized it for what it was, the restless energy of a child who'd learned that stillness meant death.

"Learned to pick pockets before I could read," Bess continued, her eyes fixed on the cup rather than her audience. "Got good enough at it that the local gang took notice. Used me for the jobs that needed small hands and big eyes." She laughed, a sound like glass breaking underfoot. "Was almost respectable, in a thieving sort of way."

Katherine leaned forward, her composed face softening slightly. "What changed?"

"Got caught," Bess said simply. "Not by the watch, might've been better if I had. Got caught by a priest who'd felt my hand in his purse during mass." Her jaw tightened. "He said he'd forgive my sin if I'd let him commit a few of his own."

Mare watched the muscle in Bess's cheek jump, the only sign of emotion on a face that had learned to hide everything that might be used against it.

"First man who bought me was that same priest," Bess spat. "Talked of God's love while he took what he wanted. Paid the gang leader to look the other way. After that, it was just business." She finally looked up, her eyes hard as river stones. "Six years of that before I grew too old for his taste. Got passed around like a bad penny after that, until the Bishop's men found me and decided I'd pay more tax alive than dead."

The room fell silent except for the muffled sounds of the brothel above, creaking floorboards, occasional laughter, the rhythmic thump that told its own story. Mare refilled Bess's cup, her movements careful, deliberate. No pity in them, pity was the one thing none of them could stomach.

Katherine's gloved fingers stroked the rim of her cup. Then, with a deliberateness that drew both women's eyes, she removed her right glove. The candlelight caught the heavy gold signet ring on her middle finger – a nobleman's crest, the kind that sealed documents that could hang a man or free him.

"My father was Lord Howard of Norfolk," she said, her accent slipping into something higher, more refined. "Third cousin to the Queen, if you traced the bloodline through enough bastards to make it matter."

Bess whistled low. "Fuck me. Always knew you talked too pretty for Southwark."

Katherine's lips curved in a smile that held no humour. "Pretty talk was all I was raised for. That and making an advantageous marriage." She twisted the ring, the gold catching the light. "My father lost his lands at cards when I was sixteen. Then his horses. Then his London house." Her voice remained even, but her fingers tightened around the ring. "When there was nothing else to wager, he bet me."

Mare felt something cold settle in her gut that had nothing to do with gin. "Against what?"

"Three hundred pounds and a racehorse," Katherine replied with bitter precision. "The horse, at least, was a thoroughbred. I was merely well-bred."

Bess swore again, more colourfully this time.

"The man who won me kept me for a year, then sold me to cover his own debts." Katherine slipped the ring off, holding it in her palm like a dead thing. "I've been sold three more times since then. The last sale brought me to Southwark and the Bishop's attention." She closed her fingers around the ring. "I keep this to remind myself that there are worse prisons than brothels, and worse jailers than pimps. At least here, the transaction is honest."

The silence that followed felt weighted with ghosts – not just their own, but all the women who'd been sold, used, discarded in the same ways. The candle guttered lower, throwing strange shadows across their faces.

Both women turned to Mare, expectation in their eyes.

Mare flexed her scarred palm, an unconscious gesture that appeared whenever trust was mentioned or tested. The raised flesh caught the candlelight; a permanent reminder etched into her skin.

"Not much to tell," she said, the lie obvious to all three.

"Horseshit," Bess replied cheerfully. "We've bled for you. Least you can do is bleed a little truth in return. I know some of it already course, but Katherine don't."

Mare stared into her cup, seeing not gin but memories best left buried. "Bess found me half-dead in the gutter, my ma had died that day. Kept me safe, taught me how to survive and then one day I got caught filching, got taken to the Bishop" she said finally. "He saw something useful in me. Sometimes I wish he hadn't."

Katherine's eyebrow raised a fraction. "That's hardly the whole story."

"It's enough," Mare replied, but something in their steady gazes broke her resolve. "I was twelve. Had been running with a gang of cutpurses. Made the mistake of cutting the purse of one of the Bishop's tax collectors." Her thumb traced the scar on her palm. "They caught me, beat me, left me for dead in an alley behind the cathedral."

Bess nodded, unsurprised. "Bishop's men don't take kindly to competition."

"It was the Bishop himself who judged me," Mare continued. "Not his men in the Clink, his grace." Her lips curled on the word. "Said he admired my audacity, if not my judgment. Had me patched up, fed, clothed. Then trained."

"Trained for what?" Katherine asked, though her eyes suggested she already knew.

"To be his shadow," Mare said. "His eyes and ears in places he couldn't go himself. To gather the secrets of Southwark for his use." She knocked back the rest of her gin. "I was good at it. Still am."

"And the scar?" Bess nodded toward Mare's palm.

Mare's expression hardened. "First lesson in loyalty. I kept a coin from my first assignment. He pressed his seal into my hand until it broke the skin. Said next time it would be my throat, not my hand."

Katherine reached for her glove, drawing it back on with practiced care. "And yet here you are, warning his whores about a fire that will cost him money."

"Here I am," Mare agreed, without explanation or excuse.

Bess scanned the room again, her eyes checking the window, the door, the ceiling beams, a habitual inventory of exits that came as naturally as breathing. "We're all dead women walking if any of this goes wrong," she observed, but there was no fear in her voice – only a weary acceptance.

"We were dead the moment we were born female in this city," Katherine replied, adjusting her gloves with precise movements. "The only choice we have is how to die, not if."

Mare stood, her chair scraping against the rough floor. "I choose not quickly and not soon," she said. "And I choose not alone."

The other women rose with her, an unspoken pact forming between them. Not friendship – such luxuries belonged to a different world – but something stronger: the alliance of survivors who recognized in each other the same bitter strength.

"To the Geese, then," Bess said, raising her empty cup. "May they fly from the fire."

"To the Order," Katherine added. "May we learn their secrets before they learn ours."

"To us," Mare finished, her scarred palm closing into a fist. "May we outlive our enemies long enough to piss on their graves."

They touched cups in the guttering candlelight, three women bound by scars both visible and hidden, by pasts they couldn't escape and futures they refused to surrender. Outside, Southwark continued its nightly dance of sin and survival, unaware that beneath its surface, smaller wars were being waged by those it had tried and failed to break. A tall man hidden by shadows of the building watched them leave, waited some moments more, before slipping away towards the bridge.

The cathedral courtyard lay in half-shadow, caught between the moon's cold scrutiny and the feeble protest of a single lantern Mare had positioned to her advantage. She leaned against the stone wall where it met an ancient oak, a spot that kept her face in darkness while allowing her to observe anyone who entered. The Bishop's residence loomed to her right, its windows mostly dark save for the occasional movement of servants preparing for their master's return. Mare flexed her scarred palm against the rough bark of the tree, counting heartbeats, waiting. Walsingham would come, his ambition was too hungry, his curiosity too keen for him to ignore her message.

The note she'd sent had been simple: information to trade, midnight, the old courtyard. No signature needed. In Southwark, anonymous messages were trusted more than signed ones; at least they made no pretence of honesty.

Footsteps on cobblestones broke the stillness, hesitant at first, then deliberately measured, as if the walker had reminded himself of his importance. Mare smiled into the darkness. Walsingham always moved like he was being watched, which in fairness, he usually was.

He appeared at the courtyard's edge; a lean silhouette momentarily caught in moonlight before he stepped into the lantern's puddle of yellow. Thomas Walsingham wore the sombre clothes of his station, the Bishop's page in public, the Bishop's spy in practice. His doublet was fine wool, though not so fine as to outshine his master's. His boots made little sound as he approached, each step placed with the careful precision of a man who knew he walked between powerful forces.

Mare didn't move, letting him scan the shadows for her. His hand drifted to his belt, where she knew he kept a slim dagger, not for fighting, but for the quick, efficient work his position sometimes required.

"You're getting careless, Thomas," she said, still concealed in darkness. "I counted four separate moments when I could have opened your throat since you entered the courtyard."

Walsingham spun toward her voice, tension visible in the set of his shoulders. "Mare," he exhaled, forcing a smile that didn't reach his eyes. "Always with the pleasant greetings."

She stepped forward, allowing the lantern light to catch half her face while keeping the rest in shadow. "Pleasant is for ladies in waiting and men who'll die in their beds. Neither of which describes us."

"Indeed." Walsingham's gaze darted around the courtyard, checking for other watchers. "Your message suggested an exchange. I assume it's something the Bishop would find valuable, or you wouldn't have risked contact."

Mare circled the lantern, maintaining her distance. "Strange days in Southwark," she remarked casually, as if commenting on the weather. "Have you noticed the Puritans growing bolder? John Stubbs was seen buying lamp oil by the barrel yesterday. Curious purchase for a man who preaches so often against the evils of late reading."

Walsingham's weight shifted subtly, his right foot sliding back half an inch, a fighter's instinct to establish better balance. Interesting, Mare thought. The mention of Stubbs had triggered something close to fear.

"The zealots are always plotting something," he replied with forced indifference. "The Bishop keeps track of their petty grievances."

"Grievances that involve enough lamp oil to burn half of Southwark?" Mare pressed. "Seems more than petty."

Walsingham wiped his brow with a quick, almost imperceptible gesture. A bead of sweat had formed despite the cool night air. "If you have specific information about Stubbs, I'm sure His Grace would compensate you appropriately."

Mare leaned against a stone pillar, her posture deliberately casual. "Not just Stubbs. There's that nun, Sister Agnes, she's gathering quite a following among the women. The Order of St. Ursula, they're calling themselves now. Very organized for a charity." She watched Walsingham's face carefully, noting how his eyes widened slightly at the mention of Agnes, how his throat constricted in a quick swallow.

"The Bishop is aware of the nun's activities," he said, his voice carefully neutral. Too neutral.

"Is he aware she's recruiting the Winchester Geese? His own tax base?" Mare raised an eyebrow. "Or that she's got a network running under Southwark's streets? Quite the operation for a woman who claims to serve God rather than herself."

Walsingham's fingers twitched at his sides. "These are serious allegations."

"They're serious times," Mare countered. She pushed off from the pillar and moved closer, close enough to see the pulse beating in his neck. "There's talk of a meeting at the old bell tower tomorrow night, thought you might want check it out yourself." she said handing him the forged document. She had done her part; the invitation was in his hands. He squirreled it away in his coat pocket to read later.

The information was false, but a carefully crafted lie designed to test Walsingham's response. If he took the bait directly to the Bishop, it would reveal one kind of loyalty. If he took it elsewhere first, or not at all, that would reveal something else entirely. If he went himself, the Order's security would be waiting for him as they had asked her to set up.

Walsingham hesitated, just a fraction too long for a man whose only master was Wickham. "I'll be sure His Grace is informed immediately upon his return," he said, the words coming out smooth but rehearsed.

"Will you?" Mare asked softly. She reached out suddenly, adjusting the collar of his doublet where it had folded in on itself. The gesture, intimate, unexpected, made him flinch. "His Grace values timely information, Thomas. Delays have a way of becoming permanent in his eyes."

Their fingers brushed as she withdrew her hand, and Walsingham tensed as if the brief contact had burned him. His eyes betrayed a flicker of something, guilt or the more complicated discomfort of a man caught between masters.

"The Bishop has always recognized my service," he said stiffly.

"The Bishop recognizes useful tools," Mare replied. "Until they're not useful anymore."

Walsingham's jaw tightened. "Is that all you wished to convey? Vague warnings about Puritans and nuns?"

Mare smiled, the expression calculated to unnerve rather than reassure. "For now. Oh, and Thomas? When you see whoever, you report to before the Bishop, you might mention that Stubbs is planning something for when His Grace is at court. Three days from now."

The blood drained from Walsingham's face, confirming what Mare had suspected. "I don't know what you're implying."

"Of course you don't," she cut him off. "Just as I don't know why the Bishop's most trusted page looks like he's about to piss himself at the mention of a bell tower invitation. "

Walsingham stepped back, his composure cracking further. "You're playing a dangerous game, Mare."

"No more dangerous than yours," she replied evenly. "The difference is, I know I'm playing."

He turned to leave, then paused, his back to her. "The Bishop returns in two days. He'll want a full accounting of your activities in his absence."

"I look forward to providing it," Mare said to his retreating form. "Every detail."

She watched him hurry away, his steps no longer measured but quick and anxious. His shoulders were hunched forward as if expecting a knife between them, the posture of a man who knew he'd revealed too much.

Once Walsingham had disappeared into the maze of streets beyond the courtyard, Mare exhaled slowly. Her hand moved unconsciously to her pocket, fingers brushing against the hard outline of the Bishop's seal. The encounter had confirmed her suspicions: Walsingham served more than one master. His reaction to Sister Agnes had been too pronounced, his hesitation too telling.

The question remained: was he collaborating with the Puritans, The Order, or some other faction altogether? And how could she use that knowledge to protect the women who would burn in three days' time if she failed?

Mare extinguished the lantern with a quick pinch of her fingers, embracing the darkness that had always been her truest ally. The game board had become clearer tonight, though the final moves remained shrouded. Walsingham was a pawn who thought himself a knight. The Bishop was a king vulnerable in his absence. And Mare herself?

She smiled grimly into the night. Mare was whatever piece the game required: pawn, knight, queen. The only rule that mattered was survival, and she'd been playing that game since before she could remember. With silent steps, she melted into the shadows, the Bishop's seal a cold weight against her thigh, a constant reminder of loyalties tested and choices yet to be made.

Mare took to her bed and dreamt of the day she woke to a strange wetness between her thighs, the discomfort pulling her from sleep like a hook tugging at her insides. As she shifted, wincing at the unfamiliar cramping low in her belly, and reached beneath the thin blanket. Her fingers came away sticky and dark in the grey pre-dawn light. Blood. Her heart lurched, mind racing through wounds, but she found no cut, no injury to explain the stain spreading across her shift and seeping into the straw mattress beneath her.

"Bess?" she whispered, voice thin with panic. Bess slept on, snoring softly, her back turned to Mare's corner of their shared room at the Cardinal's Cap.

Mare slipped from the bed, bare feet flinching at the cold floor. The cramping intensified as she stood, a dull ache that made her curl forward slightly. She pulled her soiled shift away from her skin, examining the rusty stain with growing horror. Had something torn inside her? Was she dying? Stories of girls who'd bled to death from mysterious ailments floated through her mind like river debris.

She gathered her courage and used the chamber pot's water to rinse her thighs, watching red swirl into the cloudy liquid. The blood had no source and no end, a steady seepage from somewhere deep inside her that defied her desperate attempts at cleanliness. Mare bit her lip, fighting tears that threatened to spill over. She wouldn't cry. Crying solved nothing in Southwark.

"What's all this, then?" Bess's sleep-roughened voice came from behind her.

Mare startled, dropping the rag she'd been using, arms crossing instinctively over her bloodied shift. "I'm bleeding," she said, the words sticking in her throat. "But I'm not cut. It's just... coming out of me."

Bess's face softened, understanding replacing confusion. She padded across the room, unbothered by her own nakedness in the chill morning air and knelt beside Mare.

"It's your monthly blood," she said, matter-of-factly. "Started coming to me when I was twelve. Bit late for you, ain't it? You must be, what, fourteen now?"

"Thirteen," Mare mumbled, shame and relief battling within her. "What do you mean, monthly?"

Bess stood, moved to a battered chest in the corner, and extracted a small carved box Mare had never seen before. From it, she withdrew several strips of clean linen, folded neatly, and a soft cloth that had been worn thin with washing.

"It means you're a woman now, properly," Bess explained, returning to Mare's side. "It'll come every month, thereabouts. Means you can get a baby in you, if you're not careful." She handed Mare the cloth. "Here, clean yourself proper. Then I'll show you how to wrap the linen, so you don't ruin every shift you own."

Mare took the cloth with trembling fingers. "Will it stop?"

"For a few days, yeah. Then it'll come back next month, regular as the tide." Bess's chapped lips quirked in a half-smile. "It's a fucking nuisance, if you want the truth of it. But it means your body's working as it should."

Mare cleaned herself as instructed, Bess turning away to offer a semblance of privacy in their cramped quarters. When she finished, Bess showed her how to fold and position the linen strips, securing them with a smaller strip tied around her hips.

"Tight enough to hold, not so tight it cuts into you," Bess instructed, her hands efficient and impersonal as they guided

Mare's. "You'll need to change it a few times a day, more if your flow's heavy. Wash the used ones in cold water, not hot, hot sets the blood."

Mare nodded, absorbing the information with the same focus she applied to learning which pockets were easiest to pick, which constables could be bribed, which alleys offered the safest escape routes. This was survival knowledge, another piece of armour against the world's cruelties.

"The pain in my belly," she started.

"Normal," Bess cut in. "Some women get it worse than others. Warm brick helps, or a tot of gin if it's really bad."

Bess moved to her trunk again and pulled out a faded shift, cleaner and better mended than Mare's usual garments. "Here," she said, holding it out. "I made this a while back. Thought I might sell it, but you need it more."

Mare stared at the offering, throat suddenly tight. The fabric was worn but solid, the stitching neat and even in a way her own clumsy attempts at sewing never achieved. A gift without expectation of return, rarer in Southwark than honest magistrates.

"I can't..." she began.

"Take it," Bess insisted. "You'll need your own things soon enough. Next month once we've put enough aside. The old man says there's a small room opening down the hall. It ain't much, but it'd be yours."

Mare slipped the shift over her head, the fabric settling against her skin like a blessing. Her own room. Her own space, with a door that locked and walls that belonged to only her. The thought was dizzying, beyond imagining for a girl who'd spent her life sleeping in corners and doorways before Bess had taken her in.

"What if I bleed on this one too?" she asked, running her fingers over the careful mending along one seam.

"Then you wash it," Bess replied with a shrug. "Blood comes and goes. Nothing to fear in it."

Mare sat on the edge of the bed, suddenly exhausted. The cramping had settled into a dull, persistent ache that seemed to hollow out her insides. Bess sat beside her, their shoulders touching, a rare moment of stillness in lives that rarely allowed for pause.

"I didn't know," Mare whispered. "About any of this."

"No one does, first time," Bess said, her voice gentler than Mare had ever heard it. "My ma told me, before the plague took her. Said it was the river of life, flowing through every woman since Eve." She snorted. "Romantic notion for something that ruins good linen and makes your belly feel like it's being twisted by the devil himself."

The candlelight caught on Bess's face, softening the hard angles earned through years of survival. Mare looked down at their hands, somehow now clasped together on the thin blanket. Bess's fingers were calloused, nails broken from work, a small burn scar on the back of her hand from a client's pipe. Hands that had pulled Mare from danger, fed her, taught her to survive. Hands that now showed her how to be a woman in a world that valued women only for what could be taken from them.

"Thank you," Mare said, the words inadequate for what she felt.

Bess squeezed her hand once, then let go. "Get dressed properly," she said, rising. "Day's wasting, and bread won't steal itself."

Mare nodded, understanding what wasn't said. Life continued, blood or no blood. Southwark didn't pause for women's mysteries, and neither could they. But something had shifted between them, a deepening of the bond that had saved Mare's life three years before. As Bess turned away to dress, Mare touched the new shift, the clean linens at her core, and felt strangely, unexpectedly powerful. Her body held secrets now, rhythms and cycles beyond men's understanding. In Southwark, any advantage, even one written in blood, was worth claiming.

Chapter Seven

The Bishop's Gambit

Mare knelt on the cold stone floor of Bishop Wickham's private chambers; head bowed in practiced deference that masked the calculations whirring behind her eyes. The Bishop's quarters reflected the man himself, devoted to God but unwilling to sacrifice earthly comforts. Gilded crosses hung on walls draped with Flemish tapestries worth more than most of Southwark's houses. Silver censers leaked incense that failed to fully mask the scent of last night's wine and roasted pheasant. Mare counted her heartbeats, waiting as the Bishop paced before her, his shadow cutting across her downturned face with each pass.

The wait was enough, to recall the time ten years back when the Bishop's study swallowed light. Despite the three-branched candelabra on his desk and the oil lamps hanging from iron hooks on the stone walls, shadows gathered in the corners like conspirators. The time when Mare stood before him, back straight, face arranged in the blank mask she wore for these meetings. The room smelled of beeswax and leather-bound books, a sharp contrast to Southwark's usual stink of mud and humanity. Even the air felt different here, still and expectant, as if the very stones were listening.

"Six landlords," Mare said, her voice pitched low enough that the Bishop had to lean forward slightly to catch her words. "Meeting at the Broken Anchor every Tuesday night. They're planning to reject your new collection rates, form a cooperative for protection. They've already approached three mercenaries who served in the Low Countries."

Wickham's fingers drummed against the polished surface of his desk, the rhythm precise and measured. His eyes never left

Mare's face, searching for any flicker of deception. She offered him nothing but flat certainty.

"Names," he said.

Mare recited them without hesitation, watching as the Bishop's scribe scratched quill against parchment in the corner. When she reached the final name, "Edward Harker of the River's Edge inn," Wickham's mouth curved into what might generously be called a smile.

"Harker," he repeated, tasting the name like a piece of questionable meat. "The ringleader, I presume?"

Mare nodded once. "He provides the room, supplies the wine. The others look to him before speaking."

The Bishop raised one hand, a small gesture that brought his captain of guards stepping forward from his position by the door. No words were needed; the captain nodded and departed, his footsteps echoing on stone. Mare knew what would happen next. Harker would be dragged from his bed or tavern, brought to one of the Bishop's private rooms near the Clink. He would return to his business days later, broken in body and spirit, a walking warning to others who might consider similar rebellion.

She felt nothing about this. Harker was neither friend nor enemy, merely a source of income, a name to trade for coin. In Southwark, loyalty went to the highest bidder, and the Bishop paid better than most.

"Excellent work," Wickham said, leaning back in his chair. His eyes assessed her with the clinical interest of a collector examining a rare specimen. "You've grown quite adept at this." The Bishop's eyebrow arched slightly.

"You've developed quite the reputation among my men. The girl who hears everything, sees everything. The shadow who slips between taverns and brothels unnoticed, collecting secrets like a magpie collects shiny objects."

Mare remained silent, waiting. These moments of reflection from the Bishop usually preceded either greater reward or greater demand. She had learned to weather them without reaction.

"Do you know," Wickham continued, "I've noticed something rather interesting about you? When you're focused, truly focused on a matter, you tilt your head precisely as I do." He demonstrated the gesture, a slight inclination to the right. "And that way you have of clasping your hands behind your back when delivering unpleasant news, my exact habit."

Mare stiffened imperceptibly. She hadn't realized she'd adopted his mannerisms; hadn't known she was studying him even as he studied her. The thought disturbed her more than she cared to admit.

"We observe what works, Your Grace," she replied carefully. "I've watched you bend men to your will with words alone. It seemed... useful to learn."

Wickham laughed, a sound as rare as genuine kindness in his presence. "Indeed. Good work, I can see some of myself in you, which is perhaps the highest compliment I can offer." He reached into a drawer and withdrew a small pouch that clinked with the reassuring weight of silver. "Your payment, as agreed. With a small addition for the detailed account of their mercenary contacts."

He slid the pouch across the desk, but as Mare reached for it, he placed his hand atop hers, trapping it against the wood. His palm felt cold and dry, like old parchment.

"Marion is too dainty a name for someone who moves through Southwark's shadows with such skill," he said. "From now on, I think I shall call you Mare, like the night-horse that brings bad dreams. It suits you better, I think."

Mare met his gaze, refusing to pull her hand away first. "My name is Mare, as you wish" she agreed, the words falling between them like stones into still water. Not a request, not a question, a declaration.

The Bishop released her hand, something like approval flickering across his face. "Mare it is, then."

She took the payment, tucked it into her bodice, and bowed slightly before backing toward the door. Only when she was outside, with the heavy oak closed between them, did she allow herself to breathe fully again.

That night embraced her as she made her way back to the Cardinal's Cap, the familiar stench of the Thames welcoming her home to Southwark proper. The pouch of silver weighed against her skin, each coin representing a secret traded, a confidence betrayed, a step further from the girl she'd been and closer to the woman she was becoming. Not the Bishop's creature, not entirely, but something shaped partly in his image, nonetheless.

Bess was awake when Mare entered their shared room, sitting on the edge of the bed with a candle guttering beside her. Her eyes found the outline of the coin pouch immediately.

"Good night's work?" she asked, voice carefully neutral.

Mare nodded, retrieving the pouch and counting out half the coins into Bess's waiting palm. Their arrangement had always been clear, split everything, hide nothing. But tonight, Mare held back three silver pieces, slipping them into her sleeve with a pickpocket's deftness.

"I love you," Mare said suddenly, the words awkward in her mouth, "but I'm leaving. Take back my bed."

Bess's hand closed around the coins, her expression unreadable in the dim light. "Been expecting that," she said finally. "Ever since your blood came. Girl becomes a woman, starts thinking she's ready to face the world alone."

"Not alone," Mare corrected. "Just... separate. The Bishop's using me more often now. It's not safe for you if I stay."

Bess snorted. "Nothing in Southwark's safe, love. Never was."

"This is different." Mare began gathering her few possessions, a spare shift, a dented tin cup, a knife with a bone handle that had been her first real purchase. "The men I name for him, they have friends. The women in the brothels talk when they think I'm not listening. They know someone's feeding information to Wickham."

"So you're protecting me?" Bess asked, scepticism sharp in her voice.

Mare paused, hands full of her meagre life. "I'm protecting us both. I can move quicker alone."

What remained unspoken hung between them: Mare was becoming someone new, someone shaped by the Bishop's cold calculations and Southwark's ruthless arithmetic of survival. Someone who couldn't afford the luxury of a fixed address or a known companion.

Bess rose, crossed to Mare, and pressed something into her hand, a small cloth pouch on a leather cord. "Dried rosemary and sage," she explained. "Keeps the fleas and lice away when you're sleeping rough. Change it every fortnight."

The simple practicality of the gift broke Mare's composure. She nodded, throat tight, and slipped the cord around her neck.

"You know where to find me," Bess said. "If you need anything."

Mare left before dawn, before she could change her mind.

The following weeks passed in a blur of rented rooms, each never occupied for more than three nights. Mare collected secrets by day, delivered them to the Bishop by evening, and moved her bedroll before midnight. She became expert at identifying which landlords asked no questions, which rooms had windows that opened onto rooftops or adjacent buildings, which streets offered the quickest escape routes.

The silver pieces accumulated in her various hiding places around Southwark, beneath loose bricks, inside hollow tree trunks, under specific flagstones marked with chalk symbols only she recognized. Mare built her fortune in fragments, piece by piece, a coin here and a coin there against some future she couldn't yet imagine but felt certain would require payment.

It was the pounding that woke her, not the cautious knock of a messenger or the firm rap of a watchman, but the frenzied hammering of someone intent on breaking through. Mare bolted upright on her thin pallet, knife already in hand, eyes adjusting to the darkness of a moonless night.

"I'll kill ya, girl!" The voice penetrated the thin wood of the door, slurred with drink but razor-edged with fury. "You named my brother to the Bishop! They broke his fucking legs!"

The landlord's voice joined in, high with panic: "Get out the back! I'll hold him off!"

Mare was moving before conscious thought, stuffing her few possessions into a sack, sliding feet into boots. She'd been careless, stayed too long in one place. Harker, it had to be Harker's brother or cousin, someone connected to the landlord she'd named three weeks past.

The door splintered as she slipped out the back window, dropping into the fetid alley behind the boarding house. Shouts followed her, heavy footsteps, but Mare knew Southwark's hidden paths better than any vengeful drunk. She ran, breath burning in her lungs, the familiar weight of fear and exhilaration pushing her forward.

Only when she reached the docks did she slow, certain she'd lost her pursuer in the maze of streets. Sweat cooled on her skin despite the warm night, her heartbeat gradually settling into a less frantic rhythm. The Thames stretched before her, black as sin under the clouded sky, carrying the city's filth out to sea with patient inevitability.

Mare stood at the water's edge, clutching her skirts, eyes fixed on the distant pinpricks of light that marked the north bank. The coin pouch at her waist felt suddenly heavy, not with silver but with the weight of choices made, loyalties traded, futures foreclosed.

The Bishop had named her truly, Mare, the night-horse, the bringer of bad dreams. She carried men's nightmares to their doorsteps, delivered ruin with a blank face and steady voice. And for what? A handful of silver, a room she couldn't stay in, a life spent looking over her shoulder.

The wind off the river carried the eternal stink of London, rot and life and struggle all mixed together. Mare breathed it in, letting it fill her lungs. This was her world, these shadowed banks, and treacherous currents. She had survived thus far by selling secrets, by trading in the weakness of others. But as she stared across the dark water toward the unseen north bank, Mare wondered what price she might eventually pay for the life she'd chosen, and whether, when that reckoning came, she would have enough hidden silver to purchase her way free.

"Look at me, Marion." The Bishop's voice cut through the chamber's thick air, sharp as a well-honed blade.

Mare raised her eyes, jolted back to the present, how long had she been reminiscing? It was only seconds, but it seemed like hours; she was careful to restore the precise balance of respect and attentiveness that Wickham demanded. The landlords uprising was years ago; this dangerous unsettling was far deeper and more urgent. The Bishop had aged since she'd last seen him, not in years but in something deeper. The skin beneath his eyes had darkened, and his fingers twitched at his sides as he walked, plucking at invisible threads. His gaze darted to the shadows in the corners of the room, scanning for threats that existed only in his mind.

"Three days I've been gone," he said, pausing to stare at a particularly dark corner. "Three days at court, securing our position while you..." He let the accusation hang unfinished.

"While I maintained your interests in Southwark, Your Grace," Mare completed, her voice carefully modulated to convey certainty without pride.

The Bishop's laugh was brittle as winter ice. "My interests. How convenient a phrase, broad enough to cover any manner of activities." He resumed pacing, the hem of his dark robe brushing the stones. "Tell me, does meeting with my enemies in taverns and crypts serve my interests? Does whispering with that playwright whoremonger serve my interests?"

Mare kept her face neutral despite the jolt that ran through her. Wickham had eyes everywhere, more than she'd accounted for. She weighed her response like a merchant calculating the worth of questionable goods.

"Knowledge is your greatest weapon, Your Grace," she replied. "I gather it wherever it grows, even in foul soil."

The Bishop stopped directly before her, close enough that she could smell the cloves he chewed to sweeten his breath. His hand shot out, fingers grasping her chin with surprising strength, forcing her face upward.

"Do not mistake me for a fool, Marion," he hissed, his breath hot against her skin. "I lifted you from the gutter. I can return you there with less effort than it takes to crush an insect."

Mare didn't flinch, didn't blink. "I have never forgotten your generosity, Your Grace."

The Bishop's eyes searched hers, looking for the lie. Finding nothing he could name; he released her with a small push that nearly unbalanced her. His hand moved to a chain around his neck, fingers worrying at something beneath his robes, the seal, she knew. His real seal, not the forgery that pressed cold against her ribs beneath her clothing.

"The Puritans are planning something," he said abruptly, turning away. "John Stubbs and his zealots grow bold. They speak openly of cleansing Southwark. Of burning my... investments to the ground."

Mare remained kneeling, though her knees had begun to ache against the unforgiving stone. "I've heard similar whispers, Your Grace."

"Whispers grow to shouts, and shouts to actions," the Bishop muttered, more to himself than to her. He moved to his desk; a massive oak piece imported from Spain at ruinous expense and traced his fingers along its polished surface. "They're gathering tomorrow night. A church hall near the docks. St. Clement's, the old one, not the new construction." His mouth twisted in distaste. "Appropriate that they plot arson in a building half-rotted with damp."

Mare catalogued the information silently, comparing it with what she already knew from the Puritan meeting she'd infiltrated. The Bishop's intelligence was accurate, if incomplete. He knew the location, but not the extent of their preparations.

"You will go to them," the Bishop continued, his voice hardening to the tone that brokered no argument. "You will join their gathering. And you will ensure it is their last."

"How would you have me proceed, Your Grace?" Mare asked, though she already suspected the answer.

The Bishop smiled, a thin stretching of lips that revealed nothing of pleasure. "You have a certain... talent for turning enemies against each other." He opened a drawer in his desk and withdrew two items: a small leather pouch that clinked with the unmistakable sound of coins, and a slender glass vial containing a dark liquid. "Expose them without exposing yourself. Create division. Suspicion. Let them tear each other apart while we watch from a comfortable distance."

He placed both items on the desk's edge, close enough for Mare to see but not to reach without rising from her position of supplication.

"The Puritans fancy themselves God's chosen soldiers," the Bishop continued. "But soldiers require discipline, hierarchy, trust. Remove those elements, and they become nothing more than an angry mob, easily dispersed." He pushed the vial forward with one finger. "Plant this where it will do the most damage. Among their prayer books, perhaps. Or in the coat of one who seems most trusted."

Mare studied the vial without touching it. The liquid inside was thick, dark blood or something meant to resemble it.

"And if I'm discovered, Your Grace?" she asked, needing to hear the answer though she already knew it.

The Bishop's expression hardened. "Then you'd best hope they kill you quickly." His voice dropped to a dangerous whisper. "Fail me, and you'll wash up like that clergyman, though I'll ensure there's enough of your face left for identification. A reminder to others who might consider... divided loyalties."

Mare's fingers brushed unconsciously against the scar on her palm, the raised flesh a permanent testament to the Bishop's idea of correction. She had long ago learned that survival in his service meant becoming whatever he required, a shadow, a weapon, a shield. Never quite trusted, but too valuable to discard without cause.

"I understand, Your Grace," she said, her tone perfectly balanced between obedience and capability.

"I wonder if you do," the Bishop mused. He gestured for her to rise, then slid the pouch of coins and the vial toward her. "Take these. Use them wisely."

Mare stood, her knees protesting after the long obeisance. She pocketed both items with practiced efficiency, feeling the weight of the vial against her thigh like a small, cold accusation.

As she turned to leave, the Bishop's hand shot out, catching her wrist with unexpected speed. His fingers dug into her flesh, finding pressure points with the precision of a man well-versed in causing pain without leaving marks.

"Remember who lifted you from the gutter, Marion, from a life of whoring," he said, his voice soft but carrying the weight of iron. "Remember who can put you back there. Or beneath it."

Mare met his gaze directly, allowing just enough fear to show in her eyes to satisfy him, while keeping the calculations, the rage, the plans hidden behind that careful veneer.

"I live to serve, Your Grace," she replied, the practiced words falling from her lips with perfect intonation. "Your enemies are my enemies. Your will, my purpose."

The Bishop studied her face a moment longer, then released her wrist. "Go," he said, turning away. "Report to me when it's done."

Mare bowed low, backing toward the door as protocol demanded. Only when she had closed the heavy oak panel behind her did she allow herself a single deep breath, flexing her fingers to restore circulation where the Bishop's grip had left red marks that would soon darken to bruises. The coins clinked softly in her pocket. The vial pressed cold against her leg. And in her mind, plans took shape like frost forming on winter glass—delicate, complex patterns that would determine whether she survived the coming days or joined the nameless corpses that floated daily past Southwark's docks.

The Bishop wanted sabotage. He would have it. But perhaps not exactly as he imagined.

The back room of The Cardinals Cap had the dubious honour of being the only space in Southwark that made Mare feel tall. Ceiling beams sagged to shoulder height, forcing even Bess to duck as she moved between the room's only table and its lopsided shelves. Candle smoke had blackened the timbers over decades, creating a permanent fog that hung just above eye level and gave the room the atmosphere of a confessional booth designed by a drunk carpenter. Mare pushed through the low doorway, her shadow stretching across the uneven floorboards like gallows at sunset.

Bess Quickly was already there; her wiry frame perched on a three-legged stool that wobbled with each breath. Her fingers were never still, currently occupied with rolling a copper penny across her knuckles in a fluid dance that made the coin appear alive. She wore a dress that had clearly begun its life on a woman of higher station, the fabric too fine, the cut too elegant, but had been taken in and resewn with the pragmatic efficiency of someone who valued function over fashion.

"You look like shit warmed over," Bess greeted cheerfully, the penny disappearing into her sleeve as she spoke. "Bishop had his claws in you, then?"

"Not as deep as he'd like," Mare replied, closing the door and testing the latch twice.

Katherine Howard emerged from the corner shadows like a ghost returning to haunt familiar grounds. Her posture remained impeccable despite surroundings that would have horrified her former peers at court. She'd arranged her hair in a simple style that somehow managed to look elegant rather than plain, and her gloves worn at the fingertips but meticulously clean, lay folded beside an untouched cup of what passed for wine in this tavern.

"Did Wickham's mood improve with his journey to court, or has it curdled further?"

Mare pulled a folded sheet of parchment from inside her cloak and placed it on the table. "The Bishop wants blood. Not his, of course." She began sketching with a piece of charcoal, rough lines forming the outline of a building. "St. Clement's, the old one by the docks. That's where the Puritans are gathering tomorrow night."

Bess leaned forward, squinting at the crude map. "Knew that place when I was picking pockets. Two main doors, front and back, plus a side entrance the priest used for sneaking in his lady friends." Her finger traced the outline Mare had drawn. "Window here's broken, covered with oilcloth. Easy access if you're thin and don't mind splinters in your arse."

"Guards?" Katherine asked, joining them at the table.

Mare added X marks at various points around the building. "Stubbs isn't a fool. He'll have lookouts here, here, and here. Men he trusts, armed with clubs at minimum. They change position every half-hour to stay alert."

Katherine nodded, her eyes measuring distances and angles with the precision of someone who had survived court politics. "A distraction would serve us well. A drunk couple arguing too close to their perimeter. Puritans are notorious for their discomfort with public displays of affection."

"I can play drunk with the best of them," Bess offered with a crooked grin. "Had enough practice."

Mare shook her head. "You need to teach me your hands, Bess. You're the only one who can plant the vial without being noticed." She reached into her pocket and produced the Bishop's dark gift, placing it carefully on the table. The glass caught the candlelight, making the thick liquid inside gleam with an almost metallic quality.

"What is that?" Katherine asked, not reaching for it.

"Blood," Mare replied. "Pig's blood mixed with something else. Red ink. The Bishop wants it planted where it will cause the most damage. In their prayer books, on their hands, anywhere that will make them turn on each other."

Bess picked up the vial, testing its weight and balance as naturally as a baker might heft a loaf. "And what do you want done with it?"

The question hung in the air, the acknowledgment that the Bishop's orders and Mare's intentions might not align perfectly. The three women exchanged glances, a silent communication built on shared dangers and mutual debts.

"I want exactly what the Bishop wants," Mare said carefully. "The Puritans divided and in disarray. But without unnecessary bloodshed that might bring the authorities down on all our heads."

Katherine's lips curved in a small, knowing smile. "How fortunate that our aims temporarily align with His Grace's."

Mare nodded, then reached back into her cloak and produced a second item, a stack of carefully folded papers sealed with wax that bore a passable imitation of the Bishop's mark. "I'll plant the blood and slip these into the coat of Stubbs's second, the tall man with the pockmarked face. His name's Ezekiel."

"Forgeries?" Katherine asked, not touching the papers.

"Convincing ones," Mare confirmed. "Letters supposedly from the Bishop, suggesting that Ezekiel has been feeding him information about the Puritans' plans."

Bess whistled low. "That'll get his throat cut if they find them."

"They're meant to be found," Mare corrected. "Just not until after I've created enough confusion to make them plausible."

The three women fell silent, contemplating the risk and precision their plan required. One mistake, one guard more observant than expected, and Mare would never leave St. Clement's alive. The Puritans were not known for their mercy toward perceived agents of Babylon.

"I need to prepare," Mare said finally, breaking the silence. "Katherine, I'll need to look the part."

Katherine nodded and produced a small cloth bundle from beside her seat. She unwrapped it to reveal pots of powder, a jar of something waxy, and a small knife. "Sit," she instructed Mare. "The good Lord gave me few useful skills for this life, but making one thing appear as another was essential at court."

Mare sat on the rickety stool while Katherine worked, applying pale powder to darken the shadows beneath Mare's eyes, adding a sickly pallor to her cheeks. Her fingers moved with practiced precision, transforming Mare's features into something softer, more docile—the face of a woman who spent her days in prayer rather than subterfuge.

Meanwhile, Bess practiced with the vial, making it disappear and reappear between her fingers. The movement was so smooth that even watching directly, Mare sometimes lost track of where the glass container had gone. After several attempts Mare got the gist of it, enough to accomplish her surreptitious task.

"Got my first beating for stealing from a priest," Bess remarked, showing Mare the vial vanishing up her sleeve and reappearing in her palm.

"This isn't about revenge," Mare cautioned, keeping her head still as Katherine worked. "It's about survival. The Puritans burn the brothels; the Bishop's income suffers. And what do you think happens to his mood when his purse lightens?"

"We all suffer," Katherine finished, applying a final change to Mare's transformation. "There. Modest, pious, and entirely forgettable."

Mare turned to the cloudy scrap of mirror Bess produced. The face that looked back at her belonged to someone else, a woman worn by hardship but sustained by faith, her eyes downcast, her bearing humble. Perfect for infiltrating zealots who valued submission in women more than anything else.

"If I'm not back by midnight, burn everything that connects us and scatter," Mare instructed, returning the blade to its hiding place. "Bess, take what coin you have and get to Dover. Katherine, your cousin in Hampshire might still remember what family loyalty means."

"And leave you to the worms?" Bess scoffed, though her eyes betrayed concern. "Not bloody likely."

"This isn't a debate," Mare said, her voice hardening. "If I don't return, it means I've failed. And the Bishop doesn't forgive failure."

Katherine met Mare's gaze directly. "Neither do we," she said simply.

The three women regarded each other in the flickering candlelight—a former noblewoman fallen from grace, a pickpocket turned survivor, and the Bishop's shadow with secrets of her own. They had no formal oaths, no blood-bonds, no promises beyond the understanding that in Southwark's brutal hierarchy, they were all they had.

Mare nodded once, accepting what Katherine offered. Then she gathered the map, the vial, and the forged documents and secreted them into her skirts.

"We're not just saving our skins," she told them, her voice low and certain. "We're buying time. Time to prepare for whatever comes next, whether it's Puritan flames or the Bishop's wrath."

Bess raised an imaginary glass. "To time, then. May we not run out of the bastard."

"To time," echoed Katherine, her transformed face solemn in the guttering light.

Mare said nothing, but her scarred palm burned as if remembering the Bishop's seal pressing into her flesh, marking her as his property, a mark she'd defy with every breath, if only she could find a way to survive what came after.

St. Clement's Church clung to its foundations like a dying man to his last confession, its walls bowing outward as if struggling to contain the righteous fury gathered within. Tallow candles guttered in iron sconces, their flames stretching and shrinking with each draft that found its way through warped timber and cracked stone. The scent of damp wool and unwashed bodies hung in the air, mingling with the sour tang of fervent belief, a smell Mare had come to recognize in her years of navigating Southwark's underbelly. She slipped through the church's side entrance with her head bowed and shoulders hunched, a grey figure among grey shadows, her transformed face a perfect mask of humble piety.

No one challenged her entrance as she passed a tall man, head bowed low, a hat concealing his face. Katherine's careful work with powders and wax had rendered Mare's features forgettable, another worn woman seeking salvation among the righteous. Her clothing, borrowed from a washerwoman who owed Bess a favour, hung loose enough to hide both her figure and the small glass vial nestled against her ribs. She kept her eyes downcast, moving with the tentative steps of someone unused to asserting her presence, and found a spot near the back wall where shadow and candlelight battled to an uncertain truce.

John Stubbs stood at the pulpit, his lean frame vibrating with barely contained outrage. The missing hand, taken years ago as punishment for writing against the Queen, was displayed rather than hidden, the empty sleeve pinned back to draw attention to his sacrifice. His remaining hand gripped the pulpit's edge with white-knuckled intensity, as if he might tear the wood apart through sheer force of conviction.

"The whores of Babylon flourish across the river!" he thundered, spittle flying from his lips to catch the candlelight like tiny, vicious stars. "While we pray, they sin. While we labour, they corrupt. While we starve, the Bishop of Winchester grows fat on the wages of their depravity!"

Murmurs of agreement rippled through the assembled faithful, eighty men and women packed tight in the small church. Mare catalogued faces and positions with practiced efficiency. Near the front sat Ezekiel, his pockmarked face lifted toward Stubbs with near-religious ecstasy. Beside him, three men Mare recognized from previous gatherings Stubbs's lieutenants, each responsible for a different aspect of the planned burning. And scattered throughout, ordinary folk whose grievances and disappointments had crystallized into a brittle, dangerous faith.

"God demands cleansing fire!" Stubbs continued, pointing to crude maps pinned to the wall behind him. Mare recognized the landmarks immediately, The Rose, The Crane, The Maiden's Head. Each brothel marked with a red cross, each a target for Puritan flames. "Just as Sodom was purified, so shall Southwark be cleansed of its corruption!"

The crowd responded with a chorus of "Amens" that shook dust from the ancient rafters. Mare joined in, her voice carefully modulated to neither stand out nor disappear entirely. She needed to be present enough to plant her whispers, but forgettable enough that no one would recall her face when chaos erupted.

As Stubbs launched into a detailed recitation of Southwark's sins, each more lurid than the last, Mare began her work. She shifted slightly, brushing against a middle-aged woman whose face bore the pinched look of perpetual disapproval.

"Praise God for true believers," Mare whispered, her lips barely moving. "Not like some here who speak righteousness by day and visit the Bishop's men by night."

The woman's head turned sharply. "What do you mean?"

Mare's eyes flicked meaningfully toward a man on the opposite side of the church, one of Stubbs's trusted followers. "Nothing," she murmured, feigning alarm at being overheard. "Forget I spoke. It's not my place to question the faithful."

She moved away before the woman could press further, leaving the seed of suspicion planted. Three more times she repeated the performance, each time implying a different betrayal, each time naming a different target. The whispers would spread, she knew. In a gathering built on shared hatred, the suggestion of betrayal was like blood in water, invisible until the sharks began to circle.

When Stubbs paused to take a drink from a pewter cup, the congregation shifted, stretching cramped limbs and exchanging quiet observations. Mare used the momentary disruption to implement the next phase of her plan. She made her way toward the front, where a stack of prayer books sat on a small table, ready to be distributed for the communal prayers that would close the gathering.

With movements too quick for the casual observer to track, Mare extracted the vial from her bodice. A practiced flick of her wrist, a movement Bess had made her rehearse until her arm ached, and three drops of the dark liquid spattered across the top books. Another twist of her fingers, and the vial disappeared back into its hiding place, leaving no evidence of her manipulation.

"Brothers and sisters, prepare your hearts for prayer," called Stubbs's wife, a gaunt woman with eyes like burning coals. She began distributing the prayer books, unaware of the contamination. Mare retreated, circling the perimeter of the room to position herself near Ezekiel.

The pockmarked man stood with his back to the wall, scanning the crowd with the practiced vigilance of someone accustomed to watching for threats. Mare didn't approach directly. Instead, she stumbled slightly, colliding with a large man who blocked Ezekiel's view of her. The man grunted in annoyance but steadied her with a meaty hand.

"Forgive me, brother," Mare murmured, her voice thin and reedy, nothing like her usual tones. "My spirit is willing, but my flesh is weak."

The distraction created, she slipped the packet of forged documents from her sleeve and, with a movement too smooth to be natural yet too casual to attract attention, tucked it into the outer pocket of Ezekiel's coat as she passed behind him. The man never turned, his attention fixed on Stubbs, who had returned to the pulpit with renewed vigour.

"The time for words has passed," Stubbs declared, his voice dropping to a growl that somehow carried more menace than his shouts. "Now comes the time for action. For cleansing. For God's judgment delivered by righteous hands."

He gestured to the maps on the wall. "Three nights hence, we move against the dens of iniquity. But first, I call for volunteers, brave souls to lead the first cleansing."

Hands began to rise throughout the congregation; eager faces turned toward the pulpit. Mare calculated her timing with precision honed through years of surviving Southwark's ruthless hierarchy. She waited until the moment hung suspended, until Stubbs's face had transformed with satisfaction at the response before she made her move.

"Blasphemy!" she cried, her voice pitched high with manufactured horror. She pointed to one of Stubbs's lieutenants, who had just opened his prayer book to find dark liquid staining the pages. "Look! The devil's mark!"

All heads turned. The lieutenant stared in shock at his hands, now smeared with blood. Another cry went up as a second book was opened, revealing similar stains.

"Treachery!" someone shouted from the back.

Mare pressed her advantage, moving swiftly to Ezekiel's side. "Brother," she said loudly enough for those nearby to hear, "what's that in your coat?"

Ezekiel's hand went to his pocket automatically, his face contorting in confusion as he withdrew papers he hadn't placed there. The seal caught the candlelight, a flash of red that drew every eye.

"The Bishop's mark!" gasped a woman, pointing a trembling finger.

Mare stepped back, melting into the crowd as Ezekiel broke the seal with clumsy fingers. His face drained of colour as he scanned the contents, understanding too late what they contained.

"This isn't mine," he protested, but the damage was done.

"Spy!" shouted one of the men with bloodied hands, eager to divert attention from himself. "Agent of Babylon!"

Stubbs fought to regain control, his voice cutting through the rising chaos. "Brothers, sisters, be not deceived by…"

"There are letters here with names!" Ezekiel cried, desperate now. "Names of our brethren! How could I have such things unless…"

"Unless someone placed them there," Stubbs snapped, his eyes narrowing as they swept the congregation. For a terrible moment, his gaze passed over Mare, then returned, sharpening with sudden recognition that cut through her disguise like a blade through cloth.

The chaos Mare had orchestrated provided her cover. As accusations flew and men grappled with one another, Ezekiel now struggling against those who had been his brothers moments before, she edged toward the side door. A woman's prayer book fell, pages splayed open to reveal more dark stains. Someone overturned a candle in the scuffle, sending shadows dancing wildly across the walls.

Mare slipped out into the night, pulse hammering in her throat. Behind her, the shouts grew louder. Stubbs's voice rose above the tumult, a command that froze her blood despite the distance she'd already put between herself and the church.

"Find her! The woman with the scarred palm! She's the Bishop's creature!"

She pressed herself into the shadows of an alley as the side door burst open, disgorging several angry Puritans with makeshift weapons clutched in white-knuckled hands. They looked in the wrong direction, and Mare used their confusion to slip further into the City's protective darkness.

Only when she'd put three winding streets between herself and St. Clement's did she pause to catch her breath. Her heart thudded against her ribs, but satisfaction curled through her veins like good wine. The Puritans would be too busy accusing each other of betrayal to organize any burning in the coming days. The Bishop would have what he wanted, his enemies in disarray. But Stubbs had recognized her. And a zealot with a grudge was a dangerous enemy indeed.

The Bishop's chambers felt different in daylight, though no less oppressive. Morning sun struggled through leaded windows, catching dust motes that danced like penitent souls in purgatory. Mare stood before Wickham's desk, her back straight, her face arranged in the careful mask of deference that had become second nature over the years. The Bishop himself seemed changed, not softer, never that, but satisfied in the way of a cat that had precisely cornered the mouse it wanted. His smile, rare as a truthful priest, curved beneath eyes that remained cold as January.

"The Puritans are scattered," he said, fingers steepled before him like a parody of prayer. "Their leadership fractured. Accusations of treachery flying like arrows in all directions." He tilted his head, studying Mare with unnerving intensity. "My sources tell me that Stubbs himself barely escaped a beating from his own followers. Three arrested by the night watch for brawling in the street outside St. Clement's."

Mare kept her expression neutral, though inwardly she catalogued the information. The Bishop's intelligence network worked quickly, or perhaps Walsingham had eyes of his own among the Puritans. "They turned on each other as expected, Your Grace."

"Indeed." The Bishop rose from his seat; his movements deliberate and measured. He crossed to a cabinet inlaid with mother-of-pearl and extracted a decanter of wine and two goblets, not the pewter cups used for lesser visitors, but actual silver, polished to a mirror shine. "You've earned your place closer to me, Mare."

He poured the wine, a dark red liquid that caught the light like fresh blood. The gesture was significant, the Bishop rarely shared his table with anyone, let alone a woman pulled from Southwark's gutters. Mare recognized it for what it was: not a reward, but a test. A new kind of danger wrapped in the appearance of favour.

"Your health, Your Grace," she said, accepting the goblet without revealing the wariness that tightened her throat.

The Bishop didn't drink immediately. Instead, he circled her like a predator assessing its next meal, his robes whispering against the stone floor. "Do you know why I value you, Mare?" he asked, his voice almost gentle. "It's not just your quick wits or your talent for moving unseen in places I cannot go."

Mare remained still, feeling his gaze like a physical touch across her shoulders. "I serve as required, Your Grace."

"You understand the value of turning enemies against themselves," he continued as if she hadn't spoken. "A direct attack creates martyrs. Persecution strengthens resolve. But doubt…" he paused, sipping his wine with obvious satisfaction, "…doubt is a poison that works from within. It requires no executioner, no public display. The victim does the work himself."

He completed his circle, coming to stand before her again. The sun had shifted, throwing his face into shadow while illuminating hers, a tactical choice of position that Mare didn't believe was accidental.

"What you did at St. Clement's was artistry," the Bishop said, rare approval colouring his tone. "Not a drop of blood spilled by your hand, yet the Puritans' unity lies in tatters. Their planned burning will not happen, at least not with any organization that might threaten my... interests."

Mare took a careful sip of the wine, feeling it warm a path down her throat. It was better than anything she'd tasted in years, worth more than most of Southwark's inhabitants earned in a month. "The Bishop's enemies are my enemies," she replied, the practiced words flowing easily.

Wickham's smile widened a fraction. "See that you remember that, Marion." His voice hardened on her full name, a reminder of the power he held over her identity itself. "Loyalty to me is the only path to survival in Southwark. Others may offer you protection, whisper promises in your ear. They lie. When the tides turn, and they always do, only those firmly in my ship will stay afloat."

The threat beneath the metaphor was clear as broken glass. Mare inclined her head in acknowledgment, careful not to spill a drop of the expensive wine. "I understand, Your Grace."

"I wonder if you do," the Bishop mused, echoing his words from their previous meeting. "But understanding comes with time, and I'm a patient man." He set his goblet down with a decisive click against the wood. "That will be all for now. Continue your usual duties. And keep your eyes open for any remnants of Stubbs's little congregation that might still pose a threat."

Mare placed her half-finished wine beside his, knowing better than to drain the cup as if she were entitled to its contents. She bowed, the movement precise, low enough to show respect, not so low as to appear servile.

"Your Grace," she murmured, backing toward the door as protocol demanded.

The corridor outside felt colder after the Bishop's chambers, though objectively the temperature was the same. Mare adjusted her cloak, fingers brushing against the hidden pocket where she kept her knife. The audience had gone better than expected, but the Bishop's new interest in keeping her "closer" was its own kind of danger. Proximity to power meant greater scrutiny, fewer shadows in which to manoeuvre.

She had taken only a few steps when she noticed Thomas Walsingham emerging from a side passage. The Bishop's page carried a stack of parchments, his thin fingers gripping them with unnecessary force. When he saw Mare, his steps faltered momentarily before he recovered his composure.

"The Bishop's faithful hound returns triumphant," he said, his voice pitched low enough that only she could hear. "Disrupting prayer meetings now, are we? How very... devoted of you."

Mare met his gaze directly. "We all serve in our ways, Thomas. Some with action, others with whispers."

Something flashed in Walsingham's eyes, respect mingled with suspicion. He inclined his head slightly, a gesture that acknowledged her victory while reserving judgment on its cost. Then he passed, continuing toward the Bishop's chambers with his burden of documents.

Mare had just reached the corridor's end when a shadow detached itself from an alcove, resolving into the lean, hard-edged form of John Stubbs. His face was a map of fury, eyes bloodshot, lips drawn back from his teeth in a snarl barely contained. A fresh bruise darkened his jaw, evidence of the chaos she'd created at St. Clement's.

"I know what you did, whore," he hissed, lunging forward to grab her arm. His fingers dug into her flesh with bruising force. "I saw through your disguise. I saw your devil's work."

Mare didn't flinch, didn't pull away immediately. Doing so would only tighten his grip. Instead, she let her body go loose, as if surrendering, a feint that allowed her to shift her weight and twist her arm in a movement learned from years navigating Southwark's dangers.

"Careful, Master Stubbs," she said, her voice level despite the adrenaline flooding her veins. "The Bishop's halls have ears, and touching his property is a sin he doesn't forgive."

Stubbs's face contorted, the piety he preached nowhere visible in his expression. "When we burn Southwark, you'll be the first to feel the flames," he spat. "I'll see to it personally, Bishop's pet or no."

Mare's hand found her hidden knife, fingers closing around its hilt. She didn't draw it, not yet, but its presence steadied her. "Bold words from a man whose followers think him a traitor," she replied, ice coating each syllable. "How many believed those letters were yours, I wonder? How many doubt your leadership now?"

Stubbs moved closer, his breath hot against her face. "They were false. Just like you. But the fire, the fire will be real, Marion Fleet. And it will purify Southwark of the Bishop's corruption and all who serve it."

The sound of approaching footsteps echoed from around the corner, the measured tread of the Bishop's personal guards making their rounds. Stubbs's head turned toward the noise, the movement instinctive.

Mare used the distraction to step back, breaking his grip with a practiced twist. "Run back to your dwindling flock, preacher," she said. "Before someone decides to shear you."

Stubbs retreated, melting back toward the alcove from which he'd emerged. But his eyes burning with a zealot's certainty remained fixed on Mare until the last moment. "This isn't finished," he promised, the words barely audible as the guards' footsteps grew louder.

Then he was gone, leaving Mare alone in the corridor with the echo of his threat hanging in the air like the scent of smoke before a fire.

She straightened her sleeve where Stubbs had gripped it, smoothing the fabric with fingers that didn't quite tremble. The guards rounded the corner, nodded to her with the casual acknowledgment given to a recognized fixture of the Bishop's household, and continued their patrol.

Mare watched them pass, her mind calculating angles and possibilities. The Puritans were weakened but not destroyed. Stubbs's rage had found a focus in her, which made him both more predictable and more dangerous. And the Bishop's approval, while useful, came with chains of its own.

She touched the scar on her palm, a habitual gesture when weighing difficult choices. Then she continued down the corridor, her step deliberately unhurried despite the urgency building in her chest. There were preparations to make, allies to warn, plans to adjust.

The game had changed again, the pieces rearranged on the board. And Mare had no intention of becoming a sacrifice, no matter who was playing.

The hidden room above The Mermaid Tavern existed in that peculiar limbo between legitimate and illegal, not a secret chamber, but certainly not on any floor plan the tavern keeper would admit to owning. Its single window had been painted black on the inside, its door reinforced with iron bands salvaged from a shipwright's scrap heap. Mare leaned against the room's only table, a scarred oak slab that had begun its life on a merchant ship before finding its way to this liminal space where Southwark's shadows did business that even darkness wouldn't witness.

Bess sprawled across the room's only chair, her legs draped over one arm in a posture that would have scandalized the Puritans they'd just outwitted. She balanced a cup of stolen wine on her stomach, her fingers tapping an irregular rhythm against the pewter as if counting imaginary coins or victims.

"To the Bishop's Shadow," she proclaimed with mock solemnity, raising her cup in Mare's direction. "May her enemies continue to kill each other while she watches from a comfortable distance."

Katherine, perched on a wooden chest with the precise posture her noble upbringing had branded into her spine, raised her own cup with more grace. "To well-placed lies and the men foolish enough to believe them."

Mare accepted their toast with a tired smile that reached her eyes for the first time in days. The wine was good, not as fine as the Bishop's, but sweet enough to wash away the taste of fear that had lodged in her throat since St. Clement's. She took a long swallow, feeling the warmth spread through her chest.

"You should have seen them," she said, setting her cup down on the table. "Stubbs's lieutenant with pig's blood on his hands, staring at it like he'd been marked by Satan himself. And Ezekiel" She shook her head, the memory drawing a genuine chuckle from her lips. "His face when he pulled those letters from his pocket. I thought he'd piss himself right there in the church."

Bess snorted, wine sloshing dangerously close to the rim of her cup. "Wish I could've seen it. Been wanting to stick a knife in those sanctimonious pricks since they started preaching about my 'sinful flesh' outside The Crane."

"Violence wasn't necessary," Katherine observed, her long fingers cradling her cup with delicate precision. "Mare's approach was far more elegant. They'll be too busy suspecting each other to organize any burning for weeks, maybe months."

"Stubbs knows it was me," Mare said, the momentary lightness fading from her voice. "Recognized me at the end. Caught me in the Bishop's corridor afterward."

Both women straightened at this, even Bess abandoning her lounging posture to sit upright.

"What happened?" Katherine asked, her tone carefully neutral despite the concern evident in her eyes.

Mare flexed her fingers, remembering the feel of her knife's hilt pressed against her palm as Stubbs had loomed over her. "He made threats. Said I'd be the first to burn when they came for Southwark."

"Empty words," Bess said, but her hand moved unconsciously to the knife she kept strapped to her thigh. "Man's power is broken. His followers think he's been playing both sides."

"For now," Mare agreed. "But zealots have long memories, especially when their pride is wounded."

Katherine studied Mare's face with the careful assessment of someone who had navigated court intrigues for years before falling from grace. "And the Bishop? How did he receive your success?"

A bitter smile twisted Mare's lips. "With rare approval. Even shared his wine. Says I've earned a place 'closer' to him."

"Dangerous ground," Katherine murmured, understanding immediately what Mare hadn't said explicitly. Proximity to the Bishop meant greater scrutiny, fewer shadows in which to hide her true allegiances.

"More dangerous than Stubbs and his fire-breathers?" Bess asked, refilling her cup from the stolen bottle.

"Different dangers," Mare replied. "Stubbs would kill me quickly, at least. The Bishop..." She trailed off, the scar on her palm itching with phantom pain. "The Bishop takes his time with those who disappoint him."

The three women fell silent, each contemplating the precarious nature of their victory. The sounds of the tavern below filtered up through the floorboards, laughter, arguments, the clatter of pewter mugs on wooden tables. The ordinary noise of Southwark continuing its daily business, unaware of the machinations that might determine whether it burned or survived.

Mare shifted, adjusting her cloak, and felt something crinkle in the pocket, paper that hadn't been there before. Her body tensed automatically, fingers sliding toward her hidden blade even as she reached with her other hand to investigate.

She withdrew a folded scrap of parchment, the quality better than what most of Southwark's inhabitants could afford. No seal marked its closure, but the folds were precise, deliberate.

"What's that?" Bess asked, sharp eyes missing nothing.

"I don't know," Mare replied, unfolding the paper carefully. "Wasn't there earlier."

The handwriting struck her first, a distinctive, flowing script that she recognized immediately. Her pulse quickened despite her attempt at outward calm.

"Marlowe," Katherine said softly, having risen to peer over Mare's shoulder. "The playwright's hand is unmistakable."

The message was brief, the ink still relatively fresh:

"The stage hides more than players. Midnight. The Rose."

Mare stared at the words, memories rising unbidden of her last encounter with Christopher Marlowe in that very theatre. His passionate talk of revolution, his hands on her body, the press beneath the stage that printed seditious pamphlets. The way he'd slipped a pamphlet into her cloak while she wasn't looking, much as this note must have been delivered.

"When did he..." she began, then stopped, mentally retracing her steps through Southwark over the past day. The market where she'd been jostled by a crowd watching a street performer. Or outside the Bishop's quarters, where she'd passed through a knot of petitioners seeking audience. Marlowe had friends everywhere, paid well for information and assistance.

"Dangerous man to be tangled with," Bess observed, studying Mare's face rather than the note. "Talented with words, they say, but too free with them for his own good."

"He has the ear of powerful men," Katherine added. "And a reputation for playing all sides of any conflict."

Mare traced the words with her fingertip, feeling the slight indentations where Marlowe's pen had pressed into the parchment. "The stage hides more than players," she repeated softly. The press beneath the stage, the secret printing operation that produced pamphlets challenging church and state alike. Was that what he referred to, or something else entirely?

"You're not thinking of going," Bess said, the statement more accusation than question.

Mare folded the note, her expression carefully neutral. "Knowledge is currency in Southwark. Marlowe trades in it like others trade in cloth or spice."

"Or flesh," Katherine said quietly. "Don't forget he moves in the Bishop's circles as well. This could be a trap."

"Could be," Mare agreed. "But Marlowe risks his neck printing sedition beneath the very boards where the Queen's men perform. He doesn't extend invitations lightly."

The three women exchanged glances, a silent communication built on shared dangers and mutual understanding. None of them needed to voice the obvious, that curiosity had killed more Southwark residents than plague and poverty combined.

Mare held the note over the room's single candle, watching as the flame caught the edge of the parchment. The fire consumed Marlowe's words, turning them to ash that drifted onto the table like black snow.

"If I don't return from The Rose by dawn," she said, echoing her instructions from before the Puritan gathering, "burn everything that connects us and scatter."

Bess snorted, draining her cup. "You said that last time, and here we are, celebrating. Man's probably just written some new play he wants to brag about."

But her light tone didn't match her eyes, which remained fixed on Mare with the sharp assessment of someone who had survived Southwark's streets by reading danger before it arrived.

Katherine gathered the cups with efficient movements, wiping away all evidence of their celebration. "Be careful," she said simply. "The playhouses have their own politics, their own dangers."

Mare nodded, watching the last of Marlowe's note curl into nothingness in the candle's flame. The smell of burning paper filled the small room, acrid and final. But the words remained in her mind, a puzzle piece that might connect to the larger game being played across Southwark; the dead clergyman in the Thames, the seal she still carried, the press beneath the stage.

The Bishop's approval sat uneasily in her stomach, like wine turned to vinegar. Stubbs's hatred burned hot but predictable. But Marlowe, brilliant, dangerous Kit with his poet's passion and spy's calculation represented a different kind of threat. Or perhaps an opportunity.

As the final ash from the note settled on the scarred table, Mare's expression shifted from triumph to wary curiosity. Whatever conspiracy brewed in the playhouses of Southwark, it had now drawn her into its orbit. And like the Bishop's reluctant shadow, she would discover its shape by moving silently through its darkness.

Chapter Eight

Shadows of Southwark

The rain fell in lazy drops that spring evening, turning Southwark's dirt streets into a treacherous paste that clung to Mare's boots as she lingered outside The Rose. The memory still burned like a coal lodged beneath her ribs. Playgoers pushed past, gentleman's silk brushing against labourer's wool in that brief democracy of entertainment, all of them too concerned with ducking the weather to notice the slight woman hovering at the edge of the crowd, counting purses, and measuring vulnerability with practiced eyes.

She hadn't come to lift coin, not really. The Bishop had sent her to gauge the mood of the crowd, to listen for whispers of sedition that might flow more freely in the shadow of players speaking borrowed rebellion. The theatre drew malcontents like flies to a turd, Wickham had said, his cold eyes watching her as if she were a blade he was testing for weakness.

A shoulder knocked into hers, harder than the usual jostle. Mare's hand went instinctively to her knife but found instead a chaos of papers fluttering into the mud like wounded birds.

"Christ's wounds!" The man dropped to his knees, heedless of the muck soaking into his breeches. "Not the Cambridge pages…"

Something in his voice, desperate yet musical, made Mare crouch beside him. Her fingers closed around a sheet half-submerged in a puddle, the ink already bleeding into abstract patterns.

"Here," she said, shaking off the worst of the wet.

He looked up, and Mare felt something shift in her chest, like a lock whose tumblers had unexpectedly aligned. His face was sharp, pretty in the strange light of dusk, with clever eyes that crinkled at the corners despite his youth. A poet's mouth, she thought nonsensically, then wondered where such foolishness had sprung from.

"My saviour in the wilderness," he said, taking the page with ink-stained fingers. "Though I fear this particular miracle comes too late for poor Tamburlaine."

"Tamburlaine?"

"The Great, no less. Though presently the Damp." His smile cracked across his face like summer lightning. "My unruly child, soon to be born on these very boards if the rain hasn't drowned his spirit entirely."

Mare handed him another sheet, less damaged than the first. "You're a player, then?"

"A writer of players' words, which makes me either their god or their servant, depending on the hour and how many have forgotten their lines." He gathered the last of the pages, grimacing at their condition. "Christopher Marlowe. Kit to those who've seen me drink under a table or weep over a verse that won't behave."

"Mare," she replied, offering nothing more. Names were coin in Southwark, and she spent hers carefully.

He straightened, and she realized he wasn't tall, barely half a head above her, but carried himself as if he were. "Mare," he repeated, rolling the name like a sip of wine. "Short for Marion? Or a warning that you're dangerous to ride?"

The crudeness should have offended her. Instead, she found herself fighting a smile. "Dangerous enough."

"The best ones always are." He glanced at the playhouse, then back to her, a decision forming behind his eyes. "Come. Help me salvage what can be saved from this wreckage, and I'll give you a private performance worth twice the penny they'd charge you at the door."

Sense told her to walk away. The Bishop was expecting her report. These papers might be nothing but a player's fancy, or they might be exactly the sort of seditious material Wickham sought. Either way, she should make her excuses and leave.

Instead, she followed Kit Marlowe behind The Rose, ducking under a sagging length of canvas that sheltered a makeshift workspace. A lantern hung from a hook, swaying slightly in the damp breeze and casting their shadows huge against the playhouse's wooden flank.

"Spread them here," he paused and smiled, "the pages" he said, indicating a table cluttered with quills and half-empty wine cups. "Let's see what Neptune has left me to work with."

They laid the pages out, separating those beyond salvage from those merely damp. Mare found herself studying his hands, quick, nimble, like a pickpocket's, but creating rather than taking. His fingers brushed hers occasionally as they worked, each contact like a small static spark.

"It's a new play," he explained, squinting at a particularly water-damaged passage. "Tamburlaine the Great. A shepherd who becomes a conqueror through will alone."

"The mighty dream small," Mare observed, thinking of Southwark's own dreamers, with their petty schemes and stunted ambitions.

Kit looked up sharply, his eyes suddenly intense. "Yes, exactly. That's exactly it." He abandoned the wet pages and moved closer, the lantern light catching the planes of his face. "The mighty begin no mightier than you or I, but they hunger differently. They swallow worlds while others nibble at crumbs."

His voice had changed, growing richer, deeper, the voice he must use on stage, she realized. It rolled over her like warm honey, sweet and strangely suffocating.

"'Nature that framed us of four elements, Warring within our breasts for regiment, Doth teach us all to have aspiring minds,'" he recited, stepping closer still. "'Our souls, whose faculties can comprehend The wondrous architecture of the world, And measure every wandering planet's course, Still climbing after knowledge infinite, And always moving as the restless spheres.'"

The words themselves meant little to Mare, but the way he spoke to them, as if they were fire he was breathing into life, made something inside her shift and stretch toward the heat.

"Did you write that?" she asked, her voice unexpectedly husky in her own ears.

"God wrote it through me," he replied with a grin that undercut the blasphemy. "Or the devil. The clergy can't seem to decide which."

Then his hand was cupping her cheek, thumb tracing her lower lip with such delicate precision that Mare's usual defences dissolved like sugar in rain. When he kissed her, it wasn't like the fumbling groping she'd endured before, but something almost conversational, a question asked and answered in the press of mouth against mouth.

That kiss became the first of many over the weeks that followed. Kit would find her at the river, appearing with a bottle of stolen wine and a fistful of wildflowers gathered from some church yard. They'd stretch on the bank watching boats pass, his head in her lap as he recited new lines and she pointed out which merchants were cheating their crews by the way they handled their purses.

He brought her words like gifts, sonnets with her name hidden in the first letters of each line, verses that made her laugh despite herself. She brought him stories from Southwark's shadows, tales of the Bishop's machinations and the desperation of the poor, which he scribbled down with hungry intensity.

For six impossible weeks, Mare allowed herself to believe in something she hadn't thought possible, that the world might contain beauty alongside its obvious cruelties. That someone might see past her usefulness to something worth cherishing.

The night of Tamburlaine's opening, she wore the only dress she owned that wasn't practical for moving through shadows. Midnight blue wool, fitted enough to display the figure she usually disguised, with sleeves she'd mended by candlelight. She even washed her hair, letting it fall loose instead of binding back as usual.

Kit had promised her a seat near the stage, not with the nobles, but close enough to see the sweat on the players' brows. She arrived early, slipping through the crowd with the strange self-consciousness of someone dressed for looking rather than hiding.

She found him behind the stage, among the controlled chaos of final preparations. But instead of the greeting she'd half-expected, she saw him bent close to a woman in silk the colour of fresh cream, his hand covering hers with familiar intimacy.

"'And ride in triumph through Persepolis,'" he was saying, in that same voice he'd used when reciting to Mare by lantern light. "'Is it not passing brave to be a king, And ride in triumph through Persepolis?'"

The noblewoman, for she was clearly that, with pearls at her throat that could feed Southwark for a year, laughed and tapped his cheek with her fan. "You'll make a believer of me yet, Master Marlowe."

Mare stood frozen, watching Kit press a kiss to the woman's wrist, the same gesture he'd used on her not two days past. The same words. The same look of boyish adoration that had made her feel, briefly, like something precious.

She waited until the woman had gone, then stepped from the shadows. Kit saw her and smiled, that same lightning crack across his face, but something in it now seemed calculated rather than spontaneous.

"Mare! You look…" He paused, eyes widening slightly at her transformation. "Different."

"I heard your lines," she said, voice flat as a blade. "The same ones you spoke to me by the river. Word for word."

A flicker of annoyance crossed his face, there and gone like a dragonfly over water. "They're good lines. That's why I wrote them."

"And do you say them to every woman whose skirts you hope to lift? A private performance, you called it."

Kit sighed, running a hand through his hair with theatrical exasperation. "Come now, Mare. Surely you didn't think…" He gestured between them, a dismissive wave. "It was pleasant diversion, nothing more. You're clever and sharp, but Lady Pembroke there has connections at court that could make or break Tamburlaine's future."

Mare felt something inside her harden like clay in fire. "I didn't think anything," she lied, her voice steady despite the hollowness spreading beneath her ribs. "Just wanted to be sure I understood the game."

"No game," Kit replied, already glancing past her to where the players were assembling. "Just the way of the world. Enjoyment where we find it, advancement where we can grasp it." He touched her cheek briefly. "You're a pragmatist, Mare. It's what I liked about you. Don't turn romantic on me now."

She stepped back from his touch. "I won't make that mistake again," she said, and meant it with every fibre of her being.

As she walked away, leaving Kit Marlowe to his opening night triumph, Mare felt the last of her girlish fancies burn away like morning mist. Men's loyalties clung to their breeches, not their hearts. The Bishop had tried to teach her that lesson with fear; Kit had taught it with false tenderness. But the lesson was learned now, branded into her like the scar on her palm.

She never wore the blue dress again.

Tonight, the Rose stood silent against the night sky, its wooden frame a hulking shadow cut with thin lines of candlelight that leaked through cracks in the walls. Mare approached from the river side, where fewer eyes might catch her silhouette moving against the backdrop of stars. The last of the evening's patrons had staggered off into the darkness of Maiden Lane and The Bankside leaving only the ghosts of their laughter lingering in the cool night air and a few scattered players gathering their pride after a mediocre performance of "The Spanish Tragedy" by the Lord Strange's men.

Midnight was two hours away, the nearby church bells having tolled their solemn count while Mare had waited in the shadows, watching for anyone who might be watching for her. Kit Marlowe's note burned in her memory as surely as she'd burned the parchment itself. "The stage hides more than players." Not a poet's metaphor but a thief's instruction, direct, purposeful, and potentially deadly if misunderstood.

She slipped through a performer's entrance the lock yielded to her touch with barely a whisper of metal against metal. Inside, the theatre smelled of humanity, sweat and perfume battling for dominance, the sharp tang of cheap ale spilled on wooden floors, and the distinctive musk of greasepaint that never quite washed out of the timbers.

Backstage lay in the organized chaos particular to playhouses, a world where appearance trumped reality and nothing was quite what it seemed. Painted flats leaned against walls like drunken revellers too exhausted to stand properly, their forest scenes and palace interiors garish up close but magical from a distance. A prop table still held the debris of the evening's drama, a wooden dagger with its tip broken off, a crown fashioned from painted tin that bore the smudges of anxious fingers, a goblet sticky with wine-coloured water.

Mare moved like water herself, flowing between the obstacles with practiced ease. Her eyes adjusted to the gloom, picking out paths invisible to those unfamiliar with the theatre's geography. A costume rack created a momentary barrier, festooned with doublets whose embroidery was painted on, and dresses whose jewels were glass beads and coloured paper. She pushed past them, the fabrics exhaling the body odour of the actors who'd worn those hours earlier.

The second trap door behind the main stage lay beneath a cluster of rope coils and canvas, deliberately obscured by what was discarded set pieces but which Mare recognized as a carefully arranged blind. She crouched beside it, listening. The muffled thump of machinery pulsed from below, a heartbeat of sedition pumping out words that could hang men if discovered by the wrong eyes.

Pressing her ear against the wooden floor, Mare caught fragments of conversation – low, urgent voices speaking quickly between the rhythmic groans of the press.

"—fifteen bundles to Fleet Street by dawn—"

"—need more ink for the Bishop's seal—"

"—Cheapside drop scheduled for Thursday—"

Mare's fingers found the edge of the backstage trap door, a seam invisible in the wooden floor. With the delicate touch she'd perfected picking locks and pockets in her youth, she eased it up just enough to create a slim opening. A crack of yellow light spilled upward, painting a thin line across her face.

The space below heaved with furtive activity. Three figures huddled around a printing press that looked like it had been assembled from parts stolen from half a dozen different machines. Each movement was practiced, efficient, one-man feeding paper, another working the lever with mechanical precision, a third gathering the damp sheets as they emerged. The air hung thick with the sharp smell of ink and the sweeter scent of the linseed oil used to clean the press.

Stacked against one wall, bundles of pamphlets waited for distribution, their titles barely visible in the lantern light: "On the Corruption of Bishops" and "A Call to Reformed Worship." Sedition masquerading as religious debate, enough to earn a traitor's death if discovered.

As Mare watched, the man collecting the printed sheets reached up to wipe sweat from his brow, his sleeve falling back to reveal a wrist bound with a strip of cloth. Even in the dim light, Mare could make out the embroidered insignia – a simple cross with the letters "St. U" stitched beneath it. The mark of Sister Agnes's order, here beneath Marlowe's stage.

The pieces clicked together in Mare's mind with the uncomfortable precision of a lock being picked. The Order of St. Ursula wasn't just sheltering women and defying the Bishop from the shadows, they were actively printing and distributing the very pamphlets that had London's authorities searching every corner of the city. And somehow, Kit Marlowe, the darling of London's stages and whispered agent of the Queen's spymaster, was involved.

A floorboard creaked overhead, not where Mare knelt, but from the stage itself. Voices approached, the casual banter of stagehands coming to strike the set and prepare for tomorrow's performance.

"—told him it was the wrong bloody prop, but does he listen? Pompous arse thinks—"

"—least he pays on time, unlike that bastard Henslowe—"

Mare eased the trap door closed, her movements careful and controlled despite the sudden hammering of her pulse. The men below hadn't noticed her observation, too engrossed in their illegal work. She rose in a fluid motion, gathering herself like a cat preparing to leap, and retreated toward the side door through which she'd entered.

The voices grew louder, accompanied by the scrape of furniture being moved across the stage. Mare slid between two massive set pieces, the facade of a church and a nobleman's bedchamber, the juxtaposition unintentionally revealing of London's twin religions.

She reached the door just as the first stagehand descended the steps into the backstage area, a lantern held high to illuminate his path. Mare slipped through the opening, pulling the door closed behind her with barely a sound. The night air hit her face like a splash of freezing water, washing away the close, inky atmosphere of the theatre's secret operation.

Her mind raced as she melted into the shadows surrounding The Rose. The connection between the Order and the seditious pamphlets explained much, why Sister Agnes knew the Bishop's business so intimately, how the women always seemed one step ahead of his men. But it raised more questions than it answered. What was Marlowe's role in all this? Why direct Mare to discover something she already partially knew? And most importantly, where did her own loyalties truly lie in this tangled web of players?

The trapdoor beneath the backstage had revealed one secret, but Mare sensed it was merely the visible corner of a much larger tapestry of conspiracy, one that somehow connected playwright, priest, and the women who'd survived both. She had another meeting to go to before she would be back to confront Marlowe, after midnight.

Mare slipped from The Rose's shadow into Rose Alley, so narrow her shoulders brushed both walls. The passage stank of excrement and rotting vegetables, the universal perfume of Southwark after dark. Above her, laundry lines crisscrossed between leaning buildings like the web of some monstrous spider, clothes hanging limp and ghostly in the moonlight. She pressed forward, each step deliberate and silent, her mind churning with what she'd witnessed beneath the stage floor.

The walls surrounding her were texts for those who knew how to read them, a poor man's broadsheet of crude drawings and desperate messages. Gallows sketched in charcoal with the Bishop's name scrawled beneath it. A pair of spread legs with a crown between them comment on the Queen's latest favourite. Three parallel lines crossed with a fourth the sign that marked a safe house for women on the run. Mare's fingers traced this last symbol as she passed, wondering how many of the marks had been left by Sister Agnes's women, guiding their sisters through the labyrinth of Southwark's underworld.

She paused at a junction where three alleys met, marking the spot where a child had been found dead last winter, frozen with a begging cup still clutched in tiny fingers. Someone had scratched a rough cross into the wall. Mare's eyes caught it, held it for a moment, then moved on. Southwark remembered its dead in its own way.

A rotted wooden door, its planks warped with age and damp, stood partially hidden behind a pile of refuse. To the casual observer, it would appear to be the entrance to an abandoned storage room, not worth the effort of breaking in. Mare pushed it open with her shoulder, the hinges protesting with a sound like a woman in labour. Beyond it stretched a passage that existed on no city map, a tunnel carved through the forgotten spaces between buildings.

The ground beneath her boots squelched with something she chose not to identify. The air hung thick and close, fouled by the river's proximity and the waste of thousands of souls living too close together. Mare moved with the confidence of a rat in a familiar sewer, one hand brushing the wall for guidance, the other ready at her knife. These passages belonged to Southwark's most desperate, those for whom even the streets above were too exposed, too regulated.

Occasionally, her path took her past crude shelters, a bundle of rags that contained a sleeping form, a niche where someone had created a nest of stolen straw and scraps of cloth. The inhabitants never stirred as she passed. In this underworld, you minded your business, or you lost the privilege of having business to mind.

The tunnel widened suddenly, opening into a small courtyard hidden between the backs of several buildings. Mare paused in the shadows, taking a moment to breathe air that, while not clean, at least moved. Across the courtyard, a narrow gap between two leaning structures offered a view of the street beyond a street where worlds collided in the peculiar geography of Southwark.

On one side stood Madame Dubois's ballroom, its windows glowing with expensive candlelight, the sounds of a violin and drunken laughter spilling into the night. Gentlemen in fine clothes arrived in pairs or small groups, their voices carrying the distinctive accents of wealth and education. Through the windows, Mare could glimpse women in silk dresses moving like exotic fish in a glass bowl, their jewellery catching the light with every gesture.

Directly opposite, huddled in the shadow of the ballroom's grandeur, a woman sat with three small children. Their faces were hollow-cheeked maps of hunger, their clothes little more than strategically arranged rags. The woman held out a wooden bowl to each passing gentleman, her voice a monotonous chant of practiced desperation.

"Spare a penny for my babes, good sir? Just a penny for bread?"

Most walked past without a glance, as if the woman and her children were simply unpleasant features of the landscape, like an overflowing gutter or a dead dog in the road. Occasionally, one would toss a coin into the dust near her, not even pausing in his conversation with his companions.

Mare watched, her face hardening into something dangerous. Her hand moved unconsciously to the hidden pocket where she kept the Bishop's seal, the token of her service to a man who grew fat on Southwark's misery while children starved outside his door. The weight of it pressed against her like a stone.

She'd been that woman once, or close enough, huddled in Southwark's shadows with hunger gnawing at her belly. The memory rose unbidden: the cold seeping through thin clothes, the gaping emptiness that came after days without food, the way the wealthy looked through you as if poverty might be catching. Her jaw clenched hard enough to ache.

A sharp cry jerked her from the memory. One of the children had ventured too close to a passing gentleman, hoping to tug at his cloak and draw attention to their plight. The man had shoved the child away with his walking stick, sending the small body sprawling into the filth of the street. The mother gathered her offspring back into her protective huddle, eyes downcast, knowing better than to protest.

Mare's hand moved to her knife, but she stopped herself. A confrontation now would serve no one, least of all the woman and her children. Instead, she filed the gentleman's face away in her memory, another debt to be collected when opportunity aligned with justice.

Turning away, she continued through the warren of passages, diving deeper into Southwark's hidden arteries. The sounds of the ballroom faded behind her, replaced by the drip of water from crumbling walls and the occasional scurry of rats seeking their own fortunes in the darkness.

A new sound brought her to a halt, male voices, slurred with drink, drawing nearer through a connecting passage. Mare pressed herself into a shadowy alcove, a space barely large enough to contain her body. She held her breath as four men stumbled past, their faces flushed with alcohol and something more dangerous, cruelty that came when men with little power found someone with less.

"Told you I saw her come this way," one said, his words mushy around the edges. "Little thief thought she could cut my purse and run."

"When we catch her, I get first turn," another replied, generating ugly laughter from his companions.

Mare remained motionless until their voices faded, then waited another full minute before emerging. Whatever woman they hunted, Mare silently wished her speed and shadows deep enough to hide in.

Finally, she emerged onto a street that made no pretence of respectability. Brothels lined both sides, their painted windows glowing with candlelight that transformed cheap glass into jewel-like mosaics. Each establishment advertised its specialties through crude symbols painted beside the doors, a whip, a pair of manacles, a child's doll with disturbing and despicable implications. Women leaned from upper windows, calling enticements to potential customers with voices that managed to sound both bored and desperate simultaneously.

Mare moved quickly through this gauntlet of flesh, her hood pulled low, her stride purposeful enough to discourage approach but not so hurried as to attract attention. Near the end of the street, where the better-maintained brothels gave way to buildings one strong wind from collapse, she paused before an abandoned tenement. Its windows were boarded over, its door hung crooked on broken hinges. Nothing distinguished it from a dozen similar structures in Southwark, buildings too decrepit even for the desperately poor to risk sleeping in.

Which was precisely why it was perfect for Sister Agnes's purposes. Mare slipped through the sagging doorway, disappearing into the darkness beyond as if Southwark itself had swallowed her whole.

The tenement's interior bore the expected scars of abandonment, floors warped from years of rain leaking through the collapsed sections of roof, walls stripped of anything worth selling, corners thick with the accumulated filth of neglect. Mare navigated by memory and touch, her fingers tracing paths along walls where rat-gnawed holes exposed the building's skeletal structure. The ground floor held nothing, but empty rooms and the ghosts of desperate lives once lived there, but Mare moved with purpose toward what had been the building's small chapel, a token gesture toward salvation in a place where God had never shown his face.

The chapel's door hung from a single hinge, creaking softly in a draft that seemed to come from nowhere and everywhere. Inside, moonlight filtered through a broken window, painting silver stripes across a floor littered with fallen plaster and shattered floor tiles. Wooden pews, too worthless to steal, remained in crooked rows like the ribs of some long-dead beast. Mare counted three from the left wall, then moved to the space behind it.

The pew had been deliberately broken, its back splintered as if from age and abuse rather than design. Behind it, the wall appeared solid, unremarkable except for a faint discoloration in the plaster that formed a rough rectangle about the size of a small door. Mare pressed her palm against it, feeling not the expected resistance of stone but a slight give that confirmed what she already knew. She rapped her knuckles against the surface in a pattern that had taken her weeks to earn: three quick, one slow, two quick.

Silence followed, heavy enough that Mare wondered if she'd mistaken the night. Then came the sounds, metal against metal, the slide of bolts, the turn of keys. Not one lock but many, each with its distinctive voice in the quiet chapel. Mare counted six different mechanisms before the hidden door swung inward on perfectly oiled hinges that made less noise than her own breathing.

Light spilled out, not the harsh glare of many candles but the controlled illumination of iron-braced lanterns positioned to reveal what needed seeing while leaving the rest in tactical shadow. The woman who opened the door didn't speak, merely stepped aside with a slight nod of recognition. Her face bore a scar that ran from temple to jaw, puckering the skin around her left eye into a permanent squint. In her right hand, she held a blade that looked like it had started life as a butcher's boning knife before being repurposed for more intimate work.

Mare stepped through the doorway and felt the familiar disorientation that came with entering a space much larger than should have been possible. The "chapel" extended far beyond the dimensions of the tenement above, expanding into what must have been adjacent buildings or underground chambers excavated over years of patient digging. The ceiling stretched higher than expected, supported by rough-hewn wooden beams that had been reinforced with iron bands.

A dozen women occupied the space; each engaged in some precise activity that clicked and whirred like parts of a single mechanism. None looked up at Mare's entrance, they had the focused intensity of those who knew their work might mean the difference between life and death. Their faces shared a quality that had nothing to do with physical features and everything to do with experience: these were women who had seen the worst Southwark could offer and survived it, their expressions carved by hardship into masks of determined competence.

At the centre of the room stood a massive oak table that might once have graced a merchant's dining hall before finding its way to this underground sanctuary. Spread across its scarred surface were the tools of rebellion: forged seals, including perfect replicas of the Bishop's own mark, laid out on squares of black velvet; half-assembled weapons ranging from daggers with hollow handles to what appeared to be a disassembled crossbow; and at the centre, a leather-bound ledger filled with neat columns of names and dates.

Mare moved deeper into the room, cataloguing details with the precision that had kept her alive through years of the Bishop's service. In one corner, three women sorted pamphlets into bundles, their fingers moving with the practiced efficiency of those who had repeated the same task countless times. The pamphlets were identical to those Mare had glimpsed beneath the theatre's stage "On the Corruption of Bishops" with its distinctive red lettering across the top.

Nearby, a rail-thin woman with fingers stained permanently black cleaned a set of daggers, testing each edge against her thumb before setting it aside with a nod of approval. Two more women huddled over what looked like a craftsman's workbench, manipulating tiny pieces of metal with lockpicks and thin wires, practicing on mechanisms of increasing complexity.

"The Rose's press is running again, I see." The voice came from behind Mare, calm and measured as a doctor diagnosing a familiar ailment.

Mare turned to find Sister Agnes standing at her shoulder, her arrival silent as a changing season. The woman's grey-streaked hair was pulled back severely from a face that had once been beautiful before life had carved it into something more useful. She wore simple clothes, a tunic and skirt of undyed wool, sturdy boots that had seen better decades, but carried herself with the natural authority of someone who expected and received obedience.

"Welcome to the real war, Marion," Agnes said, the use of Mare's full name a deliberate reminder that here, at least, she stood stripped of pretence.

Mare's spine stiffened, not with fear but with the sudden realization that Agnes knew precisely who she was, not just the Bishop's agent or a Southwark survivor, but Marion Fleet in all her contradictions and divided loyalties.

"Your war seems well-equipped," Mare replied, her voice carefully neutral despite the rapid calculations happening behind her eyes.

Agnes smiled, a quick flash of teeth that held no warmth. "We fight as we must, with whatever weapons are available." She gestured toward the table. "Including information. The Bishop leaves for Windsor on Thursday morning, traveling with a smaller guard than usual due to his confidence in the recent disruption of the Puritan threat."

The casual revelation of information that should have been known only to those in Wickham's innermost circle sent a chill across Mare's skin. The implications bloomed like bloodstains on white linen, the Order's reach extended further than she'd imagined, their eyes and ears present in places Mare had believed secure.

"Our sisters work in noble houses as maids, in taverns as serving girls, in brothels as, well, you know what they do there." Agnes moved to the table, her fingers trailing over the ledger's open pages. "They hear things. See things. Things powerful men discuss when they believe only the furniture is listening."

Mare glanced at the ledger, catching glimpses of familiar names arranged in columns with dates and cryptic notations. The Bishop's private secretary. The Queen's Chamberlain. The Earl of Essex's favourite manservant. Each connected to women whose names Mare recognized from Southwark's brothels or the Bishop's own household staff.

"You've built quite a network," Mare observed, the understatement deliberate.

"We've built what necessity demanded," Agnes corrected. "When the holy men and nobles use women's bodies as currency, we use their carelessness as our coin." She closed the ledger with a decisive movement. "They never imagine that the girl warming their bed might remember their secrets, or that the maid scrubbing their floor might recognize the significance of a document left carelessly unattended."

Around them, the women continued their work, the quiet industry of revolution unfolding in precise, measured movements. The click of lock mechanisms, the whisper of papers being sorted, the soft scrape of blades against whetstones, a symphony of preparation conducted by Agnes's calm presence.

"Why show me this?" Mare asked, the question that had been building since the door opened. "You know who I serve."

"I know who employs you," Agnes replied, her eyes sharp as a midwife's knife. "But service? That's a matter between you and your conscience, Marion."

She stepped closer, close enough that Mare could smell the herb sachets Agnes kept in her clothes to ward off the stink of Southwark, rosemary, and something bitter, medicinal.

"You've been playing a dangerous game, standing between the Bishop and those he'd crush beneath his heel," Agnes continued. "Warming the Puritans, helping the Geese fly before the fires could reach them. Did you think such actions went unnoticed?"

Mare's hand moved instinctively toward her hidden knife, but Agnes made no threatening movement. Instead, she smiled again, this time with something that might have been genuine amusement.

"We don't want your death, Marion. We want your choice." She gestured around the room. "This is the true battlefield of Southwark, not the streets or the brothels, but the flow of information, the collection of secrets, the quiet recruitment of those who've seen enough to know that men like Bishop Wickham must fall."

The offer hung in the air between them, unspoken but unmistakable. Mare felt the weight of it pressing against her chest, heavier than the Bishop's seal she still carried. The women around them had paused in their tasks, attention shifting subtly toward the exchange between Agnes and the Bishop's shadow.

"Think carefully," Agnes said, her voice softening to something almost maternal. "You've already chosen sides a dozen times without admitting it to yourself. The only question is whether you'll finally acknowledge what you've become."

Mare stood frozen in place, awed by the scope of what she'd discovered and terrified by the implications of Agnes's words. The Order was not just a sanctuary for broken women or even a thorn in the Bishop's side, it was a fully realized resistance with roots that reached into the very heart of power. And somehow, without fully understanding how, Mare had already entangled herself in its web.

"The war has always been here," Agnes said, turning away with the confidence of someone who knew they had planted a seed that would grow whether tended or not. "You've simply been fighting on too many fronts at once."

She moved back toward the table, leaving Mare to absorb the magnitude of what she'd witnessed, a network of the despised and discarded who had transformed their exploitation into a weapon, who had learned to fight with the only tools left to them: secrets, misdirection, and the invisible power of being perpetually underestimated.

Behind her, the door closed silently, the locks re-engaging one by one. Before her stretched a decision that would reshape everything, she thought she knew about survival in Southwark's unforgiving landscape.

Chapter Nine

Playwright's Betrayal

The Rose theatre stood silent against the midnight sky, its wooden frame creaking with secrets in the gentle river breeze. Mare slipped through the actor's entrance, a door whose lock had surrendered to her talents as easily as a drunk surrenders to sleep. Inside, darkness pooled in corners and gathered beneath benches where, hours earlier, apprentices and merchants had crowded to watch bloody tales unfold on stage. Now the only audience was the rats, scuttling between discarded apple cores and nutshells, witnesses to a different kind of drama about to unfold.

Mare uncovered her lantern just enough to cast a thin blade of light across the floor. The meagre illumination turned familiar shapes strange, rope coils became sleeping serpents; costume racks transformed into waiting spectres. Her pulse hammered against her ribs; each beat a reminder of the risk she took coming here. Marlowe's note had been deliberately vague: "The stage hides more than players." But his handwriting had carried an urgency that spoke louder than the words themselves, the ink pressed deep into the parchment as if driven by fear or desperation.

She knew the path to the trap door by memory. The boards beneath her feet groaned with age and damp. She paused at each sound, counting heartbeats until satisfied no other movement answered hers. The theatre felt alive around her, breathing with drafts that slipped through ill-fitted walls, settling its weight like an old man finding comfort in familiar discomfort.

The backstage trapdoor lay hidden beneath a cluster of rope and canvas; a deliberate blind she'd helped arrange on the previous visit. Mare crouched beside it, setting her lantern on the floor. She pressed her ear to the wooden planks and held her breath.

From below came the distinctive rhythm of a printing press, the groan of the lever, the slap of the plate, the whisper of paper being lifted.

She eased the trap door up with practiced care, just enough to spill light from below onto her face. The smell hit her first, ink and linseed oil, sweat and cheap tallow candles burning low. The hidden room beneath the stage was cramped but efficiently arranged. A table dominated the centre, stacked with freshly printed pamphlets still damp with ink. And hunched over it, back to the trapdoor, was Christopher Marlowe.

His fine doublet was cast aside; sleeves rolled to the elbows as he worked. Marlowe's shoulders, normally carried with the arrogant ease of a man confident in his wit and charm, were tense as bowstrings. He moved with frantic energy between table and press, gathering pages, collating, binding.

Mare widened the opening and slipped her head and shoulders through for a better view. The papers nearest her bore titles that sent ice through her veins: "God's Cleansing Flame. A Call to Righteous Action" and "The Bishop's Sins: A Record of Corruption." Puritan tracts, not the political sedition Marlowe usually trafficked in. And beside them, something worse a leather pouch, carelessly open, revealing the distinctive red wax of church seals. Mare recognized the Bishop's personal mark among them, identical to the one she carried.

Her scarred palm throbbed as if the skin remembered the Bishop's brand and burned anew with the betrayal she witnessed. Marlowe wasn't just printing anti-Bishop rhetoric, he was actively supporting Stubbs and his zealots, the very men who had planned to burn Southwark to the ground. The same men whose plans she had disrupted at notable risk to herself.

As Mare eased herself through the opening, the full scope of Marlowe's deception lay spread before her. Notes detailing guard rotations at key buildings. Maps of Southwark with the brothels marked the same brothels that had been targeted for burning. Receipts for lamp oil and other supplies, marked with forged versions of the Bishop's seal to deflect suspicion. Everything needed to reignite Stubbs's campaign of fire once the confusion she'd sown had settled.

Her boot caught the edge of a wooden prop, a crown meant for some player's king, sending it rolling across the floor with a hollow, accusatory rattle. The sound seemed to explode in the cramped space.

Marlowe spun, ink-stained fingers reaching instinctively for the dagger at his belt. When he saw Mare half-emerged from the trap door, his face drained of colour so rapidly she could almost track its recession like a tide pulling back from shore. His eyes, which had charmed nobles and commoners alike, widened with naked fear.

"Mare," he breathed, her name falling from his lips like a prayer or a curse.

She dropped fully into the room, landing with the controlled silence of a predator. "You lying bastard," she hissed, her voice low and dangerous in the cramped space.

Marlowe scrambled to gather the papers, to hide the evidence of his betrayal, but the task was impossible. There was too much, and she had seen too clearly. His elegant hands, which had written verses that made queens weep and drafted plays that stirred London's heart, now trembled like those of a guilty child caught stealing sweets.

"This isn't what you think," he said, the words tumbling over each other in their rush to escape. "There are necessities you don't understand, larger concerns. "

"Larger concerns?" Mare advanced, each step measured, her fury cold and precise. "Like burning women alive in their beds? Like helping fanatics 'cleanse' Southwark with fire while you watch safely from across the river?" She snatched a pamphlet from the table and thrust it toward him. "This is Stubbs's work. The same Stubbs who'd see me burn as the Bishop's creature."

Marlowe retreated until his back pressed against the printing press. "It's complicated, Mare. There are powers at work beyond the Bishop, beyond Southwark. Sometimes we must align with unlikely allies for the greater good."

"The greater good," she echoed, the words tasting like ash on her tongue. "And what 'greater good' is served by helping zealots murder women whose only crime is surviving the way this world allows them to?"

His face twisted with something that might have been shame or might have been frustration at being caught. "You don't understand the game being played…"

"I understand betrayal," Mare cut him off. "I understand that while I was disrupting Stubbs's plans, risking my neck to save the Geese, you were printing the very pamphlets that would send new fanatics to finish what he started."

Marlowe's hand reached for her arm, a playwright's instinct to direct the scene unfolding before him. "Mare, please. Listen. There are wheels within wheels here. The Bishop, the Puritans, they're both tools in a larger mechanism. I'm trying to steer things towards, that's why I called for you."

"Don't touch me," she snapped, jerking away from his grasp. "How long have you been feeding Stubbs information? How long have you been playing me for your puppet?"

The words hung between them, heavier than the low ceiling pressing down from above, darker than the shadows gathering in the corners beyond the candles' reach. In his silence, Mare found her answer.

Mare snatched a stack of papers from the table, her fingers leaving smudges on the still-damp ink. Lists of names, dates, locations, all written in Marlowe's distinctive hand, the same flowing script that had once penned sonnets comparing her eyes to midnight skies. Now it marked drop points for Puritan propaganda, detailing the corners and taverns where zealots could collect the fuel for their righteous anger. Her stomach twisted as she recognized streets where she had walked freely, believing herself invisible to all but the Bishop's men.

"The Bell and Anchor. The crossing at Cheapside. The abandoned tannery." She read aloud, each location striking like a hammer on an anvil. "Christ's wounds, Kit, these are places I pass daily. Places where I've met you." Her voice dropped to something dangerous. "Was I being watched each time? Was I followed back to…" She cut herself off, suddenly unsure how much of her own movements had been compromised.

Marlowe stepped forward, hands raised in what might have been supplication or defence. "It's not what you're thinking. The pamphlets go out, yes, but I control what's printed in them. I direct the anger where it needs to go."

"And where is that, exactly?" Mare thrust another paper toward him, this one bearing a crude woodcut of the Bishop with horns sprouting from his mitre. "Toward the women who'll burn when Stubbs whips his followers into righteous fury again? Toward me, when they realize I disrupted their plans?"

The cramped printing room felt smaller with each passing moment, the ceiling pressing down like a hand on the back of her neck. The smell of ink and sweat hung thick in the air, mingling with the sharp tang of betrayal that seemed to rise from the papers clutched in Mare's hand. She turned to a fresh stack of pamphlets, these bearing red seals that matched the Bishop's with uncanny precision. "How long?" she demanded, her voice cracking with rage she refused to fully release. "How long have you been playing me for a fool?"

Marlowe's face worked through a series of expressions defiance, calculation, a flash of something like regret before settling into the smooth mask of reasonableness he wore when convincing theatre owners to stage his more controversial works.

"Mare, this isn't about you. We have always had an understanding, ever since you wore that blue dress. There are forces at work in London beyond Southwark's petty struggles. The Queen's counsellors, the church, foreign powers all moving pieces on a board larger than you can see." He gestured at the printing press. "This is merely one gambit in a greater game."

"A game where women burn?" Mare's finger jabbed at a list of targets, the same brothels that had been marked on Stubbs's map in the barn. "These aren't pieces on a board, Kit. These are people. People I know. People I…" She swallowed the word "protect" before it could escape, unwilling to reveal more of herself than she already had.

Marlowe circled to her left, attempting to reach the leather pouch with the seals. Mare matched his movement, keeping herself between him and the evidence. They began a slow dance around the small space, predators assessing each other's weaknesses.

"You've been feeding information to both sides," Mare said, the realization dawning as she connected threads that had seemed separate. "Telling the Puritans about the Bishop's movements while selling the Bishop information about court intrigues." Her eyes narrowed. "And where do I fit in your scheme? A convenient source? A useful distraction?"

Marlowe's shoulders tensed beneath his linen shirt. "You were never meant to be involved. You were supposed to remain the Bishop's loyal hound, reporting what he wanted to hear."

"Until I disrupted Stubbs's plans." The pieces clicked together in Mare's mind with the terrible precision of a hangman's trap. "That's why you sent the note. Not to warn me, but to expose me to your operation, to gain leverage."

"I needed to know how much you'd discovered!" Marlowe's composure slipped, frustration bleeding into his voice. "When word came that someone had infiltrated the Puritan meeting, had turned them against each other, I knew it had to be you. Only you could have done it so perfectly, so completely."

There was something like admiration in his tone, which made the betrayal cut deeper. Mare pressed her back against the table, feeling the edges of pamphlets dig into her spine. The walls of the small room seemed to lean inward, as if the theatre itself were listening to their hissed accusations.

"Your mastery of deception is impressive," she said, her voice flat and cold as a winter puddle. "The Bishop thinks you his creature, the Puritans believe you serve their righteous cause, and all the while you play your own game."

"Not my game," Marlowe corrected, an edge of desperation entering his voice. "Francis Walsingham's game. The Queen's game. Do you think I'd risk my neck printing sedition for my health? There are plans within plans, Mare. England's future hangs on movements we make now."

"England's future?" Mare laughed, a sound like breaking glass. "You speak of nations while standing in the filth of Southwark, plotting to burn women who've never known a day's security in their lives." She snatched up a receipt marked with the Bishop's forged seal. "You used this to purchase lamp oil for Stubbs's men. Oil meant to burn The Rose, The Crane, The Maiden's Head."

Marlowe's hand slashed through the air, cutting off her words. "Those buildings were never the true targets! The plan was always to redirect the Puritans toward the Bishop's personal holdings, to strike at his wealth, not his whores."

The casual cruelty of the word struck Mare like a physical blow. In that moment, she saw through the elegant veneer of the playwright to the calculating manipulator beneath. A man who viewed Southwark's struggles as pieces to be moved on a board, who saw the women of the brothels not as human beings fighting to survive but as faceless pawns in a greater scheme.

"You never understood what was at stake in Southwark," she said, each word precise as a knife cut. "You saw only opportunity in our desperation."

"And you never looked beyond its borders!" Marlowe countered, his poet's voice rising with conviction. "While you scurry through the shadows of one district, powers are moving that could reshape the entire kingdom. The Bishop is part of a Catholic faction that would see England back under Rome's thumb. The Puritans would replace one tyranny with another. Someone must balance these forces, must…"

"Must sacrifice the powerless to influence the powerful?" Mare finished for him. She gathered more documents, scanning dates and locations. "You've been at this for months. Every meeting, every 'chance' encounter, was any of it real, Kit? Or was I always just another source to be mined for information?"

The hurt in her voice surprised her as much as it surprised Marlowe. His face softened, his hand reaching toward her in a gesture that might have been genuine or might have been another calculated move in his endless game of manipulation.

"Mare, please. What passed between us was separate from this. I never lied about…"

Her laugh cut him off, sharp enough to draw blood. "You lie as easily as you breathe. It's your profession, after all, creating worlds from empty air, making audiences believe in ghosts and kings and love that never existed."

He moved toward her suddenly, frustration overriding caution. "Damn you, will you just listen? There are greater stakes than…"

Mare's instincts took over as his hand reached for her arm. She shoved him hard against the printing press, her forearm across his chest, her weight leveraging against his taller frame. The press rocked backwards from the impact, its metal frame scraping against the floor. Loose type scattered like startled insects, the small metal pieces skittering across the floorboards in a chaotic constellation.

"Don't," she hissed, her face inches from his, "touch me again."

Marlowe's eyes flashed with something darker than fear; a playwright's wounded pride or a spy's calculation of odds suddenly turned against him. His hand shot out, fingers closing around a wooden frame used for holding type. He swung it in a wild arc that whistled past Mare's ear as she ducked, the frame splintering against the table behind her. Papers scattered like startled birds, fresh ink spattering across the floor in black tears.

Mare moved with the fluid economy of someone who'd learned to fight in Southwark's unforgiving streets, where every battle was potentially fatal and hesitation meant death. Her hand closed around the nearest weapon, an ink roller abandoned beside the press. She lunged forward, driving the wooden handle toward Marlowe's midsection while the ink-soaked roller end swept upward in a vicious arc that caught him across the face.

A black streak painted his features from jaw to temple, the sudden sharp reek of ink filling the cramped space. He staggered back, cursing with a poet's elaborate fury. "God's wounds, Mare! This isn't what you think…"

She didn't bother responding to words she knew were as hollow as a stage prop. Instead, she pressed her advantage, driving him back toward the corner where puppet heads from some forgotten morality play stared with painted eyes like unsympathetic witnesses.

Marlowe grabbed a candlestick from the workbench, wielding it like a club. The candle itself tumbled free, rolling beneath the printing press where it guttered but didn't die, casting wild, dancing shadows across the underground room. Light and darkness chased each other across their faces as they circled, transformed into grotesque masks of rage and desperation.

"I wasn't betraying you," Marlowe insisted, his breath coming in short gasps. "I was protecting you, keeping your name off the Puritans' lists of the Bishop's agents." He feinted left, then swung the candlestick in a wide arc that Mare easily sidestepped.

"My name," she spat, "which you knew because I trusted you." She kicked a wooden tray toward his feet, the small metal letters scattering like caltrops across the floor. Marlowe stumbled, his fine leather shoes sliding on the loose type.

She drove forward again, the ink roller connecting with his shoulder hard enough to make him drop the candlestick. It clattered to the ground, rolling beneath the table. They grappled in the increasingly chaotic space, knocking into the printing press, sending it rocking on its base. A jar of red ink, the same used to forge the Bishop's seal, tipped and shattered, splashing across the floor like fresh blood.

Mare fought with the cold calculation that had kept her alive in Southwark, each movement efficient, each strike aimed at vulnerable points. Marlowe fought like a man unaccustomed to physical confrontation, all desperate energy and untrained strength. He had height and weight on his side, but Mare had survived far worse than an ink-stained playwright.

"You're making a terrible mistake," he gasped, catching her wrist as she aimed another blow with the roller. "There are forces at work you don't understand, the Bishop isn't who you think..."

"Save your lies for your patrons," Mare snarled, twisting in his grip and driving her knee upward and into his groin. Marlowe released her wrist, doubling over with a pained wheeze. She used the moment to scan the room, looking for an exit or a more effective weapon.

The second candle toppled as Marlowe stumbled back against the table, plunging the room into darkness broken only by thin streams of moonlight filtering through cracks in the stage above. In the sudden gloom, shapes became menacing abstractions, the printing press a crouching beast, stacked papers the outlines of watching figures.

Something caught Mare's ankle, Marlowe had grabbed a coil of rope used for binding pamphlets and yanked it across her path. She went down hard, the air driven from her lungs as she hit the floor. Before she could recover, Marlowe was on her, his weight pinning her as he wrapped the rope around her arms.

"Listen to me," he gasped, his face inches from hers, still streaked with black ink that made him look like some pagan deity of chaos. "The Bishop is planning something far worse than taxing whores. There's a Spanish connection; documents I've seen with my own eyes. Walsingham knows but needs proof. "

Mare drove her head upward, connecting with Marlowe's jaw hard enough to send stars dancing behind her eyes. He reeled back with a curse, his grip on the rope loosening just enough. She rolled, tangling herself further but gaining the leverage to plant her foot against his chest and shove with all her strength.

Marlowe flew backward into a stack of freshly printed pamphlets, sending them cascading around him like dead leaves. He scrambled to his feet, abandoning the rope and lunging for the ladder that led to the trap door. Mare struggled against her bonds, the hemp biting into her wrists as she worked to free herself.

"The Puritans are being used," Marlowe called down, already halfway up the ladder. "The Bishop, too, all puppets in a greater design. For God's sake, Mare, look at the documents. Look at the Spanish correspondence!"

The trap door banged open, moonlight spilling down into the chaos below. Mare finally worked one arm free of the ropes, then the other, but too late. Marlowe disappeared through the opening, the sound of his boots heavy on the stage above.

She cursed and gave chase, scaling the ladder with the agility born of a childhood spent climbing through Southwark's architectural chaos. By the time she emerged onto the stage, Marlowe was already a fleeing shadow, knocking over a painted flat as he ran. It crashed to the boards with a sound like distant thunder, the canvas forest scene fluttering in the draft from the open stage door.

Mare stood in the centre of the empty stage, breathing hard, surrounded by the fictional world of The Rose, painted castles and cloth forests, thrones made of gilded wood and crowns of painted tin. Everything false, everything a lie designed to make audiences believe in worlds that never existed.

Much like Marlowe himself.

The theatre creaked around her, ancient timbers settling as if sighing in relief now that the violence had ended. Moonlight streamed through the open roof, turning the stage into a silver island in a sea of shadows. In that cold, unforgiving light, Mare felt something crack inside her, not her resolve, but whatever remnant of trust she'd foolishly preserved.

She returned to the trap door and descended into the wreckage below. With trembling fingers that betrayed her emotional state more than any words could, she began gathering the scattered documents. The pamphlets with their calls for cleansing fire. The forged seals. The receipts for supplies purchased with the Bishop's stolen authority. The maps of drop locations throughout Southwark.

And beneath it all, partially hidden by an overturned tray of type, a stack of letters bearing a seal she recognized from her time in the Bishop's service, the mark of a Spanish noble house with connections to Philip's court. She added these to her collection, her mind already calculating their value as leverage, as protection, as weapons in the war she hadn't chosen but now found herself fighting on multiple fronts.

The spilled ink had begun to dry, turning from glossy black to dull matte on the wooden floor. Mare's hands were stained with it, dark whorls and patterns marking her palms and fingers like some pagan ritual of vengeance. The scar on her palm throbbed beneath the ink, a reminder of loyalties both forced and chosen.

As she bundled the evidence together, tying it with the same rope that had briefly bound her, Mare felt a cold clarity replace the heat of betrayal. Marlowe had made her a piece in his game without her knowledge or consent. The Bishop had branded her as his property. Sister Agnes offered a third path, but with its own invisible chains.

In the silent aftermath of violence, surrounded by the tools of deception and manipulation, Mare made a decision that belonged to her alone. The evidence she gathered would serve neither Marlowe's schemes nor the Bishop's control. It would be her leverage, her protection in a Southwark suddenly more dangerous than she'd believed possible.

She climbed the ladder one final time, emerging onto the empty stage with her bundle of damning papers clutched to her chest. In the silver moonlight, she stood where kings and fools had strutted their brief hours, another player forced onto a stage not of her making but determined to write her own ending to the tale.

Chapter Ten

Mother's Blood

Mare's boots struck the wet cobblestones with deliberate force, each step carrying her deeper into Southwark's tangled guts. Her mind still churned with Marlowe's betrayal, the ink-stained evidence now hidden in a pouch against her ribs where it pressed like a bruise with every breath. Night had fallen hard on the district, the kind of darkness that erased moral boundaries and transformed ordinary men into monsters or exposed the monsters they'd always been.

The streets exhaled their nightly stench of piss and desperation, familiar as a mother's voice to Mare. She flexed her scarred palm, the old habit surfacing whenever danger pressed close. And danger was everywhere tonight, in the shadows that followed her movements, in the unusual quiet that had settled over normally raucous taverns, in the prickling awareness that travelled like lightning down her spine.

She heard it before she saw it, the distinctive sound of violence that couldn't be mistaken for anything else. Not the theatrical brawling of drunks or the calculated efficiency of thieves, but the wet, dull thuds of hatred given physical form. The sounds came from ahead, down an alley that connected two of Southwark's main thoroughfares, a shortcut known to locals that tourists and marks never discovered.

Mare quickened her pace, one hand sliding to the knife at her belt. As she rounded the corner, the scene hit her with the force of a physical blow.

The alley had become a trap. At one end, two carts lay overturned, their contents, rotting vegetables and fish guts spilled across the cobblestones in a putrid barricade. At the other, the gate that normally stood open had been chained shut. Between these makeshift barriers, a pack of men surrounded a group of women pressed against the alley wall.

Mare recognized the women instantly; Winchester Geese, their distinctive dresses now torn and dirty, their faces masks of terror as they huddled together like animals cornered by hunters. The men wore the drab browns and greys favoured by Puritans, their hair cropped short against their skulls, their faces twisted with the entitled madness of those who believe God sanctions their violence.

"Filthy whores of Babylon!" One man swung a makeshift club, a table leg with nails driven through its end, which whistled through the air inches from a woman's face. "The fire was meant to cleanse you! If it failed, our hands would finish God's work!"

Mare assessed the situation with the cold calculation of someone for whom survival was a daily negotiation. Seven men. Five women. One narrow alley with limited escape routes. The Puritans carried an assortment of crude weapons—clubs, knives, a length of chain that one swung in lazy circles. The women had only their terror and whatever makeshift defences they could improvise from the rubbish around them.

She moved without conscious decision, her body flowing from shadow to action with the grace of long practice. Her knife found the nearest zealot's kidney with a sound like a spoon pushing into over-ripe fruit. He went down without a cry, blood blooming across his back in a dark flower.

"Run!" Mare shouted to the women, using the momentary confusion to create space. "To me! Now!"

Two of the Geese broke from their huddle, scrambling toward Mare with the desperate energy of drowning women spotting a rope. The others remained frozen, trapped between terror and the zealots who now turned their attention to this new threat.

"The Bishop's Shadow!" One of them spat the title like a curse. "God has delivered two prizes tonight, whores and their protectors!"

Mare backed toward the overturned carts, positioning herself to defend the women who'd reached her. "I count five of you still standing," she said, her voice winter cold. "Not good odds for men facing judgment."

The zealot with the chain laughed, the sound devoid of humour. "We do God's work. Our righteousness is armour enough."

"Let's test that theory," Mare replied, her knife catching the moonlight as she shifted stance.

The first man charged with more enthusiasm than skill, his club raised high for a killing blow that telegraphed his intentions to anyone with eyes. Mare sidestepped, her blade opening his forearm to the bone. He howled, dropping his weapon with a clatter that echoed between the close-set buildings.

The others came together then, a wave of righteous fury crashing toward her. Mare met them with cold precision, her knife finding gaps in their guard, her free hand wielding a broken bottle she'd snatched from the filth underfoot. Blood sprayed across her face, warm and copper-scented, as her bottle connected with one man's cheek, shredding it to red ruin.

But numbers began to tell. A blow caught her shoulder, sending pain lancing down her arm. Another nearly took her legs from under her. She backed further toward the carts, gathering the terrified women behind her like a shepherd collecting scattered sheep. Three of the zealots pressed forward, while two circled to cut off any escape through the barrier of upended carts.

Then a new sound cut through the chaos, a woman's voice, pitched to carry over the grunts and cries of combat.

"To me, sisters! Form ranks!"

A figure vaulted over one of the carts, landing with impossible grace on the slick cobblestones. Sister Agnes moved like water given human form, flowing between the two zealots who'd circled behind Mare. In her hands, a pair of thin blades caught the moonlight, then disappeared into darkness as they found their targets with surgical precision.

"Throat or groin," Agnes called to the cowering women, her voice a battlefield commander's. "Nothing in between matters. Strike once, strike hard, then move!"

As if her words carried some magical property, the Winchester Geese transformed from terrified victims to desperate fighters. They scrambled for weapons amid the rubbish—broken chair legs, shards of glass, a discarded metal poker that one woman wielded like a spear.

Agnes carved a path through the remaining zealots, her movements displaying a brutal efficiency that spoke of years of similar combat. Where Mare fought with the calculated precision of someone who'd learned to kill as a last resort, Agnes attacked with the ruthless commitment of a woman who saw death as a tool to be wielded without hesitation.

They converged in the centre of the alley, backs nearly touching as they faced opposite directions, creating a defensive core around which the Geese could rally.

"Behind you!" Mare shouted as a zealot lunged toward Agnes with a rusted knife.

Agnes spun, her hood falling back as she moved. Her face, normally hidden in the shadows of her habit, caught the moonlight in full, the strong jaw, the grey-streaked hair pulled back severely from a face that had once been beautiful before life had carved it into something more useful. The scar along her cheek, mirror to the one Mare had seen in her own reflection a thousand times. A zealot's club whistled toward her head, missing by inches as she recovered just in time, muscle memory compensating for her mind's sudden paralysis.

The fight swirled around them, demanding all their attention. Mare parried a thrust aimed at her belly, her eyes never leaving Agnes's face even as her body continued the dance of survival. The resemblance she'd never noticed before now seemed blindingly obvious, the same high cheekbones, the same slate-grey eyes, the same way their lips pressed into a thin line when concentrating.

A scream cut through Mare's shocked haze. One of the Geese had fallen, a deep gash across her thigh pumping blood onto the filthy cobblestones. The zealot who'd struck her raised his blade for a killing blow.

Agnes moved like a vengeful spirit, her blade taking the man's hand at the wrist. Blood fountained in the moonlight as he fell to his knees, howling. Mare snapped back to full awareness, driving her knife into the shoulder of a zealot who'd tried to flank them during her moment of shock.

"Protect her!" Agnes shouted, gesturing toward the fallen woman. "Form up!"

Together, they created a human barrier around the wounded Goose, the other women falling into position with desperate determination. Mare and Agnes stood at the centre of this makeshift phalanx, their blades extending outward like the spines of some defensive sea creature.

Agnes's hand, slick with blood, brushed against Mare's as they adjusted stance. Agnes's palm bore a scar that mirrored Mare's own, though hers ran diagonally where Mare's crossed horizontally.

"Ready?" Agnes asked, her eyes meeting Mare's with a question that went beyond the immediate battle.

Mare gave a short nod, words impossible past the knot in her throat. They moved together then, as if they'd fought side by side for years rather than minutes. Where Agnes struck high, Mare went low. When Mare feinted left, Agnes capitalized from the right. Their bodies seemed to communicate without conscious thought, a language of blood and movement that transcended their twenty-eight years of separation.

The remaining zealots, facing this unexpected resistance, began to falter. One broke and ran, scrambling over the overturned carts with more concern for speed than dignity. Another followed, then a third. The last man standing the one who'd wielded the chain backed away slowly, his face a mask of hatred and fear.

"This isn't over," he spat, blood dripping from a cut above his eye. "God's cleansing fire will come for all of you!"

"Tell your God," Agnes replied, her voice deadly calm, "that when he sends his next messengers, he should choose ones who can fight better than they preach."

The man turned and fled, leaving behind three of his companions who would never rise again and two more who moaned in the filth, clutching wounds that might yet send them to meet their maker before dawn.

Mare and Agnes stood amidst the carnage, their breaths coming in ragged gasps, blood both theirs and others' cooling on their skin as the night air chilled it. The Geese gathered around the wounded woman, tearing strips from their dresses to bind her leg.

"They'll bring more men next time," Sister Agnes said finally, pushing down the storm of emotions threatening to overwhelm her. "And the Bishop's men won't be far behind. The wounded need shelter. Somewhere the zealots won't think to look."

"I know a place," Mare replied, her voice steadier than she felt. She released Agnes's hand and turned to the Geese. "Can you walk?" she asked the injured woman, who nodded despite her ashen face.

As they helped the wounded woman to her feet, Mare felt Agnes's eyes on her searching, assessing, blade in hand and blood on her face.

The weight of that gaze pressed against Mare's back as they moved deeper into Southwark's shadows, heavier than any weapon she'd ever carried.

The alcove sat wedged between two crumbling buildings like a secret kept between drunken friends, not well hidden but overlooked by those without reason to notice it. Mare pushed aside the rotted planks that formed a makeshift door, revealing a space barely large enough for their bloodied company. The stench of old violence hung in the air, mingling with the fresher scents they brought with them, copper-bright blood, sweat, and the distinctive smell of fear slowly giving way to exhaustion.

"In here," Mare instructed, her voice clipped as she helped the wounded woman through the narrow opening. The Geese filed in, their once-gaudy dresses now torn and darkened with filth, their faces hollow with the emptiness that comes after surviving something you were certain would kill you.

The space had once been a storage room for a tavern long since burned down, its walls blackened by that ancient fire, its corners softened by years of rats and rot. A single high window, more hole than glass, allowed a thin shaft of moonlight to penetrate the gloom. Mare knew this place from her earliest days in Southwark, one of many boltholes she'd discovered as a child when running from those who saw her as prey.

Agnes entered last, her movements careful and controlled despite the fresh cut across her forearm that leaked blood in a slow, steady pulse. She scanned the alcove with the practiced assessment of someone who had evaluated hundreds of similar spaces for defensibility, escape routes, and immediate threats.

"Water," she said, gesturing toward the wounded woman who now lay against the far wall, her companions creating a protective huddle around her. "And clean cloth, if any exists in this place."

Mare pulled a leather flask from her belt and a clean handkerchief from an inner pocket. These she handed to Agnes without a word, their fingers deliberately not touching during the exchange. Then she stepped back, creating distance between herself and the woman who had so casually spoken the words that had redefined Mare's entire existence.

Agnes knelt beside the injured Goose, her hands moving with the confident efficiency of someone long accustomed to patching wounds inflicted by men's violence. She cleaned the gash, her touch gentle despite the clinical detachment in her eyes.

"The blade missed the major vessels," she reported to no one in particular. "She'll live, if infection doesn't set in."

Mare watched Sister Agnes work, noting the small details that suddenly seemed laden with significance borne with confusion, the way Agnes tucked escaped strands of grey-streaked hair behind her ear with the back of her wrist to keep blood from her face, the same unconscious movement Mare had made a thousand times. The slight furrow between her brows as she concentrated, identical to the one Mare had seen in her own reflection. The economy of motion that wasted no energy, a trait Mare had always believed she'd developed through hard experience rather than inheritance.

The other Geese huddled together, murmuring quiet reassurances to one another, taking inventory of cuts and bruises that had been ignored during the fight. One kept watch at the makeshift door, her eyes darting nervously to the shadows beyond.

"Three streets over," Mare said to her, "there's a cellar beneath the candlemaker's shop. Entrance through the back alley. Tell him the Bishop's Shadow sent you. He'll hide you until morning."

The woman nodded, gratitude flashing across her face before being replaced by the wariness that was the Winchester Geese's natural expression. She gathered her companions with whispered instructions, helping the less injured to their feet.

"What about her?" she asked, nodding toward the wounded woman.

"We'll bring her when she can be moved," Agnes answered before Mare could speak. "Go now, while the streets are still quiet."

The women slipped out into the night, their departure leaving the alcove feeling suddenly larger and more confining simultaneously. The wounded Goose had drifted into unconsciousness, her breathing shallow but steady beneath the bandage Agnes had fashioned from strips of her own underskirt.

In the sudden quiet, the weight of unspoken words pressed down like a physical force. Mare stood with her back against the wall, watching her Sister Agnes clean blood from her hands with the methodical care of someone who had performed the ritual countless times.

"You saved me." The words escaped Mare's lips like birds suddenly freed from a cage ragged and desperate for flight. "Why?"

Agnes didn't look up from her task, her fingers continuing their precise movements as if Mare had commented on the weather rather than voiced the question that had haunted her entire existence.

"I had no choice. The church would've killed us both." Her voice remained level, stripped of emotion.

"And yet you survived." Agnes's voice hardened, an undercurrent of something like pride bleeding through her composure. "Look at you, the Bishop's Shadow, feared throughout Southwark, moving between worlds that destroy most who try to navigate them."

"Thanks to the Bishop who found me half-dead and saw something useful rather than disposable," Mare countered, the confused irony bitter on her tongue. "The same Bishop you and your Order now plot against."

Agnes's expression flickered with something complex, regret, or calculation. "Richard Wickham is many things, but a saviour isn't one of them. What he gave you came with chains you're still wearing."

The wounded woman stirred, a soft moan escaping her lips. Agnes immediately returned her attention to her patient, checking the bandage with careful fingers.

Agnes looked up, her eyes reflecting the shattered moonlight from the broken window. For a moment, her carefully maintained control cracked, revealing a glimpse of raw pain beneath.

She reached for Mare's hand, but Mare pulled back, unwilling to allow the physical connection that might soften her resolve. The wounded Goose whimpered again, the sound cutting through the tension between mother and daughter. Agnes immediately turned her attention back to her patient, checking the bandage with practiced hands that never betrayed the emotion in her voice.

"Her fever's rising," she said, pressing a palm to the woman's forehead. "We need to move her somewhere cleaner, with access to proper medicines."

Mare stood frozen, caught between conflicting impulses, the urge to continue extracting answers from the mother who had appeared like a ghost from her past, and the practical necessity of addressing the immediate danger surrounding them.

"The Order has a safe house near the old bell tower," Agnes continued, her voice returning to its practical cadence. "We can treat her there, and it's well defended if the Puritans or the Bishop's men come looking."

She rose to her feet, brushing dirt from her knees with an automatic gesture. "We can't stay here. The Puritans will regroup, and the Bishop's men won't be far behind. Word of a skirmish travels fast in Southwark."

Mare's mind raced, calculating risks and alternatives. The evidence from Marlowe's printing operation still pressed against her ribs, its implications now complicated further by the revelation of her mother's identity. Her loyalties, already stretched thin between self-preservation and reluctant duty to the

Bishop, now faced the additional pull of blood ties she'd never known existed.

"What happens after?" Mare asked, the question encompassing far more than the immediate future.

Agnes met her gaze directly. "That depends on choices neither of us has made yet."

The simple truth of the statement hung in the air between them. Mare nodded curtly, decision made for the moment.

"I'll take her legs," she said, moving to help lift the wounded woman.

Together, they managed the unconscious Goose into a carrying position, their movements unconsciously synchronized despite their years of separation. As they prepared to slip back into Southwark's dangerous night, Agnes paused, her eyes finding Mare's in the dim light.

"Marion," she said softly, using the full name that Mare had abandoned years ago. "I have always looked out for you. Even when I couldn't approach you, I watched."

Mare absorbed the words without response, filing them away with all the other revelations that would need to be examined when survival wasn't the immediate concern. The weight of their shared history pressed down on her shoulders as they stepped into the alley, moving deeper into the shadows that had shaped both their lives in ways neither had fully chosen.

Chapter Eleven

The Bishop's Wrath

Bishop Wickham paced the length of his private chamber; each step measured despite the storm brewing beneath his skin. The silver crucifix hanging from his neck caught the firelight as he moved, casting reflections across tapestries worth more than most of Southwark's hovels. His fingers, adorned with rings that marked his station, traced the edge of a parchment bearing news that threatened to shatter his carefully constructed world. The Bishop's eyes, cold as January frost, flickered between the document and the man standing at rigid attention before his desk.

"The whore has played us both," Wickham finally said, his voice deceptively soft, like a blade wrapped in silk. He slammed his fist onto the mahogany desk with enough force to send a golden chalice toppling. Wine spilled across a map of Southwark, bleeding into the paper like an omen.

Thomas Walsingham didn't flinch at the outburst. His thin lips curved into the barest suggestion of a smile, quickly hidden behind a mask of appropriate concern. "The evidence is irrefutable, Your Grace. Mare Fleet has been undermining your authority for months. The disruption of the Puritan gathering was merely a feint to gain your trust while she strengthened her position with the Winchester Geese."

The Bishop snatched up another report, this one detailing a clandestine meeting between Mare and Sister Agnes at an abandoned tenement. His hand trembled slightly, the only visible betrayal of the rage coursing through his veins.

"I lifted her from the gutter," Wickham hissed, crumpling the parchment. "I saw potential where others saw nothing but

Thames filth. I educated her, clothed her, gave her purpose." His voice hardened with each sentence, his accent slipping from cultivated Church Latin toward something rougher, a reminder of his own climb from obscurity. "And this is how she repays my generosity."

Walsingham's gaze followed the Bishop's movement, cataloguing each twitch and tremor with the precision of a man who survived by noticing such details. "Your kindness has often been repaid with betrayal, Your Grace. The Winchester Geese have never truly understood their place in God's order."

The Bishop turned abruptly, his heavy robes swirling around his ankles like disturbed water. Behind him, the chamber's walls bore testament to his power and piety, or at least the appearance of it. Gilded crosses and religious paintings hung alongside maps marked with his properties. Bookshelves groaned beneath leather-bound volumes few in Southwark could read. A silver censer leaked incense that failed to fully mask the scent of last night's indulgences.

"She was different," the Bishop muttered, more to himself than to Walsingham. "I moulded her myself. Taught her to read when she could barely speak without gutter cant. Showed her how to move among the powerful." His fingers unconsciously sought the chain around his neck, worrying at the seal that hung beside the crucifix. "I gave her my trust."

Walsingham stepped forward, producing another document from inside his doublet. "You treated her as if she was your own and she used that trust to betray you. This was found in the possession of a dead Puritan, a map of your Southwark holdings with guard rotations noted in Fleet's hand."

The Bishop took the parchment, studying it with narrowed eyes. His jaw clenched tight enough that a muscle jumped beneath the skin, the only outward sign of the cold fury building inside him.

"She knows everything," he said finally. "Every property, every transaction, every arrangement with the authorities." He crossed to a small writing desk inlaid with mother-of-pearl and ivory, its craftsmanship a stark contrast to the crude furnishings found in the hovels visible through his leaded-glass windows. From a drawer, he withdrew several blank parchments and a stick of red sealing wax.

"Prepare the men," he ordered, seating himself with the rigid posture of a man accustomed to command. "Every brothel, every safe house, every miserable hole where these treacherous whores hide, I want them raided tonight."

Walsingham's eyes gleamed with something that might have been anticipation. "All of them, Your Grace? Even The Cardinal's Cap and The Maiden's Head? Those establishments pay significant…"

"All of them," the Bishop cut him off, his pen scratching against parchment as he began writing with swift, angry strokes. "The infection must be purged completely." He glanced up, eyes narrowed. "Unless you harbour some reservation about carrying out my orders?"

"None whatsoever, Your Grace," Walsingham replied smoothly. "I merely sought clarification on the scope of our response."

The Bishop continued writing, his hand steadier now, as if the act of ordering violence had calmed the tremors of rage. "Mare Fleet has information that could destroy everything I've built. Every alliance, every arrangement with the Queen's ministers, every transaction with our friends across the Channel." He finished the first document with a flourish and reached for his seal.

The red wax dripped onto the parchment like drops of blood. The Bishop pressed his personal seal into it with practiced precision, a stylized wolf beneath a bishop's mitre, the same mark that had been found on the murdered clergyman pulled from the Thames three weeks prior. The wax cooled quickly, hardening into a perfect impression that carried the weight of both church and criminal authority.

"I want her head," Wickham said, his voice dropping to a dangerous whisper as he prepared another warrant. "Not captured, not questioned. Dead. She knows too much, has seen too much." The seal came down again, another death sentence stamped with the finality of God's judgment. "Bring it to me personally."

Walsingham bowed slightly, the motion precise but not overly deferential. "And the Winchester Geese who sheltered her?"

"Burn every brothel harbouring these traitors," the Bishop replied without looking up. "Let the Puritans believe God has answered their prayers if it suits our purpose. But the women who knew Mare Fleet, who might have heard her whispers or carried her messages" He stamped another warrant with damning force. "those must disappear completely."

"Consider it done, Your Grace." Walsingham collected the finished warrants, careful not to smudge the still-tacky seals. "How many men should I commit to this task?"

The Bishop finally looked up, his face settling into the mask of pious authority he wore in public. Only his eyes betrayed the malice beneath, cold and calculating as a winter predator's. "All of them. Empty the Clink if you must. This ends tonight."

Walsingham nodded, tucking the death warrants inside his doublet with the care one might give to love letters. "I'll see to the preparations personally." His lips twitched into another barely perceptible smile. "By dawn, Marion Fleet will be nothing, but a cautionary tale whispered among those who might consider betraying your trust."

After Walsingham departed, Bishop Wickham remained at his desk, staring at the spilled wine that had now dried into a dark stain across the Southwark map. His hand returned to the seal hanging from his neck, the twin of the one he'd just used to authorize slaughter. He'd worn it for fifteen years, since his elevation to his current position, and in that time, it had marked countless documents that had built his empire of flesh and secrets.

Now it would mark its destruction, if necessary, rather than let it fall into hands beyond his control.

The Bishop rose and moved to the window, looking out over the squalid buildings of Southwark, where even now his former agent might be hiding. His reflection in the glass showed a man of imposing presence, silver hair, strong features, the trappings of ecclesiastical authority, but beneath that reflection, the night's darkness seemed to gather, as if sensing the violence soon to be unleashed.

"Run if you must, Marion," he whispered to the glass. "There is nowhere in Southwark I cannot reach."

The Clink's courtyard exhaled the stink of damp stone and old blood as Thomas Walsingham strode through the gathered men. Torchlight caught in the droplets of rain that fell like God's half-hearted tears, turning leather armour to gleaming scales and making weapons shine with deadly promise. Walsingham's face, typically a careful mask of subservience in the Bishop's presence, now animated with the barely contained excitement of a man finally granted permission to settle old scores.

"The Bishop's justice comes to Southwark tonight," he announced, his voice carrying across the yard where thirty men stood in formation. Rain slicked his dark hair against his skull, making his features appear carved rather than grown, all sharp angles and calculating eyes. "And with it, a lesson about loyalty that won't soon be forgotten."

He gestured to a lieutenant who stepped forward bearing a leather satchel. From it, Walsingham extracted several folded parchments, their edges worn from frequent handling. The men shifted, water dripping from the brims of their hats as they craned to see.

"These maps," Walsingham continued, unfolding one with theatrical precision, "were created by Marion Fleet herself." He allowed himself a thin smile, satisfaction seeping through like poison from a slow blade. "The Bishop's pet thought she played both sides, gathering intelligence on the Geese for His Grace while secretly helping them escape his justice."

He held up the map so the gathered men could see the detailed renderings of Southwark's twisted streets and alleyways. Specific buildings were marked with small, precise crosses, notations in Mare's distinctive hand indicating entry points, guard positions, escape routes.

"She created these to help the Bishop monitor the whores," Walsingham said, his voice dropping to a conspiratorial tone that forced the men to lean forward. "But tonight, her diligence serves us instead. Every bolthole, every secret passage, every hiding place she discovered, all now weapons in our hands."

A murmur ran through the assembled men. Most had encountered Mare in the Bishop's service, had seen her slip through Southwark like a living shadow, had witnessed her return with information no one else could extract. Some had feared her.

Others had desired her. All had understood she carried the Bishop's protection like an invisible shield.

"Tonight, that shield is broken," Walsingham declared, as if reading their thoughts. He passed the maps to his lieutenants, who began distributing them among the squad leaders. "The Bishop himself has signed the warrants. Marion Fleet is to be executed on sight, no questions, no mercy."

He paced before them, boots splashing through puddles that reflected the torchlight in fractured, patterns. "The Winchester Geese who harboured her are to be treated no better. Their houses burned, their possessions seized, their lives forfeit to the Bishop's justice."

One of the men, a scarred veteran with grey streaking his beard, cleared his throat. "All of them, sir? Even the younger girls who…"

"All of them," Walsingham cut him off, his voice sharp as a gutting knife. "His Grace was quite explicit. The infection has spread too far for half measures." He fixed the man with a stare that promised consequences for further questions. "Do you find yourself unable to carry out the Bishop's commands?"

The veteran straightened, his face going carefully blank. "No, sir. Just clarifying the orders."

Walsingham held his gaze a moment longer before continuing. "You'll operate in five squads, each with specific targets." He pointed to a grizzled man with a face like crushed gravel. "Benson, you'll take The Rose and The Crane. Flush them out, put them to the sword, then burn what remains."

He moved to the next squad leader. "Phillips, The Maiden's Head and the tenements behind it. There's a network of rooms connected by passages in the walls. Mare's notes indicate at least twenty women might be hiding there."

One by one, he assigned targets to each squad, his finger stabbing at locations on the maps with the precision of a surgeon identifying where to cut. The rain fell harder as he spoke, drumming on helmets and shoulders, turning the courtyard's dirt to sucking mud that pulled at their boots.

"The Puritans will be moving too," Walsingham warned, his voice grave. "Stubbs and his zealots have their own grievances with the Geese, and with Fleet for disrupting their little gathering. Don't mistake them for allies." His lip curled in contempt. "They'll kill you as readily as the whores if you cross their path. Their God makes no distinction between the Bishop's men and the sinners we police."

He surveyed the gathered forces, noting which men met his gaze and which looked at the ground. The eager ones, the ones whose hands rested too casually on sword hilts or whose eyes held that gleam of anticipated violence, he made mental note of them. Such men were useful for tonight's work, if properly directed.

"Check your weapons," he ordered. "We move on the cathedral's midnight bell."

The courtyard erupted into controlled activity. Men tightened straps on leather cuirasses, tested the edges of blades against calloused thumbs, checked crossbow mechanisms with practiced fingers. Some spoke in low murmurs, sharing flasks of cheap spirits to ward off the rain's chill. Others remained silent, their faces set in the vacant expression of men deliberately not thinking about what they'd been ordered to do.

Walsingham's lieutenant approached, his voice pitched for his commander's ears alone. "Some of the men have concerns about attacking The Rose, sir. The owner pays well for protection, and his cousin sits on the…"

"The Bishop's seal overrides all previous arrangements," Walsingham interrupted, his eyes hard. "Anyone who finds their loyalties... conflicted... should declare so now. I'm sure His Grace would appreciate knowing which of his men value coin over obedience."

The lieutenant nodded, message received. He hesitated, then added, "And Fleet herself? If she's taken alive?"

Something flickered across Walsingham's face, a complex emotion that might have been anticipation or something more personal. "She won't be," he said simply. "But if circumstances prove otherwise, she's to be brought directly to me before the Bishop is informed."

Rain plastered his fine doublet to his shoulders as he moved among the men, offering a word of encouragement here, a pointed reminder there. Unlike the Bishop, who ruled through fear and distant authority, Walsingham cultivated a different relationship with these men. He knew which ones had families to feed, which ones harboured ambitions beyond their station, which ones simply enjoyed inflicting pain. Each received the exact motivation needed to ensure their dedication to the night's grim task.

The cathedral bells began to toll, the sound muffled by rain but still carrying across Southwark's cramped streets and alleyways. One, two, three…the men counted silently, checking weapons one final time. By the twelfth toll, they stood in perfect formation, torches sputtering in the downpour but still casting enough light to transform the raindrops into falling sparks.

"For the Bishop," Walsingham declared, drawing his sword. The blade caught the torchlight and held it, gleaming with malicious purpose. "For Southwark's purification."

The main gates of the Clink swung open, revealing Southwark's twisted streets beyond. The squads moved out in precise order, breaking into their assigned groups at the first intersection. Their torches formed rivers of light that flowed through the narrow alleys, dividing and rejoining like blood through veins.

Walsingham watched them go, rain streaming down his face in rivulets that might have been mistaken for tears on a more compassionate man. When only his personal guard remained, he smiled, a genuine expression that transformed his features from merely handsome to something almost boyish, if one ignored the cold calculation in his eyes.

"Now, Marion," he murmured, "let's see how well you taught your whores to fly before the hawk descends."

He stepped out into the rain-slick streets, his sword still drawn, his stride purposeful. Behind him, the Clink's gates swung closed with the final resonance of the midnight bell still hanging in the wet air.

The copper pot struck with a wooden spoon sent its alarm clanging through the building like a death knell, jerking Mare from uneasy sleep to instant alertness. Her hand found her knife before her eyes fully opened, muscle memory born of a lifetime's vigilance. Around her in the cramped attic room, women stirred from pallets and crumpled blankets, confusion giving way to the startled terror of prey recognizing the hunter's approach. Mare's boots were already on, her clothes never removed, a precaution that now seemed prophetic as torchlight flickered beyond the grimy windows like distant lightning.

"Up," Mare commanded, her voice pitched low but carrying through the sudden panic. "Gather only what you can run with."

The Geese erupted into frantic motion, young women in various stages of undress grabbing at scattered clothes and meagre possessions. Fingers fumbled with laces, curses replaced prayers, and the scent of fear, sharp and animal, filled the close air. An older woman with white-streaked hair moved with the practiced efficiency of someone who'd fled similar raids before, pulling a loose dress over her shift and directing the younger girls with hissed instructions.

Mare crossed to the far corner where a loose floorboard concealed her insurance. She pried it up with the tip of her knife, revealing a leather satchel nestled in the cavity beneath. The rough-hewn leather felt cool against her fingers as she withdrew it, the weight confirming its contents remained undisturbed, documents that could hang men or save women, depending on whose hands held them, and a dagger with an edge keen enough to split a hair.

"They know everything," Mare announced to the room, her voice steady despite the pulse hammering in her throat. She scanned the dozen frightened faces turned toward her, committing each to memory in case some didn't survive the night. "Walsingham's men are coming from the north, Puritans likely from the east."

"How many?" asked the madam, a woman called Mother Coyle whose face bore a scar from jaw to temple, the mark of a client who'd objected to her price years before.

"Too fucking many," Mare replied simply. She unrolled a crude map on the table, beckoning the women closer. "They'll have the maps I made for the Bishop every tunnel, every passage I documented."

The women exchanged glances, the unspoken accusation hanging in the air. It was Mare's intelligence turning against them, Mare's careful documentation of escape routes now a weapon in their pursuers' hands. No one voiced the thought, but their eyes held the question, nonetheless.

Mother Coyle broke the moment by upending a wooden chest, revealing an arsenal of crude weapons, butcher knives with handles wrapped in cloth, clubs fashioned from table legs, a few rusted daggers that had opened more purses than flesh.

"Take what you can use," the madam ordered, distributing the weapons with the brisk efficiency of a quartermaster. "Aim for the throat or the balls, they're the only targets that matter."

A girl no more than sixteen clutched a knife with white-knuckled terror, the blade trembling in her grip. Mare crossed to her, gently adjusting her hold.

"Like this," she demonstrated, wrapping the girl's fingers more securely around the handle. "And remember the tunnels we practiced last week. The second right, then the passage that smells of tallow."

The girl nodded, fear making her eyes seem twice their normal size in her pale face. "What if they're waiting in the tunnels too?"

"Then we fight," Mare said simply. "We're Winchester Geese. We've survived worse than men with swords."

Outside, the first shouts became audible, voices raised in command, the distinctive clink of weapons against armour. Mare moved to the window, peering through a gap in the shutters. To the north, torches moved in organized formation, the disciplined approach of Walsingham's men. To the east, more scattered lights advanced with the chaotic energy of zealots driven by righteousness rather than orders.

"Split into three groups," Mare instructed, stepping back from the window. "Mother Coyle, take four girls through the cellar passage. Head for the old tannery. Sister Agnes's people should have it secured."

The madam nodded, already selecting which women would accompany her.

"Beth, you'll lead the second group through the tunnel behind the false wall in the kitchen. Go to the chapel ruins if you can, St. Clement's if you can't."

A tall woman with burn scars on her hands nodded grimly, tucking a knife into her belt.

"The rest come with me," Mare finished. "We'll draw their attention to the front while the others slip out the back."

In the dim candlelight, they dared not light more for fear of making themselves easier targets. Mare studied the women's faces. Some were streaked with tears, others set in grim determination. The youngest looked terrified, the eldest resigned, as if they'd always known this night would come. All looked to Mare with the desperate hope of those who had no choice but to trust her judgment, her knowledge, her ability to navigate Southwark's dangers.

The weight of their trust pressed against her chest like a stone. These women had sheltered her after her confrontation with Marlowe, had bound her wounds and shared their meagre food without question when she'd appeared bloodied at their door. Now her very presence had brought death to their sanctuary.

Mother Coyle approached, her scarred face softened briefly by something like compassion. "This isn't your doing, girl," she said quietly, reading Mare's expression. "The Bishop was always going to turn on us eventually. You just gave us warning enough to maybe survive it."

Mare nodded, not trusting herself to speak. The madam squeezed her arm once, then turned to organize her group.

Through the window, Mare could see the approaching forces more clearly now. Walsingham's men moved in tight formation, crossbows at the ready, swords drawn. Their torches illuminated grim faces beneath leather helmets, men following orders, some reluctantly, others with the eager anticipation of violence soon to be unleashed.

The Puritans were fewer but more frenzied, their torches waving wildly as they advanced, voices raised in psalms that sounded more like war cries in the rain-slick night. Their leader not Stubbs himself, but one of his lieutenants, carried a book in one hand and a burning brand in the other, the incongruity of holy text and weapon perfectly encapsulating their insanity.

"They're surrounding the building," Mare announced, stepping back from the window. "We need to move. Now."

Mother Coyle's group disappeared down the narrow stairs that led to the cellar, each woman clutching her weapon and a small bundle of possessions. Beth herded her charges toward the kitchen; their faces set in the blank expression of those moving through terror into a strange calm beyond.

Mare gathered the remaining women with a gesture. "Stay close. Move when I move, stop when I stop." She adjusted the satchel across her body and drew her dagger. "And if I fall, don't stop for me. Just run."

A crash from below announced the first breach, the sound of wood splintering as a door gave way beneath a battering ram or axe. Shouts echoed up the stairwell, men's voices calling to each other as they entered the building.

"Ready?" Mare asked, meeting each woman's eyes in turn.

They nodded, some steely with determination, others trembling but holding their ground. In that moment, Mare saw not whores or victims but survivors, women who had endured Southwark's cruelty and still found the courage to face whatever came next.

The floor beneath them shuddered as more men poured into the building. Footsteps pounded on the stairs, heavy with purpose and the weight of weapons.

"Remember," Mare said, her voice steady as she positioned herself before the attic door, "we are not what they name us. We are what we choose to be."

And with those words hanging in the air like a blessing or a battle cry, she raised her dagger and prepared to carve a path through the coming storm.

Southwark fractured into pockets of hell as the midnight hour stretched toward dawn. Buildings that had stood for generations surrendered to hungry flames, their timber bones collapsing in showers of sparks that drifted upward like perverse prayers. The screams formed a terrible chorus, women fleeing through alleyways, men shouting commands, the wounded crying out for mercy that wouldn't come. And beneath it all, the wet thud of steel meeting flesh, of clubs finding bone, of bodies falling to cobblestones slick with blood and rain.

Thomas Walsingham personally led the raid on Mare's safe house, his sword already bloodied from the throat of a serving girl who'd tried to block his path. His men moved with practiced efficiency, kicking down doors and dragging occupants into the street with mechanical precision. Unlike the zealots who attacked with religious fervour, Walsingham's forces operated with the cold calculation of butchers at their trade, impersonal, thorough, and utterly remorseless.

"Find Fleet!" he shouted as his men tore apart the building, methodically checking behind every false wall and under every floorboard Mare had documented in her reports to the Bishop. "Turn this rat's nest inside out if you must!"

A lieutenant approached, his face splattered with someone else's blood. "Sir, we found tunnel entrances in the cellar and behind the kitchen wall. Fresh footprints. They can't have gone far."

Walsingham's face contorted with frustration and something darker, a personal hunger that went beyond duty to the Bishop. "Send men through every passage. Flush them toward the river where the other squads can intercept them." He wiped his blade clean on a torn bedsheet. "The whores are secondary. It's Fleet I want."

Three streets away, a different kind of violence unfolded. A band of Puritans, led by a preacher with eyes burning like twin coals in a gaunt face, had cornered a group of half-dressed women in a dead-end alley. The zealots advanced slowly, savouring the fear of their trapped prey, torches held high to illuminate their righteous work.

"Behold the harlots of Babylon!" the preacher cried, his voice cracking with ecstatic hatred as he brandished his Bible in one hand and a burning torch in the other. "Their flesh has corrupted Southwark; their sin has poisoned godly men!" Sputum flew from his lips as he spoke, catching the torchlight like tiny diamonds. "Cleanse them with fire!"

The women huddled together against the brick wall that trapped them, some weeping openly, others silent with the frozen terror of rabbits before a fox. One stepped forward, an older woman whose face bore the lines of a hard life, placing herself between the zealots and the younger girls.

"We're just trying to live," she said, her voice steady despite the tremor in her hands. "Same as anyone."

The preacher's response was to throw his torch at her feet. The flames caught her tattered skirt, and within seconds, she was engulfed in fire, her screams cutting through the night like a knife.

From her perch atop a steeply pitched roof across the narrow street, Mare watched the scene unfold, her face a mask of horror and cold fury. She had escaped the safe house through a passage even Walsingham didn't know about, a chimney flue modified years ago to serve as an emergency exit. Now she crouched among the chimney pots of a tanner's workshop, calculating angles and options with the detached precision that had kept her alive through years in Southwark's unforgiving hierarchy.

The women in the alley had seconds, not minutes. The Puritans were working themselves into a frenzy, encouraged by their leader and the first taste of blood. Mare counted eight zealots, all armed with improvised weapons, table legs studded with nails, butcher knives, a rusted sword that had been stolen from some noble's wall display.

She shifted position, testing the weight of a loose roof tile beneath her fingers. The drop to the alley was steep but survivable. If she timed it right, surprise might compensate for the disadvantage of numbers.

Meanwhile, across Southwark, the pattern repeated with cruel variations. At The Maiden's Head, the Bishop's men moved with military precision. A battering ram reduced the front door to splinters, and armoured figures poured through the opening like rats into a granary. Women scattered before them, some fleeing upstairs only to find more soldiers entering through windows accessed by ladders. Others ran for hidden passages, only to encounter blades waiting at the exits, Mare's carefully documented escape routes now death traps.

The madam of The Maiden's Head stood her ground in the main parlour, a loaded crossbow in her weathered hands. She got off one shot taking a soldier through the eye with accuracy born of desperation before three blades opened her from navel to neck.

At The Crane, the Puritans struck first, their attack chaotic but devastating. They set fire to the lower windows, trapping occupants upstairs, then blocked the main entrance with a cart to prevent escape. Their psalm-singing formed a macabre backdrop to the screams emanating from the burning building, their faces lit with the righteous satisfaction of those convinced God smiled upon their cruelty.

The two forces, Walsingham's disciplined troops and the Puritans' frenzied mobs, created a net that tightened across Southwark with each passing minute. Where they encountered each other, brief, confused skirmishes erupted. Neither recognized the other as ally, both saw only obstacles to their holy work of purification.

Back in the dead-end alley, Mare made her decision. She slid the roof tile free and took careful aim at the preacher's head. The heavy clay projectile struck with satisfying force, splitting his scalp, and sending him crashing to the ground, his torch rolling from limp fingers. The sudden attack from above created the moment of confusion Mare had counted on.

She swung down from the roof, using a drainpipe to control her descent, and landed in a crouch behind the rearmost zealot. Her dagger found the gap between his ribs before he registered her presence, the blade sliding home with the precision of a key entering a lock. He died without sound, collapsing as she withdrew the blade and moved to her next target.

"Run!" she shouted to the cornered women, creating a path with her blade and her body. "Through the tanner's! Second door on the left!"

Two of the zealots turned toward her, recognition dawning on their faces.

"The Bishop's Shadow!" one cried, raising his makeshift club. "God has delivered her to us!"

Mare ducked beneath his wild swing and opened his femoral artery with a precise slash. Blood fountained across the cobblestones as she pivoted toward the next attacker, her movements economical and lethal—not the elegant violence of a trained soldier but the desperate efficiency of someone who had learned to kill purely to survive.

The trapped women seized their chance, rushing past the distracted zealots toward the escape route Mare had indicated. The older woman, her dress still smouldering, grabbed a fallen torch and thrust it into the face of a Puritan who tried to block their path. His screams added to the cacophony as the women fled.

Mare found herself facing the remaining zealots alone, her back to the wall where the women had been trapped moments before. The odds were poor, but she'd faced worse. She adjusted her grip on her dagger, mind calculating vulnerabilities, escape routes, the likelihood of help arriving.

Across Southwark, the night sky glowed orange with multiple fires, black smoke rising in columns that merged into a single dark canopy above the district. The rain had stopped, as if even the heavens had withdrawn to watch the destruction unfold. The glow illuminated figures running through streets and alleys, some fleeing, some pursuing, all caught in a dance of violence that transformed familiar geography into a nightmare landscape.

From her position in the alley, Mare could see another brothel collapsing in flames two streets over, its windows vomiting fire as its roof caved inward. The screams from within had stopped, either everyone had escaped, or there was no one left to scream.

The guilt sat in Mare's chest like molten lead, burning through muscle and bone. Her maps, her intelligence, her careful documentation of Southwark's secret geography, all now weapons in Walsingham's hands, turned against the very women she'd sought to protect. The Bishop's vengeance was absolute, but it was her knowledge that gave it precision.

As the zealots closed in, Mare felt the weight of that knowledge press against her like a physical force. But alongside the guilt came cold determination. She hadn't survived Southwark's brutality, hadn't endured the Bishop's ownership, hadn't navigated the treacherous waters between rival powers only to die in a filthy alley at the hands of men who thought themselves God's instruments.

She shifted stance, blade ready, eyes calculating distances and vulnerabilities. The women she'd freed had a chance now. Perhaps a small one, but more than they'd had moments ago. And for tonight, in a Southwark consumed by flames and hatred, that was the only victory possible, not stopping the destruction but creating small pockets of survival within it.

The nearest zealot lunged forward, his face contorted with righteous fury. Mare stepped into his attack rather than away from it, her blade finding the soft flesh beneath his jaw with unerring accuracy. As he fell, she was already moving toward the next, her mind cold and clear despite the horror surrounding her.

She would survive this night. And then she would make the Bishop pay for every drop of blood spilled in his name.

They came from the shadows like vengeance made flesh, a dozen women moving with the coordinated precision of wolves rather than the scattered panic of prey. Sister Agnes led them, her face carved from stone and fury, the habit she normally wore replaced by practical clothing dark enough to blend with the night. Where Walsingham's men brought military efficiency and the Puritans brought zealous chaos, Agnes's women brought something else entirely, the cold, methodical violence of those who had studied their oppressors' methods and improved upon them.

The flames from the burning brothels painted their faces in flickering orange and black, highlighting scars both visible and hidden. Each carried weapons concealed beneath dark cloaks, not the military steel of Walsingham's forces but tools repurposed with deadly intent: butcher knives honed to surgical sharpness, iron pokers weighted for skull-cracking force, garrottes fashioned from wire and wooden handles. Some wore leather guards on their forearms, others had padding sewn into strategic locations on their clothing, protection born of experience rather than formal training.

Agnes raised a hand, halting her force at the edge of the shadows cast by a burning tannery. Her eyes, the same slate grey as her daughter's, scanned the chaos with the calculating assessment of a general surveying a battlefield. Three streets converged before them, each presenting a different tableau of violence: to the left, Walsingham's men dragged screaming women from a two-story brothel; straight ahead, Puritans had cornered several fleeing Geese against the wall of a chandler's shop; to the right, a mixed group of younger women cowered behind overturned market stalls as zealots advanced with torches held high.

"Judith," Agnes called softly to a tall woman with a face mapped by old burn scars, "take three and deal with those Puritans by the chandlery. No survivors, no witnesses."

The woman nodded, selecting her team with quick gestures. They melted away, moving not in a group but splitting to approach their targets from multiple directions simultaneously.

"Mary, the market square. Get those girls to the tunnels beneath St. Clement's. They're open and guarded." Agnes directed her next lieutenant, a compact woman whose grey-streaked hair was bound tightly against her skull. "The path through the old brewery is clear."

Agnes turned to the remaining women. "The rest with me. We'll create enough chaos to cover their escape." Her lips thinned into a hard line as she surveyed the burning buildings, the running figures, the bodies already cooling on cobblestones. "Save who you can. The rest is God's judgment."

They dispersed with practiced efficiency, moving through Southwark's burning streets like ghosts made solid only when striking. Unlike the Bishop's men who attacked openly or the Puritans who announced their presence with psalms and condemnation, the Order women appeared suddenly, struck with precise violence, and vanished before their victims fully registered the attack.

Agnes herself led the assault on a group of Puritans who had trapped three young women in the doorway of a burning building. She approached openly, her posture altered to suggest age and harmlessness, her steps deliberate as if struggling to hurry. The zealots barely glanced at her, just another old woman caught in the night's violence, hardly worth noting.

Their mistake became apparent when Agnes reached the rearmost man. Her hand emerged from her cloak holding an iron hook attached to a short length of chain. The hook found the soft underside of the zealot's jaw, tearing through flesh and lodging in bone. He fell without a sound as Agnes yanked backward, already moving toward her next target.

The other women of her group struck simultaneously, emerging from different approaches with weapons already in motion. Two Puritans died before they registered the attack; a third managed to raise his club before a garrotte closed around his throat, cutting off both breath and the psalm he'd been chanting.

"Run," Agnes ordered the trapped Geese, pointing toward a narrow alley. "Third door on the left. Knock twice, pause, then three more. Say 'Saint Ursula guides me' and they'll let you in."

The women fled without question, clutching tattered clothing around themselves as they disappeared into the darkness. Agnes watched them go, then signalled her group to move to their next target.

As they reached an intersection, Agnes paused, her attention caught by movement on a rooftop across a narrow alley. A figure crouched among chimney pots, observing the chaos below with the stillness of a predator selecting its prey. Even in the inconsistent light of the fires, Agnes recognized the set of those shoulders, the precise angle of that head, her own posture reflected at her across twenty-eight years of separation.

Mare.

Their eyes met across the distance, recognition flowing between them like a current through water. No words were necessary; they had fought side by side in the alley mere days ago, had moved together with the unconscious coordination of shared blood. Now, amid Southwark's burning chaos, they established a different kind of connection, the silent communication of strategists recognizing a potential ally.

Agnes pointed toward the old tenement chapel where they had taken refuge after the alley fight, then made a slashing gesture across her throat while nodding toward a group of the Bishop's men moving in formation down a nearby street. The message was clear: the Order was targeting Walsingham's forces specifically, delaying for the Geese to escape.

Mare nodded once, sharply, understanding flowing between them. She gestured toward a cluster of younger women huddled behind a water trough, then toward the sewers, followed by a questioning tilt of her head.

Agnes confirmed with a quick hand signal, a leftward slash followed by two fingers held upright. The tunnel beneath the tannery was clear, guarded by her people.

This silent exchange took mere seconds yet conveyed a battle plan more precise than many commanders achieved with lengthy orders. The connection between them transcended their brief reunion; somewhere in Mare's blood and bone lived the same instincts that had kept Agnes alive through decades of fighting from the shadows.

A shout from nearby broke their visual link. A squad of Walsingham's men had spotted Agnes's group and were advancing with drawn swords, their torches illuminating grim faces beneath leather helmets.

Agnes signalled her women with a sharp gesture, spread out, engage, withdraw. They responded instantly, forming a loose skirmish line that presented multiple targets rather than a solitary group. As the Bishop's men charged, the women scattered like water droplets on hot iron, drawing their pursuers into the maze of narrow alleys where their superior numbers became a disadvantage.

From her rooftop vantage, Mare watched her mother's tactical genius unfold. Agnes's women didn't attempt to defeat the larger force directly; instead, they created confusion and division, separating the soldiers from each other, leading some down blind alleys while others were drawn toward noise that seemed to come from everywhere and nowhere.

Meanwhile, other members of the Order used the distraction to guide terrified Geese toward safety, appearing beside groups of huddled women, leading them through doors that seemed solid but concealed passages, or into cellars with hidden exits to the sewers below. Some Order women stood guard at key intersections, redirecting fleeing Geese away from approaching danger with quick gestures and whispered directions.

The discipline of their operation stood in stark contrast to the chaos surrounding them. While Southwark burned and screams filled the night air, the Order moved with the practiced precision of those who had prepared for this exact scenario, as indeed they had. Agnes had spent years mapping escape routes, establishing safe houses, training her women to fight when necessary and disappear when possible.

Mare recognized her own tactical thinking reflected in her mother's methods, the same calculated assessment of threats and opportunities that had kept her alive in the Bishop's service. But where Mare had worked alone, Agnes had built an army of shadows, women dismissed as powerless who had transformed their invisibility into their greatest weapon.

Another group of Walsingham's men appeared at the end of the street, moving toward Agnes with purposeful strides. She met Mare's eyes once more across the distance, made a sharp cutting motion with her hand, go, save who you can, then turned to face the new threat, drawing a long knife from beneath her cloak as her women regrouped around her.

Mare hesitated for just a moment, torn between joining her mother's fight and continuing her own mission to save as many Geese as possible. Agnes made the decision for her, pointing emphatically toward the huddled women Mare had indicated earlier, then making a shooing gesture that brooked no argument, the same gesture mothers had used to direct children since time immemorial.

With a final nod of acknowledgment, Mare slipped away across the rooftop, moving toward her own battle while Agnes prepared for hers. Between them, they might not save all of Southwark's trapped women, but those they did save would carry forward the knowledge that even on this night of fire and death, they had not been abandoned.

Smoke hung in the air like a shroud, turning Southwark's narrow streets into a shifting labyrinth of half-seen threats and sudden dead ends. Mare moved through this transformed landscape with seven terrified women trailing behind her like ducklings following their mother through a storm. Her lungs burned with each breath, her eyes watered from the acrid sting of burning timber and melting fat, but her steps never faltered. She had mapped these streets in her mind years ago, had learned their secrets as a child when knowledge of hidden corners meant the difference between eating and starving, between safety and violation.

"Stay close," she urged over her shoulder, pausing at a corner to assess the street beyond. The women huddled against the wall behind her, their faces streaked with soot and terror. Mare had gathered them from the wreckage of The Crane after spotting them cowering in its burning kitchen, paralyzed by fear until her sharp commands had shocked them into movement.

Torchlight flickered at the far end of the street, a patrol of Walsingham's men moving with the methodical precision that made them more dangerous than the frenzied Puritans. Mare gestured sharply, and the women pressed themselves into a shadowed doorway, bodies crushed together, breath held collectively as the patrol passed within arm's reach of their hiding place.

When the soldiers' footsteps faded, Mare led them forward again, her pace deliberately unhurried despite the urgency cramping her muscles. Running attracted attention; calm movement blended with the chaos. They slipped past a burning tavern, its windows belching black smoke that provided momentary cover. Ahead, the street opened into a small market square where toppled carts and abandoned stalls created a maze of potential hiding places.

"Cross in pairs," Mare instructed, pointing toward a narrow alley on the far side. "Duck behind the carts if you hear anything. I'll go last."

She watched as the women scurried across in pairs, their movements jerky with fear but obedient to her directions. The youngest barely sixteen, with burn marks on her arms from The Crane's collapse stumbled halfway across. Mare's hand shot out, steadying her before she could fall, then pushing her gently toward the alley where the others waited.

The sound of boots on cobblestones froze Mare before she could follow. A patrol approaching from the east, moving quickly toward the square. No time to cross unseen. She ducked behind an overturned fishmonger's cart, pressing herself against its wooden side as the patrol entered the square.

"Spread out," ordered a voice Mare recognized with a jolt, one of Walsingham's lieutenants, a man who had once nodded respectfully to her in the Bishop's courtyard. "Check every shadow. Fleet can't have gone far."

The women in the alley would be discovered within minutes if the patrol completed their search. Mare calculated odds and angles with the cold precision of someone for whom violence was a tool rather than an emotion. Three men, well-armed but separated as they moved between market stalls. The nearest was approaching her hiding place, sword drawn, torch held high in his other hand.

She didn't hesitate. As he passed the cart, Mare exploded from her hiding place, her dagger already in motion. The blade found the soft spot beneath his jaw with deadly accuracy, driving upward into his brain. She caught him as he fell, easing his body to the ground to muffle the sound, the warm gush of his blood soaking her sleeve.

But the lieutenant had spotted the movement. "There!" he shouted, pointing toward Mare as she straightened from the corpse. "Take her alive if you can!"

The third soldier charged from behind a bread stall, his face twisted with the maniacal hatred reserved for traitors. Mare ducked his wild sword swing, calculating her next move with the clarity that came in moments of mortal danger.

Before she could strike, movement erupted from the alley. The Geese women swarmed forward, improvised weapons clutched in white-knuckled grips, a broken chair leg, a heavy cooking pot, a knife likely taken from a dead Puritan. They fell upon the charging soldier with the desperate fury of those with nothing left to lose, their collective weight bearing him to the ground as their weapons rose and fell.

Mare didn't waste the opportunity their bravery provided. She crossed the distance to the lieutenant in three swift strides, evading his sword thrust by inches. Her dagger found his throat in the same moment his blade sliced across her upper arm, drawing blood that felt hot against her skin in the cool night air.

"This way," she urged the women, blood splattered across her face as she wrenched her blade free from the lieutenant's neck. The Geese abandoned the fallen soldier, his face now unrecognizable beneath their frenzied attack and hurried to her side, eyes wide with the shock of what they'd just done.

Mare led them down a side street barely wide enough for two to walk abreast, then into an even narrower alley that ended at a blank wall. The women exchanged nervous glances, but Mare simply crouched down, fingers finding the edge of an iron grate set into the cobblestones.

"The sewers?" asked one woman, her voice thick with dread. "We'll drown down there, or worse."

"We'll die up here," Mare replied simply, straining to lift the heavy grate. Two of the women rushed to help, and together they heaved it aside, revealing a dark hole that exhaled the stench of Southwark's collective waste. "I know these tunnels. Trust me or stay here, your choice."

She paused only long enough to retrieve her dagger from the dead lieutenant's throat, wiping the blade on his cloak before sheathing it. Then she lowered herself into the darkness, hanging from the edge of the opening before dropping down with a splash that echoed in the confined space.

One by one, the women followed, each making a small sound of disgust as they landed in knee-deep filth. The last pulled the grate back into place above them, sealing them in darkness broken only by thin slivers of light from street level.

"Stay close enough to touch the person ahead of you," Mare instructed, producing a stub of candle from a waterproof pouch at her belt. She struck a spark with flint and steel, and the tiny flame cast grotesque shadows on the curved brick walls. "The water gets deeper in some places, shallower in others. There are side passages that lead nowhere or to dead ends. Follow only me."

They moved forward into the fetid darkness, the sludge sucking at their legs with each step. Rats swam around them, their eyes reflecting the candlelight like malevolent stars. The stench was overwhelming, human waste, rotting food, the decomposing bodies of animals and worse things.

One woman began to sob quietly, the sound echoing off the tunnel walls. Mare paused, turning back to find a girl barely out of childhood, her face a pale oval in the dim light.

"I can't," she whispered, her body shaking with terror or revulsion or both. "I can't do this. The rats, the smell, the dark..."

Mare reached through the filth and found the girl's hand, squeezing it firmly. "We're Winchester Geese," she reminded her, voice low but carrying to all of them. "We've survived worse than this shit. Men have used our bodies, beaten us, treated us like less than dogs. But we're still here." She strengthened her grip. "This isn't pretty, but it's a path to living. Focus on that."

The girl's fingers clutched Mare's like drowning hands finding rope, her breathing steadying despite the tears still tracking through the dirt on her cheeks. Mare nodded once, then turned to continue leading them through the underground maze.

They moved in silence after that, each woman locked in her own thoughts as they waded through the physical manifestation of Southwark's hidden filth. Mare navigated by memory and touch, one hand trailing along the slimy brick wall, counting intersections and turns. Third left, second right, straight past the fallen grating that admitted a shaft of moonlight from above.

The tunnels grew older as they progressed, the neat brickwork giving way to rougher stone, then to sections that seemed carved directly from the earth. These passages predated much of Southwark, originally built to channel rainwater but expanded over centuries to serve the growing district's needs. Mare had discovered them as a child, had mapped them in her mind during years of using them to move unseen through the Bishop's domain.

Now those same tunnels offered the only chance of escape for women whose existence the Bishop had exploited, then tried to erase when they were no longer useful to him. The irony wasn't lost on Mare as she led them deeper beneath the burning streets, away from the violence above but through a different kind of hell below.

"Not much further," she assured them as they passed beneath a section where voices could be heard above; Walsingham's men, from the sound of it, discussing search patterns with cold efficiency. "The tunnel widens ahead, then connects to an old cellar. From there, we can reach the river."

The women followed without question, their initial disgust now replaced by grim determination. They had chosen life through filth over death in flames, and having made that choice, committed to it fully. Even the youngest had stopped crying, her face set in the blank expression of someone who had moved beyond fear into a strange, detached calm.

Mare felt a grudging pride as she glanced back at them, not the Bishop's whores or Southwark's rubbish, but survivors navigating this latest horror with the same tenacity that had carried them through all the others. She had unwittingly contributed to the violence through the maps now in Walsingham's possession. But these seven, at least, might live to see morning because of her. It was a small victory in a night of overwhelming defeat. But in Southwark, Mare had learned to count such victories carefully, to hold them close against the darkness that always threatened to swallow everything.

Chapter Twelve

Ashes Of Trust

Mare crouched in the filth-choked alley, the muck of Southwark's gutters soaking through her already ruined breeches. Three hours had passed since she'd emerged from the sewers with the seven Geese, pointing them toward the river where Agnes's people waited with a small boat. Three hours of skulking through the wreckage of her world like a rat in burned ruins, counting the dead and the missing with a tally that grew with each street she dared to cross.

Her hands trembled, from rage, from exhaustion, from the shallow knife wound across her forearm that she'd bound with a strip torn from her shirt. Blood had soaked through the makeshift bandage, drawing flies that she absently swatted away. She hadn't slept in thirty hours. Hadn't eaten in longer. Her body screamed for rest, but her mind remained painfully alert, registering every sound, every movement, every threat in this broken landscape that had once been her kingdom.

Southwark lay gutted around her. Buildings that had stood for generations were now blackened skeletons, their timber bones exposed to the morning air like the ribcages of beached whales. Smoke still rose from the ruins of The Cardinal's Cap, The Crane and The Maiden's Head, thin grey tendrils twisting skyward as if carrying the souls of those who'd perished inside. The streets that normally bustled with traders, whores, and thieves were emptying, patrolled by clusters of the Bishop's men who stalked between burned-out buildings with the arrogant swagger of conquerors.

Those few citizens who dared venture out moved with the hunched, furtive posture of prey, eyes downcast, steps hurried. They skirted the worst of the destruction, crossing themselves as they passed makeshift shrouds covering bodies not yet collected bundles of rags and flesh that had been women with names and voices just hours before.

Movement at the end of the main thoroughfare snapped Mare's attention forward. A squad of the Bishop's men marched in tight formation, half a dozen armoured figures surrounding three stumbling women whose hands were bound before them. Mare's breath caught in her throat as recognition hit her with physical force. Winchester Geese, her Geese, captured alive rather than slaughtered in the night's purge.

She pressed deeper into the shadows as they drew closer, her eyes cataloguing details with the precision that had kept her alive through years in the Bishop's service. The women's dresses hung in tatters, exposing flesh marked with burns and bruises. Their faces were barely recognizable beneath masks of dried blood and soot. Two were strangers to her younger girls who must have been new to The Crane. But the third.

"Bess," Mare whispered, the name escaping like a prayer or curse.

Bess Quickly. Forty years old and still working the bar and rooms at The Cardinal's Cap when younger women might have a night off. Bess who had found Mare half-frozen in an alley twenty years ago, who had shared her meagre dinner and taught her to pick pockets with fingers nimble enough to feed herself. Bess who had laughed like summer thunder and cursed like a sailor even as she bandaged Mare's first knife wound with surprising gentleness.

Now Bess stumbled between two guards, her right eye swollen shut, her grey-streaked hair matted with blood. But her shoulders remained straight, her steps as dignified as her shackles allowed. She'd survived worse than the Bishop's men, that's what she'd always told the younger girls. "You'd be surprised what a body can live through if the spirit's stubborn enough."

The guards yanked their prisoners toward the Clink, that stone monument to the Bishop's authority that squatted like a malevolent toad at the edge of his domain. Mare's fingernails dug into her palms hard enough to draw blood as she watched them disappear through the prison's iron-bound doors.

Her hands shook with a rage so pure it felt like fever, but beneath it burned something worse, guilt, hot and acrid in her chest. Her maps. Her intelligence. Her careful documentation of every hiding place and secret passage. All now weapons in Walsingham's hands, turned against the very women she'd sworn to protect. Bess was being dragged to the Clink because of her. Because Mare had been the Bishop's creature for too long, had trusted her own cleverness to keep her balanced between worlds that were never meant to coexist.

A different kind of commotion drew her attention—a town crier had appeared at the crossroads, his bell cutting through the morning air with irritating persistence. Citizens gathered, hunger for news briefly overcoming their fear of lingering in the open.

"Hear ye, hear ye!" The crier's voice echoed between buildings, bouncing off stone and charred wood. "By decree of Her Majesty's Privy Council, all works of the playwright Christopher Marlowe are henceforth banned from performance or publication throughout the realm!"

A murmur ran through the gathered crowd, swelling as the crier continued.

"Said works having been found to contain seditious content and heretical ideas contrary to the peace of the realm and the authority of church and crown! Any persons found in possession of such works shall be subject to fine and imprisonment!"

The crowd's reaction split like fabric along a seam, cheers from some quarters, muttered curses from others. A group of labourers spat in the dust, their disappointment obvious; Marlowe's bloody spectacles had been their favourite entertainment after a week's brutal work. Nearby, a cluster of merchants nodded in solemn approval, their faces pinched with the sardonic satisfaction of those who enjoy seeing brilliance punished.

"Good riddance to that sodomite," declared one, loud enough for those nearby to hear. "His plays were naught, but filth dressed in fancy language."

His companion, a man whose velvet doublet strained across an ample belly, leaned in with the eager excitement of sharing fresh gossip. "They say he fled London two nights past, after being named in that Puritan plot. My cousin's boy works at The Rose, swears he saw Marlowe burning papers before he vanished."

"Burning evidence, more like," the first merchant replied. "Word is, he'd been passing information to both sides for months, telling the Puritans about the Bishop's movements while selling court secrets to Walsingham."

The second man lowered his voice, though not enough to prevent Mare from catching every damning word. "They say he was fucking the Bishop's whore-spy too. That shadow woman, what's her name? Fleet. Marion Fleet."

"Fleet? The one who betrayed the Bishop?"

"The very same. Rumour says she helped the Puritans plan their fires, then turned on them when it suited her purpose. Playing both sides, just like her playwright lover."

Mare's fingers closed around the dagger hidden in her cloak, knuckles whitening with the effort of restraining herself. She could cross the distance in three strides, could open both their throats before they registered her presence. The image flashed vivid in her mind, their blood spilling hot across cobblestones, their eyes widening in shock as they recognized who had killed them.

But such action would only confirm their version of events, would only solidify the narrative being built around her name. Marion Fleet, traitor. The Bishop's Shadow turned against her master. Marlowe's whore. The woman who had helped burn Southwark to the ground.

She pulled her hood lower, obscuring features already disguised by soot and dried blood. Revenge against gossipmongers would satisfy nothing but her immediate rage. There were larger targets deserving of her blade, Walsingham who had led the night's slaughter, the Bishop who had ordered it, Marlowe who had betrayed them all and somehow escaped the consequences.

And there was Bess, now languishing in the Clink's darkness, waiting for whatever torments the Bishop had planned for those who had survived his initial purge.

Mare slipped deeper into the alley, moving away from the crowd with the silent grace that had earned her the title of Shadow. Her mind cleared, rage and guilt crystallizing into something colder, more useful, purpose. She would find Agnes first, gather whatever remained of the Order. Then she would do what she'd been trained to do, hunt, gather intelligence, identify weaknesses.

And then, when the moment was right, she would make the Bishop bleed for every drop spilled in his name.

The abandoned church of St. Bartholomew squatted at the edge of Southwark like a beggar forgotten by both God and man. Its stone walls, blackened by decades of London's filth, rose jagged against the afternoon sky where the roof had partially collapsed years before. No one came here to pray anymore, no one except the women who had carved a different kind of sanctuary beneath its rotting floorboards. Mare approached from the river side, using the overgrown cemetery as cover, her eyes tracking the movements of the Bishop's patrols that still combed the district like lice through a corpse's hair.

She knew the sanctuary's entrance better than most, had helped design some of its defences during those few brief days when she and Agnes had acknowledged their shared blood. A mausoleum whose stone door hung crooked on rusted hinges. Inside, behind the empty coffin of some forgotten merchant, a narrow shaft descended fifteen feet to a tunnel that connected to the church's ancient crypt.

Mare slipped inside the mausoleum and secured the door behind her with practiced movements. The air inside hung thick with dust and the stillness of places long abandoned by the living. She moved the coffin with effort that sent fresh pain lancing through her wounded arm, revealing the iron rungs set into the wall.

The climb down was awkward, her body protesting each movement after a night of violence and a day of tense hiding. At the bottom, the tunnel stretched before her, low enough that taller men would need to stoop. Mare moved forward with one hand brushing the wall, the other on her knife, every sense alert for signs of ambush or surveillance.

The first indication that something was wrong came from the smell. The tunnel had always carried a damp, earthy scent tinged with the herbs Agnes's women burned to ward off disease and vermin. Now the air hung heavy with the metallic tang of blood and something worse, the stink of burned flesh.

Mare's pace quickened despite her caution. The tunnel opened into the church's crypt, where generations of wealthy Southwark citizens had mouldered in sealed tombs before the district's decline had left the building to rats and the desperate. The Order had transformed this space, clearing debris, setting up cots and worktables, creating a command centre for their operations throughout Southwark.

What greeted Mare now barely resembled the organized sanctuary she'd visited before. Overturned tables lay splintered across the flagstone floor. Storage chests gaped open, their contents, medicine, food, clothing scattered and trampled. The small altar where Agnes had led her women in prayer was shattered, its candles broken, its modest cross snapped in half and tossed aside like rubbish.

Blood painted the walls in broad smears and smaller droplets, already turned brown with time. Some spots showed the distinctive patterns of arterial spray someone had died here, violently and without mercy. Mare's eyes tracked the evidence of struggle across the room, reading the story written in broken furniture and bloodstains. The women had fought back. Overturned benches positioned as barricades. Broken bottles that had held oil, turned to weapons in desperate hands.

But most telling were the prayer books. Dozens lay torn apart, their pages ripped and scattered like fallen leaves across the stone floor. Not merely knocked aside in struggle but deliberately destroyed, an act of desecration rather than simple violence.

"Agnes," Mare whispered, the name escaping unbidden as she moved deeper into the ruined sanctuary, scanning for any sign of her mother. Her boot slipped in a dark puddle, and she caught herself against a wall, her hand coming away sticky with half-dried blood.

She searched methodically, checking each alcove, each overturned cot, dreading what she might find yet needing to know. But no body with Agnes's face stared back with death-glazed eyes. No corpse with her mother's distinctive, grey-streaked hair lay crumpled in a corner.

A faint sound, the whisper of cloth against stone, froze Mare mid-step. She pivoted toward a small door she knew led to a storage closet where Agnes kept her precious supply of medicines and herbs. The sound came again, a pained intake of breath quickly muffled.

Mare approached with her knife drawn, pushing the door open with her foot to keep both hands free for whatever might wait inside. The closet's interior lay in shadow, shelves upended, glass bottles shattered across the floor. In the corner, a darker shape huddled, barely distinguishable from the surrounding gloom.

"Don't move," Mare commanded, her voice hard as the stone beneath her feet.

"Please," came the reply, a woman's voice cracked with pain and thirst. "Please don't hurt me."

Mare crouched, keeping her knife visible as she pulled a tinderbox from her belt and struck a spark to a small candle stub, she carried. The flame illuminated a woman in the torn remains of a nun's habit, her face so swollen and bruised that Mare hardly recognized Sister Catherine, one of Agnes's most trusted lieutenants.

"It's me," Mare said, setting the candle on a broken shelf. "Mare. Marion Fleet."

Recognition dawned slowly in the nun's one eye that wasn't swollen shut. "Marion?" Blood bubbled at the corner of her mouth when she spoke. "They said... they said you were dead."

"Not yet," Mare replied, sheathing her knife and moving closer to assess the woman's injuries. They were extensive, her left arm bent at an unnatural angle, her ribs visibly misshapen beneath her torn habit, deep cuts across her face and neck that had been clumsily bandaged with strips of cloth.

"The Bishop's men," Catherine whispered, each word clearly causing pain. "They came at dawn... just after we'd gathered the survivors from The Crane."

Mare helped the woman sit more comfortably, noting the fever heat radiating from her skin. "Agnes? Was she here?"

Catherine nodded weakly. "She led the defence... told the others to run while she... while she faced them." A rattling cough shook her frame. "Sister Agnes told them nothing, even when they..." Her voice broke, tears cutting clean tracks through the blood and dirt on her face.

"When they what?" Mare pressed, her stomach clenching with dread.

"Walsingham himself... he questioned her. About you. About the Order's hideouts. About the Puritan pamphlets." Catherine's uninjured hand clutched Mare's sleeve. "She said nothing... not even when they put out candles against her skin."

Mare's face remained expressionless, a mask of control that betrayed nothing of the storm raging beneath. Her hands, however, trembled slightly as she checked Catherine's wounds with gentle precision.

"Did they take her?" Mare asked, her voice steady despite the churning in her gut.

"Dragged her away alive. Said the Bishop wanted to question her personally." Catherine's breathing grew more laboured. "But that's not the worst of it. While Walsingham was here, Stubbs and his zealots found our refuge at the old brewery."

A cold premonition settled in Mare's chest. "What happened?"

"They called us papist whores while they burned our sisters alive," Catherine whispered, tears flowing freely now. "Barred the doors and windows from outside. Fifteen women. Some were just girls we'd rescued from the brothels."

Mare helped the woman drink from a small flask of water she carried, her mind racing with calculations and contingencies. "Are there other survivors? Other safe houses still intact?"

Catherine nodded faintly. "The tunnels beneath the old tannery... Agnes made us memorize different locations, told us never to share all of them with any one person." Her fingers dug into Mare's arm with surprising strength. "Even you. She said especially you, because of... because of what you might be forced to tell the Bishop."

The words struck Mare like a physical blow, but she kept her face carefully neutral as she finished examining Catherine's wounds. "You can't stay here. They'll come back to check for survivors."

"I can't move," Catherine replied simply. "We both know that."

Mare unhooked the small pouch from her belt, her last coins, enough for a week's food and lodging at the worst inn in Southwark. She pressed it into Catherine's hand, followed by the small knife she kept in her boot.

"Someone will come for you," Mare promised, though they both recognized the lie for what it was. "The tannery people, they'll send help when they can."

Catherine's lips, cracked and bloodied, curved in a faint smile. "Go find her, Marion. Find Agnes." Her good eye held Mare's with surprising clarity. "She never stopped watching over you,

you know. Even when you served him. Even when you didn't know she existed."

Mare nodded once, sharply, unable to trust her voice. She arranged what intact blankets she could find around the injured woman, positioned the water flask within reach, and placed the knife where Catherine's right hand could grasp it easily. Then she rose, her face settling into the cold mask of calculation that had served her through years in the Bishop's shadow. The time for grief would come later. The time for rage was now, but rage harnessed and directed like a blade rather than splashed uselessly like water.

She left as she had come, silent as a ghost through the defiled sanctuary, the names of the dead and missing adding weight to her shoulders with each step. But beneath that weight, her spine remained straight, her purpose clear. Find Agnes. Find the survivors. And make the Bishop pay for every drop of blood spilled in his holy name.

Chapter Thirteen

Captive of The Past

Mare woke with a jolt in absolute darkness, her consciousness returning like a swimmer breaching the surface after too long underwater. Pain bloomed across her skull, radiating outward in waves that made her stomach clench with nausea. She tried to lift her hand to her throbbing head, but her wrists wouldn't move, bound tight behind her back, the rough hemp digging into flesh already raw.

"Fuck," she hissed, the word escaping through cracked lips. Her mouth tasted of copper and bile, her tongue a swollen stranger. How long had she been unconscious? Hours? Days?

Memory returned in fractured pieces: leaving The Rose's ruins, the leather packet of Marlowe's papers tucked against her ribs, dawn breaking over Southwark's charred skyline. Then footsteps behind her, too many to fight alone. A cloth pressed over her face, reeking of something bitter and chemical. Darkness.

She twisted her wrists experimentally, wincing as the movement sent fresh pain lancing through her wounded arm. The knife cut she'd received during the escape from the brothel had reopened, warm wetness seeping into the ropes that bound her. She flexed her fingers, relieved to find them still responsive despite the tightness of her bonds.

Her eyes strained against the perfect blackness, seeking any edge or shape to orient herself. Gradually, her other senses compensated for her blindness. Cold stone pressed against her back and thighs, not a chair but something more substantial, older. A throne or an altar. The air hung heavy with damp and decay, the mustiness of underground spaces abandoned by all but rats and spiders. Beneath that familiar stench lay something else, the cloying sweetness of incense, faint but unmistakable.

Water dripped somewhere to her left, each drop striking stone with metronomic precision. The sound echoed slightly, suggesting lofty ceilings and solid walls. Not a cellar, then. Something larger. A crypt or one of the abandoned chapels that dotted Southwark like forgotten prayers.

Mare pulled against her restraints again, more methodically this time. Her ankles were bound to the stone chair's legs, the rope there even tighter than at her wrists. Whoever had tied these knots knew their business, no slack to work with, no give in the fibres. Her fingers sought purchase on the hemp, searching for a loose strand, a frayed edge, anything that might offer leverage.

"Come on, you miserable bitch," she muttered to herself, the sound of her own voice strangely comforting in the pressing darkness. "You've escaped worse than this."

But had she? The Bishop's men had never taken her captive before. She'd always been the hunter, not the prey. The fact that she still lived suggested they wanted information before executing her; information about the surviving Geese, about the Order, about the evidence she'd collected from the ruins of The Rose.

The thought sent fresh panic coursing through her veins. Marlowe's papers, where were they? She couldn't feel the familiar weight against her ribs. Had they found them? Taken them? The documents were her only leverage, her only chance of bargaining for Agnes's life and her own.

A new sound cut through her racing thoughts, footsteps approaching from somewhere beyond the darkness. Heavy boots on stone, unhurried and deliberate. Mare tensed, forcing her breathing to steady, her mind to clear. Whatever came through that door, she would face it with the cold calculation that had kept her alive in Southwark's unforgiving hierarchy.

Light spilled suddenly into the chamber as a door creaked open on ancient hinges. Mare squinted against the sudden brightness, the flame of a single torch momentarily blinding after such complete darkness. The footsteps entered, then stopped. The door closed with a finality that echoed through the chamber.

As her vision adjusted, details of her prison emerged from shadow, walls of fitted stone now black with centuries of damp, a vaulted ceiling lost in darkness above the torch's reach, niches carved into the walls where saintly statues had once stood watch but now gaped empty like eyeless sockets. A crypt, then, beneath one of Southwark's forgotten churches.

The torch found its home in an iron sconce, its flame casting long shadows that danced across the stone floor. And in that flickering light stood not Thomas Walsingham, not the Bishop's men, but Sister Agnes—tall and straight-backed in her simple dark habit, her face half-hidden in shadow, her grey-streaked hair bound severely beneath her veil.

Mare's mind struggled to make sense of this apparition. Agnes should be in the Bishop's custody, should be suffering under Walsingham's interrogation. Yet here she stood, unharmed, carrying a small wooden box in hands that bore no visible signs of the torture Catherine had described.

"Finally awake, I see," Agnes said, her voice unnervingly calm, as if she were greeting Mare for morning prayers rather than in this underground prison.

"Untie me now," Mare snarled, yanking against her bonds hard enough that fresh blood trickled down her wrists, "or I swear I'll gut you when I get free you old bitch."

Agnes approached slowly, her footsteps silent on the stone floor. Her face, as it came into the torch's full light, revealed nothing, no fear, no anger, no guilt. Just the measured composure that Mare had first mistaken for piety when they'd met in that blood-soaked alley.

"Such language from my daughter," Agnes said, setting the wooden box on the floor beside Mare's chair. "Though I suppose I shouldn't be surprised, given your upbringing."

"My upbringing?" Mare laughed, the sound scraping raw from her throat. "I'm not your daughter, my stepmother was Margaret Fleet, washerwoman, worked her socks off to provide for me after my real mother died in childbirth…before the plague took Margaret, I was only eight." Mare barked back.

"Marion, listen to me, I am your mother, that was what Margaret, and I agreed you would be told until you were old enough to know, to understand who you were and where you came from. A lie to protect you."

Mare froze, her mind reeling as the words settled over her. It was as if a heavy, invisible cloak had been draped over her shoulders, pressing down with a weight she hadn't anticipated. Her heart pulsed in her chest, each beat resonating with the gravity of the moment. Agnes straightened, studying Mare with eyes that matched her own in colour if not in expression. "You've been running your whole life, Marion," she said softly. "It's time you stopped."

"Don't call me that," Mare spat. "Marion died in the gutter where you left her. I'm Mare now. The Bishop's Shadow. The woman who's going to see his head on a pike for what he's done."

"The Bishop's Shadow," Agnes repeated, her tone making the title sound like a child's game rather than the fearsome reputation

Mare had built. "Is that really who you want to be? His creature, even in your rebellion?"

Mare strained against the ropes until her shoulders screamed in protest. "Better his creature in rebellion than your puppet in captivity. At least I choose my own chains."

Agnes's lips curved in what might have been a smile on another woman's face, but on hers looked more like a scar reopening. "Choice," she said, the word heavy with meaning Mare couldn't decipher. "We'll see how much choice you have when you know the truth."

She knelt beside the wooden box, her fingers hovering over its lid. "Your whole life has been built on lies, Marion. It's time you learned which ones are mine, and which are his."

Agnes rose to her feet with the fluid grace of someone who had learned to move silently through hostile spaces. She began to circle Mare's stone chair, her plain habit whispering against the floor like secrets passed in confessional. Her eyes never left Mare's face, studying every flicker of expression with the patient assessment of a falconer who knows the hawk must tire eventually, must submit to the hood and jesses.

"You've made quite a name for yourself in Southwark," Agnes said, her voice pitched low but carrying in the stone chamber. "The Bishop's Shadow. His eyes and ears in every brothel, his knife in the dark when necessary." She completed a full circle, stopping directly before Mare. "Twenty-seven confirmed kills in his service. Though I suspect the actual number is higher."

Mare kept her face blank, though her mind raced. The number was correct, precisely correct. Not even Walsingham knew the exact count.

"You have a particular method," Agnes continued, resuming her slow orbit. "A single thrust beneath the ribs when possible. Clean, efficient. You learned that from a river pirate named Cord when you were fourteen. He taught you after you saved his son from a press gang."

The hair on Mare's neck rose. No one knew about Cord. The old pirate had died years ago, his secrets dying with him.

"You're well-informed for a nun," Mare said, forcing bored disinterest into her tone. "Been keeping a little book on me, have you? Collecting rumours and gossip?"

Agnes's lips twitched, faintly a smile. "Not rumours. Facts." She paused behind Mare, close enough that Mare could feel her breath stirring the hair at her nape. "Like the fact that you sleep with a knife under your pillow. That you can't abide the smell of lavender because it reminds you of the plague pits. That you have nightmares about drowning despite never having set foot on a ship."

Each detail struck like a physical blow. Mare's chest tightened, her breathing shallow as Agnes moved back into view, her grey eyes reflecting the torchlight.

"You've had spies watching me," Mare accused, but the words sounded hollow even to her own ears. These weren't details a spy could know, they were intimate fragments of a life observed up close, over time.

"I've had no need of spies," Agnes replied simply. "I've watched over you myself since the day I left you by the Thames." Her voice remained steady, but her hands betrayed her, a slight tremor as she touched the wooden cross hanging at her waist. "I know about the scar on your left knee from falling through rotted floorboards when you were nine. I know about the time you stole apples from the orchard behind St. Saviour's and gave them all away to the younger children before eating one yourself."

Mare's defiance curdled into something colder, more primal. These weren't just facts; they were memories she herself had nearly forgotten, moments no one had witnessed, or so she'd believed.

"You're lying," Mare insisted, but doubt had crept into her voice. "You've pieced this together from multiple sources. The Bishop's records, Marlowe's notes, gossip from the Geese."

Agnes shook her head slowly. "I know about the crescent-shaped birthmark on your right shoulder," she said quietly. "The one that looks like a new moon, just below your collarbone."

Mare froze, her body going rigid as if struck by lightning. The birthmark was her most closely guarded secret, a distinctive mark that could identify her if she were ever caught, stripped, and interrogated. She kept it covered always, had never shown it to anyone, not even to lovers in the most intimate moments.

"How could you possibly know that?" The question emerged as little more than a whisper.

Agnes held Mare's gaze as she slowly rolled up the sleeve of her habit, exposing her right forearm. There, just below her own collarbone, was an identical crescent-shaped mark—the same size, the same distinctive curve.

"Because I gave it to you," Agnes said simply.

Mare's breath caught in her throat, her pupils dilating with shock. The world seemed to tilt beneath her, certainties crumbling like sand underfoot. She stared at the mark on Agnes's skin, the mirror image of the one she'd carried her entire life, the one she'd sometimes traced with her fingers in private moments, wondering if it might be the only inheritance from a mother she'd never known.

Agnes knelt before the wooden box again, opening it with reverent care. From inside, she removed two objects, a small knife with a distinctive bone handle carved with intricate patterns, and a scrap of cloth so faded and worn its original colour was indiscernible.

"You were born during the Feast of Saint Agnes," she said, placing the items on the floor between them. "In a room not unlike this one, cold stone walls, a single candle for light And wrapped you in this before I ran and left you with Margaret."

"No," Mare said, the word tearing from her throat. She struggled violently against her bonds, the chair rocking beneath her. "No, you're lying! I was told my mother was a whore who died in childbirth!"

"I was a whore, a whore to a powerful man. A man that would have you killed if he found you, and so I hid you with a woman whose own child was stillborn. Someone who could nurse you, bring you up as hers and hide you in plain sight. She was wonderful to you before the plague got her, and you were still so young and vulnerable." Agnes replied, her voice steady even as Mare thrashed against her restraints. She rose to her feet, towering over Mare's bound form. "I'm so sorry that she died, but I didn't."

Mare stared ahead, rapt in astonishment, and shook her head slowly, incredulous.

With movement too quick to anticipate, Agnes's hand cracked across Mare's cheek, the slap echoing in the stone chamber. Mare's head snapped sideways, more from shock than force. Agnes had struck her with the precise calculation of someone who knew exactly how much pressure to apply, enough to shock, not enough to truly harm.

"I did not endure twenty-eight years of watching my daughter from shadows, did not build an army of broken women into warriors who rescued me when I was being carried away by the Bishop's men to be killed after Walsingham's interrogation, only to listen to you deny the truth when it stands before you," Agnes said, each word sharp as the knife that lay between them. "I am your mother. You are my blood. And we are running out of time to finish what I began when I first defied the Bishop's predecessor and stole you from his plans."

Mare tasted blood where her teeth had cut the inside of her cheek. The sting grounded her, pulling her back from the precipice of panic the revelation had pushed her toward. She stared up at Agnes, at the woman who claimed to be her mother, searching for lies in that severe face that so eerily mirrored aspects of her own.

"If what you say is true," Mare said finally, each word deliberate and heavy, "then you've had twenty-eight years to claim me. Why now? Why let me serve the very man you claim to have saved me from?"

Agnes's face softened fractionally, something like regret passing across her features. "Because I thought I was protecting you," she said. "Until I realized I was merely postponing your destruction."

The revelation hung in the air between them like a physical presence, reshaping the very atmosphere of the stone chamber. Mare's mind rebelled against it, searching desperately for some alternative explanation, some reason this woman would fabricate such an elaborate lie. But the birthmark couldn't be dismissed, identical in shape and placement, a crescent moon that had followed Mare through every year of her solitary life.

"Tell me," Mare said finally, her voice scraped hollow by emotion she refused to name. "If you're my mother, tell me everything."

Agnes nodded once, sharply, then retrieved the torch from its sconce. She moved it closer, casting warmer light across the damp walls, chasing shadows from the corners where they might hide secrets or listeners. When she spoke, her voice carried the familiar cadence of a story long rehearsed but never shared.

"I was sixteen when the Bishop's predecessor brought me to Southwark," she began, her eyes fixed on some middle distance as if watching scenes unfold on the blank stone wall. "Not Wickham, but the man before him, Bishop Harland. He claimed to be rescuing me from a life of sin." Her mouth twisted in bitter amusement. "What he actually wanted was young flesh to sell to his noble friends without the complications that came with established whores."

She paced a small circle, the torch's flame wavering with her movements. "I was kept in a special brothel, The Cardinal's Hat, it was called then, reserved for clergymen and their favoured associates. That's where I met your father."

Mare's breath caught. "My father?"

"A young clergyman called Father Thomas Leech, he had kinder words, treated me as a person, and kept me for himself. The spirit was weak and the flesh willing, they all were, the Bishop's clan."

The name screamed at Mare, like a dagger pushed into her heart up to the hilt. A name that jolted her memory where she stored everyone and everything that moved about Southwark. That was the man she found face up lying in the Thames a month hence. He had been kind to her once, years ago, when she was nothing but a half-starved girl with a bloodied lip and lice in my braids.

He found Mare outside the Clink, bruised and barefoot, He gave her bread and had said,

"The Lord watches the birds and the whores both, child. It's only men who choose between them." Little had he known he was giving scant care for his daughter.

Her expression hardened again. "But Harland had other plans. A pregnant whore was useless to him, but a child born within his domain had value.

"The church branded me a heretic for speaking against a priest who used his position to rape women in the confession booth," Agnes continued, her words precise as surgical cuts. "They would have burned me, and any child of mine would have been taken by the same men who condemned me, raised to believe their mother was a servant of Satan."

Mare's jaw tightened, her teeth grinding against the unwelcome understanding that threatened to undermine her righteous anger. "So, you left me to chance instead."

"I left you where I knew you would be found," Agnes corrected. "I watched from the shadows until a woman I trusted took you in. I planned for your care until..." She stopped abruptly, the memory still sharp enough to wound. "Until circumstances forced me to flee London entirely."

"And when you returned? When you became Sister Agnes, rescuing fallen women?" Mare's voice cracked despite her effort to maintain control. "Did you ever look for the daughter you abandoned?"

"Every day," Agnes replied simply. "But by then, you belonged to the Bishop. Protected and watched. Approaching you would have meant exposing everything I'd built."

Agnes knelt beside Mare's chair, close enough that Mare could see the fine lines radiating from her eyes, could smell the herb-scented soap that clung to her skin.

"When my time came, they took me to a room beneath the cathedral. No midwife, just Harland and two of his priests. I laboured for eighteen hours." Her voice remained steady, but her fingers trembled as they traced patterns in the dust on the floor. "When you finally came into this world, Harland declared you would be raised in service to the church. Not as a nun or servant, as a tool. A child with holy blood who could be placed in certain households, trained to listen and report."

Mare could picture it suddenly, vivid as her own memories, a younger Agnes, her face contorted with pain and determination, lying on a stone altar like the chair where Mare now sat bound. Candlelight glinting off the bone-handled knife as Agnes secreted it beneath her skirts while the Bishop examined her newborn child.

"I waited until they left me to rest," Agnes continued, the words coming faster now. "Then I cut my bonds with the knife, this knife, that I'd stolen, wrapped you in a blanket I'd hidden beneath the altar, and ran. It was raining that night, a storm that covered the sound of my escape."

The image unfolded in Mare's mind: Agnes running through Southwark's twisted streets, rain lashing her face, a bundle clutched protectively against her chest. Her bare feet slipping on cobblestones slick with filth and rainwater, her breath coming in desperate gasps as church bells tolled in the distance, signalling the alarm.

"I knew I couldn't keep you," Agnes said, her voice dropping to barely above a whisper. "They would search every boarding house, every hovel where I might hide. So, I left you where I knew you would be found, in the house of a woman named Margaret Fleet who had lost her own child the week before."

Another image: Agnes crouched in shadow across from a riverside shack, watching as a grey-haired woman was handed the bundle at her doorstep, lifted it with surprised tenderness, and carried it inside out of the rain.

"I watched over you when I could," Agnes continued. "But Harland's men were hunting me. I had to leave London or die, and my death would have meant no one knowing the truth of your origins, no one to protect you from afar."

Mare's throat ached with unspoken questions, with the weight of a history suddenly made flesh before her. "Where did you go?"

"North, to a convent where Harland's influence couldn't reach. I took vows, not out of piety but necessity, the church's protection against the church's own corruption." Agnes's lips curved in a humourless smile. "The irony wasn't lost on me."

She rolled up her sleeve again, but this time turned her palm upward, revealing the scar that Mare had noticed during their fight in the alley, a mark identical to the one the Bishop had carved into Mare's own palm years later.

"Ten years ago, I returned to London after Harland's death. I found you had been taken in by Wickham, his successor. He had marked you as his own, was using you exactly as Harland had planned to use you, as a spy, a tool, a weapon fashioned from flesh and blood."

"The Order," Mare said slowly, pieces falling into place. "You formed it to fight him. To undo what he was doing."

Agnes nodded. "I gathered women like me, those the church and its men had used and discarded. I taught them to fight, to gather intelligence, to move unseen through Southwark just as you did for the Bishop." Her eyes met Mare's directly. "But while you served him, we worked to undermine him, protecting the Geese when possible, disrupting his more vicious schemes, slowly building toward his downfall."

The torchlight caught the unshed tears in Agnes's eyes, turning them to molten silver. "I watched you from afar, unable to approach without endangering everything I'd built. Unable to tell you the truth without putting your life at risk. The Bishop kept you close, kept you visible. Any connection between us would have meant death for both."

"Why now?" Mare's voice came out raw, the question that had burned in her since Agnes's revelation finally finding voice. "Why tell me this now when you've watched me for years?"

Agnes reached forward, her fingers hovering just above the rope binding Mare's wounded wrist. "Because the Bishop has marked you for death," she said simply. "The same way he marked me twenty years ago."

Mare's body slumped, the fight temporarily draining from her limbs as this final truth landed. She had known, of course, had seen the orders with her own eyes, had understood that her usefulness to Wickham had ended. But hearing it confirmed made it suddenly, terribly real.

"He discovered your connection to me a month ago," Agnes continued, her fingers working at the knots binding Mare's wrists. "One of my women was captured, broke under torture. Told Walsingham about my interest in you, my orders to watch over you specifically. Told him about Father Leech who in one small act of decency, out of doing right, out of guilt, maybe both, was passing me word of the Bishop's work. He ended up in the Thames the following day, as you found him and as we watched you. A warning to any others like him. News travels fast in Southwark, especially bad news."

Agens applied the cut, the rope gave way, freeing Mare's bloodied wrists. "He's already written the warrant for your execution, not capture, not interrogation. Death on sight."

Mare brought her arms forward slowly, wincing as circulation returned in painful prickles. Agnes moved to the ropes at her ankles, working them loose with practiced efficiency.

"So, you captured me yourself," Mare said, understanding dawning. "Brought me here instead of letting him find me."

"I had to make a choice," Agnes replied, not looking up from her task. "Let you run until they caught you or take you myself and offer you the truth." The final rope fell away. "And a chance."

Mare stood slowly, her legs unsteady after hours bound to the stone chair. Agnes straightened to face her, making no move to block the chamber's single door, but her posture making it clear she would not step aside easily.

"You have a choice now," Agnes said, her voice taking on the formal cadence of ritual. "Join us, join your mother, or walk away. But know that if you return to him, neither of us will survive the month."

Their eyes met across the small space, slate grey matching slate grey, the same determination reflecting between them like light bouncing between mirrors. Agnes extended her scarred palm, the gesture both invitation and challenge.

"I've lived my life in shadow, Marion," she said softly. "First as the Bishop's property, then as his enemy. Don't make my mistakes. Don't spend another day as his creature, even in rebellion."

Mare looked down at her own scarred palm, the Bishop's brand that had defined her existence for as long as she could remember. Then at the identical mark on her mother's hand, not a brand of ownership but a scar of resistance, a wound taken willingly in defiance.

Between them lay choice, and blood, and the weight of histories both shared and separate, a chasm twenty-eight years wide that could be crossed only by the most dangerous of leaps.

Rising from the Thames

Mare's consciousness returned bringing fresh pain with it. First came the throbbing in her skull, a steady drumbeat of agony that matched the sluggish pulse in her veins. Then the searing burn on her forearm, where flesh had met hot iron and surrendered. Last came memory, Agnes's outstretched hand, her own refusal, the struggle that followed, and finally darkness delivered by multiple pairs of hands that held her down while something sweet and bitter was forced between her lips.

"Fuck," she whispered, the word scraping past a throat dried to parchment.

The cell materialized around her as her eyes adjusted to the gloom, four walls of ancient stone slick with damp, a ceiling lost to darkness, a floor of packed earth that smelled of mould and piss. A single torch guttered in an iron bracket outside the cell door, its feeble light squeezing through a small, barred window set at eye level. The door itself was solid oak banded with iron, old but sturdy.

Mare tested her bindings, rough hemp rope wrapped too tight around her wrists, securing her to a rusted iron ring set into the wall. Similar rope bound her ankles. The skin beneath the hemp was raw and weeping, testament to earlier struggles she couldn't fully remember. Her clothes had been taken, replaced with a shapeless grey shift that stank of previous occupants. Blood had dried in the creases of her elbows, under her fingernails.

And on her right forearm, angry and fresh, the mark of The Order, a cross bisected by a vertical line, the brand still weeping clear fluid, the flesh around it an angry red halo of tortured nerve endings.

"Mother," Mare spat the word like poison. Agnes had offered choice with one hand while holding betrayal in the other. How quickly her promises of truth and protection had transformed into imprisonment and pain once Mare had rejected her offer. The sweet words about watching over her for twenty-eight years had dissolved like sugar in rain the moment Mare had made clear she would forge her own path, neither the Bishop's creature nor The Order's convert.

She remembered fragments of what followed, her refusal, Agnes's face hardening, her own lunge for the door, the women who had materialized from shadows to restrain her. Agnes watching with those slate-grey eyes, the same eyes Mare saw in puddles and polished metal, as they forced something bitter down her throat. Then darkness.

And now, this cell. This pain. This betrayal that cut deeper than the Bishop's ever had, because she'd never expected anything better from him. Mare drew a deep breath that sent pain lancing through her ribs, then began systematically testing her bonds. She twisted her wrists against the hemp, feeling for weak spots, for places where the fibres might give. The rope was competently tied, but not by an expert; there was a slight looseness on the underside of her right wrist, where the knot hadn't been pulled completely taut. She worked her hand back and forth in microscopic movements, feeling the fibres stretch ever so slightly.

Footsteps approached from the corridor outside, heavy, unhurried, the gait of someone unconcerned about detection. Keys jingled, metal scraped against metal as a lock turned. A small panel at the bottom of the door slid open.

Mare instantly went limp, her head lolling forward, her breathing slowed to the shallow rhythm of the deeply unconscious.

"Still out, then," a woman's voice muttered. "Sister Agnes won't be pleased."

A clay bowl scraped across the stone floor as it was pushed through the opening—thin gruel from the smell of it, water with the merest suggestion of grain. The panel began to slide shut.

"Wait," another voice called from further down the corridor. "Check her bindings again. The last one nearly got loose."

The door panel remained open. Keys jangled again, and the lock turned once more. Mare kept her breathing shallow, her muscles completely slack, as the cell door creaked open. Heavy footsteps approached, smelling of tallow and sweat.

"Bindings look secure enough," the guard said, nudging Mare's leg with a booted foot. "She'll be out for hours yet, with what they gave her." The woman yawned audibly. "I'm for a rest. Wake me when Sister returns."

"Don't sleep too deeply," the second voice warned. "This one's dangerous. The Bishop's Shadow, they say."

"Not anymore," the guard replied, her voice receding as she moved toward the door. "Now she's just another apostate waiting for judgment."

The door closed. The lock turned. Footsteps retreated down the corridor.

Mare remained motionless for ten slow breaths, counting each inhale and exhale with the patience of a hunter. When silence had settled back around her like dust, she resumed working at the weak spot in her bindings, this time with more urgency.

The rope gave slightly, enough to create a fraction more space between hemp and skin. Mare twisted her wrist at a painful angle, using a technique learned from a river pirate who'd specialized in escaping the Queen's justice. The movement dislocated her thumb with a muted pop that sent bile rising in her throat. Pain flared white-hot up her arm, but the extra flexibility allowed her hand to slip through the widened loop of rope.

One hand free, she made quick work of the other bindings, relocating her thumb with another nauseating pop once both hands were liberated. She flexed her fingers, ensuring they still responded to her commands, then set about searching the cell with methodical precision.

The walls first, pressing against each stone, testing for loose mortar or hidden openings. Nothing. The floor next, her fingers probing the packed earth for irregularities. Near the far corner, the ground felt different—harder, less yielding. Mare scraped away the thin layer of dirt to reveal a flat stone, the size of a dinner pate, set into the floor.

She pried at its edges with bleeding fingernails until it shifted, then lifted free. Beneath lay darkness, a narrow shaft that disappeared into the earth, just wide enough for a human body. The scent that rose from it carried memories of her childhood, the distinctive smell of Southwark's underground tunnels, the hidden network she'd mapped for the Bishop, the same passages that had saved her life countless times.

A faint smile twisted Mare's cracked lips. Agnes might know her birthmark, might have watched her from shadows for years, but she didn't know every secret Mare had uncovered in her service to the Bishop. This tunnel, its entrance hidden beneath what had once been a monastery before The Order claimed it, connected to the main sewer line that ran beneath all of Southwark.

Muffled snoring drifted from the corridor. The guard, asleep at her post. Mare moved to the door, peering through the small, barred window. A woman slouched on a three-legged stool, her chin dropped to her chest, a small knife tucked into her belt within arm's reach of the door.

Mare's fingers slipped through the bars like eels through weeds, extending to their full length, straining toward the knife handle. Too far. She withdrew, assessing options, then tore a strip from the bottom of her shift. One end she pushed through the bars, the other she held tightly. With careful manipulation, she looped the cloth around the knife handle and slowly, painstakingly drew it toward her.

The knife came free with a soft scrape of metal against leather. The guard stirred, mumbled something unintelligible, then resumed her rhythmic snoring.

Weapon in hand, Mare returned to the tunnel entrance. She took one last look around the cell, at the ropes that had bound her, at the brand still weeping on her arm, at the gruel congealing in its bowl on the floor. Each a reminder of Agnes's betrayal, of The Order's hypocrisy, of promises broken before they were made.

She lowered herself into the darkness of the tunnel, her body remembering its dimensions from years of mapping Southwark's hidden veins. As she pulled the stone back into place above her, sealing herself into the fetid darkness, a grim satisfaction settled in her chest.

Let them discover her gone. Let them search. Let Agnes feel the sting of loss that Mare had carried her entire life.

Mare Fleet belonged to only herself now, not the Bishop's Shadow, not The Order's convert, not a mother's reclaimed daughter. Just Mare, armed with a stolen knife and a lifetime of survival instincts, slipping into the darkness that had always been her true home.

The tunnel closed around Mare like a throat, its ancient brick walls slick with slime that glowed faintly green in the darkness. She moved by touch and memory, one hand trailing along the wall, the other clutching the stolen knife. Her feet found purchase on the uneven floor with the surety of someone who had traversed these passages before, though each step sent fresh pain lancing through her body, ribs bruised from the Order's handling, brand throbbing on her forearm, dislocated thumb a dull ache beneath the sharper pains.

Blood seeped through the makeshift bandage she'd torn from her shift, wrapping it around the brand in a futile attempt to soothe the burning. The Order's mark, Agnes's mark, her mother's mark, was meant to be permanent, a claim of ownership no different from the Bishop's seal carved into her palm years before. Another person declaring possession of her flesh, her loyalty, her very existence.

"Fuck both of them," Mare muttered, her voice swallowed by the pressing darkness.

She recognized this section of tunnel, an older Roman construction that had been repurposed centuries later to channel rainwater away from the cathedral. Seven years ago, she'd mapped it for the Bishop, noting the curious joins where ancient stonework met medieval brick, measuring the distance between access points, marking where the ceiling had begun to sag dangerously low. Her fingertips found familiar cracks in the mortar, confirmed locations that existed in her mind as precisely as if she were reading a parchment chart.

The passage narrowed abruptly, forcing Mare to turn sideways, her shoulder blades scraping against damp stone as she inched forward. Her lungs burned with each breath of the stagnant air a noxious blend of rot, human waste, and the ever-present fungal stench that thrived in perpetual darkness.

Three hundred paces from her cell, the floor dipped sharply. Chilly water lapped at her ankles, then rose quickly to her knees as the tunnel's grade steepened. The Thames was high tonight, backing up into Southwark's sewer system, turning what should have been merely damp passages into treacherous, half-submerged labyrinths.

Mare pushed forward, each step a deliberate calculation. The water, foul with shit and rubbish washed down from Southwark's streets, soaked her shift, the sodden fabric clinging to her legs like grasping hands. Something brushed her calf beneath the surface, a rat or something worse.

Behind her, faint but unmistakable, came the sounds of pursuit. A shout echoed through the tunnels, followed by the scrape of boots on stone, the splashing of multiple bodies entering the water. The Order had discovered her absence sooner than expected. Someone must have checked her cell, the sleeping guard roused or replaced.

"Find her!" a woman's voice commanded, the words distorted by the tunnel's acoustics but still recognizable as Agnes. "She can't have gone far."

Another voice, lower, urgent: "Release the hounds!"

The baying began moments later, the sound bouncing off stone walls, seeming to come from everywhere at once. The Order kept mastiffs trained to track through Southwark's foulest corners. Mare had seen them tear a man's throat out during a raid on a Puritan meeting house, had watched their powerful jaws lock onto limbs with the terrible certainty of death.

She quickened her pace, ignoring the protests of abused muscles. The passage widened slightly, allowing faster movement, but the water deepened to mid-thigh. Something sharp scraped her leg beneath the surface, broken pottery, or discarded metal, adding fresh blood to the filth swirling around her.

Fifty paces ahead, the tunnel forked. Mare hesitated, calculating. Left led toward the cathedral, where Order members would be stationed. Right angled toward the river, a longer route but less likely to be guarded. She veered right, ducking beneath a low-hanging section of ceiling where ancient bricks had shifted, creating a gap barely wide enough for a human head.

As she straightened on the other side, her foot struck something that shifted beneath her weight a trigger stone. Mare froze, recognition flashing through her mind a moment too late. A mechanism grated somewhere in the walls, the sound of rusted metal protesting after decades of disuse.

She lunged forward as a section of ceiling collapsed behind her, brick and mortar splashing into the foul water, blocking the passage she'd just traversed. Dust filled the air, choking her, coating her wet skin with gritty film.

The tunnel fall would slow her pursuers, but not for long. They knew these passages too, had set the trap themselves for unwanted visitors.

Mare pressed on, the water gradually receding as the tunnel sloped upward again. When she reached a dry section, she paused, leaning against the wall, allowing herself ten heartbeats of rest.

In the dim phosphorescence of the tunnel's fungal growth, she examined the brand on her forearm. The Order's mark glared back at her, raised and angry against her pale skin. Not just a symbol of ownership, a declaration of judgment. Apostates received this mark before their final penance. Agnes had not merely imprisoned her; she had marked her for cleansing.

The memory of Agnes's face, so like her own yet hardened by years Mare couldn't fathom flashed behind her eyes. The mother who had watched from shadows for twenty-eight years, who had claimed to protect while preparing to possess. Who had offered choice with one hand while holding iron-hot betrayal in the other.

The baying of hounds grew louder, jolting Mare from her bitter reverie. They had found a way around the collapse. She pushed off from the wall, ignoring the screaming protest of exhausted muscles, the dizziness that threatened to topple her into the filth at her feet.

The tunnel narrowed again, then jogged sharply left. Mare followed its twisting path with the surety of long practice, though each step now came harder than the last. Her lungs struggled to extract oxygen from the fetid air, her wounded arm throbbed in time with her racing heart, and somewhere behind, the dogs bayed with the excited fever of predators who have caught their prey's scent.

She rounded another bend and stopped abruptly. Twenty paces ahead, two figures stood with torches raised, women in the plain dark clothing of Order scouts, their faces illuminated in the wavering flame. They had approached from the opposite direction, sent to cut off her escape route while the main force pursued from behind.

"There!" the taller one shouted, raising her torch higher. "It's her! The Bishop's whore!"

They drew knives from their belts, advancing with the confidence of those who believe they have cornered wounded prey. Mare didn't give them time to close the distance. She charged forward, water splashing around her calves, stolen knife gripped in her right hand.

The scouts hesitated, surprised by the direct attack, a fatal mistake. Mare feinted left, then slashed right, opening the first woman's thigh from hip to knee with a single stroke. The blade sliced through wool and flesh with equal ease, drawing a scream that echoed through the tunnel like a struck bell. Blood fountained into the filthy water as the woman collapsed.

The second scout lunged forward, torch thrust ahead like a weapon. Mare ducked beneath the swinging flame, her shoulder driving into the woman's midsection with enough force to expel the air from her lungs in a strangled gasp. They staggered together, locked in a desperate clinch, until Mare's boot found the edge of a collapsed section of floor. With a final surge of strength, she shoved the scout backward, sending her tumbling into the gap with a startled cry that ended abruptly as stones shifted, settling over the woman's lower body with a sickening crunch.

"Surprise, you fucking Order rats," Mare muttered, stepping past the fallen scout.

She didn't look back at the women she'd left broken in her wake. Sentiment was a luxury she couldn't afford, not with the hounds drawing closer, their excited baying telling her they had found fresh blood to follow.

The tunnel ahead sloped sharply downward, the floor giving way to crude steps carved into stone. Mare descended into deeper darkness, toward the muffled roar that could only be the Thames, swollen with rains and flowing swift enough to carry her beyond Agnes's reach, if she could survive its treacherous embrace.

The hatch loomed above her, a rusted circle of iron set into the tunnel's ceiling that separated her from freedom and death in almost equal measure. Mare's hands shook as she reached up to test its weight, her fingers finding the ancient release mechanism, a simple lever worn smooth by centuries of smugglers' touch. The rushing sound beyond told her all she needed to know: the Thames waited just above, swift, and hungry with spring rains, eager to swallow anything that fell into its churning maw. Including her if the current proved stronger than her already taxed body.

Behind her, the baying of hounds grew closer, their frenzied chorus punctuated by shouts as the Order closed in. No time for hesitation, no space for fear. Mare gripped the lever and pulled with what strength remained in her trembling arms.

The mechanism resisted, then surrendered with a screech of protesting metal. The hatch swung open, revealing a square of night sky framed by the stone embankment of the Thames. River wind gusted through the opening, carrying the stink of London's great artery.

Mare pulled herself up and through, emerging onto a narrow ledge of stone barely wider than her shoulders. The river churned below, its black surface broken by white-capped waves that reflected the scattered lights of the city. The gap between her perch and the water stretched five feet, a dizzying drop into darkness.

She hesitated for one heartbeat, her childhood terror of drowning rising like bile in her throat. Twenty years ago, she'd nearly died in these waters, pushed from a dock by older boys who thought it sport to watch a skinny girl struggle. She remembered the blind panic, the burn in her lungs, the certainty of death as the current had dragged her under.

The memory paralyzed her for a crucial moment, long enough to hear boots splashing through water in the tunnel below, to feel the vibration of approaching bodies through the stone beneath her feet.

No choice. No time.

Mare stepped off the ledge and plummeted toward the waiting river.

The cold hit first, a violent shock that stole her breath and contracted every muscle in her body. Then the disorientation as dark water closed over her head, swirling her in three directions at once, stripping away any sense of up or down. Instinct opened her eyes to blackness, her lungs burning with the need to breathe while her mind screamed to keep her mouth shut against the filthy water.

She fought the panic, forcing her limbs to move in the powerful strokes Cord had taught her years later, after she'd survived that first drowning. Kick. Pull. Angle the body. Use the current rather than fight it directly.

Mare broke the surface with a desperate gasp, her lungs filling with sweet, fetid air. The current had already carried her thirty feet downstream, past the sewage outlet, toward the tangle of docks and piers that crowded the river's edge. Above, the sky stretched black and vast, pricked with stars that seemed impossibly distant from the churning chaos of the water.

A shout from the embankment, figures silhouetted against the night sky, pointing toward her bobbing form. The Order, already spreading out along the shore, preparing to follow her downstream.

Mare ducked beneath the surface again, swimming with the current but angling toward the opposite bank, away from Southwark and the Bishop's territory. Her lungs burned, muscles screaming with the effort of fighting the river's pull. The wound on her arm trailed ribbons of blood that dispersed into the darkness like smoke.

When she surfaced again, she had been pulled by the current beyond the safety of the bank. The north bank loomed ahead, its jumbled buildings cutting jagged shapes against the night sky. She swam with renewed purpose, her movements more efficient now as her body remembered its training despite the exhaustion weighing down every limb. The cold had numbed the worst of her pain, transformed the burning in her branded arm to a distant ache. But that same cold was stealing her strength, leaching heat from her core with each passing moment in the frigid water.

Something bumped against her legs, debris carried by the current, or something that had once lived and breathed before the river claimed it. Mare kicked harder, pushing the thought away along with whatever had touched her.

The memory of her childhood drowning surged back, the helpless flailing, water filling her nose and mouth, the strange peace that had come with surrender just before rough hands had dragged her back to life. A riverman had pulled her from the Thames that day, had pounded her back until she'd vomited river water and drawn ragged breath. She'd never learned his name, had run as soon as she could stand, afraid he'd want payment she couldn't give. No one would save her tonight. No rough hands waited to pull her from the current if her strength failed.

The thought stiffened her resolve. Three more powerful strokes brought her within reach of the starling, one of many pillars supporting London's only bridge between its North and South Banks. She had to make it, a desperate lunge to the stone footing or be swept beyond it and downstream to a certain death. Nobody could swim its width, the currents too strong, the water so filthy. Her feet scraped the bottom of the plinth, finding purchase on slick stones and her fingernails dug into its coarse facade, as if scratching her epitaph into its skin. Mare dragged herself from the Thames's grasp, crawling up the incline on hands and knees, her sodden clothes weighing her down like mail.

She collapsed onto her back, staring up at the huge bridge, its' one hundred buildings bundled across to its base, overbearing and dangerously set. Her chest heaved with the effort of drawing air into abused lungs. For ten precious heartbeats, she allowed herself to simply exist, to feel the solid stone beneath her, to breathe without fighting for each inhale.

Then reality intruded, the frigid wind against her wet skin, the distant shouts from the south bank as Order members searched for signs of her emergence, the knowledge that she had minutes, not hours, before they would be on to the bridge from the south side in pursuit.

Mare forced herself to her feet, fingers fumbling with the sodden garments that clung to her shivering frame. First came the nun's hood she'd taken from the Order cell, a grey scrap of wool that had once been part of a habit, now reduced to a disguise that hadn't served its purpose. She tore it from her head and dropped it into the muddy water, watching as the river's edge lapped at the fabric, drawing it back into the current.

Next, she unwound the sash she'd worn for years as the Bishop's secret-keeper, a length of fine dark cloth embroidered with symbols only his inner circle would recognize. It had marked her as untouchable within Southwark, had opened doors and loosened tongues with its mere presence. Now it represented just another chain, another claim on her identity she could no longer afford.

The sash joined the hood in the mud, two pieces of a past self-abandoned to the river's hunger. Stripped to the simple shift, Mare moved with purpose up the rotting planks that supported the great beast that straddled the Thames. She emerged at Nonsuch House, the largest of the parasitic buildings that leeched off their host, so called because there were none other such like it on the crossing. She ran across to the North, side stepping the crowded street amid bumps without permission or apology.

She skipped down the far side steps on the bankside, down to the muddy banks, where mudlarks would sift through its gunk, and back under a pier that stood lonely and forgotten. She ducked beneath its sagging boards, feeling along the underside of the structure until her fingers found what they sought, a small leather satchel, sealed with wax and tied securely to a crossbeam just above the water's highest reach.

The cache had been one of her insurances for over a year, supplies hidden throughout London in case she ever needed to disappear completely. This one contained the basics: a man's simple shirt and breeches, a hooded cloak, a small knife in a leather sheath, flint and steel, a purse containing enough silver to survive for a week, and a folded parchment bearing a crude map of safe routes out of the city.

Mare changed quickly, ignoring the discomfort of pulling dry clothes over wet skin. The men's garments hung loose on her frame but would draw less attention than a woman's dress in the places she needed to go. She bound her hair back with a strip of leather, tucking the wet strands beneath the hood of the cloak.

Before leaving the shelter of the pier, she paused at the river's edge, drawn by her own reflection in a puddle formed by the receding tide. The face that stared back was barely recognisable, hollowed by exhaustion and pain, streaked with mud and blood, eyes dark with a fury that seemed to burn from within. The Order's brand stood out livid against the pale skin of her forearm, its lines precise and deliberate. Mare touched the mark gently, tracing its outline with one finger. Not so different from the Bishop's seal carved into her palm years before, both marks of ownership, both attempts to name her, claim her, define her.

"Not anymore," she whispered to her reflection, to the river, to the ghosts of her past selves.

She straightened, shouldering the leather satchel. Across the water, torches moved along Southwark's embankment, the Order still searching for any sign of her. Behind them, the glow of fires still burning from the Bishop's purge painted the night sky orange. Two powers that had each tried to possess her, now set against each other in a battle that would consume Southwark if she played her cards right.

Mare turned away from the river and slipped into the warren of streets beyond the embankment, disappearing into London's darkness like a knife into its sheath, purposeful, dangerous, and answerable only to the hand that wielded it.

The abandoned boathouse reeked of dead fish and rotting timber, its sloped roof missing enough shingles to map the constellations through the gaps. Mare claimed a corner where the floor remained sound, sweeping aside fish bones and ancient netting with the edge of her boot. She emptied her satchel onto a splintered table that listed drunkenly on three legs, the fourth having long since surrendered to wood rot or been repurposed as a weapon in some forgotten dockside brawl. The items scattered across the warped surface represented the total of her resources, and the foundation of Southwark's coming conflagration.

Three sheets of parchment, stolen months ago from the Bishop's own study. A small pot of ink, its contents thick but still usable. Two quills, one fresh, one worn to a nub. Sealing wax in deep crimson, the colour of arterial blood. And most precious of all, a small silver seal, a replica of the Bishop's own mark, like the one she'd kept this past month, crafted by a forger who'd disappeared the day after completing the commission. Mare had ensured his silence with coin rather than violence; the man's skills were too valuable to waste.

She arranged the materials with methodical precision, aligning the parchments perfectly, testing the quill's point against her thumb. The wooden table wobbled with each movement, but she adjusted her posture to compensate, her body remembering the countless hours spent at the Bishop's side, recording his thoughts and orders in neat, practiced script.

Mare began with the message for the Bishop himself, the most straightforward of the three deceptions she would craft tonight. On the first parchment, she sketched a crude map of Southwark, marking specific locations with small crosses. Then, in a hand deliberately different from her own customary script, she detailed battle plans for an Order attack on the Bishop's remaining properties.

"The Bishop's man in the brewery district has been compromised," she wrote, the quill scratching softly against parchment. "Sister Agnes believes his records contain evidence of the Spanish correspondence. The attack must proceed before dawn on the third day. The Puritan zealots will provide distraction at the cathedral while our forces secure the documents from his private chambers."

She added details only the Bishop and his inner circle would recognize, references to secret meetings, to transactions recorded in ledgers kept locked in his personal strongbox, to communications with agents across the Channel that could implicate him in treasonous activity if discovered. Each word calculated to stoke the rising paranoia that had driven him to order Southwark's purge.

The second parchment required a different approach. For the Puritans, she created a blood-spattered pamphlet—using a drop of her own blood from the still-weeping brand wound, smeared artfully across the top corner to suggest a document rescued from violence.

"BROTHERS IN CHRIST," she wrote in the blocky capitals favoured by Puritan pamphleteers, "THE WHORE OF BABYLON SITS NOT IN ROME BUT IN SOUTHWARK, WHERE BISHOP WICKHAM HAS PLEDGED THE SOULS OF ENGLISHMEN TO PAPIST MASTERS."

She continued in the same vein, mimicking the breathless outrage of Puritan rhetoric, detailing a fictional arrangement between the Bishop and Catholic forces, secret masses conducted in the cathedral's crypt, payments to Rome disguised as charitable donations, plans to undermine the Queen's Protestant reforms from within. The claims were outrageous but contained just enough truth to be plausible to those already inclined to believe the worst of the Bishop.

"THE WINCHESTER GEESE WERE SACRIFICED NOT TO CLEANSE SIN BUT TO SILENCE WITNESSES," she concluded. "THE FLAMES THAT PURIFIED SOUTHWARK CONCEALED THE GREATER ABOMINATION OF POPISH CONSPIRACY."

For the Order's message, Mare switched to a cipher she knew Agnes used for communication among her lieutenants. She had memorized it during their brief collaboration, noting the pattern of substitutions with the same careful attention she'd given to the Bishop's codes years before.

In this encrypted text, she outlined an alliance between the Bishop and Stubbs, the Puritan leader, a pact to eliminate the Order completely, dividing its assets between church and zealots once Agnes and her women were destroyed. She included specific details about Order safe houses that only an insider could know, suggesting the Bishop had infiltrated their ranks at the highest levels.

"Trust no one," she wrote in plain text at the bottom, knowing these words would echo Agnes's own frequent warning to her followers. "The Bishop's Shadow has revealed all our secrets to our enemies."

Mare sat back, studying the three documents laid side by side on the wobbling table. Each contained enough truth to be believable, enough falsehood to be deadly. Each played upon existing suspicions, deepening cracks already present in the uneasy balance of power that had governed Southwark for years.

She reached for the sealing wax, holding a stub of candle beneath until red drops fell like blood onto the folded parchments. While the wax remained soft, she pressed the Bishop's seal into each, but with a crucial modification. Using the tip of her knife, she added a small notch to the edge of each impression, a mark so subtle it would be missed by casual inspection but instantly recognizable to her if the documents ever found their way back to her hands.

When the wax had cooled, Mare gathered the messages and moved to the boathouse door. The fog had thickened while she worked, transforming London's familiar skyline into looming shadows punctuated by the occasional glow of torchlight. Perfect conditions for her purposes, visibility limited enough to conceal movement, but not so poor as to prevent her messengers from finding their targets.

She let out a low whistle, a pattern of notes that carried just far enough through the fog to reach its intended recipients.

They materialized from the mist like spectres, three children with the hollow-cheeked look of London's forgotten offspring. The oldest, a boy of twelve with a scar bisecting his upper lip, approached first. The others, a girl with hair cropped close to her skull and a smaller boy who moved with the wariness of a feral cat, hung back, eyes darting between Mare and the potential escape routes with practiced calculation.

"Job?" the oldest asked, his voice cracking between childhood and whatever came after for those who grew up on London's streets.

Mare held up the sealed messages but didn't immediately hand them over. "Three destinations. Three silver pieces. Each delivered directly to the intended recipient, no one else."

The children exchanged glances, a silent negotiation passing between them in the language of those who survived by mutual reliance.

"Five silver each," the girl countered, her voice surprisingly deep for her slight frame. "Bishop's men are stopping everyone crossing the bridges since the fires."

Mare's mouth twitched in what might have been appreciation. "Four silver, and an extra for each of you if the messages are delivered before dawn."

Another wordless exchange, then the oldest boy nodded. "Names?"

Mare handed him the first message. "The Bishop's private secretary. He'll be in the Clink, not the cathedral. Tell the guards you have information about the fires." She turned to the girl, passing over the second parchment. "For Stubbs himself. You'll find him at the printer's shop on Bell Lane. Say you were sent by a friend of Master Marlowe."

The smallest boy stepped forward, hand extended for the final message. Mare studied him for a moment, the calculation behind his eyes, the tension in his thin shoulders, the way he balanced on the balls of his feet, ready to flee or fight as circumstances demanded. A survivor, like herself.

"This goes to Sister Agnes," she told him, placing the Order's message in his dirt-streaked palm. "She'll be at St. Clement's, or the old tannery if St. Clement's has been compromised. Tell whoever challenges you that you have word from Marion Fleet."

The boy nodded once, tucking the message into some hidden pocket in his ragged clothing. Mare counted out twelve silver coins, distributing them equally among the children.

"The rest when you return here after delivery," she said. "I'll know if you've failed."

It wasn't entirely a bluff. The messages themselves contained certain phrases, certain details that would prompt specific reactions if delivered properly. By morning, those reactions would ripple through Southwark in ways visible even from across the river.

The children pocketed the coins and melted back into the fog without another word, each heading in a different direction like arrows loosed from a single bow. Mare watched them go, calculating probabilities, alternative scenarios, potential complications. Contingency had been her watchword under the Bishop's tutelage; she'd learned to anticipate failure points and plan accordingly.

But tonight's plan required no backup, no safety net. The messages would reach their destinations, or they wouldn't. The recipients would believe the deceptions, or they wouldn't. Either way, the result would be chaos, the Bishop, the Puritans, and the Order each convinced of betrayal by the others, each acting to protect themselves against imagined conspiracies that would quickly become real in the crucible of suspicion and fear.

Mare gathered her remaining supplies, wiping the table clean of ink and wax drippings. She swept the fish bones back over the spot where she'd worked, erasing evidence of her presence through the simple application of existing filth. Then she shouldered her depleted satchel and stepped out into London's fog-choked night.

For a moment, she paused on the edge of the dock, looking back toward Southwark. Through the mist, she could still make out the orange glow of fires not yet extinguished, could imagine the Bishop in his chambers, Agnes in her sanctuary, Stubbs among his zealots, all believing themselves righteous, all certain of their authority, all destined to tear each other apart in the coming days.

Let them burn each other to the ground. Let them destroy what they'd each tried to claim. Let them feel, just for a moment, what it was to be powerless in a world where others decided your fate.

Mare turned away from the view and disappeared into London's labyrinthine alleys, another shadow among many in a city built on secrets and blood. Behind her, the three children carried her vengeance into the night, unwitting agents of a war none of the recipients would see coming until the first blades were drawn.

By dawn, Southwark would be at war with itself. And Mare Fleet would be gone, carrying nothing but the scars that marked where others had tried, and failed to own her.

Chapter Fifteen

Southwark's Reckoning

Southwark split open like a rotten fruit, spilling its interiors onto cobblestones still slick with morning dew. Dawn had barely broken when the first Puritan torches appeared at the district's edge, a wavering line of flame advancing through fog thick enough to choke on. John Stubbs led them, Bible clutched in one hand, burning brand in the other, his gaunt face illuminated from below like a carnival devil's mask. Behind him surged his followers, shopkeepers and labourers transformed by religious fervour into instruments of divine wrath, their ordinary tools repurposed as weapons for God's cleansing fire.

"Behold Sodom!" Stubbs bellowed, his voice cracking with the strain of righteous hatred. "Behold the whores of Babylon who corrupt the souls of godly men!" Spittle flew from his lips as he jabbed his torch toward the brothels that lined the street ahead. "The Lord commands us to cleanse this filth with flame!"

His followers took up the cry, their voices merging into a psalm that sounded more like a war chant as they advanced through the morning mist. They carried makeshift weapons, hammers still crusted with nails, butcher knives tied to broomsticks, clubs studded with metal fragments. Their faces glowed with the righteous madness of those convinced God's hand guided their violence.

Half a mile away, moving like liquid shadow through the narrower streets, came a different force. The Order of St. Ursula operatives slipped between buildings with the practiced silence of those accustomed to moving unseen. Their dark cloaks concealed both their identities and the weapons they carried, garrots fashioned from wire and wooden handles, slim blades designed for the spaces between ribs, iron bars wrapped in leather to muffle the sound of impact against bone.

They converged on the Bishop's properties with methodical precision, each team targeting a specific location according to plans memorized days before. Three women scaled the wall behind the Bishop's counting house while two more disabled the guards at the wine cellar entrance, their movements quick and economical, leaving no witnesses to sound alarms. Others positioned themselves at key junctions, prepared to intercept messengers or reinforcements.

In the cramped street between these advancing forces, a third group moved with similar purpose but rougher execution. The Winchester Geese, those whores and tavern women Mare had cultivated as her own network, had abandoned their usual haunts for this one desperate morning. They wore simple clothes, their faces partly concealed by hoods or scarves, nothing to mark them as the Bishop's former property except the hard knowledge in their eyes and the scars that remained hidden beneath their garments.

The collision came at the crossroads where Fish Street met the alley leading to The Golden Horn brothel. Stubbs' zealots rounded the corner just as an Order team emerged from a side passage. For one suspended moment, they stared at each other across twenty feet of cobblestones, Puritans with their torches held high, Order women with knives half-drawn from concealed sheaths.

"Papist witches!" shouted a barrel-chested man at Stubbs' right hand, raising a blacksmith's hammer. "They've come to protect their whorehouse!"

The Order women didn't waste breath on words. They scattered into practiced formations, three moving to engage while two melted into the shadows, circling to attack from behind. Steel flashed in the torchlight as the first Puritan charged forward, his hammer swinging in a wide arc that found only empty air as his target stepped inside his reach. Her blade found the soft underside of his jaw with practiced precision, opening his throat in a single motion that sent blood fountaining across the cobblestones.

Chaos erupted as the groups collided, their mutual hatred ignited by Mare's carefully planted lies. Puritan zealots swung their improvised weapons with more fervour than skill, while Order women moved with the deadly efficiency of those trained to kill quickly and disappear. Bodies fell on both sides, blood darkening the stones beneath their feet.

In an upper window overlooking the melee, a curtain twitched aside. Bess Quickly, her face still bruised from her time in the Clink, her eyes hard as river stones, surveyed the battle with cold satisfaction. When a young prostitute fled past the building, pursued by two Puritans with burning brands, Bess slipped down the back stairs and out a side door.

The girl stumbled at the corner, her bare feet sliding on the slick cobblestones. She fell hard, crying out as her pursuers closed the distance, their faces twisted with the cruelty of men who enjoyed female fear. One reached down, grabbing her by the hair, yanking her head back to expose her throat.

"Let's send this whore to meet her master below," he sneered, raising his torch.

Something flashed in the morning light, a small knife sliding from Bess's sleeve into the trapped girl's hand. The prostitute drove it upward without hesitation, finding the soft flesh between the zealot's legs with unerring accuracy. His scream cut through the general chaos as he collapsed, clutching himself, his torch rolling away.

"Run, girl," Bess urged, pulling her toward a narrow passage between buildings. "Three streets east, basement door with a red mark. Tell them Bess sent you."

The girl fled without looking back, the borrowed knife still clutched in her bloodied hand.

Across the district, another Geese operative with a face mapped by old burn scars pressed close to an Order lieutenant in the confusion of a three-way skirmish between Puritans, Order women, and the Bishop's guards.

"Sister Agnes says the Bishop's men have taken the tannery," she whispered, her lips barely moving. "They knew the tunnel entrance. You're to redirect to St. Clement's immediately."

The Order woman's eyes widened in momentary shock before narrowing with renewed purpose. She nodded once, then slipped away to spread the false information to her companions. Within minutes, the Order forces began a strategic withdrawal from their original targets, regrouping to defend a sanctuary that faced no actual threat—#, exactly as Mare had planned.

From her perch atop a disused bell tower, Mare watched the pieces move across Southwark's board. Her face remained impassive despite the throbbing pain from the Order's brand on her forearm, still raw and weeping beneath a crude bandage. She'd removed her hood, letting the morning breeze cool her fever-hot skin as she tracked the movement of forces through the district's twisting streets.

The Puritans had already set fire to two brothels, the flames licking up wooden walls with hungry enthusiasm despite the damp morning air. The Order had successfully penetrated two of the Bishop's strongholds before Mare's false intelligence had drawn them away. And the Bishop's men, responding to the threat, had abandoned several key positions, creating vulnerabilities Mare intended to exploit in the next phase of her plan.

It was working. Three factions tearing at each other's throats, each convinced the others had betrayed some unspoken covenant. Each believing they fought from righteous necessity rather than manipulated paranoia.

Mare's fingers traced the brand on her arm, the Order's mark that Agnes had seared into her flesh. Beside it, the older scar on her palm where the Bishop had marked her as his property years before. Two claims of ownership, two attempts to define her existence through pain and obligation. Both, weaponised against their makers.

She descended the tower's rotting steps with careful movements, her body still aching from her escape and swim in the Thames, her mind focused entirely on the next phase of her plan. The chaos in the streets would provide perfect cover for her approach to the Bishop's inner sanctum. While Wickham's attention remained fixed on the external threats to his domain, she would slip inside through passages only she and the Bishop himself knew existed.

Mare pulled her hood back into place as she reached street level. Three Geese waited in the shadow of the tower, their faces grim but determined. Without words, she gestured toward the cathedral, then made a series of quick hand signals they acknowledged with short nods. They would create the diversion she needed, drawing the remaining guards away from the western approach to the Bishop's chambers.

As she moved through Southwark's burning streets, Mare felt a strange detachment from the destruction surrounding her. This district had been her prison and her kingdom, the maze she'd learned to navigate before she could properly read, the cesspit where she'd been discarded and the fertile ground where she'd grown strong. Now she walked its cobblestones for what might be the final time, watching it convulse in the death throes she'd orchestrated.

Ahead, the Bishop's residence rose from the chaos like a fortress, its stone walls and iron-bound gates standing firm while Southwark burned around it. Behind those walls, Richard Wickham would be watching, calculating, preparing to crush whatever forces threatened his domain. He wouldn't expect the true threat to come from within, from the shadow he himself had shaped and honed.

Mare smiled, a cold baring of teeth that held no mirth. The time had come to show the Bishop exactly what his finest creation had become.

The statue of Saint Peter guarded the cathedral's western alcove, his stone face worn smooth by centuries of supplicants' touch. Mare pressed her fingers to the exact spot where the saint's sandaled foot met its pedestal, feeling the hidden mechanism give way with a soft click that resonated through the hollow space behind. The section of wall pivoted inward on silent hinges, a testament to the craftsmanship of those who had built the Bishop's secrets into Southwark's bones generations before either Mare or Wickham had drawn breath.

Mare slipped through the narrow opening, closing the passage behind her with practiced care. Darkness enveloped her, absolute and familiar. She didn't need light to navigate these hidden veins of the Bishop's domain; she had mapped them in her mind years ago, when Wickham had first shown them to her, his prized Shadow, the only one he trusted with knowledge that could destroy him.

"Remember these passages well," he'd told her then, his hand heavy on her shoulder as they'd stooped through the low tunnel. "They've saved the lives of three Bishops before me."

Now they would help end the fourth.

Mare moved forward, her fingers trailing along the damp stone wall, counting intersections by touch. The air hung thick with the must of enclosed spaces where nothing grew but secrets and resentment. Water dripped somewhere ahead, each splash marking time like a dying man's heartbeat. Rats scurried in the darkness, their claws scratching against stone, fellow travellers in Southwark's underbelly, survivors by any means necessary.

The passage narrowed, forcing Mare to turn sideways where ancient foundations intersected with more recent construction. Her wounded arm scraped against rough stone, sending fresh pain lancing through the branded flesh. She welcomed it, let it fuel the cold purpose that had carried her this far.

Three turns later, the passage began to slope upward. Mare paused at a junction where a rusted iron grating set into the floor would have dropped an unwary intruder twenty feet onto waiting spikes, the first of the Bishop's security measures. She stepped carefully over it, remembering Wickham's smile as he'd shown her the skeletons of previous trespassers still impaled below.

The second trap came fifty paces further, a tripwire that would have released a shower of poisoned darts from the ceiling. Mare ducked beneath it, her movements economical and precise despite exhaustion that made her limbs feel leaden.

Ahead, voices echoed through the stone, guards stationed outside the Bishop's private chambers, their conversation drifting through hidden vents designed to carry sound to ears that needed to hear.

"...never seen him like this," one said, his voice tight with tension. "Pacing like a caged beast, breaking things."

"You'd pace too if half your properties were burning," his companion replied. "My cousin says the Puritans have already taken the north brewery district, and those Order bitches hit three guard posts at once."

"It's that Fleet woman behind it. Must be. The Bishop's been raving about her since yesterday."

Their voices faded as Mare passed the vent, continuing toward the final approach to Wickham's sanctuary. The passage ended at a blank wall that appeared solid but concealed the most ingenious aspect of the Bishop's security system, a false panel set into the ornate woodwork of his private chambers, disguised as part of an elaborate carved depiction of Christ's crucifixion.

Mare pressed her ear against the wood, listening for movement within. Nothing but the distant sounds of chaos from outside, shouts, the crash of breaking glass, the muffled roar of growing fires. The Bishop was alone, then. Perfect.

She found the release mechanism by touch, a specific knot in the wood that, when pressed just so, disengaged the locks holding the panel in place. It slid aside with barely a whisper, revealing a gap just wide enough for Mare to slide through sideways.

The Bishop's chamber assaulted her senses after the tunnel's damp simplicity. Rich velvet draperies in deep crimson hung from ceiling to floor, blocking the windows and muffling sound. Gilded icons and crucifixes dotted the walls, interspersed with paintings of saints in various stages of martyrdom. Thick Venetian carpets covered the floor, their intricate patterns visible even in the dim light provided by a dozen beeswax candles in silver holders.

The massive oak desk dominated the centre of the room, its surface covered with maps of Southwark, reports from Walsingham's men, letters bearing the seals of noble houses and royal ministers. Several had been torn apart, ink spilled across their remains like blood from opened veins.

And before the largest window, a tall figure stood with his back to the room, hands clasped behind him, shoulders rigid beneath rich ecclesiastical robes. Bishop Richard Wickham stared out at his burning domain through a gap in the curtains, his silver hair catching the orange glow of distant fires.

"I wondered when you'd arrive," he said without turning, his voice steady despite the destruction evident on his desk. "Though I expect you've come with a blade."

Mare eased fully into the room, letting the panel slide shut behind her. She moved laterally, maintaining distance between them, her eyes never leaving his back as she circled toward the opposite side of the desk.

"Blades are crude," she replied, her voice calm despite the hatred burning beneath her breastbone. "I prefer to watch you destroy yourself."

Wickham turned then, his handsome face composed in the mask of authority he wore like a second skin. Only his eyes revealed the rage beneath, blue ice over bottomless depths, pupils contracted to pinpricks.

"You think yourself clever," he said, moving to the desk but remaining standing, his fingers splayed across the scattered papers. "Setting my dogs against each other while you slip away in the confusion."

Mare kept circling, putting the massive desk between them. "Not just your dogs," she corrected. "Your enemies as well. The Puritans believe you've been conducting secret masses in the church crypt. Something about payments to Rome disguised as charitable donations."

A muscle twitched in Wickham's jaw, the bare tell, but one Mare knew well. She'd spent years learning to read the micro expressions that preceded his rages.

"Stubbs has always been a fool," he dismissed, though his fingers curled into the papers beneath them. "His zealots will be dealt with once this rebellion is crushed."

"Hard to crush a rebellion when your own forces are divided," Mare observed, trailing her fingers along a bookshelf as she continued her circuit of the room. "The Order seems convinced you've allied with the Puritans to eliminate them. They're fortifying positions you never threatened, abandoning targets you left exposed."

Wickham's composure slipped further, a flush creeping up his neck. "Agnes always was too clever by half," he growled. "A trait she passed to her unfortunate daughter."

The casual cruelty of the statement struck Mare like a physical blow, but she kept her face impassive, refusing to give him the satisfaction of a reaction. "She also believed you had infiltrated her ranks," she continued, voice steady. "That someone had revealed all her secrets to her enemies."

"And had I managed that, she would already be dead," Wickham snapped, his control fraying visibly now. "Instead, she slips through my men's fingers like smoke while her women bleed my guard posts dry."

"A shame about your guard posts," Mare said, allowing herself the ghost of a smile. "Particularly those at the north and east gates. So unfortunate that they received orders to redeploy to the church just before the attacks began."

Wickham went still, the kind of stillness that preceded his most violent outbursts. "What have you done?"

"I simply ensured your men would be in the wrong places," Mare replied, picking up a small silver crucifix from a side table, examining it with false interest. "It wasn't difficult. Your seal is remarkably easy to reproduce if one has studied it closely enough. And your guards are trained to obey written orders without question."

The Bishop's hands curled into fists against the desk, knuckles whitening with strain. Papers crumpled beneath his grip, ink smearing across expensive parchment. "You forged my orders," he said, voice dropping to a dangerous whisper. "You deliberately exposed my properties."

Mare replaced the crucifix, her movements unhurried despite the tension crackling between them. "Just as I told the Puritans which brothels held your most valuable ledgers. Just as I informed the Order which of your men could be turned against you with the right pressure." She met his gaze directly for the first time. "Your pieces are all moving exactly as I positioned them."

"You treacherous girl," Wickham snarled, his composure shattering completely. He swept an arm across the desk, sending maps and documents flying, a crystal inkwell smashing against the wall in a spray of black that resembled arterial blood. "I raised you from nothing! I made you what you are. I…I made you. You are my flesh and blood!"

Mare jolted back, the words piercing her composure, her eyes widened, maddening.

“My mother is Sister Agnes” she exclaimed, with some doubt in her tone.

“Yes, and I am your father, Marion.” The Bishop spoke in hushed tones, but ready to explode.

“But my Mother, told me not one day ago of Father Leech, kind and loving.”

“Father Thomas Leech? It could never be Father Thomas Leech, your mother was the wrong sex and at sixteen, too old for his preference. She would not tell you the truth, she could not prompt you to hold any hint of empathy for me, her sanctimonious scorn cannot be absolved. We met before I became Bishop, she was my whore, she fell in love with me. She was cock struck, I was young, handsome, yes even if I say so, but I was, and I treated her tenderly. When she fell pregnant, and you were mine no doubt. She was in dedicated service to me, do you understand, no goose was going to bite me, I could not take the risk, to have the pox is as much a death sentence as plague.”

“You kicked her out, and with me in her belly” scowled Mare.

“I gave her coin to have you removed, wormwood, artemisia, herbal abortifacients, inducements from one of the midwives, but she refused. When you were born she was to hand you over to the church, she ran and hid. Before she left London, you were left with a woman who had not long since lost her own. She thought she had you hid, but I knew, I always knew, I’ve had eyes on you since the day you were born Marion. How do you think you came into my service? Was it coincidence that you were caught finger smithing at the market by the bridge and brought before me?”

"Perhaps not" Mare agreed, her tone conversational despite the maelstrom of emotion beneath her skin. "You shaped me into your perfect weapon. Taught me to observe weaknesses, to exploit vulnerabilities, to strike where the damage would be most severe." She smiled, the expression never reaching her eyes. "You were a thorough teacher."

Wickham stalked around the desk toward her, his face contorted with a rage she had seen directed at others but never at herself.

"You were my finest creation," he snarled, closing the distance between them. "My masterpiece. My fucking daughter. It was I that called you Mare, do you remember? Have you ever wondered why?"

Mare didn't retreat, standing her ground as he loomed over her. She gazed up at him, her eyes as cold and impenetrable as the Thames in winter.

"A mare, a ghost of the dark, they bring on asphyxiating dreams, by sitting on men's chest while they sleep, they ride their victims chests, straddle them like a horse, or their cocks like a whore, that's why when they wake, if they wake, they are called nightmares. You are my nightmare, Marion, a ghost of the dark underbelly that is Southwark, my Southwark, its farmyard full of swine and gaggles of my geese. I taught you everything Marion."

"And that," she said softly, "was your greatest mistake. You still don't understand what you've lost," Mare said, circling back toward the window. Outside, columns of smoke rose from a dozen locations across Southwark, black against the morning sky. She ran her fingers along the heavy velvet curtains, appreciating their quality one final time. "Your men are scattered. The Puritans and the Order are tearing each other apart in your streets. But that's just the surface." She turned back to face him, something like pity crossing her features. "You've lost the foundation itself."

Wickham's eyes narrowed, calculation replacing rage for a crucial moment. "Speak plainly. Your theatrics bore me."

"The tunnels," Mare said, watching comprehension dawn on his face. "Those ancient passages you showed me so proudly. The ones only you and I knew completely." She smiled, the expression devoid of warmth. "They make excellent channels for distributing black powder."

The Bishop went still, disbelief warring with dawning horror. "You're bluffing," he said, though doubt had crept into his voice. "You couldn't have brought enough powder into Southwark without my men noticing."

"Your men," Mare echoed, almost laughing. "The same men who've been searching for me above ground while I moved below. The same men who've been chasing Order shadows and Puritan phantoms for three days?" She shook her head. "I've had access to your tunnels for years, Wickham. I've been placing caches for months, lesser amounts, nothing to draw attention. A pregnant washerwoman here, a limping beggar there. People your guards don't see because you taught them not to look."

She reached into her cloak and produced a small metal object, a flint striker, its steel catching the candlelight as she turned it between her fingers. "The first cache is directly beneath the cathedral north transept. The second beneath the Clink's foundations. Three more at key junctions throughout your domain including this place. Prolonged fuses, long enough to give me enough time to come here and watch you watch it all burn."

"You wouldn't dare burn it all," Wickham growled, advancing toward her with measured steps. "This district made you. These streets shaped you as surely as I did."

"I was born in the mud and shit of this place," Mare replied, her voice suddenly raw with emotion she'd kept carefully banked. "I'll gladly see it burn to be rid of you and its already lit, nothing can stop it now."

Something broke in Wickham's expression, the last restraint of civilization giving way to the predator beneath. He lunged across the desk with unexpected speed for a man his age, papers scattering as his body propelled forward, hands outstretched toward Mare's throat.

She pivoted, but not quickly enough. His fingers caught the edge of her cloak, yanking her off balance. Mare stumbled backward, colliding with a bookshelf that sent leather-bound volumes cascading to the floor. Wickham pressed his advantage, closing the distance before she could fully recover.

His fist connected with her jaw, snapping her head back against the shelf. Stars burst behind Mare's eyes, copper flooding her mouth as teeth cut into soft flesh. The Bishop had fought men in his youth, had killed with those manicured hands before rising to power and delegating violence to others. The knowledge of this had made her cautious, but experiencing it firsthand was something else entirely.

Mare ducked his next blow, driving her shoulder into his midsection with enough force to expel air from his lungs in a pained grunt. They staggered together across the room, knocking over a side table, sending a silver candlestick clattering across expensive carpet.

She broke free, creating space between them, her hand finding the knife concealed at her back. Wickham saw the movement and smiled, a wolf baring its teeth.

"There's my girl," he said, circling to cut off her path to the door. "I knew you'd come with a blade eventually. It's your nature."

Outside, the sounds of battle drew nearer, shouts and the clash of weapons, the distinctive crack of timber giving way to flame. Wickham's guards would soon abandon their posts to protect their master, drawn by the approaching danger regardless of previous orders.

Mare feinted left, then lunged right, her knife slashing toward Wickham's exposed side. He twisted away with surprising agility, catching her wrist, and using her momentum to slam her against the wall. Pain exploded through her shoulder blade, the knife clattering from suddenly nerveless fingers.

The Bishop's hand closed around her throat, pinning her to the wall with crushing force. His face loomed inches from hers, close enough that she could smell the expensive wine on his breath, could see the broken blood vessels mapping his rage across the whites of his eyes.

"I should have had you killed years ago," he raged through closed teeth, his fingers tightening until black spots danced at the edges of Mare's vision. "Should have drowned you the moment Agnes fled north."

Mare clawed at his hand, her lungs burning for air that wouldn't come. The brand on her arm throbbed in counterpoint to her racing heart, the twin claims of mother and Bishop both seared into her flesh against her will. Her free hand scrabbled against the wall behind her, searching for purchase, for weapon, for escape.

"Perhaps you were never really mine," Wickham continued, watching her struggle with clinical detachment. "Never truly loyal. I see that now. Something in your blood resisted me from the start."

Mare's fingers found a small groove in the wood panelling, the secondary release for the hidden passage she'd used to enter. As darkness began to crowd the edges of her consciousness, she summoned her remaining strength and pressed the mechanism.

The wall shuddered beneath them just as the first explosion rocked the building's foundation.

The blast came from deep below, a roar like the earth itself splitting open, followed by a tremor that rippled through stone and timber. Dust rained from the ceiling as the floor pitched beneath their feet. Wickham's grip loosened in surprise, giving

Mare the moment she needed. Her knee drove upward, finding the soft flesh between his legs with unerring accuracy.

The Bishop doubled over with a strangled cry, stumbling backward as a second, larger explosion tore through the foundation directly beneath the building. This one was no distant rumble but an immediate, violent upheaval. The floor buckled, stone cracking with sounds like pistol shots. A fissure opened in the expensive carpet, revealing the void beneath as huge timbers gave way, one landing on his ribs, compressing his diaphragm. The Bishop gasped as he struggled to breath, a waking nightmare, one dark ghost sitting heavy on his chest and one slipping away, smirking.

Mare dove toward the hidden panel, now hanging ajar from the force of the blast. Behind her, Wickham regained his footing, lunging for her with a roar that seemed to come from somewhere inhuman. His fingers brushed the back of her cloak as she slipped through the opening, the fabric tearing but holding just long enough for her to clear the passage.

"Marion!" His voice followed her into the darkness, raw with hatred and something else, something that might have been fear. "This isn't finished between us!"

Mare pulled the panel shut behind her as the third explosion shook the tunnels, more violent than the previous two. Dust and debris rained down as she ran, navigating by memory through passages now transformed by destruction. Some had collapsed completely, forcing her to backtrack and find alternate routes. Others had partially caved in, leaving spaces she squeezed through with desperate haste, plaster and stone scraping her skin raw.

The air grew thick with dust and smoke, burning her lungs with each ragged breath. Behind her, the rumble of collapsing masonry pursued like a living thing, hungry for her flesh. Ahead, the tunnel forked, left toward the church, right toward the river. Mare chose right without hesitation, running now with the single-minded focus of prey with death at its heels.

She reached the exit as another explosion tore through Southwark's underbelly. This blast wasn't one of hers, something else had caught fire, something that burned hot enough to ignite forgotten stockpiles of materials in abandoned cellars. Mare burst from the tunnel's mouth into a narrow alley choked with smoke, gasping clean air into starved lungs.

The streets of Southwark had transformed in the hour she'd spent beneath them. Fires burned unchecked across the district, buildings that had stood for generations now reduced to blazing skeletons. People ran in all directions, some fleeing with bundles of possessions clutched to their chests, others moving purposefully toward targets of opportunity, taking advantage of the chaos to settle old scores or acquire what they'd never been able to afford.

Mare staggered to the relative shelter of a recessed doorway, wiping blood from a cut above her eye. From this vantage, she could see the Bishop's residence beginning to collapse in on itself, stone walls that had stood for centuries now crumbling as their foundations gave way. The intricate stained glass of its windows, scenes of saints and martyrs rendered in jewel-like colours, shattered outward in glittering clouds as the structure failed.

Men in the Bishop's livery scrambled from the building, abandoning dignity in their flight from certain death. Some carried wounded comrades, others clutched valued possessions or documents. Mare searched their faces for Wickham himself but couldn't distinguish individual features through the thickening smoke.

Had he escaped the collapsing chamber? Had his men reached him in time? Or was he buried beneath tons of stone and timber, crushed by the weight of his own pride and ambition?

Mare found she didn't, particularly care. Alive or dead, her father, Bishop Richard Wickham's power was broken. His carefully constructed domain lay in ruins around her, his web of control incinerated by the very flames he had used to terrify others.

She pushed away from the doorway, moving with the stumbling gait of the exhausted toward the river. Southwark burned at her back, transformed by her vengeance into something unrecognisable, no longer the Bishop's kingdom nor Agnes's battleground, but a scorched wasteland where nothing of value remained.

Blood matted Mare's hair to her scalp, ran in thin rivulets down her face. The brand on her arm throbbed in time with her pulse, a constant reminder of chains broken but not forgotten. She felt hollow, emptied of everything but pain and a strange, floating detachment.

Behind her, the Bishop's palace completed its collapse with a roar that shook the very air. Mare didn't turn to look. She had seen enough destruction for one lifetime, had caused enough to last for several more. The time for watching came later. For now, there was only the river ahead and whatever lay beyond, a future without bishop or mother, without branded palm or scarred forearm defining her path.

For the first time in her life, Mare Fleet belonged truly and only to herself. The knowledge settled like ash on her tongue, bitter, choking, but undeniably real.

Chapter Sixteen

The Aftermath

Mare stood atop the collapsed scaffold like a carrion bird surveying a battlefield, her boots planted firmly on charred beams that had once supported the roof of the Bishop's granary. Ash drifted through the morning air, settling on her shoulders and in her hair like premature aging, painting the world in shades of grey that matched her mood. Below, Southwark smouldered, her handiwork, her vengeance, her liberation rendered in fire and rubble.

The district that had birthed her, raised her, used her, and finally betrayed her now lay gutted before her eyes. Buildings that had stood for generations were reduced to blackened skeletons, their timber bones jutting toward the sky like accusatory fingers. Streets that had once teemed with merchants, whores, and thieves were now choked with debris, splintered wood, shattered glass, collapsed stone, and here and there, the unmistakable shape of human remains partially buried beneath the wreckage.

The central square, where the Bishop had once held his public judgments, was now a crater filled with standing water from broken cisterns and the hasty efforts of those who'd tried to battle the spreading flames. Thin spirals of smoke still rose from a dozen locations, carrying the stench of wet ash, scorched flesh, and the acrid smell of dreams burned to cinders.

Mare's eyes, red-rimmed from smoke and lack of sleep, moved methodically across the scene, cataloguing damages with the same precision she'd once used to map the district for the Bishop. Her body ached with the aftereffects of her escape, a deep cut along her shoulder had stopped bleeding but pulled painfully with each movement, and burns on her left calf throbbed beneath hastily applied bandages. Dried blood caked her knuckles and flaked from a split in her lower lip.

The physical pain was nothing, a familiar companion she'd learned to ignore years ago. What surprised her was the hollow feeling in her chest, the curious emptiness where she'd expected satisfaction to bloom. She'd burned Southwark to be free of the Bishop and the Order, but standing above the smoking ruins, she felt not triumph but a strange, uncomfortable heat she recognized as guilt.

Her fingers found the scar on her palm; the Bishop's seal carved into her flesh years ago as a mark of ownership. The brand throbbed with phantom pain, as if the destruction of his domain had somehow awakened the mark rather than erased it. On her other arm, the Order's brand, Agnes's brand, felt similarly alive, a constant reminder of her mother's final betrayal.

Movement caught her eye, figures picking their way through the devastation below. Not the Bishop's men, who moved with military precision, nor the Puritans with their stiff-backed righteousness. These were women moving with the careful grace of those accustomed to navigating dangerous terrain while avoiding unwanted attention. Winchester Geese, survivors of the brothels and the Bishop's purge, now emerging from whatever hiding places had sheltered them through the night's destruction.

Mare watched as they went about their business with the grim efficiency of those well-acquainted with catastrophe. Some tended to wounded companions, using strips torn from their own clothing to bind injuries. Others moved systematically through the ruins of their former quarters, salvaging what little remained worth taking, a cooking pot here, an intact blanket there, the occasional glint of hidden coins or jewellery recovered from secret caches.

They worked together without unnecessary words, communicating through gestures and shared understanding born of collective suffering. Mare recognized many of them, women she'd helped escape the Bishop's men, women who'd provided her with information over the years, women who'd tended her wounds when she'd returned bloodied from the Bishop's errands. None had known her full plans, but all had understood her hatred for the man who'd claimed ownership of their bodies and lives.

One woman, older than most, with iron-grey hair and the map of hard years etched into her face, paused in her scavenging to look up at Mare's perch. Their eyes met across the distance, recognition flowing between them like a current. The woman straightened, ignoring the protests of what were clearly broken ribs, and gave Mare a single, solemn nod.

Not gratitude, these women were too practical for such sentiments. Not forgiveness, Mare had caused destruction that had claimed friends alongside enemies. Just acknowledgment, one survivor to another. Recognition that while Mare had struck the match, the tinder had been laid by years of cruelty and exploitation.

Mare returned the nod, then turned away. This view had served its purpose; she'd seen enough to confirm that her plan had succeeded. The Bishop's domain was destroyed, his power broken, his carefully constructed hierarchy reduced to ash and memory. What would rise from these ruins remained to be seen, but it would be built on different foundations.

She descended from her perch, climbing down the twisted metal and splintered wood with the same careful precision she'd used to navigate the Bishop's political landscape. Her boots hit solid ground with a jolt that sent pain lancing up her injured leg, but she didn't pause to acknowledge it. Pain meant life, meant survival, meant purpose not yet fulfilled.

The air grew thicker as she moved into the heart of the destruction, smoke and ash coating her tongue with each breath. The sounds changed too, from the distant, almost abstract chaos of screams and collapse she'd heard from above to the immediate, intimate noises of suffering and survival. Groans from the injured, the scrape of debris being moved, the occasional sob quickly stifled.

Mare pulled her hood lower, partly to shield her lungs from the worst of the smoke, partly to obscure her features from those who might recognize the Bishop's Shadow moving through the wreckage she'd created. Not from fear, she was beyond that now, but from purpose. There were still tasks to complete, loose ends to gather, certainties to confirm before she could truly count her vengeance finished.

Chief among them: the Bishop himself. She needed to confirm his death with her own eyes, to stand over his body and know that his influence was truly ended. Until then, the hollow feeling in her chest would remain, the brands on her flesh would continue their phantom burning, and the ghosts of Southwark would follow at her heels, demanding the completion of what she'd begun.

Mare moved with renewed determination toward the ruins of the Bishop's private chapel, where his body, if found, would have been taken. Each step carried her deeper into the devastation she'd orchestrated, ash rising around her boots like the disturbed memories of what had once been home.

The Bishop's private chapel stood like a wounded animal at the edge of the destruction, one wall collapsed entirely, its roof partially caved in to expose rafters that pointed skyward like broken ribs. Mare approached through what had once been a prayer garden, now reduced to churned mud and uprooted rosebushes. Glass crunched beneath her boots, fragments of the stained windows that had once depicted saints with faces suspiciously like the Bishop's own benefactors. Morning light streamed through the remaining-coloured panes, casting blood-red and bile-yellow patterns across the ruined interior.

Mare stepped through the gaping hole where ornate doors had once controlled access to the Bishop's sanctum. Inside, the destruction was more complete than the exterior had suggested. Wooden pews lay splintered and scattered like discarded toys, some still smouldering from the fire that had swept through hours earlier. The marble altar had cracked down the middle, its gilded candlesticks melted into grotesque shapes that resembled weeping figures. Prayer books and psalters formed small pyres across the floor, their pages curling and blackening in the lingering heat.

At the front of the chapel, elevated on a platform of imported stone, sat the Bishop's chair, a throne, really, though he'd called it a "seat of spiritual authority" to mask his worldly arrogance. The carved oak was scorched but intact, its cushions of Venetian velvet now soaked with water from the collapsed ceiling. Empty. The space around it told a story to Mare's practiced eye, scuff marks where multiple boots had gathered, a trail of blood leading toward a small door at the side, the disturbed ash suggesting a body had been dragged rather than carried.

A sudden movement drew her attention. Behind the altar, half-hidden by a fallen beam, a thin figure in the remains of fine livery struggled to stuff papers into a leather satchel. Thomas Walsingham, not the hardened lieutenant who'd led the raids on the Winchester Geese, but his cousin of the same name who served as the Bishop's personal page. A boy of later teenage years with scholarly hands and nervous eyes, promoted beyond his abilities through family connection.

The boy froze at her appearance, recognition widening his eyes to perfect circles of terror. The ledger he'd been attempting to salvage slipped from his trembling fingers, landing with a wet thud in a puddle of melted snow and ash.

"You," he stammered, backing against the wall. "They said you died in the explosions."

Mare approached slowly, deliberately placing one foot before the other, her gaze never leaving his face. "The Bishop," she said, her voice flat as a blade. "Where is he?"

Thomas swallowed visibly, his prominent Adam's apple bobbing like a cork in water. "Gone," he managed, gesturing vaguely eastward with a soot-blackened hand. "They carried him out before the main explosion. His legs..." The boy's voice cracked. "His legs were crushed when the floor collapsed, but he was conscious. Ordering everyone about even as they lifted him."

Mare kept her expression neutral, though frustration curled in her gut like a living thing. The Bishop alive meant her vengeance incomplete, her freedom still contingent. She moved closer to Thomas, close enough to see the sweat beading on his upper lip despite the chapel's chill.

"Before he left," she said, her voice deceptively gentle, "what did he say?"

Thomas's eyes darted to the door, calculating his chances of escape. Mare shifted slightly, blocking his path without appearing to do so.

"He swore vengeance," the boy finally whispered. "Said your name like a curse. Said you'd pay for your betrayal with more than just your life." Thomas's gaze dropped to the floor. "He said he'd find you if he had to crawl on the stumps of his legs."

Mare allowed herself a small, cold smile. "Good," she said, the word falling between them like a pebble into still water. "Let him waste what remains of his life hunting me."

She stepped past Thomas to examine the scattered papers he'd been gathering, ledgers bound in calfskin, correspondence sealed with the wax of noble houses, lists of names and figures that represented the true foundation of the Bishop's power. Not faith, not spiritual authority, but information, the secrets of powerful men, the debts of merchants, the sins of nobles carefully recorded and preserved for leverage.

Mare knelt beside a partially burned ledger, scanning its water-stained pages with practiced efficiency. This one contained record of payments from brothel owners, protection money gathered monthly, with notations of those who had failed to pay and the consequences they'd suffered. Another ledger, its cover bearing the Bishop's personal seal, listed "donations" from merchants who had received favourable treatment in disputes brought before his court.

Most valuable was a thin volume bound in red leather, containing names and details of nobles who had visited the Winchester Geese, lords of the Queen's court, foreign diplomats, even a bishop from the north whose proclivities ran to noticeably young girls. The Bishop had used this information to secure his position, to guarantee that those who might have challenged his authority remained silent for fear of their own exposure.

Mare slipped this volume inside her cloak, along with several folded letters bearing the seals of prominent families. She selected two more ledgers, one detailing the Bishop's financial holdings across London, another listing his agents in other districts. Information was currency in this new landscape; these documents might purchase her safety or provide leverage against those who would continue the Bishop's work.

The rest she left where they lay, scattered and vulnerable. Thomas watched with growing alarm as Mare kicked over a still-burning candle stand, sending flames licking across the pile of remaining papers. The fire caught quickly, spreading through the dry parchment, sending up curls of black smoke that carried the scent of burning ink.

"What are you doing?" Thomas cried, lunging forward. "Those are worth a fortune to the right buyers!"

Mare caught his wrist, her grip like iron despite her exhaustion. "They're worth nothing now," she said evenly. "Just like your master."

She released him, watching as he clutched his wrist to his chest, his eyes filling with tears of pain or desperation or both. "He'll find you," Thomas said, a final attempt at bravado. "The Bishop never forgets a betrayal."

Mare turned to leave, pausing at the ruined doorway as flames began to climb the walls behind her, consuming the last physical records of the Bishop's corrupt domain. "Let him come," she said without looking back. "I'll be waiting."

She stepped out into the ashen morning, leaving Thomas to choose between salvaging what he could from the burning chapel or fleeing while escape remained possible. It made no difference to her. The page was insignificant, a footnote in the Bishop's eulogy, and nothing at all in hers.

Mare tucked the stolen documents more securely inside her cloak, their weight against her ribs a reminder of purpose not yet fulfilled. The Bishop lived, wounded but dangerous still. Knowledge of his survival should have disappointed her, should have felt like failure after all her careful planning. Instead, she found herself smiling thinly as she moved away from the burning chapel.

The game continued. The Bishop would hunt her with whatever resources and allies remained to him. She would hunt him in return, armed now with his own secrets and the freedom to use them however she chose. It was almost fitting, the Shadow and her former master, locked in a final dance of vengeance and survival.

Behind her, the chapel's remaining wall collapsed with a sound like distant thunder, sending up a fresh plume of smoke and ash to join the pall hanging over what remained of Southwark.

The Puritans had established their makeshift camp at Southwark's eastern edge, where the district's buildings gave way to muddy fields dotted with skeletal trees. Mare spotted their pathetic gathering from a hundred paces away, a cluster of men huddled around smoky fires, their once-pristine robes now tattered and filthy, their righteous bearing replaced by the slumped shoulders of the defeated. She approached without attempting concealment, her boots squelching in the mud loud enough to announce her presence. Let them see her coming. Let them remember her face when they recalled the night their holy crusade had crumbled to ash.

Two dozen men remained of what had been a hundred zealots the previous day. Some nursed wounds bound with strips torn from their own garments, burns, cuts, broken limbs sustained during their disastrous assault on the Bishop's territory. Others simply stared into the smoking fires with the vacant expressions of men whose certainties had been stripped away, leaving nothing but confusion and doubt in their place.

Their camp reeked of defeat, not just the physical stench of unwashed bodies and poorly tended wounds, but the sour smell of broken faith. These men had marched into Southwark bellowing scripture, convinced God's hand guided their clubs and torches. They had burned women alive in the name of purity, had beaten unbelievers senseless in service to their righteous cause. Now they sat in mud and ash, their prophet silenced, their divine mission revealed as nothing more than manipulation.

"False prophecies," one muttered as Mare drew closer, his voice cracking with either smoke damage or suppressed tears. "We were led astray."

"God has abandoned us," whispered another, rocking back and forth, clutching a scorched Bible to his chest like a talisman.

At the centre of this pathetic congregation sat John Stubbs himself, perched on an overturned barrel, his head cradled in hands that had once gestured dramatically as he called for holy fire to cleanse Southwark's sin. His fine black cloak hung in tatters around his shoulders, one sleeve entirely burned away to reveal blistered skin beneath. The prophet's beard, once neatly trimmed to frame his pronouncements of doom, was singed on one side and matted with what might have been blood or mud or both.

Mare stopped at the edge of their circle, making no move to conceal her identity. The stolen documents crinkled inside her cloak as she shifted her weight, a subtle reminder of purpose that steadied her. She had come not just to witness their defeat but to ensure Stubbs understood exactly how thoroughly he had been played, another loose end tied before she left Southwark behind.

Gradually, the Puritans noticed her presence. Their reactions varied from blank indifference to sudden fear, a few reaching instinctively for weapons no longer at their belts. One man made the sign of the cross before catching himself, the Catholic gesture at odds with his Protestant zealotry, a telling slip that revealed how thin their convictions ran.

Stubbs sensed the change in his followers, lifting his head slowly from his hands. His eyes, once alight with fervour that could ignite crowds to violence, now appeared sunken and dull within a face streaked with soot and despair. Until they found Mare standing before him, then recognition sparked, followed immediately by hatred so pure it transformed his features into something barely human.

"You," he spat, the word emerging like poison from his cracked lips. He struggled to his feet, swaying slightly, his right leg dragging as he took a step toward her. "The whore who brought us down."

Mare stood unflinching before his rage, her posture relaxed, almost bored. The very casualness of her stance inflamed Stubbs further, his hands curling into claws at his sides.

"Your cause was built on lies," she stated coldly, her voice carrying to every man in the circle. "Just like the Bishop's." She extracted a folded paper from inside her cloak, one of the documents she'd just recovered from the chapel, bearing the Bishop's seal. "These lists payments made to you over three years. Your 'divine mission' was funded by the very corruption you claimed to oppose."

Stubbs lunged toward her with surprising speed for a wounded man, his face contorted in fury. "Liar! Jezebel!" he snarled, hands outstretched toward her throat.

He never reached her. Two of his own followers caught him, restraining his flailing limbs with practiced movements that suggested this wasn't the first time their prophet had needed physical restraint. Stubbs struggled against their grip, spittle flying from his lips as he hurled invectives, "whore" and "deceiver" mixed with scriptural condemnations that blurred together into incoherent rage.

Mare tucked the document away, her expression never changing. "Your holy war was nothing but the Bishop's distraction," she continued, addressing not just Stubbs but all the gathered men. "While you burned brothels, believing you served God's will, you were merely puppets dancing on strings pulled by men cleverer and more corrupt than yourselves."

"She lies to divide us, brothers!" Stubbs cried, still struggling against those who held him. "The Lord tests our faith through this demon in woman's form!"

A bitter laugh escaped one of the men restraining him, a stocky fellow with a burned face and empty eyes. "The Lord?" he echoed. "Where was the Lord when our brothers were cut down? Where was divine protection when we followed your visions straight into the Bishop's trap?"

Murmurs of agreement rippled through the gathering. Mare watched as doubt spread visibly among them, faith crumbling faster than she could have hoped. Her work here was nearly complete.

"Your crusade is finished," she said, her voice quiet but carrying. "Southwark has suffered enough from men who claim to know God's will while serving their own ambitions."

She turned to leave, sensing no further threat from these broken men. Behind her, Stubbs's voice rose in one final, desperate pronouncement.

"This isn't over!" he shouted, the words ragged with emotion. "God's judgment will find you, Marion Fleet! Neither the Bishop's gold nor the devil's protection will shield you from divine wrath!"

Mare didn't bother looking back, didn't dignify his impotent threats with acknowledgment. She had seen what she came to see, another power that had claimed authority over Southwark now reduced to mud and recrimination. The Puritans might linger, might even rebuild their movement elsewhere, but their hold over this district was broken.

As she walked away, Mare heard the argument behind her intensifying, follower turning against follower, accusations of false faith mingling with demands for explanation. Stubbs's voice rose above the others, still trying to assert control, but the power had gone from it, leaving only the hollow echoes of a man confronting his own irrelevance.

One more piece cleared from the board. One more threat neutralized. Mare turned her steps toward the tannery, where the final confrontation, the one she had both dreaded and anticipated awaited.

The tannery stood at Southwark's northern edge, its stone walls blackened but largely intact compared to the wooden structures that had collapsed throughout the district. Mare approached through the remnants of the outer courtyard, stepping over fallen timbers and around a massive oak door that had been blown clear of its hinges by the force of the explosion she'd orchestrated. Inside, the cavernous main floor where hides had once been stretched and cured before the Order claimed the building as sanctuary, lay in shadow broken only by shafts of light penetrating holes in the roof. The air hung heavy with a nauseating blend of scents: old leather, fresh blood, burning flesh, and the cloying sweetness of approaching death.

The space bore the devastation of a place destroyed from within rather than without. Walls remained standing while floors had collapsed, exposing the warren of rooms below where the Order had established their command centre. Support beams hung at precarious angles, creaking occasionally as they settled further into their new, unstable configurations. The explosion had originated in those lower chambers, precisely placed charges that

Mare had helped design weeks earlier when she'd still been playing both sides, when Agnes had still been a mentor rather than a mother who had betrayed her.

The tannery was eerily quiet compared to the chaos elsewhere in Southwark. No shouts, no crackling flames, just the muted sounds of suffering, soft moans from the wounded, whispered prayers, occasional sobs quickly stifled. In the dim light, Mare could make out figures moving through the debris with the practiced care of battlefield nurses. Sisters of the Order, their habits torn and stained, tending to fallen comrades or gently covering the faces of those beyond help.

None challenged Mare as she picked her way across the ruined floor. They didn't recognize her in the gloom, or they simply lacked the strength or will to confront yet another enemy. She followed a trail of blood, not droplets but a continuous smear, as if someone grievously wounded had been dragged toward the tannery's eastern corner, where old tanning pits had been converted to sleeping quarters.

The blood led to a small alcove formed by a partially collapsed wall. There, on a makeshift pallet of cloaks and sacking, lay Sister Agnes, Mother Agnes to her followers, Marion Fleet's mother by blood if not by choice. Her body appeared broken beyond repair, limbs twisted at unnatural angles, burns covering much of her visible skin. The Order's brand stood out starkly on her exposed forearm, a mirror to the one Mare carried, though Agnes's was an old scar while Mare's remained an angry wound.

Agnes's eyes were closed, her breathing shallow and wet with the unmistakable rattle of approaching death. Someone had attempted to bind her wounds, but the bandages had soaked through, dark and wet against her ashen skin. Her grey-streaked hair, usually bound severely beneath her veil, spilled loose around her face, emphasizing how small she suddenly appeared, no longer the formidable leader of a shadow army but simply a dying woman.

Mare stood motionless, studying the woman who had given her life, then abandoned her, then found her again only to betray her once more. She had imagined this moment differently confronting Agnes at the height of her power, forcing her to acknowledge her manipulations, even exacting some physical retribution for the brand burned into her flesh. But this broken figure before her offered no satisfaction, no target for the rage that had driven Mare through the long night of Southwark's destruction.

A sound escaped Agnes, not quite a moan, more a sigh of pain. Her eyes fluttered open, unfocused at first, then sharpening as they found Mare standing above her. Recognition dawned slowly, followed by something Mare hadn't expected to see, relief.

"You came," Agnes whispered, blood bubbling at the corners of her lips. "I didn't think you would."

Mare knelt beside the pallet, not from compassion but from a need to hear the dying woman's words, to witness her last moments with her own eyes. Close up, Agnes's injuries appeared even worse, her right cheekbone shattered, several fingers clearly broken, a deep gash across her collar that had been roughly stitched but continued to seep.

"Why wouldn't I?" Mare replied, her voice deliberately flat. "I orchestrated all of this. Shouldn't I see the results of my handiwork?"

Agnes's lips curved in what might have been a smile on a less ruined face. "Still so much anger," she murmured. "You get that from me. Your father was the gentle one."

Mare felt something twist in her chest, not grief, she told herself, but irritation at this attempt to forge connection in last moments. "Don't," she warned. "Don't pretend we're family now, when it's convenient for your conscience."

"Not pretending," Agnes managed, each word clearly causing pain. "Never stopped being your mother. Even when I couldn't claim you." She coughed, fresh blood speckling her lips. "Even when you hated me."

Against her will, Mare found herself taking her mother's hand, the one with fewer broken fingers, its skin cool and dry against her own. Agnes's fingers tightened around hers with surprising strength, as if this physical connection might bridge the chasm of years and betrayals between them.

"Was it worth it?" Mare asked, her voice barely controlled now, the question encompassing everything, Agnes's life of resistance, the Order she'd built, the daughters she'd abandoned, the destruction they'd both contributed to. "All of this?"

Agnes's eyes found hers, the same slate grey that stared back at Mare from still water or polished metal. Despite her broken body, those eyes remained sharp, penetrating, seeing too much.

"Freedom always costs," she rasped. "Sometimes more than we can bear to pay." Her grip tightened as another spasm of pain crossed her features. "I paid with your childhood. You paid with your innocence. Southwark pays now with its very foundations." She drew a laboured breath. "But yes. Worth it. To break what was corrupt beyond saving, to clear ground for something new."

Mare felt an uncomfortable heat behind her eyes, a pressure in her throat that threatened to become something dangerous. "The Bishop survived," she said, partly to change the subject, partly because Agnes deserved to know her ancient enemy lived still.

"Of course he did," Agnes whispered, unsurprised. "Men like him always crawl from the wreckage." Her breathing grew more laboured, her words coming in shorter bursts. "He'll come for you. With whatever remains of his power."

"Let him try," Mare replied, echoing her words to Thomas in the chapel.

Agnes's lips twitched again in that almost-smile. "So much like me," she murmured. "But you're more than just my anger, Marion. More than the Bishop's weapon." Her fingers squeezed Mare's with the last of her strength. "Remember who you are. Not what they made you."

The pressure tightened. Then released. Agnes's final breath escaped in a soft sigh, her eyes losing focus but remaining open, fixed on Mare's face as if trying to memorize it for whatever journey came next.

Mare sat motionless for several heartbeats, still holding her mother's cooling hand. Then, with a gentleness she hadn't known she possessed, she reached out and closed Agnes's eyes. The gesture felt ancient, inherited from some collective memory of how the living should honour the dead, even when the relationship between them had been broken beyond repair.

She should feel triumph, Mare thought distantly. Or at least satisfaction. Agnes had been her enemy as much as her mother had imprisoned her, branded her, tried to force her into yet another role not of her choosing. But the hollow feeling in her chest wasn't satisfaction. It wasn't grief either, she told herself firmly. Just emptiness where purpose had been now that another piece of her vengeance lay complete.

Mare stood, releasing her mother's hand to rest on the rough pallet. Around her, the Order sisters continued their grim work, a few glancing her way but none approaching. They had their own grief to manage, their own wounded to tend. Whatever vengeance they might desire against the Bishop's Shadow would wait for another day.

As Mare turned to leave, she caught sight of her reflection in a shard of broken mirror propped against the wall, a face streaked with ash and blood, eyes hard as flint, jaw set in determination that mirrored the dead woman's behind her. Mother and daughter, bound by blood and rage and the strength of women who had survived Southwark's brutal crucible.

"Remember who you are," Agnes had said with her dying breath. As if Mare had ever been allowed to discover that for herself, between the Bishop's manipulations and Agnes's expectations. As if identity was something solid to be reclaimed rather than a void to be filled with whatever might serve survival.

Mare moved away from her mother's body without looking back, refusing to acknowledge the wetness on her cheeks that could have been sweat or blood or something more dangerous still.

What remained of the Winchester Geese's quarters stood like broken teeth in the jawbone of a beaten fighter, some buildings completely collapsed, others partially standing with walls sheared away to expose intimate spaces to open air. Mare picked her way through the debris-strewn path that had once been Rose Alley, where the cheaper brothels had housed those women too old or too damaged to command premium prices from the Bishop's clients. The cobblestones beneath her boots were slick with a mixture of water from burst pipes, ash from collapsed roofs, and here and there, darkening patches that could only be blood. Around her lay the scattered remains of interrupted lives, a child's wooden doll with one arm missing, a comb with most of its teeth broken, a red shawl fluttering from a splintered beam like a surrender flag.

The destruction felt more personal here than elsewhere in Southwark. The church's ruins spoke of institutional power broken; the Bishop's chapel represented corrupt authority toppled. But these modest buildings had been homes of a sort, however meagre, to women who had few other options. Here, Mare could read individual stories in the wreckage, a collection of cheap tin brooches spilled across stone steps, carefully hoarded treasures now exposed to theft or weather. A painted wooden box containing scraps of ribbon and dried flowers, the small luxuries of someone who had little else to call her own. A broken mirror still hanging crookedly on a partially collapsed wall, reflecting nothing now but smoke-stained sky.

Mare had orchestrated this destruction, she had known these buildings would fall, had understood women would lose what little they possessed. The knowledge sat uneasily in her chest, not guilt but something adjacent to it, the recognition that her vengeance had claimed collateral damage among those she'd sought to free.

Women had begun to gather, drawn by the sight of Mare's familiar figure, or simply by the human instinct to cluster after disaster. Some Mare recognized from years of moving through the Bishop's domain; others were newer to Southwark, their faces less familiar but their wary expressions identical to women who had learned young that survival often came at terrible cost.

All bore the marks of the night's violence, burns, cuts, bruises flowering across exposed skin. All watched Mare with the caution of those accustomed to calculating which authority figure currently held power over their lives. The realization twisted something in Mare's chest, that these women might see in her simply another master replacing the Bishop, another hand holding the leash they'd worn so long they'd forgotten the feel of its absence.

Mare reached into her cloak again, this time withdrawing a small leather pouch that clinked softly with the weight of its contents. The coins inside represented what she'd saved during her years as the Bishop's Shadow, payment for services rendered, blood money she'd intended to use for her own escape once her vengeance was complete.

Mare untied the pouch and began distributing its contents, pressing silver coins into startled hands. "Go north if you want," she told them as the pouch grew lighter. "York, Edinburgh places beyond the Bishop's reach, even if he survives his wounds. Or stay. Southwark will need new leadership now."

The women exchanged glances, weighing options they'd never been offered before. Bess watched the distribution with sharp eyes, neither approving nor condemning, simply observing as she had observed all of Southwark's upheavals over decades of survival.

"And you?" one asked when Mare had emptied the pouch, her voice neutral but her gaze penetrating. "Where does the Bishop's Shadow go when there's no Bishop left to cast her?"

Mare tucked the empty pouch back into her cloak, her face revealing nothing of the uncertainty that question provoked. "I have unfinished business," she said simply. "The Bishop lives. And I made promises to the dead."

She didn't elaborate, didn't need to, debts in Southwark were always collected, one way or another.

Mare moved away from the gathered women, leaving them to decide their own fates for the first time since the Bishop had claimed them. Behind her, she heard their voices rise in tentative discussion, some already planning journeys north, others talking of rebuilding, of claiming abandoned properties, of creating something new from Southwark's ashes.

She didn't look back. Their choices were their own now, not hers to make or influence. For the first time since she'd returned to consciousness in the Order's cell, Mare felt something close to peace, not for herself, but for these women who might build lives outside the shadow of men who saw them as nothing but flesh to be used and discarded.

Chapter Seventeen

Echoes of the past

Dawn broke over Southwark like a bruise spreading across flesh, purples and yellows seeping into the smoke-stained sky. Mare's boots sent ash swirling as she picked her way through streets rendered unrecognizable by her own calculated destruction. The air tasted of char and copper, catching in her throat with each laboured breath. She'd spent the night finding shelter in an abandoned boathouse across the river, sleeping fitfully on rotting planks while her dreams filled with Agnes's dying face and the Bishop's promise of vengeance. Now she returned to the theatre's skeleton, knowing Marlowe's secrets might be the only currency valuable enough to keep her alive in the coming days.

Her body catalogued each step with fresh complaints. Burns stippled her forearms where she'd pushed through a curtain of falling embers during her escape from the Bishop's chambers. Her left ankle throbbed with each step, twisted when she'd leapt from a collapsing floor. Dried blood crusted beneath her fingernails, some hers, some belonging to the Order sister who'd tried to block her exit from the tannery. Mare ignored these discomforts with practiced indifference. Pain meant survival; the dead felt nothing.

The theatre loomed ahead like the carcass of some magnificent beast, picked clean by the fires that had swept through Southwark. What had once been the pride of London's south bank, a place where queens and cutpurses stood shoulder to shoulder, united in their temporary surrender to illusion, now stood as nothing more than blackened timber reaching toward the sky like supplicant fingers.

Mare paused at what had been the main entrance, now just a jagged hole torn into the building's face. She remembered he second time she'd passed through these doors, Marlowe himself had greeted her, his clever hands warm against the small of her back as he'd guided her to his private box. "My muse arrives," he'd whispered, his breath wine-sweet against her ear. "Come see how I've immortalized you." The memory curdled in her stomach, acid rising in her throat. That same night, she'd discovered his papers, evidence of his collaboration with the Puritans, his plans to use her connection to the Bishop for his own advancement.

She stepped through the ruined entrance, and glass crunched beneath her boots like broken promises. The great hall where merchants and labourers had once stood transfixed by Marlowe's words lay open to the sky, its roof entirely gone. Charred beams crisscrossed the space like the ribs of some prehistoric creature, draped with the tattered remains of decorative banners that had once proclaimed the theatre's name in gold thread on crimson velvet.

Mare moved carefully around a collapsed balcony, her eyes tracking potential threats out of habit, unstable beams, protruding nails, weakened floorboards that might give way beneath her weight. The great stage where kings had died and lovers had swooned night after night was now a jumble of splintered wood and sodden ash. Half the platform had collapsed into the space below, revealing the cramped quarters where actors had waited for their entrances, where stagehands had operated the primitive machinery that had transformed mundane reality into magic.

Her hands became black with soot as she shifted debris, searching for the trapdoor she knew existed. Something caught her eye amid the wreckage where Marlowe's writing desk had once stood in the small antechamber behind the stage. A charred quill lay atop a pile of ash that might once have been manuscripts, its feather blackened but still recognizable, its metal nib warped but intact. Mare knelt and picked it up, turning it over in her fingers with a care that belied her earlier detachment.

This quill, or one identical to it, had scratched across countless pages in her presence, forming words that had moved audiences to tears or laughter or rage. Marlowe had wielded it like a weapon, claiming it more powerful than any sword. "Kings rise and fall, my sweet shadow," he'd told her once, twirling the quill between clever fingers, "but words, the right words, mind you, words are immortal."

Words and betrayal. That had been Marlowe's true legacy to her. Words of love whispered against her skin in private moments. Words of revolution muttered in shadowed taverns with Puritan zealots. Words of submission murmured in the Bishop's chambers as he sold her secrets alongside his talent. All false, all calculated, all designed to advance his own ambitions while using her as a stepping stone toward his imagined greatness.

The weight of it crashed down on Mare suddenly, not just Marlowe's betrayal, but everything she had lost. Her mother, dead by her own orchestration. The Geese, scattered to uncertain futures. Southwark itself, the only home she'd ever known, now burning around her. Her purpose fulfilled yet somehow hollow in its completion. Her identity, carved away piece by piece until she wasn't sure what remained beneath the layers of necessary deception.

Her knees buckled without warning, depositing her gracelessly onto the ash-covered floor beside the quill's resting place. Mare clutched the blackened feather to her chest as her shoulders began to shake with silent, terrible sobs that seemed wrenched from some place inside her she hadn't known existed. Blood from a half-healed cut on her forehead, received during her escape from the Bishop's chambers, trickled down her temple, mixing with tears she couldn't control to carve clean tracks through the soot on her cheeks.

She allowed herself this moment of weakness, this private surrender, knowing no witnesses remained in this destroyed temple of illusion. Here, just once, she could acknowledge the cost of her vengeance, not just in blood and fire, but in the hollowing out of her own humanity. The Bishop had shaped her into a weapon. Agnes had tried to forge her into a soldier. Marlowe had used her as a muse and informant. Between them, they had carved away everything that might have been simply Marion, until only Mare remained, efficient, deadly, and terribly alone.

Her tears fell on the charred quill, darkening the ash that coated it. Mare wondered distantly if this was grief or merely exhaustion if the pressure in her chest was sorrow or simply the accumulated strain of the past days. Did it matter? The result was the same this moment of surrender, of acknowledgment that victory tasted of nothing but ash and blood.

Something glinted amid the ash, a tarnished silver coin caught in a crack between floorboards. Mare pocketed it without thinking, an instinct born of childhood poverty that had never fully left her. She moved deeper into the wreckage, ignoring the pricking sensation of being watched. Nothing lived here now except rats and memories, both equally untrustworthy companions.

Near what had been stage left, Mare's toe struck something solid. She crouched, brushing away layers of soot to reveal a wooden chest, its lid cracked but intact. Inside lay the theatre's treasures, costumes and props that transformed dockworkers into emperors, serving girls into goddesses. Her fingers sifted through the contents: a tarnished crown missing half its paste jewels; a wooden dagger with its tip broken off; a leather-bound book of cues, its pages warped by water and heat.

At the bottom of the chest, her hand closed around something smooth and cool. She withdrew a mask, half-melted by the fire's heat, its once-white surface now bubbled and grey on one side while the other remained eerily intact. Mare's breath caught in her throat as memory surged unbidden.

Marlowe behind that same mask, his eyes gleaming through its narrow slits as he'd played the villain in his own production. His voice carrying across the crowded theatre: "Who dares challenge God's appointed?" The crowd had hissed and booed, never suspecting the author himself lurked behind the villain's face. Later, in his chambers, he'd kept the mask on while taking her to his bed, a game that had thrilled her then but now seemed another layer of his perpetual deception.

"Fucking charlatan," Mare whispered, her voice scraping raw in the silence of the ruined theatre. She turned the mask over in her hands, tempted to crush it beneath her boot, to obliterate this remnant of Marlowe's many faces. Instead, she set it carefully aside, knowing sentiment was a luxury she couldn't afford, not when survival demanded she think clearly.

She moved to where the stage's centre had partially collapsed, revealing the space beneath. Here, in this dark cavity below the boards where actors had strutted and fretted, Marlowe had hidden his most dangerous possession, not the press itself, which was too large to conceal completely, but the manuscripts and correspondence that would have seen him hanged had the Bishop discovered them.

Mare knelt at the edge of the collapsed section, ignoring the protest of her injured ankle. Her fingers probed the broken edges of the stage floor, searching for the latch that would reveal the trapdoor Marlowe had worked from. The wood felt different here, not just charred but deliberately cut, a section designed to be removed.

She found the hidden catch beneath a layer of ash, a small metal lever disguised as a nail head. Something tight uncoiled in her chest, relief that fire and collapse hadn't destroyed everything. That somewhere in this wasteland of her own making, Marlowe's secrets might still exist, waiting to serve a purpose their creator had never intended.

Mare pulled the lever, and a section of flooring shifted with a groan of warped wood. She braced her weight against it, pushing until the trapdoor reluctantly swung open on heat-damaged hinges. Darkness gaped below, smelling of ink, secrets, and possibilities yet to be explored.

The space beneath the trapdoor gaped like a toothless mouth, exhaling the stale breath of secrets long hidden. Mare lowered herself into the darkness, her boots finding the rungs of a narrow ladder bolted to the wall. The wood creaked beneath her weight, weakened by heat and water, threatening to give way with each cautious step. Ten feet down, her soles touched packed earth, and she paused to let her eyes adjust to the gloom. Marlowe's sanctuary, the womb where his most dangerous ideas had gestated before being birthed onto parchment lay before her, where she had uncloaked his duplicity, transformed by fire and collapse into something barely recognizable but still potent with possibility.

Water dripped steadily from the ceiling, pooling in depressions in the dirt floor. The press itself stood in the centre of the small chamber a hulking shadow of metal and wood, its frame warped by heat, one side partially crushed by a fallen beam. Mare circled it slowly, her fingers trailing over its surface. The machine that had printed words powerful enough to incite riots, to question kings, to challenge bishops reduced now to scrap, its potential energy spent.

Her fingers encountered the oiled leather wrapping she remembered, Marlowe's paranoid protection against London's damp. She tugged the bundle free, backing carefully out from under the ruined stage with her prize clutched to her chest like something precious and fragile.

In the relative open of what had been the orchestra pit, Mare unwrapped the leather with hands that betrayed none of the turmoil brewing beneath her ribs. The contents emerged unscathed, packets of paper bound with twine, sealed letters bearing the marks of various noble houses, a small journal with gilt-edged pages.

She arranged them in neat rows on a flat piece of fallen timber, then pulled a stub of candle from her pouch. The tiny flame did little to push back the theatre’s encompassing darkness, but it was enough to read by if she held the papers close.

The first packet contained pages of Marlowe's handwriting, an unfinished play about Edward II, the lines flowing across the page in his distinctive script, complete with crossed-out phrases and marginal notes to himself. Mare set it aside. Marlowe's literary ambitions meant nothing to her now.

The second bundle proved more relevant. Letters, carefully preserved, from various Puritan leaders to Marlowe. The earliest dated back three years, cordial, cautious communications discussing matters of theology and literature. But the more recent ones spoke of "our mutual friend in the Bishop's household" and "intelligence regarding Southwark's sinful quarters."

Mare's jaw clenched as she read her own activities described in coded but recognizable terms. Reports of her movements, her investigations, her meetings with the Bishop, all detailed with damning precision. Marlowe had been watching her for years, using their relationship to monitor her actions and report them to the very men who had tried to burn Southwark to the ground.

Her hands trembled as she set those letters aside and opened the small journal. Inside, in cipher she recognized as one she herself had taught him, Marlowe had kept meticulous records of his double-dealing. Notes on information passed to the Puritans about the Bishop's activities. Intelligence provided to the Bishop about court intrigues. Observations about Mare's movements and habits, catalogued with the clinical detachment of a naturalist studying some interesting species of insect.

And beneath these records, the true evidence of his betrayal, detailed notes of meetings with Thomas Walsingham, the Bishop's most trusted lieutenant. Not the playwright's cousin of the same name, but the man who had led the raids on the Winchester Geese. The man who had tortured Agnes for information about Mare.

Marlowe had been playing all sides against each other, using his position as the Bishop's occasional informant, his reputation among the Puritans, and his relationship with Mare to gather secrets he then sold to the highest bidder. His true allegiance, it seemed, had been only to himself and his ambitions.

"You lying bastard," Mare whispered, the words falling like stones into the burned theatre's silence.

The final parcel contained letters addressed but never sent. One to the Earl of Southampton, begging patronage. Another to some Catholic nobleman whose name Mare didn't recognize, offering information about the Queen's movements. And at the bottom of the stack, one addressed simply to "Mare."

She stared at her name in his handwriting, the elegant loops, and flourishes so at odds with the crude betrayal they represented. For a moment, she considered casting it into the darkness unread, denying him even this final communication. But the need to know, to understand, overwhelmed her anger.

The seal broke with a satisfying crack beneath her thumb. The letter was brief, written in haste judging by the blots and uncharacteristic messiness of the script:

“Mare

Forgive what you cannot understand. Some causes are worth any sacrifice. By the time you read this, I will be across the Channel, where neither the Bishop nor Walsingham can reach me. I could not take you with me, your face is too well known, your connection to me too easily traced.

What I've done may seem like betrayal, but there are powers and purposes beyond Southwark's petty struggles. The Queen's ministers play a game of chess while you and the Geese fight over scraps beneath the table.

I saved what pieces of you I could. Remember that when they tell you otherwise.

Kit"

Mare's fingers crumpled the parchment, crushing his words into a tight ball as if she could squeeze the meaning from them like water from a rag. Her hands shook not with fear or grief but with a rage so pure it felt like fever beneath her skin.

"Saved what pieces," she whispered, striking a fresh spark to her candle stub. "While selling the rest."

She held the crumpled letter to the flame, watching as the fire caught and spread across Marlowe's final words to her. The parchment blackened and curled, adding its small contribution to the theatre's larger destruction. The flames illuminated her face for brief seconds, revealing tracks of moisture cutting clean lines through the grime on her cheeks.

Not tears, she told herself. Just the smoke and the body's natural response. Nothing more.

She gathered the remaining papers, the evidence of Marlowe's entanglement with Walsingham, the cipher notes about the Bishop's operations, the correspondence with Puritan leaders. These she rewrapped carefully in the oiled leather. They might prove useful in whatever came next. Weapons or bargaining chips if her plans went awry. As the last of Marlowe's letter crumbled to ash between her fingers, Mare settled onto a fallen beam, suddenly too exhausted to move further. Around her, the theatre's ruins stretched like the aftermath of some pagan sacrifice, all that art and beauty reduced to charred wood and twisted metal.,

She sat alone among the ashes of her former life, surrounded by the ghosts of those who had betrayed her and those she had failed to protect. The burden of names pressed against her shoulders, Bess in the Clink awaiting torture, Agnes in the Bishop's hands, the Geese burned alive in their sanctuary, the Order women hunted through Southwark's streets. All because she had trusted where she shouldn't have. Because she'd believed she could move between worlds without being claimed by any of them.

In the east, the sky began to lighten, the first pale suggestion of dawn breaking over London's jumbled rooftops. Mare watched it spread with the detached interest of someone observing a scene in one of Marlowe's plays, the symbolic light arriving after darkness, the visual cue that a new act was beginning.

She rose stiffly, tucking the leather packet inside her shirt where it pressed against her skin like a second conscience. The weight of it, of all it represented, seemed to straighten her spine rather than bend it. The time for grief had passed with the night. The time for vengeance had arrived with the dawn.

"Enough," she said to the theatre's ghosts, to Marlowe's memory, to her own failures. The word fell from her lips like a blade, clean, sharp, and final.

What interested her more lay scattered around the press: papers, hundreds of them, some charred at the edges, others sodden and illegible, many still intact enough to read. They had spilled from a metal strongbox that lay on its side, its lock broken, its contents vomited across the earthen floor. The box itself bore the seal of

Cambridge University, stolen, no doubt, during Marlowe's academic years. The irony wasn't lost on her; the very institution that had shaped his mind had unknowingly protected his most seditious thoughts from destruction.

Mare crouched beside the scattered parchments, methodically gathering those that remained most intact. Her hands blackened quickly with soot and ink, leaving dark smudges on each page she touched. She wiped her palm absently against her thigh, creating streaks of black against the already filthy fabric of her breeches.

"Let's see what secrets you kept, Christopher," she murmured, the sound of his name bitter on her tongue.

More interesting were markings she didn't recognize, a different code, one that suggested connections beyond London's borders. References to "northern friends" and "Continental brothers" hinted at a network more extensive than she had imagined, stretching as far as Scotland or even France.

Mare spread the pages across the dirt floor, arranging them in patterns that might reveal connections, her mind working with the precision that had made her valuable to the Bishop. She brushed dirt from a particularly intact sheet and discovered a list of names, some struck through, others marked with symbols indicating position or influence. Among them, she recognized lords of Elizabeth's Privy Council, merchants who controlled trade routes to the Americas, and most damning of all, a bishop from the north whose name had been circled repeatedly in red ink.

The pieces clicked together in her mind like the tumblers of a lock falling into place. Marlowe hadn't simply been writing seditious pamphlets; he had been coordinating a network that extended into the highest levels of power, using the theatre as cover for meetings that could change the religious and political landscape of England itself.

And the Bishop, her Bishop, had known or suspected enough to want Marlowe silenced, but not enough to understand the full scope of the conspiracy.

Mare gathered the most revealing documents, careful to collect fragments that named names and detailed connections. Her movements became more urgent as she recognized the value of what she held, not just as historical record or literary curiosity, but as protection and power in the dangerous weeks ahead. The Bishop might be wounded, but his reach remained long. These papers could serve as shield or sword, depending on how she wielded them.

A sudden shifting of weight above, wood groaning against wood, sent a cascade of dirt and ash raining down through the open trapdoor. Mare froze, every sense alert for threat. A rat scurried across a fallen beam, its claws scratching against charred wood. Nothing more. Still, the reminder of her vulnerability in this underground chamber sent urgency through her limbs. She had lingered too long already.

She worked faster now, sorting the papers into that worth taking and those better left to rot. The most damning pages she folded carefully and tucked into a hidden pocket sewn into her bodice, a modification she had made years ago for carrying the Bishop's more sensitive communications. The pocket sat against her skin, between her breasts, where no casual search would discover its contents.

As she worked, a mirthless smile twisted her lips. Marlowe would have appreciated the irony his revolutionary words pressed against her heart, his greatest work preserved by the woman whose trust he had betrayed. In death, he served her purposes as thoroughly as she had once served his in life.

"Everything circles back," she murmured, gathering the remaining useful papers and securing them inside her shirt, against the small of her back. The rest she left scattered across the dirt floor, physical remnants of dreams and schemes rendered impotent by fire and betrayal.

Mare emerged from the hidden chamber as the last threads of daylight unravelled across Southwark's broken skyline. Shadows stretched like fingers through the theatre's skeleton, reaching toward her as if to reclaim what she'd stolen from their depths. Her body ached with the accumulated weight of exertion and discovery, muscles protesting each movement as she hauled herself onto the ruined stage. The papers against her skin felt unnaturally warm, as if Marlowe's words still burned with the revolutionary fire that had animated him in life, a fire that had consumed him, as it had nearly consumed her.

Twilight would soon surrender to full darkness. Mare scanned the rubble, eyes adjusting to the dimming light. Near what had once been the playwright's private box, she spotted a small oil lamp, miraculously intact amid the destruction. A quick search of nearby debris yielded flint and the stub of a candle, enough to transfer flame to the lamp's wick. Her hands moved with practiced efficiency, striking spark to tinder, nursing the infant flame until it caught and steadied inside the lamp's glass chamber.

The warm light pushed back the encroaching darkness, creating a small island of illumination amid the theatre's ruins. Mare settled onto an intact section of flooring, her back against a charred support beam that still bore traces of gilt paint, remnants of some elaborate backdrop that had transformed this space into palace, battlefield, or fairy wood with nothing more than paint and audience imagination.

She withdrew the papers from her hidden pockets, spreading them across her lap in the lamp's gentle glow. By day, these documents had revealed their basic shape and significance. By night, with time to study them properly, their true power emerged in more intricate detail.

One sheet contained a map, not of physical terrain but of influence. Lines connected names in a complex web that spanned from London's slums to Edinburgh's royal court. Marlowe had marked certain names with symbols she recognized from ciphers she'd used in the Bishop's service, stars indicating direct access to Queen Elizabeth, crosses marking those with Catholic sympathies, circles for those with control of physical resources like ships or warehouses.

"You weren't just writing plays, were you, Christopher?" Mare murmured, tracing the connections with her fingertip. "You were mapping the entire bloody power structure of England."

Another document detailed meeting locations throughout London and beyond; taverns, private homes, even a chamber within the Queen's own palace where sympathizers gathered to discuss reform. Names and dates had been recorded in a shorthand that Mare decoded with growing appreciation for Marlowe's methodical mind. For all his poetic reputation, the playwright had possessed an intelligence agent's attention to detail.

The most valuable pages contained financial information, who funded the network, how money moved between supporters, which nobles contributed while maintaining public personas loyal to church and crown. Mare recognized several names from the Bishop's own circle, men who had dined at his table while secretly supporting the very movements he sought to crush.

As full night settled over Southwark, Mare leaned back against the beam, the papers rustling in her lap as she contemplated their significance. In her hands lay enough evidence to destroy reputations, end careers, even send men to the Tower. The Bishop would pay handsomely for such intelligence. So would his enemies. So might the Queen's own spymaster, another Walsingham, Francis, if she could find a way to approach him without risking her neck.

She could destroy these papers, burn them in the lamp's flame, and walk away, severing all connection to Marlowe's schemes and the danger they represented. The thought held momentary appeal, a clean break, a fresh start beyond London's intrigues. She could sell the information to the highest bidder, using the proceeds to flee England entirely, find passage to the colonies where even the Bishop's long reach might not follow.

Or she could do what neither Marlowe nor the Bishop nor even Agnes had expected of her she could use these secrets herself, wielding them not as anyone's agent but as her own master.

Mare's fingers tightened on the papers, decision crystallizing in her mind with the clarity that came from having nothing left to lose. These words, Marlowe's final legacy, would become her weapon, her currency, her means of ensuring that what rose from Southwark's ashes served her purposes rather than those of men who saw her as merely a pawn in their greater games.

"Your words will outlive you, Christopher," she said to the empty air, her voice steady in the theatre's hollow acoustics. "But I'll decide who hears them."

She carefully folded the most damning pages, those naming the Queen's councillors, those detailing meetings within the palace itself, those mapping the flow of money from noble houses to revolutionary causes and returned them to the hidden pocket against her breast. The remaining papers she gathered into a neat stack beside the lamp.

Mare rose, brushing ash from her breeches, her decision bringing with it a strange lightness. For the first time since childhood, her path belonged to only herself, not the Bishop who had shaped her into his tool, not Agnes who had claimed her by blood, not Marlowe who had used her trust to further his ambitions. Whatever came next would be of her own choosing.

She looked around the ruined theatre one last time, taking in the skeleton of a place that had once housed illusions crafted to reveal deeper truths. Marlowe had understood the power of words to transform reality to make kings of beggars, to turn women into queens, to reshape how men saw their world and their place within it. Now his words would serve her transformation from shadow to substance, from instrument to instrumentalist.

With a decisive movement, Mare kicked dirt over the lamp, extinguishing its flame. Darkness reclaimed the theatre, broken only by starlight filtering through the absent roof. She turned toward the exit, her silhouette sharp-edged against the smouldering skyline of Southwark visible through the ruined wall.

Behind her lay the ashes of her past, the Bishop's domain destroyed, Agnes's Order scattered, Marlowe's sanctuary exposed. Before her stretched a London painted in possibilities, its streets, courts, and palaces unknowing targets for the secrets she now carried against her heart. Mare stepped through the jagged opening that had once been the theatre's grand entrance, her stride purposeful despite her injuries. The night air carried the mingled scents of smoke and river mist, of destruction and possibility. She pulled her cloak tighter against the chill, the papers crinkling softly beneath her garments, Marlowe's final verses transformed into the opening lines of her own story, one she would write in whatever ink the future required.

Mare Fleet had been the Bishop's Shadow, Marlowe's lover, the Winchester Geese's reluctant guardian. Those roles lay in ashes around her, consumed in Southwark's flames. What emerged from the ruins was something new, a woman with nothing left to lose and everything to avenge.

She stepped from the theatre's skeleton into the grey light of early morning, leaving behind the charred remains of who she had been. Ahead lay the Bishop's reckoning, and her own.

Chapter Eighteen

The last flight

Southwark rose from its own ashes like a half-formed creature, its bones exposed to the grey morning light. Mare's boots sent up small clouds with each step, the settled debris of collapsed lives clinging to her soles as she navigated streets that had shifted from familiar to foreign in the space of a single night. Her destruction. Her liberation. The weight of both pressed against her chest with each breath of smoke-tinged air.

Four days had passed since the fires. Four days of fitful sleep in borrowed corners, of washing river water through her hair to rid it of ash that seemed determined to make a home there. Her face, reflected in a puddle she stepped over, looked hollowed and sharp, her eyes darkened not just by lack of sleep but by something deeper, a knowledge that couldn't be unlearned, a line that couldn't be uncrossed.

Workers swarmed the district like ants rebuilding a trampled hill, their bodies bent to the task of resurrection. Hammers struck rhythmically against wood and stone, a heartbeat returning to streets that had briefly died. Men Mare recognized as dockworkers now hauled splintered beams from pathways, tossing them into growing piles that would eventually feed new construction or winter fires. Women with soot-blackened hands sorted through debris, separating salvageable items from refuse with the efficiency of those accustomed to making use of whatever fate provided.

"Watch yourself there," called a man as a timber swung precariously close to her head. Mare stepped aside without comment, her eyes following the wood's journey from the collapsed tavern wall to a waiting cart. The King's Arms, where she'd once listened to Marlowe recite lines from his newest play while his hand traced patterns on her thigh beneath the table. Now just a jagged shell with half its foundation exposed like a rotten tooth pulled from gum.

Her branded forearm throbbed beneath her sleeve, a persistent ache that flared with each shift in temperature or brush against fabric. The wounds would never fully heal, she knew. Some marks were meant to be carried like permanent reminders of lessons learned at too high a cost.

At the corner where Rose Alley met the main thoroughfare, Mare paused. A massive beam, charred at both ends but somehow intact at its centre, lay half-across the path. It had once supported the roof of Madame Voss's dress shop, where the more successful Winchester Geese had purchased gowns with coin earned on their backs. Mare's fingers reached out, of their own accord, to touch the scorched wood. Beneath the soot, she could still make out carved roses that had decorated the beam, Madame's attempt at refinement in a district that valued function over beauty.

Her fingers trembled slightly against the wood, a betrayal of the calm she maintained in her face. For a moment, the street around her disappeared, replaced by the roaring chaos of that night, flames climbing walls like hungry creatures, screams cutting through smoke-thick air and the sound of timbers giving way beneath their own weight. The satisfaction she'd felt watching the Bishop's domain collapse had been sharp as a blade, sweet as the first sip of wine. Now it sat differently in her chest, an uncomfortable heat she recognized as guilt.

Mare withdrew her hand, wiping soot onto her already stained breeches. Guilt served no purpose, not when survival remained her priority. The destruction had been necessary, the only way to break the foundations of power that had trapped her, trapped all of them, for generations. What rose from these ashes might be better, or merely different. Either way, she wouldn't be here to see it.

A woman emerged from a partially collapsed building across the street, her arms filled with blackened linens that might, with enough scrubbing, be salvaged. Behind her, two children carried a cracked cooking pot between them, their faces smudged with soot but set with the determination of the young who haven't yet learned to surrender to circumstance. Mare watched them pick their way through debris, the woman calling out warnings about unstable footing, the children adjusting their path accordingly.

All around her, similar scenes unfolded, survivors extracting what remained of their lives from the wreckage, already beginning the work of rebuilding not just structures but routines, relationships, purpose. Mare observed them with the distance of someone who has already stepped away, mentally if not yet physically. Her decision to leave hung in her mind like a door left ajar, waiting only for her body to follow where her thoughts had already gone.

She continued toward what had been the brothel district, her path requiring detours around collapsed walls and still-smouldering ruins. The landscape of her childhood had been rewritten in fire and rubble, landmarks erased or transformed beyond recognition. Where The Crane had stood with its red-painted door and perpetually listing sign, only a pile of stone and charred timber remained. The narrow passage where she'd first learned to pick pockets was now blocked by the collapsed roof of the building that had once provided its sheltering shadow.

The metallic film of ash coated her tongue, mixed with the sharper stench of things that had burned less cleanly than wood, cloth, oil, flesh. Mare breathed through her mouth, a technique she'd perfected during childhood visits to the tanneries. The air tasted of endings, of clearing ground, of possibilities not yet defined enough to be called beginnings.

A group of men worked to clear a large section of wall that had fallen across what had been the district's main well. Their faces streamed with sweat despite the cool morning air, muscles straining against the weight of stone that refused to yield. One man caught Mare's eye as she passed, his gaze lingering just long enough to register recognition before returning to his task. She'd seen him before in the Bishop's chambers, delivering reports about shipments along the river. Now he hauled debris like any common labourer, the hierarchy that had elevated him washed away in the tide of destruction.

Mare felt the weight of her small leather satchel against her hip, packed with everything she intended to take from Southwark, a change of clothes, the silver she'd salvaged, Marlowe's papers pressed flat between layers of fabric. Light enough to carry for miles, heavy enough to contain the seeds of a different future. Her hand drifted to it briefly, confirming its presence as she moved between piles of rubble that had once been places with names, with purposes, with inhabitants who had called them home.

Bess Quickly sat atop an overturned barrel like a queen on a makeshift throne, her back straight despite the pain that tightened the corners of her mouth. Her hands worked methodically at her own ribs, winding dirty linen around her torso with the practiced movements of someone who'd patched herself up more times than worth counting. Blood had seeped through the bandage in three distinct spots, dark against the grimy fabric, marking the places where her ribs had punctured through skin during her escape from the collapsing brothel.

She looked up at Mare's approach, her weathered face splitting into a grin that showed three missing teeth, casualties of a client's fist years before Mare had even learned to walk. "Well, fuck me sideways," Bess rasped, her voice roughened by smoke and shouting. "Thought you'd be halfway to France by now."

Mare stepped over a fallen beam to reach the older woman. "Not France," she replied, kneeling to examine Bess's bandaging job. "Too many fucking Frenchmen there."

Bess's laugh turned into a wince, her hand pressing against her side. "Shit," she hissed through clenched teeth. "Don't make me laugh, girl. Every breath feels like being stabbed by the Bishop himself."

"He'd enjoy that too much," Mare muttered, gently nudging Bess's hands away from the bandage. "Let me. You're making it too loose." Her fingers worked quickly, unwinding the soiled linen to reveal the mottled purple-yellow bruising spread across Bess's rib cage. Three distinct lumps protruded beneath the skin where bones had broken and shifted.

"Thought you were dead when that wall came down," Bess said, her eyes fixed on some point beyond Mare's shoulder. "Half expected to see your corpse when we dug through the rubble."

Mare rewound the bandage, pulling it tighter than Bess had managed alone. The older woman sucked air between her teeth but didn't complain. "Sorry to disappoint," Mare said, her tone flat but her fingers gentle as they worked.

"Disappointed? Christ, girl, I was fucking relieved." Bess's hand caught Mare's wrist, stilling her movements for a moment. "Not many of us left now, is there?"

Something shifted in Mare's chest, not pain, not relief, but the uncomfortable space between. She resumed bandaging without answering, focusing on the mechanical task of wound care rather than the weight behind Bess's words.

"Heard the Bishop survived," Bess continued, releasing Mare's wrist. "Dragged away by his dogs, half his body crushed but still breathing. Still giving orders, they say."

"He's a cockroach," Mare replied, tying off the bandage with a firm knot. "Survives what would kill any decent creature."

"And that cunt Agnes?" Bess asked, adjusting her position on the barrel as Mare sat back on her heels.

"Dead." The word fell between them like a stone dropped in still water. "I watched her go."

Bess nodded once, satisfaction tightening her mouth. "Good. That bitch got what she deserved, playing mother only when it suited her." She spat on the ground, the gesture conveying more than words could about her opinion of the Order's leader. "And that fucking playwright? The one who had you wrapped around his ink-stained finger?"

Mare's hand moved unconsciously to her satchel, where Marlowe's papers pressed against her hip. "Gone, before all this." She straightened, surveying the ruins of what had once been The Cardinal's Cap, Bess's establishment, not the finest of Southwark's brothels but far from the worst. "Your girls?"

"Five dead. Seven made it out." Bess shrugged, the motion causing another wince. "Maggie lost an eye. Katherine got that pretty face sliced open. The rest have the usual, burns, broken bones, nightmares that wake the whole fucking street." She reached for a bottle nestled in the rubble beside her barrel, uncorked it with her teeth, and took a deep pull before offering it to Mare. "Building's gone, but we've claimed that old warehouse by the tannery. Not so many windows, but the walls are stone. Won't burn so easy next time."

Mare accepted the bottle, cheap gin that burned her throat like liquid fire. "Next time?"

"There's always a next time in Southwark, isn't there?" Bess reclaimed the bottle. "Different men, different reasons, same result. We burn, we rebuild, we survive." Her eyes, sharp despite the pain clouding them, fixed on Mare. "Most of us, anyway. Some run."

"I'm not running," Mare said, the words emerging with more heat than she'd intended. "I'm just... done."

"Done," Bess repeated, testing the word like an unfamiliar taste. "What's that feel like, I wonder? To be done with a place?" She gestured to the ruins surrounding them, to the women picking through debris, to the men hauling timber for new construction. "Some of us don't have the luxury of running, of being done. Do we?"

Mare held Bess's gaze, neither apologizing nor defending. "You could come. There's enough silver I have."

"For fuck's sake, girl." Bess cut her off with a dismissive wave. "Look at me. Broken ribs, forty or so years of Southwark ground into these bones, and girls who need looking after. What would I do out there?" She nodded toward the world beyond the Thames. "This shithole is mine. If I'm to die choking on its filth, at least I'll do it on my own terms."

They fell silent, the space between them filled with the sounds of reconstruction, hammers striking nails, voices calling instructions, the groan of timber being set into place. Mare realized with a sudden clarity that this might be the last time she'd speak with Bess, the woman who'd taught her to survive Southwark's streets when she was barely old enough to walk them. The woman who'd cleaned her wounds after the Bishop's first punishment, who'd shown her how to pick locks and men's pockets with equal skill, who'd never once pretended the world was anything but what it was, cruel, unfair, and occasionally survivable if you were clever enough.

"I see you've packed light," Bess said finally, her eyes dropping to Mare's satchel. "Smart. Heavy baggage slows you down when you're making a new start."

Mare nodded, relieved that Bess understood without requiring explanations she wasn't sure she could provide. "I'll be gone by nightfall."

"Good. The Bishop's men were sniffing around yesterday. What's left of them, anyway." Bess shifted, wincing as her ribs protested. "Asking questions about the Bishop's Shadow. Offering coin for information."

"And?" Mare asked, her voice carefully neutral.

Bess looked affronted. "And I told them to fuck themselves sideways with a rusty poker. What do you take me for?" She reached into a pocket hidden within the folds of her skirt, withdrawing something small that gleamed dully in her palm. "Here. Been saving this for something special."

Mare accepted the object, a small silver pendant on a leather cord, tarnished with age. A crude bird with outstretched wings had been stamped into the metal, its edges worn smooth by years of handling.

"My mother's," Bess said, looking away as if embarrassed by the sentimentality of the gesture. "Only thing I had of hers. Silver's real. You can sell it if you need to."

Mare closed her fingers around the pendant, the metal warm from Bess's body heat. She slipped it over her head without comment, tucking it beneath her shirt where it settled against her collarbone.

"Don't get yourself killed out there," Bess said gruffly, reclaiming her bottle. "You're the only friend I've got left."

Mare stood, brushing ash from her knees. The word "friend" hung between them, neither acknowledged nor rejected. "Stay alive, Bess," she replied, the closest to affection she could manage. "I'd hate to have to come back and avenge you."

Bess's laugh followed her as she walked away, the sound breaking into a pained cough that Mare pretended not to hear. She didn't look back, didn't need to see Bess watching her go. Some goodbyes were better left unwitnessed, their weight carried forward rather than observed in the moment of their making.

Rose Alley existed now only in memory; its physical form reduced to a tangle of timber and stone that bore no resemblance to the narrow passage where girls had once called to passersby from red-curtained windows. Mare stepped over what had been the alley's entrance, marked by a twisted iron post that had once held a lantern perpetually lit to guide customers through even the blackest nights. Now the post jutted from rubble like a sentinel guarding ruins no one would think to plunder.

Katherine glanced up at Mare's approach, recognition flashing across features made unfamiliar by recent violence. The fresh scar bisecting her left eyebrow stood livid against skin still young enough to heal without permanent creases. It began at her temple and cut diagonally through the eyebrow, ending just short of her eyelid, a gift from one of the Bishop's men who'd found her hiding in a root cellar during the initial purge. The wound had been stitched by inexpert hands, the black thread stark against her pale skin, pulling the flesh into a permanent expression of scepticism on that side of her face.

"Still alive then," Katherine said by way of greeting, her hands never pausing in their work of sorting. "Was wondering if you'd gotten yourself killed after setting all this in motion." Her tone held no accusation, just the resigned flatness of someone too exhausted for anger.

Mare crouched beside her, examining the collection of salvaged items. "Not yet," she replied. "Though not for lack of trying on the Bishop's part."

"Or the Order's," Katherine added, setting aside a bent silver fork that might fetch a few coins from a metalsmith willing to melt it down. "Sister Catherine's been through here twice, asking after you. Called you a traitor and murderer, said Agnes died by your hand."

"Agnes died by her own choices, same as the rest of them."

Katherine's fingers stilled momentarily on a cracked leather pouch. "The Bishop's men are still looking for you," she said, her voice lowered though no one stood close enough to overhear. "And what's left of the Order wants your head."

"Let them look. I'll be gone by nightfall."

Something flickered across Katherine's face, not disappointment, not relief, but some complicated emotion that existed in the space between. She touched her scar absently, tracing its path from temple to eyebrow in an unconscious gesture she'd developed since receiving the wound.

"Of course you are," she said finally. "Why stay and help clean up the mess?"

The accusation hung in the air between them, sharp enough to draw blood if either of them moved carelessly against it. Mare remained still, watching Katherine's fingers move from her scar to sort through more recovered trinkets with methodical precision.

"There's nothing left to stay for," Mare said, her tone deliberately neutral. "The Bishop's broken. The Order's scattered. Southwark will rebuild or it won't, but either way, it won't be what it was."

Katherine snorted, the sound startlingly inelegant from someone whose face, even marred by violence, retained the delicate beauty that had once commanded the highest prices in the Bishop's brothels. "And what was it, exactly? A shithole where men like the Bishop grew fat on our backs? Where women like Agnes traded in flesh while claiming some higher purpose?" She pushed a strand of hair behind her ear, revealing a second, older scar along her jawline. "Or was it home? The only one some of us have ever known."

The question contained no right answer, and Mare offered none. Instead, she reached for a small ceramic pot in Katherine's collection, turning it to examine the unbroken rose painted on its side. "Yours?" she asked.

"Ruby's," Katherine replied, mentioning one of the women who hadn't survived the fires. "She kept her earrings in it. Said her mother gave it to her, but Ruby was a fucking liar, so who knows?" She took the pot from Mare's hands, placing it carefully among the items she'd deemed worth keeping. "Doesn't matter now, I suppose. It's mine until someone takes it from me. Just like everything else in this life."

Mare recognized the bitterness in Katherine's voice, it was the acrid tone of someone young enough to still feel betrayed by the world's fundamental unfairness. The fact that she could recognize it meant she'd moved beyond it herself, though she couldn't pinpoint when that transition had occurred.

"Where will you go?" Katherine asked abruptly, her eyes meeting Mare's directly for the first time. Despite the new hardness in her gaze, she looked impossibly young, twenty at most, with half those years spent in Southwark's brothels after being sold by a father who'd run out of options and daughters in equal measure.

Mare shrugged, the gesture encompassing the world beyond Southwark's broken boundaries. "Somewhere I don't owe anyone a fucking thing."

"Does such a place exist?" Katherine's hand moved to her scar again, as if the still-healing wound anchored her to reality when thoughts threatened to drift toward dangerous shores.

"I'll let you know when I find it," Mare replied, the closest she could come to acknowledging that Katherine's scepticism might be warranted.

They worked in silence for several moments, sorting through the recovered items with the unspoken understanding of those who have survived the same storm. Mare separated rusted nails from the collection, setting them aside where builders might salvage them. Katherine folded a smoke-damaged length of ribbon, adding it to her small pile of kept treasures.

"Bess says you're going alone," Katherine said finally, not looking up from her task.

Mare nodded, though the younger woman wasn't watching for her response.

"Probably smarter that way," Katherine continued. "No one to slow you down. No one to betray you when things get difficult." She straightened, brushing dirt from her skirt with hands that looked too delicate for the calluses they carried. "No one to watch your back either."

"I've managed alone before," Mare said, rising to her feet in a single fluid movement that belied her exhaustion.

Katherine stood as well, her height bringing them eye to eye. "You never were, though, were you? Alone. Even when the Bishop had you running his errands, when that playwright was using you for his schemes, you had connections. People who gave a shit whether you lived or died." She gestured to the ruins surrounding them, to the figures moving through collapsed buildings with the determination of those rebuilding rather than merely scavenging. "That's what you're really leaving."

Mare felt the weight of Katherine's words press against her chest, not guilt, exactly, but recognition of a truth she'd been avoiding. She had survived Southwark because of connections formed in its dark corners and filthy alleys. Because Bess had taught her to fight dirty, because Ruby had shown her how to identify safe targets, because even the Bishop, in his manipulative way, had trained her to navigate dangers that would have claimed a truly solitary soul.

"Maybe," Mare acknowledged, offering the concession like a parting gift. "But connections are chains too, if you're not careful."

Katherine's mouth curved in a smile that pulled at her stitches. "Says the woman with two different brands burned into her skin." She stepped forward suddenly, arms wrapping around Mare in a brief, fierce embrace that ended before Mare could decide whether to return it. "Don't die out there," Katherine said, already turning back to her work. "Someone should make it out of this shithole alive."

Mare stood for a moment, watching as Katherine returned to her methodical sorting, her scarred face set in lines of concentration that made her look older than her years. Then she turned away, moving toward the river where her final cache waited beneath a pier that had somehow survived the destruction that had claimed more solid structures.

By midday, she would retrieve her final cache from beneath another pier. By evening, she would cross London Bridge, leaving Southwark and its ghosts behind. The thought should have brought relief, or at least the cold satisfaction of a mission completed. Instead, it settled in her stomach like a stone, not regret, exactly, but acknowledgment of a transition more significant than merely changing location.

The tide had receded, exposing the slimy wooden supports of the dock. Mare slipped beneath it, her boots sinking into mud that sucked at each step with hungry persistence. She counted posts until she reached the seventh, then crouched to feel along its base where water met wood during high tide. Her fingers found the loose board exactly where she'd left it months earlier, when the possibility of needing an escape route had been theoretical rather than immediate.

Mare pried the board free, reaching into the small cavity behind it to extract a waterproof leather pouch sealed with wax. Inside, she found everything she'd hidden for this moment: a man's shirt and breeches, practical for travel and less conspicuous than women's clothing; a small knife in a worn leather sheath, its blade oiled to prevent rust; a pouch containing silver coins sewn into its lining to prevent telltale jingling; and a folded scrap of parchment bearing a crude map of routes north, marked with symbols only she could interpret.

At the bottom of the pouch lay one impractical item, a small wooden horse, crudely carved but polished smooth by years of handling. Mare's fingers closed around it, the familiar contours fitting perfectly against her palm. The Bishop had given it to her on her tenth birthday, one of his rare moments of something approaching genuine affection. She'd kept it through years of his manipulation and cruelty, a reminder not of his kindness but of her own capacity for survival.

Mare tucked everything into her traveling satchel, then carefully replaced the board, erasing evidence of the cache's existence. Rising, she wiped mud from her hands onto her breeches, leaving dark streaks across the already filthy fabric. The tide was turning, water beginning its slow creep back toward the pier's supports. By the time it reached the seventh post, she would be far from Southwark, leaving no trace for those who might follow.

London Bridge stretched before Mare like the spine of some ancient beast, its hunched buildings crowding the edges as if they might topple into the Thames with the next strong wind. She stood at its southern entrance, a solitary figure against the gathering dusk, her silhouette sharp-edged where it cut through the mist that rose from the river in ghostly tendrils. Behind her, Southwark smouldered still, occasional flames licking at the darkening sky like the last defiant gestures of a dying animal. Ahead, London proper waited, indifferent to her arrival or departure, eternal in its willingness to swallow lives without acknowledgment.

The Thames flowed beneath, dark, and constant, its surface broken occasionally by floating debris, splintered timbers, sodden cloth, unidentifiable objects that might once have been furniture or might have been something else entirely. The river accepted Southwark's remains without judgment, carrying away the physical evidence of destruction as it had carried the evidence of countless human dramas before. Mare watched a child's wooden hoop spin lazily in the current before disappearing beneath the bridge's first arch, bound for the sea that would eventually claim all of London's discarded pieces.

Everything she owned hung from her shoulder in a small leather pouch that pressed against her hip with each shift of her weight. Inside: the clothes from her cache, practical and plain; silver coins sewn into hidden pockets; Marlowe's papers, their edges softened by repeated folding; the knife she'd carried since childhood; the wooden horse that represented her one concession to sentiment; and now, Bess's silver pendant warm against her collarbone beneath her shirt. Her possessions amounted to less than most beggars carried yet contained enough secrets to upend lives across England if wielded properly.

Mare's gaze drifted between the two landscapes divided by the bridge, Southwark behind, London ahead, the river flowing indifferently between. The buildings across the water emerged and disappeared as fog shifted, their outlines softened and then hardened by the whims of air and moisture. Lights appeared in windows as darkness crept across the sky, candles and oil lamps transforming structures into constellations grounded by gravity rather than suspended in night's expanse.

On the Southwark side, fewer lights appeared. Entire sections remained, dark buildings collapsed beyond repair, streets rendered impassable by rubble, districts where survivors huddled around fires rather than returning to unstable structures. Mare could trace the pattern of destruction from her vantage point, could see where flames had burned hottest, where buildings had fallen most completely, where her orchestrated chaos had left the deepest scars on the landscape of her birth.

The brands on her arm and palm throbbed in unison, their pain intensified by the damp evening air that rose from the river. The Bishop's seal on her palm felt hot beneath the glove she'd donned to hide it, as if the wound recognized its proximity to the man who had inflicted it. The Order's brand on her forearm pulsed with duller pain, the newer injury still pink at its edges where damaged skin struggled to heal. Mare flexed her fingers, feeling scar tissue pull taut across her palm, a permanent reminder of ownership she had rejected but could never fully escape.

A bell tolled somewhere in the City, marking the hour with seven solemn notes that carried across water and stone to reach her ears. The sound mingled with closer noises, merchants on the bridge calling final prices as they packed away goods, apprentices shouting to one another as they closed shop for the night, the constant backdrop of the river slapping against the bridge's supports. A cart rumbled past, its wheels clattering on uneven stones, its driver hunched against the evening chill, oblivious to Mare standing motionless amid the flow of homeward-bound travellers.

The bridge itself seemed alive with movement, people crossing in both directions, their purposes as varied as their appearances. A group of apprentices jostled past, laughing too loudly, drunk on cheap ale and youth's invincibility. A woman in a finer dress than the district typically saw hurried toward Southwark, her face partially concealed by a hood, her steps quick with purpose that Mare recognized as the urgency of secret assignations. Two merchants argued over the price of wool as they walked, their hands gesturing expansively, their voices rising and falling with the rhythm of practiced negotiation.

Mare drew a deep breath, tasting smoke and river water on her tongue. The air carried Southwark's essence, ash and mud and the tang of too many lives pressed too closely together but also London's promise of anonymity, of reinvention, of paths leading beyond city walls to places where her name meant nothing and her scars told stories only she could translate. She touched Bess's pendant through her shirt, feeling its outline against her fingertips, then adjusted her satchel more securely across her body.

There would be no dramatic farewell, no final glance back at the district that had birthed her, raised her, nearly destroyed her. Mare had never been one for gestures without purpose, and sentiment served no practical end. Instead, she simply pulled her hood lower against the thickening fog and stepped forward onto the bridge proper, her boots striking stone with deliberate force, as if testing the bridge's willingness to bear her weight and the weight of what she carried, physically and otherwise.

The crowd absorbed her as she moved, her figure becoming one more shadow among many. A woman in men's clothing drew few glances in the gathering darkness, particularly one who moved with the confidence of belonging wherever she stood. Mare adjusted her stride to match the flow of bodies crossing the bridge, neither hurrying nor dawdling, giving no cause for attention or memory. Her face beneath the hood remained impassive, revealing nothing of the calculations that continued behind eyes the colour of the river at dusk.

The Bishop lived, wounded but dangerous still. His reach might extend beyond Southwark, beyond London itself. Mare carried enough of his secrets to protect herself or destroy him, depending on how events unfolded. She also carried Marlowe's legacy, papers that implicated men in high positions, connections that stretched to court and beyond. And she carried her own history written in scars visible and invisible, in knowledge earned through blood and betrayal, in skills honed under the tutelage of those who had sought to use her for their own ends.

The bell tolled once more, a single note that seemed to hang in the air before dissolving into the ambient noise of the city. Mare passed the midpoint of the bridge without acknowledging the significance of the crossing. The river flowed beneath her feet, carrying away the last physical connections to Southwark, to the Bishop, to Agnes, to the life she had known. Ahead, London's maze of streets offered a thousand paths, each leading to futures she could now choose rather than merely survive.

Mare disappeared into the thickening fog, her figure becoming indistinct among the crowds that crossed London Bridge each evening. The mist swallowed her as it swallowed all who passed, the wealthy merchant, the tired apprentice, the woman of negotiable virtue, the pickpocket eyeing unwary travellers. Just another shadow moving between worlds, poised between a past written in fire and blood and a future she would inscribe herself, one careful step at a time.

Chapter Nineteen

Fog on the Thames

The corridors of Whitehall Palace reeked of power, a scent as distinct as Southwark's blend of river mud and desperation but disguised with rosewater and beeswax polish. Mare moved through it like a current of chilly air, her steps silent on marble floors that had never known the press of bare feet, or the splatter of blood shed for something as common as survival. Three months had passed since she'd crossed London Bridge, and still the opulence of Elizabeth's court felt like a costume she'd donned rather than a world she inhabited.

She wore that costume well enough, a dark blue dress of modest cut but fine material, her hair tamed into a simple knot at the nape of her neck, her scarred hands concealed in soft leather gloves that never left her flesh, not even in the Queen's presence. The Bishop's mark remained beneath the left glove; a constant reminder pressed against her palm. The Order's brand on her forearm stayed hidden beneath carefully chosen sleeves, never revealed even to the chambermaids who might have glimpsed it while helping her dress, had she allowed such intimacies.

Afternoon light streamed through tall windows, catching dust motes that swirled in her wake. Mare followed their dance with eyes that missed nothing, not the pageboy slipping a folded note to a lady-in-waiting, not the courtier whose fingers tapped a nervous rhythm against his doublet, not the servant who paused too long while polishing a silver candlestick near the Queen's private chambers. Court was a different kind of battleground than Southwark, its dangers wrapped in silk rather than steel, but her survival depended on reading its patterns just the same.

Ahead, voices murmured from an alcove half-hidden behind a massive tapestry depicting the triumph of English ships over the

Spanish Armada five years earlier. Mare slowed, her attention shifting like a predator scenting more promising prey. Four men huddled near the hanging, their fine clothes marking them as ministers of the Queen's Privy Council. Lord Cecil's hunched shoulders were unmistakable, his shrewd eyes peering from a face that reminded Mare of a rat that had learned to wear human skin. Beside him stood the Earl of Essex, younger and more handsome, his beard trimmed to fashionable precision, his rings catching light as he gesticulated in barely contained frustration.

Mare drifted toward a nearby column, her movements casual yet precise. She extracted a small leather-bound book from the pocket hidden in her skirts, one of Marlowe's journals, its contents less important than the shield it provided. A woman reading was invisible, dismissed as occupied, her attention presumed elsewhere.

"...situation in the north grows more precarious," Essex was saying, his voice pitched low but carrying to Mare's practiced ears. "The Puritan factions gain strength daily. They speak of Southwark as proof that corruption can be purged through fire."

"Fools," Cecil muttered. "They miss the obvious lesson, that fire consumes indiscriminately. Besides, that destruction served no godly purpose, merely the vendetta of a woman scorned."

Mare's fingers tightened imperceptibly on her book, but her face remained a mask of polite disinterest, her eyes fixed on the page before her.

"And did you hear about Marlowe? Died like a tragic hero from one of his plays" said a third minister, Lord Howard, whose family controlled much of England's naval interests. "

"People who play with fire get burnt, nothing tragic about that or heroic" Cecil countered.

Mare felt numbed by the news that she had garnered from another conversation earlier that day. Kit, a man the same age as Mare, they shared their bodies, but nothing else, dead before thirty years old and a miracle Mare had not suffered the same fate; a wild and fatal stab in the eye following a disturbance in a tavern.

"Not, unlike our disgraced friend from Winchester." Added Lord Howard.

The men fell silent at the reference, glancing over shoulders as if the mere mention might summon unwanted attention. Mare turned a page she hadn't read, her ears straining to catch every word.

"Has there been word?" Essex finally asked, his voice dropping further. "Of his whereabouts?"

Cecil shook his head, jowls quivering with the motion. "Nothing certain. Rumours place him in Scotland, in France, even in Rome seeking papal protection." His mouth twisted in distaste. "Though how a man half-crippled could travel so far..."

"He had resources we never fully mapped," Howard said. "Connections beyond his diocese, coffers we never located."

"What of the woman?" asked the fourth minister, a slender man whose name Mare couldn't immediately place. "The one who brought him down. The Bishop's Shadow, they called her in the broadsheets."

Mare kept her eyes on her book, though the words blurred before her. Her pulse remained steady through long practice, even as she felt the weight of her name, or title, hanging in the corridor's still air.

"Vanished," Cecil said, his tone suggesting the mystery irritated him personally. "Like smoke. Some say she died in the fires. Others claim to have seen her in a dozen different places." He glanced around, his gaze sweeping past Mare without lingering. "The Queen expressed interest in meeting this woman. Someone capable of dismantling the Bishop's network might prove... useful to the Crown."

Essex snorted softly. "If she exists at all. These tales grow more fantastical with each telling. A woman single-handedly destroying Southwark's power structure? More likely it was simply the culmination of long-simmering tensions, with no single architect."

Mare turned another page, a smile threatening at the corners of her mouth. Men like Essex could never quite believe a woman capable of orchestrating what they themselves would consider a complex political manoeuvre. It was a blindness she had exploited in Southwark; it served her equally well in court.

"The Bishop believed she existed," Howard said quietly. "His last known correspondence spoke of her betrayal in rather biblical terms. Vengeance, hellfire, divine retribution—language unbecoming a man of the cloth."

The ministers exchanged uncomfortable glances, as if the Bishop's rage might extend to those who discussed him. Cecil made a dismissive gesture with jewelled fingers.

"Regardless, both the Bishop and his Shadow are ghosts now, useful for frightening children and nervous courtiers, but of little practical concern. We have more pressing matters."

As the conversation turned to French diplomatic envoys and Spanish trade disputes, Mare closed her book with careful deliberation. She had what she needed, confirmation that the Bishop lived, that his whereabouts remained unknown even to the Crown's intelligence network, that her own identity remained secure despite the stories circulating through London.

She stepped away from the column, moving toward the corridor's opposite side where a smaller passage led to the servants' areas. As she walked, she felt eyes on her back, not the ministers, who had already dismissed her presence, but someone else. Mare turned slightly, her gaze meeting that of a young page boy who stood frozen in the act of delivering a sealed message.

The boy stared too long, his eyes widening as they locked with hers. Something in her face, the flatness of her expression or the dispassionate coldness of her eyes made him flinch as if physically struck. Mare held his gaze for one heartbeat, two, three, until the boy dropped his eyes and scurried past, his shoulders hunched as if expecting a blow.

She continued toward the servants' passage, satisfied. Fear was useful currency in any realm, whether in Southwark's brutal hierarchy or Whitehall's perfumed corridors. The boy would remember her face but think twice before mentioning her presence to others, a small victory in the constant battle to remain seen but not remembered, present but not noteworthy.

The passage opened before her, narrow and dimly lit compared to the main corridor's grandeur. Mare slipped into its shadows with the relief of someone returning to more familiar territory. Here, away from watching eyes, she moved faster, her skirts gathered in gloved hands, her steps sure despite the uneven flagstones. The passage twisted, descended, then emerged through a small door that servants used for discrete entrances and exits from the palace grounds.

London spread before her, its rooftops catching the late afternoon sun, its streets already filling with shadows as day waned toward evening. Mare pulled her cloak around her shoulders, its dark fabric settling like wings as she descended the worn steps to street level. The city swallowed her immediately, one more figure among thousands, unremarkable to any but the most observant eye.

Behind her, Whitehall's windows blazed with light as courtiers prepared for evening entertainments. Mare didn't look back. The court was simply another hunting ground, another source of information to be gathered and utilized. The true game lay elsewhere, in discovering the Bishop's hiding place, in finishing what she had started in Southwark's flames.

Her cloak billowed behind her as she turned into a narrow street where fading sunlight never reached. Within three steps, she had vanished into London's labyrinth, leaving nothing behind but the fading impression of a woman who moved like shadow given form.

The Cardinals Cap wore its scars with the same pride as its patrons. Smoke stains crawled up the newly plastered walls like black vines reaching for the ceiling, where salvaged beams, some still bearing char marks from the fires, stretched across the room like the ribs of a ship turned inside out. The tavern had been one of the first establishments to rise from Southwark's ashes, cobbled together from whatever survived: a door from the old church, window frames rescued from the collapsed brothels, floorboards pried from buildings that couldn't be saved but might still contribute to what would come next.

Behind a bar fashioned from the Bishop's overturned carriage, a particular bit of spite that delighted the locals, a grizzled man with one ear missing poured ale from a dented pewter pitcher. His remaining ear twitched occasionally toward the table of sailors near the hearth, their voices rising and falling with the discordant rhythm of men who'd been drinking since midday and planned to continue until their coins or consciousness gave out.

"Another," demanded a dockworker, slamming his empty mug down. The barkeep filled it without comment, his eyes never leaving the rowdy sailors even as his hands performed their task with practiced precision.

The tavern hummed with the sounds of Southwark's resurrection, hammers striking in the distance as new construction continued even into evening, the scrape of chair legs against uneven floorboards, laughter that carried the edge of relief from those who had survived when others hadn't. The air hung thick with the smell of bodies pressed too closely together, of spilled ale soaking into wood, of the perpetual damp that rose from the Thames and settled into the district's foundations.

"They've put stone footings under the new brothels," said a heavyset man to his companions, gesturing with a half-eaten piece of bread. "Twice the cost, but the merchant syndicate won't risk another collapse. Bad for business, they say."

"Everything's 'bad for business' with that lot," replied a woman with hair gone grey despite her young face. "They'd put a toll on breathing if they could figure out how to collect it."

"Still better than the Bishop's men," muttered a third, his eyes darting around as if the name might summon unwelcome ghosts. "At least these new masters don't claim to be saving our souls while emptying our pockets."

A fourth dockworker snorted into his ale. "Give 'em time. Power's power, no matter who wields it."

Conversation flowed around the tavern in similar currents, talk of rebuilding, of new authorities establishing themselves, of old debts being settled and new alliances being formed from necessity. Southwark adjusted to its altered landscape with the stoic resilience of a place that had burned and risen repeatedly throughout its history, each incarnation carrying the bones of what came before.

Then someone, a thin man near the door whose clothes marked him as a scribe, mentioned "the Bishop's Shadow" while recounting a rumour heard in a Fleet Street printshop. Conversation halted as if a blade had been drawn, mugs paused halfway to lips, words died in throats, and heads turned subtly toward the speaker. The silence lasted only a heartbeat before talking resumed with forced casualness, but the momentary tension lingered like smoke after a candle's extinguishing.

In a corner booth constructed from the salvaged pews of a burned chapel, Katherine Howard leaned toward a younger woman whose unblemished face and nervous eyes marked her as relatively new to Southwark's oldest profession. The scar across Katherine's eyebrow had faded from angry red to a pale line that bisected her face like a permanent sceptical expression, pulling slightly at her left eyelid.

"You see that?" Katherine murmured, nodding toward the scribe who'd unwittingly silenced the room. "Six months gone, and still they lower their voices at the mention of her name."

The younger woman, barely seventeen, with bitten nails and the hollow-cheeked look of someone who'd known hunger long enough to consider it a constant companion shrugged one thin shoulder. "People get superstitious after disaster. Need someone to blame or credit, easier than admitting life's just shit happening without reason."

Katherine's laugh held no humour. "Is that what you think she was? Just a convenient explanation?"

"I think she's a story," the girl replied, tearing a piece of bread into smaller and smaller fragments that she didn't eat. "Like the headless monk they say haunts the old churchyard, or the river ghost that drags drunks into the Thames. Something to whisper about when the night gets too dark."

"They say she still walks these streets," Katherine continued, her voice dropping lower, forcing the girl to lean closer. "Collecting secrets like coins, building a new hoard to replace what she spent bringing down the Bishop."

The younger woman rolled her eyes. "Ghost stories to scare children."

Katherine's gaze sharpened, the scar pulling her eyebrow into a more pronounced arch. "Then why does Bess Quickly still leave an empty chair at her table every third Thursday?" She nodded toward the far corner of the tavern, where the oldest surviving madam in Southwark sat holding court with three younger women. True to Katherine's words, a single chair at their table remained conspicuously empty, though the tavern was crowded enough that any available seat would normally be claimed.

The girl followed Katherine's gaze, her expression wavering between dismissal and uncertainty. "Sentiment? Respect for the dead?"

"Bess Quickly hasn't got a sentimental bone in her body," Katherine replied, touching her scar absently, a habit she'd developed in the months since receiving it. "And she doesn't waste respect on the dead, who can't do anything useful with it."

The corner table sat directly beneath a small window, its leaded glass salvaged from the Bishop's private chapel, another deliberate choice in the tavern's reconstruction. Light filtered through the coloured panes, casting jewel-toned patterns across the weathered wood. Bess's face, lined with decades of Southwark's hardships, shifted between blue and amber as she gestured, clearly recounting a story that made her companions lean forward with the eagerness of those receiving valuable instruction.

"Look at this place," Katherine continued, gesturing around the tavern with her mug. "Built from pieces of what came before. That door? Pulled from the old King's Arms before the rest collapsed. The bar itself made from the Bishop's own carriage. The mirror behind it salvaged from Madame Voss's reception room." Her eyes returned to the younger woman's face. "Nothing ever truly disappears in Southwark. It just changes form."

The girl's gaze drifted across the tavern, taking in details she'd previously overlooked. The candle holders hammered from metal once used as brothel signage. The stone hearth constructed from blocks that had survived the cathedral's collapse. The wooden panels lining one wall, their edges still blackened from the fires that had claimed their original building.

"She burned it all down," Katherine said, her voice so quiet it barely carried across the small table. "But she was clever enough to ensure certain pieces survived, certain people, certain information, certain connections. Do you think the reconstruction happened by accident? That Bess and the others just got lucky?"

The younger woman's expression shifted, suspicion replacing dismissal. "You sound like you knew her."

Katherine's mouth curved in a smile that didn't reach her eyes. "Everyone in Southwark knew her, one way or another. Some better than others." She lifted her mug in a small toast toward the empty chair at Bess's table. "And some of us are still paying debts we owe, in whatever currency we have available."

From the street outside came the sound of the night watchman calling the hour, his voice carrying through the tavern's open windows. Conversations shifted, patrons signalling for final drinks or settling debts before heading home. The sailors by the hearth launched into a bawdy song, their voices surprisingly melodic despite their intoxication.

Bess Quickly rose from her table, her movements revealing the stiffness of partially healed ribs that would never set quite right. She placed a hand briefly on the empty chair beside her, not the superstitious gesture of someone warding off ghosts, but the deliberate acknowledgment of an absence that might, one day, be filled again. Then she made her way toward the bar, exchanging nods with various patrons, her authority established not through any official position but through the simple fact of her survival when so many others had perished.

As she passed Katherine's table, Bess paused, her eyes flicking toward the younger woman with the assessing gaze of someone weighing potential value. "Teaching the new ones our history, Kate?" she asked, her voice raspy from decades of smoke and cheap gin.

Katherine shrugged, her scar catching the light. "Someone has to. Otherwise they might think Southwark sprang up fresh from the ashes, with no debts carried forward."

Bess's laugh was a harsh sound, like rusty hinges forced into movement. "No such luck in this life." She continued toward the bar, calling for the one-eared barkeep's attention with a tone that ensured immediate service despite the crowded room.

The younger woman watched her go, then turned back to Katherine, confusion evident in her expression. "You all talk about her like she's coming back. But if she's the one who burned everything, why would she return to the scene of her crime?"

Katherine's eyes drifted toward the empty chair at Bess's table, then to the window beyond, where London's rooftops stretched toward a darkening sky. "Maybe because destruction wasn't her only purpose," she said finally. "Or maybe because even those who burn bridges sometimes find they've left something valuable on the other side."

Outside, the watchman called the hour again, his voice fading as he moved deeper into Southwark's reconstructed streets. Inside the Cardinals Cap, patrons continued their conversations, their laughter, their arguments, life flowing forward as it always did, around and through the broken pieces of what had come before.

London Bridge stretched before Mare like a spine connecting two worlds, its hunched buildings stark against a sky the colour of old bruises. Fog rolled in from the Thames in thick, ghostly billows, swallowing the bridge's southern end where Southwark's reconstructed skyline should have been visible. The mist brought with it the river's particular scent, mud and salt and the accumulated debris of a city that discarded its unwanted into water that never judged, merely carried away. Mare stood midway across, a solitary figure against the gathering darkness, her cloak drawn tight against the damp that sought to penetrate cloth and skin alike.

Three months had passed since she'd last stood here, looking back at Southwark's smouldering remains, everything she owned hanging from her shoulder in a small leather pouch. Now she carried different burdens, knowledge gathered in whispers at court, secrets extracted from ministers who never noticed the shadow listening at the edges of their conversations, plans forming like the slow crystallization of salt from evaporating seawater.

Below, the Thames flowed black and relentless, its surface disturbed by the passage of boats whose outlines appeared and vanished like apparitions in the thickening fog. A wherry emerged from the mist, its outline softened to a smudge of darker grey, the boatman's figure barely distinguishable as he guided his craft beneath the bridge's central arch. A larger vessel followed, a merchant ship returning from the day's trade, its lanterns glowing orange through the fog like dying embers, the calls of its crew muffled by the mist that wrapped around every sound.

Mare watched them pass with the mute stillness she'd perfected at court, a motionlessness that rendered her almost invisible despite standing in plain sight. The gloves she wore, fine leather now, rather than the rough pair she'd owned in Southwark, concealed both her brands from casual observation. The left one covered the Bishop's seal carved into her palm; the right hid the calluses that might betray her as something other than the minor lady's companion she pretended to be in Whitehall's corridors.

With deliberate movements, she removed the left glove, exposing her hand to the chill evening air. The scar stood livid against her skin, the pattern of the Bishop's seal still clearly legible despite the months that had passed. She traced its outline with her right thumb, feeling the raised tissue that would never fully heal, the permanent reminder of her first lesson in betrayal. The brand on her forearm throbbed in sympathetic memory, though it remained hidden beneath her sleeve.

"Where are you hiding, old man?" Mare murmured to the fog, her words immediately swallowed by the damp air. The ministers' conversation echoed in her mind, rumours placing the Bishop in Scotland, in France, in Rome. A man half-crippled yet still dangerous, still connected, still burning with the rage of the powerful brought low by those they'd considered beneath them.

She had spent months gathering information, sifting court gossip for grains of truth, mapping connections between nobles who might shelter a disgraced bishop for reasons of their own. Francis Walsingham, the Queen's spymaster had noticed her, not as Mare Fleet, the Bishop's Shadow who had burned Southwark, but as the quiet companion who seemed to fade into tapestries yet somehow retained every word spoken in her presence. He had used her twice already, placing her near conversations he wished to monitor. She had allowed this use, recognizing it as currency to be spent later when her own purposes required royal resources.

A merchant passed, nodding respectfully at the sight of a woman alone on the bridge at dusk. His eyes skipped over her face without truly seeing it, registering only the quality of her cloak, the modest but fine cut of the dress visible beneath it. Mare returned the nod with the precise degree of acknowledgment appropriate to her assumed station, not so friendly as to encourage conversation, not so cold as to be remembered as rude.

When he had passed beyond hearing, she withdrew a small leather-bound book from within her cloak. The volume resembled Marlowe's journals, deliberately so, as she had commissioned it from a bookbinder near St. Paul's who asked no questions about why a lady's companion required a replica of a dead playwright's personal records. The binding was worn as if from frequent handling, the pages inside filled with her own careful script, names, dates, connections recorded in the same cipher Marlowe had used, though the information it concealed had nothing to do with revolutionary poetry.

Mare opened the book to a specific page, examining the neat rows of encoded text by the fading light. Each entry represented a piece of information gathered, a rumour confirmed or discredited, a connection mapped between the Bishop's allies. Taken together, they formed a pattern that pointed not at distant Scotland or continental Europe, but somewhere much closer, a place the Bishop might believe himself beyond her reach because she would never willingly return.

She tore the page from the book with precise movements, the sound of ripping paper oddly loud in the fog-muffled quiet of the bridge. From another pocket she produced a small writing implement, not the quill favoured by court secretaries, but a piece of charcoal wrapped in leather that left bold, black marks without requiring ink. Mare wrote a single sentence across the bottom of the page, the words clearly legible despite the growing darkness:

"The fox returns to the henhouse he believes abandoned."

The cipher above it contained the details, a location in Southwark itself, a date three days hence, the names of those who would accompany the Bishop on his secret return to recover documents hidden before his hasty departure. Mare folded the page into a tight square fashioned by a small string tied into a fastened knot. A scrap of a girl appeared with eyes that shone keenly like a torch and scurried off with the paper with nimble steps that evaded the bustling throng. She jinked her way across the bridge to Southwark, to be taken to the woman in the Cardinal's Cap where an empty chair awaited every third Thursday.

The information would spread through channels the Bishop believed destroyed, whispers passing between former Winchester Geese, signals exchanged by dockworkers who had once been the Bishop's informants but now served a different purpose, preparations made by those who had survived the fires with debts unpaid and grudges unresolved.

Mare replaced her glove, the leather sliding over her scarred palm like a second skin. The fog had thickened while she stood on the bridge, reducing visibility to arm's length in all directions. She could no longer see the buildings that clung to the bridge's edges, could barely make out the stone beneath her feet. London's sounds reached her as if from great distance, muffled voices, the creaking of cartwheels, the distant call of the night watchman announcing the hour.

She turned, facing north toward the City rather than south toward Southwark. Her next tasks lay in Whitehall's shadowed corridors, in whispered conversations with the Queen's spymaster, in the gradual accumulation of power that came from knowing what others wished kept secret. The Bishop would emerge from hiding, drawn by the belief that his Shadow had moved on to other hunting grounds. He would find instead a trap laid with the patience and precision he himself had taught her.

As Mare moved forward, the fog embraced her, wrapping around her figure until her outline became increasingly indistinct. Her cloak, the colour of wet slate, melded with the grey mist. Her steps, always light, made no sound on the damp stones. With each pace, she seemed to dissolve further into the fog itself, her form becoming impossible to distinguish from the swirling vapours that claimed the bridge.

Within moments, the spot where she had stood showed no evidence of her presence, just empty with fog swirling in patterns that might have been formed by a passing figure or simply by the river's restless breath rising to meet the evening air. London Bridge stretched into darkness, connecting past to future, Southwark to City, destruction to reconstruction. The mist claimed it all, rendering judgment impossible, leaving only possibility suspended between water and sky.

Epilogue

The Cardinal's Cap heaved with bodies like a ship riding rough seas. Pipe smoke hung thick as morning fog, turning the already dim lantern light into smudges of dull gold against the darkness. Men's voices fought against each other for dominance, merchant sailors boasting of distant ports, labourers cussing over dice games, and the occasional clerk from across the river trying to sound rougher than his soft hands suggested. The stink of sweat, spilled ale, and fear-tinged hope permeated every wooden beam of the place that had seen too many secrets spilled alongside its drinks.

A woman slipped through the doorway, her face shadowed by a deep hood despite the muggy warmth inside. She moved with the careful precision of someone accustomed to not being noticed, her steps light against the rush-strewn floor. The patrons parted unconsciously before her, as if sensing a current of something dangerous beneath the calm surface of her movements.

Bess stood behind the scarred oak bar, her sleeve-covered forearms planted firmly as she poured ale with the mechanical efficiency that came from years of practice. Her eyes, sharp as a magpie's, caught the hooded figure moving through the crowd. Something in the stranger's gait made her pause mid-pour.

"Take a seat. What can I get…" The practiced greeting died on her lips as the figure drew closer. "Fuck me, it's you."

The hood tilted slightly, revealing a slash of pale face and dark eyes that caught the light like wet stone. "Upstairs," Mare said, her voice barely audible above the din yet carrying the unmistakable weight of command.

Bess nodded, gestured to a gangly youth to mind the bar, and ducked under the counter. She caught Kathryn's attention with a quick jerk of her chin toward the back stairs. Kathryn, halfway through collecting empty tankards, widened her eyes in question before spotting Mare. Her mouth formed a perfect circle of surprise.

The stairs to the upper floor creaked beneath their feet, each step releasing the ghosts of a thousand previous ascents, some made in joy, others in desperation, most in business. Mare led the way, her back straight as a church spire, her shoulders set with the same rigid determination that had always defined her. But there was something different now, an edge of shadows that clung to her even as she stepped into the candlelit room above.

"Christ's balls, Mare, where've you been hiding?" Bess shut the door behind them, dropping her tavern-keeper's smile for the harder lines of her true face. "Three months with not a bloody word."

Mare threw back her hood, revealing features that made both women stare. The same Mare, yes, but changed, like a familiar building viewed in different light. Her cheekbones stood stark against her skin, her eyes deeper set, their darkness more pronounced. Her black hair, once kept short, now fell in a tangle past her shoulders, framing a face that had grown both sharper and more commanding.

"Busy," Mare said, removing her cloak and draping it over the back of a chair. She sat with the careful poise of a lady, though her eyes still darted to exits and windows with the wariness of a street child. "And the less you knew of my whereabouts, the safer for all concerned."

Kathryn approached cautiously, as if Mare might vanish if startled. "You look... different. Like..."

"Like the fucking shadow of the bishop himself," Bess finished, folding her arms. "Same eyes. Same way of looking at you like she's deciding whether you're worth the trouble of talking to."

A ghost of a smile touched Mare's lips. "A family resemblance I've stopped fighting." She reached inside her sleeve and pulled out a small leather purse that clinked heavily as she set it on the table. "I've money. And position at court, of a sort."

Bess raised her eyebrows. "A sort that doesn't involve spreading your legs, I hope."

"There are many ways to fuck someone," Mare replied coolly. "I prefer the kind that leaves my dignity intact and my purse heavier. Selling information is good business."

Kathryn's eyes widened. "Those parchments? The ones from…"

"From Marlowe. Yes." Mare's fingers drummed once on the table before going still. "They opened doors. Doors that needed opening."

Bess poured three cups of wine from a flagon that had been warming by the small hearth. The liquid gleamed dark red in the candlelight, almost black. "Well, while you've been opening doors, shit's been changing here too. The 'liberty of the clink' has been dissolved. No more church authorities running things. Thanks to your message, the Bishop indeed appeared, and since disappeared, no more word of him, the Thames waters run harsh, and deep. "

"Good fucking riddance," Kathryn muttered.

"New authority's been set up," Bess continued. "Not church, though who they answer to isn't clear yet. Even this place has new ownership." She gestured around them at the familiar walls of the Cardinal's Cap. "Haven't seen him yet, whoever he is. Left a man to deliver the message that it's not to be a whore house anymore. Just a tavern with ale and food."

Mare took a sip of wine, watching the women over the rim of her cup. Her eyes, so like her father's in their calculation, revealed nothing. "He is she."

"What?" Kathryn frowned.

"I own this place." The words fell like stones into still water.

Silence stretched between them, broken only by the muffled sounds of revelry from below. Bess's mouth opened, closed, then opened again. "You? How in God's name…"

"That old bastard owed me. For my silence, for my service." Mare's voice remained even, matter of fact, as she thought of the evil controlling father who was no more. "His legacy has paid in property, not promises. The deed is signed, witnessed, and sealed. The Cardinal's Cap is mine." Her mouth twisted in a humourless smile. "Though I'm thinking of changing the name to The Winchester Goose. Seems fitting, don't you think?"

Kathryn barked a laugh, sharp with surprise. "Bold as brass, you are."

"What exactly are you planning to do with a tavern, Mare? You've never struck me as the type to settle for pouring ale and wiping tables." Bess studied her with narrowed eyes.

Mare leaned forward, her elbows on the table. The candlelight carved her face into planes of light and shadow, emphasizing the newfound hardness there. "I'm not settling for anything. I'm building something. But I'll need help running it." She paused, eyes flicking between the two women. "Bess, beer and front of house. You know how to handle the rowdy ones, how to make a man feel welcome without promising more than a full cup.

Kathryn, the business, figures, supplies, keeping the books straight."

"And you?" Kathryn asked.

"I'll provide protection. Connections. Make sure no one interferes with what we build here. You can take the girl out of Southwark, but you can't take Southwark out of the girl." Mare's hand rested flat on the table, her fingers splayed. A thin scar marked her left palm, white against the skin.

Bess and Kathryn exchanged glances, years of silent communication passing between them.

"Sounds like you've thought it through," Bess said slowly. "But why us? You could hire anyone."

"Because you're survivors. Because you know this place, these streets." Mare's voice softened imperceptibly. "Because I trust you. And that's not something I say lightly."

The words hung in the air, unexpected and weighty. Trust was a rare currency in Southwark, more valuable than gold.

"Partners, then?" Kathryn ventured.

Mare nodded. "Partners. Equal share in the profits, though the property remains in my name."

Bess let out a low whistle. "The Winchester Goose. Fuck me, that's rich." A slow smile spread across her face, carving lines beside her eyes that spoke of hard years but refused to surrender to them. "Southwark's changing, that's certain. Maybe it's our turn to change it back."

"To new beginnings, then." Mare raised her cup.

The women clinked their vessels together, the sound sharp and clear against the backdrop of murmuring voices below. Wine splashed dark onto the table, like blood spilled in oath-making.

"The Winchester Goose," Kathryn said, testing the name on her tongue. "Has a ring to it."

"Speaking of rings," Bess nodded toward Mare's hand, "that's new."

Mare glanced down at the simple silver band on her finger. "A necessary fiction for court. Makes me less of a target."

"And who's the lucky husband?" Kathryn smirked.

"A ghost," Mare replied flatly. "Men find widows less threatening than unmarried women. Easier to move about without questions."

She drained her cup and stood, a sudden tension in her movements. "I have to leave. The hour grows late, and I'm expected elsewhere."

"You just got here," Bess protested.

"And I'll return." Mare reached for her cloak. "Keep a chair vacant for me at your table. You never know when I might come in."

Something passed across her face, a grimace quickly suppressed. Her hand moved reflexively to her stomach before dropping away.

"Mare?" Kathryn's eyes narrowed in concern.

"It's nothing. Just tired." Mare settled the cloak around her shoulders, pulling the hood forward to shadow her face once more. "I'll send a man tomorrow with the papers. His name is Finch. Small fellow, nervous hands. He'll bring everything you need to start properly."

Bess followed her to the door. "You sure you're alright? You look..."

"I'm fine." Mare cut her off with a sharp gesture. "Better than I've been in years." She paused, her hand on the latch. "Southwark's changing. It's still a hard place, still full of shit and danger. But there's room now for something different. Something better."

"Hope's a dangerous thing to carry around these streets," Bess said quietly.

"So am I." Mare's lips curved in a smile that didn't reach her eyes. "Good night, ladies. I'll see you soon."

They watched her descend the stairs, her movements deliberate and careful. At the bottom, she paused to exchange words with a rough-looking man who nodded respectfully and melted back into the crowd. Then she was gone, swallowed by the press of bodies. Outside, Mare stood in the narrow street, the sounds of the tavern fading behind her as the door swung shut. She took a deep breath of night air, tainted with the Thames' familiar stink and the smoke of a hundred fires. Her hands moved to her belly, feeling the firm swell hidden beneath the loose folds of her dress.

Four months along now. Soon enough, it would be impossible to hide.

She looked out across Southwark, the tangled maze of streets and alleys she knew better than the lines on her own palm. The fog was rolling in from the river, transforming the familiar into something ghostly and uncertain. Yet beneath the mist, the streets remained solid, unchanged in their essential nature despite the shifting authorities that claimed dominion over them.

Mare pressed a hand against the small of her back, easing the ache that had become her constant companion. She could never truly leave this place, it was bone-deep in her, the dirt of these streets mixed with her blood. But neither could she live here now, not with what she carried. Not with who she had become.

If it were a boy, she would name him Christopher, for the man whose words had given her the key to her own freedom, and the life that grew inside her. If a girl, Agnes, after the woman whose strength had shown her what was possible, whose dark eyes and unflinching will Mare now saw reflected in her own face each morning.

The child kicked, a flutter of movement beneath her palm. Mare's lips pressed into a thin line, not a smile, neither a grimace. Another survivor. Another story beginning.

She pulled her hood lower and moved forward into the gathering fog, her footsteps sure despite the darkness. She had business yet to finish before the night was through. Behind her, the glow from the Cardinal's Cap, soon to be The Winchester Goose, spilled golden light onto the cobblestones, a beacon in the mist that would remain long after she had disappeared.

Printed in Dunstable, United Kingdom

70197675R00218